THE ROAD TO PARADISE ISLAND

By Victoria Holt

THE ROAD
TO PARADISE
ISLAND

Victoria Holt

Doubleday & Company, Inc.
Garden City, New York
1985

Designed by Virginia M. Soulé

Library of Congress Cataloging in Publication Data
  The road to Paradise Island.
  I. Title.
PR6015.I3R6   1985   823'.914

Library of Congress Catalog Card Number 85-4538
ISBN 0-385-19110-3
Printed in the United States of America
  First Edition

CONTENTS

THE ROAD
TO PARADISE
ISLAND

THE NIGHT
OF THE STORM

On the night of the great storm, our house, like so many in the village, was damaged; and it was due to this that the discovery was made. I was eighteen years old at the time and my brother Philip twenty-three; and in the years to come I was often to marvel at what followed and to speculate how different everything might have been but for the storm.

It came after one of the hottest spells on record when the temperature soared into the nineties, and there was hardly a topic of conversation which did not concern the weather. Two old people and one baby died of it; there were prayers for rain in the churches; old Mrs. Terry, who was ninety and after a frivolous youth and less than virtuous middle age, had taken to religion in her seventies, declared that God was punishing England in general and Little and Great Stanton in particular by starving the cattle, drying up the streams and not providing enough moisture for the crops. The Day of Judgement was at hand, and on the night of the storm even the most sceptical of us were inclined to think that she might have a point.

I had lived all my life in the old Tudor Manor House on the Green, presided over by Granny M. The M stood for Mallory, which was our family name, and she was called Granny M to distinguish her from Granny C—Granny Cresset—for at the time of my mother's death, which coincided with that of my birth, the War of the Grannies had waged.

"They both wanted us," Philip had told me when I was about four and he a knowledgeable nine. That made us feel very important to be so wanted.

Philip told me that Granny C had suggested that she have one of us and Granny M the other—dividing us as though we were two strips of land over which the generals were fighting. It was a long time before I could trust Granny C after that for the person who mattered most in my life was Philip. He had always been there, my big brother, my protector, the clever one, possessed of five glorious years of experience beyond my own. We quarrelled occasionally, but such differences only made me realize more fully how important he was to me, for during the periods of his displeasure I suffered acute misery.

The suggestion of parting us had fortunately aroused the indignation of Granny M.

"Separate them! Never!" had been her battle cry, while she stated with no uncertain emphasis that as the *paternal* grandmother she had the greater claim. Granny C was at length vanquished and forced to accept the compromise, which entailed brief summer holidays once a year at her home in Cheshire and the occasional day visit, gifts of dresses for me and sailor suits for Philip, stockings and mittens for us both and presents at Christmas and birthdays.

When I was ten years old Granny C had a stroke and died.

"A nice state she would have got us into if she had had the children," I heard Granny M comment to Benjamin Darkin. Old Benjamin was one of the few who ever stood up to Granny M, but he could afford to because he had been at the "shop" from the day he was twelve years old and he knew more about the business of map making than any man alive, so said Granny M.

"The lady can scarcely be blamed for the acts of God, Mrs. Mallory," he said on that occasion with mild reproof; and presumably because he was Benjamin Darkin, Granny M let it go at that.

Granny M behaved as the lady of the manor in Little Stanton, and when she went into Great Stanton, as she did at that time every day, she rode in her carriage with John Barton the coachman and little Tom Terry, a descendant of that prophet of doom, the now virtuous nonagenarian Mrs. Terry, in his place at the back of the carriage.

Philip said, when he was about eighteen and as far as I was concerned the wisest man in Christendom, that people who "Came into things" were often more dedicated to them than those who had been born into them. What he was implying was that Granny M had not been born into the squirarchy. She had merely married Grandfather M and thus had become one of the Mallorys who had lived in the Manor House since it had been built in 1573. We knew this because the date was engraved on the stonework on the front of the house. But there could not have been a prouder Mallory than Granny M.

I had never known Grandfather M. He had died before the great Battle of the Grannies had begun.

Granny M managed the village as efficiently and autocratically as she did her own household. She presided over fêtes and bazaars and kept our mild vicar and his "woolly-minded" wife in order. She made sure there was a good attendance at morning and evening services, and every servant was expected to be in his or her place at church every Sunday—and if certain essential duties prevented attendance, there must be a rota so that anyone who missed one Sunday must be there the next. Needless to say Philip and I were always present and walked sedately—Sunday fashion—across the Green from the Manor to the church, on either side of Granny M, to take our places in the Mallory pew at the side of which was the stained-glass window depicting Christ in Gethsemane, presented by one of our ancestors in 1632.

But perhaps what claimed Granny M's greatest devotion was the "shop." It was unusual for squires to be connected with business and pay such respect to a shop. But this was no ordinary shop.

It was a shrine, as it were, to the glory of long-dead Mallorys, for the Mallorys had been great circumnavigators of the globe. They had served their country well since the days of Queen Elizabeth and it was Granny M's conviction that the country owed a great deal of its maritime supremacy to the Mallorys.

A Mallory had sailed with Drake. In the seventeenth century they had also gone off on their adventures; but there was one great interest which set them apart. It was not their determination to capture the ships of enemy Spaniards and Dutchmen, but their fierce desire to chart the world.

They, said Granny M, had carved their name on the world's history, and not merely that of England; they had made navigation easier for hundreds—no, thousands—of great adventurers all over the world; and what these intrepid sailors—and not only sailors but those who explored the terrain of the Earth—owed to Mallory's maps was inestimable.

The "shop" was situated in the main street of Great Stanton. It was an ancient three-storeyed building with two bow windows on the ground floor, one on either side of the stone steps which led up to the front door.

At the back of the shop, across a yard, was another building in which were situated three steam-driven machines. This was forbidden territory unless we were accompanied by an adult. The machines did not greatly interest me but Philip was immensely interested in them.

In one of the bow windows was a great globe painted in the most beautiful blues, pinks and greens, which in my early days had held immense fascination for me. When I was a child and had visited the shop in the company of Granny M, Benjamin Darkin would show me a similar globe which was in the front room and he would twirl it round and round and show me the great blue seas and the land and its boundaries; never hesitating to point out the pink bits on the globe—the parts which were British. Made so, I presumed, by the glorious Mallorys who had made the maps to show the explorers the way.

Philip had been equally excited by visits to the shop and would talk to me about it. We had maps in our schoolroom and when she visited us there, Granny M would ask us questions about the atlas. Geography was a subject which took precedence over all others, and Granny M was delighted by our interest in it.

In the other bow window of the shop there was a huge map of the world. It looked magnificent spread out before us with the continent of Africa on one side and the Americas on the other. The sea was a vivid blue, the land dark brown and green mostly. There were our own islands looking quite insignificant just to the left of the funny-looking tiger which was Scandinavia. But, most glorious of all, was the name of our ancestor written in gold on the right-hand corner: *Jethro Mallory 1698.*

"When I grow up," said Philip, "I am going to have a boat and I am going to measure up the seas. Then I'll have *my* name in gold at the bottom of a map."

Granny M overheard that remark and her face was one deep happy smile, for it was just what she intended; and I guessed she was congratulating herself that she had rescued her grandson from the clutches of Granny C who might have tried to make an architect or even a politician of him, for her family had harboured people in these professions.

I learned a little of the family history over the years and discovered that Granny M had never entirely approved of her son's marriage to Flora Cresset. Flora, judging by her portrait which hung in the gallery, had been very pretty but frail, which seemed to have been borne out by her death at my birth; but then so many people died in childbirth—babies too—so that to survive was, in a way, a minor triumph. I said to Philip that it was an indication of the tenacity of women that the human race went on, to which he replied: "You do talk nonsense sometimes."

Philip was more down-to-earth than I was. I was a dreamer, a romancer. He was interested in the practical side of map making, calculations and measurements, and his fingers itched to take up compasses and such scientific instruments. For me it was so different. I wondered who would be living in those remote places. I wondered about their lives; and when I looked at those islands in the midst of the blue tropical seas, I wove all sorts of stories about my going there, living among the people and learning their ways.

We were quite different in outlook—Philip and I. Perhaps that was why we got on so well together. We each supplied something which the other lacked. No doubt because we were motherless—fatherless in a way, although our father was not dead—we had turned to each other.

When my father had brought his bride to the Manor, he was working in the family business. Naturally he had been brought up to it as Philip was being. Perhaps if my mother had not died he would still be there, doing more or less what Granny M wanted him to. But when my mother had died he had been unable to endure life at the Manor. There must have been too many memories. He might well have a dislike for the child who had seized her place in the world at the expense of one who was more greatly loved. However, he decided to go away for a while, to work in Holland with another firm of map makers—just for a short time to enable him to recover from the loss of his wife. Holland was a country which had given birth to some of the leading map makers from the earliest days and Granny M had, at the time, thought it was a good plan to help him recover from his grief and acquire new experience at the same time.

But my father stayed on in Holland and showed no desire to return, and in time he married a Dutch girl, Margareta, whose father was a wealthy export merchant, and to Granny M's disgust my father joined him in his business, deserting the glorious profession of map making for one to which Granny M contemptuously referred as "Commerce." I had half brothers and a sister whom I had never seen.

There was talk about Philip's going over to stay with his father, but Granny M always prevented that. I think she was afraid that Philip might be lured away by the fascination of the export business. So my father settled down with his new family and seemed content to leave his first one in the care of Granny M.

On my eighteenth birthday, which was in May and about three months before the great storm, the governess whom I had had for seven years left, and since I was no longer in need of such services, I knew that Granny M was beginning to think about finding a husband for me. Not one of the young men who were being invited to the house appealed to me so far. Nor did I see romance in such a prosaic charade. There were the Galtons from Great Stanton who had a son, Gerald. They were very wealthy and had interests in London—which was some twenty miles from Great Stanton—and not so far off as to cut Galton père completely off from his family. Gerald accompanied his father on trips to London where they often spent several weeks, and their visits to the country house were of fairly short duration. Gerald, as a husband, would not be at home a great deal and when I realized that was a point in his favour, I saw at once that he did not fit into my dreams of romance.

There was Charles Fenton, the son of the squire of Marlington—a fox-hunting, shooting, sporty type. Quite jolly, laughing at almost everything, so that one longed for a little gloom in his company. I enjoyed being with both of these young men but the idea of spending my life with them was far from exciting.

Granny M said: "You must learn more social graces, my dear. A young woman has to make a choice sooner or later and choose from what is available. Those who delay the choice too long often find there is nothing to choose from."

Dire warning, which fell on deaf eighteen-year-old ears.

What was wrong with life as it was?

Granny M was more wary about Philip. His wife would be brought into the Manor. She would become a Mallory, whereas when I married I would relinquish that illustrious name. I had no doubt that Granny M had thought with some misgivings of the coming of Flora Cresset into the Manor. True, she had provided Granny M with two grandchildren, but the frailty of Flora had cost Granny her son who now, as Granny M put it, had been "Commandeered by that Dutch woman."

After the marriage she had not had a good word to say for the Dutch.

"But Granny," I reminded her, "you used to say that some of the best map makers came from that part of the world. Some of the earliest explorers ... and Mercator himself was Flemish. Think what we owe to him."

Granny M was torn between the pleasure she always felt when I showed interest in the business and her dislike of being contradicted.

"That was long ago. Besides it was a Dutchman who first started buying old black and white maps and colouring them. Then selling them at a great price."

"A practice which those who came after followed to great advantage," I said.

"You are very perverse," said Granny M, but she was not displeased, and she did what she always did when not sure of winning the point—she changed the subject.

She was delighted that I considered it a treat to visit the shop, and on certain afternoons, after lessons in the schoolroom of course, I and my governess would go into Great Stanton where I would spend some very pleasant hours in the shop.

For one thing talking to Benjamin always intrigued me.

His life was maps. Sometimes he took Philip and me over to the building where the printing was done and he would ramble on about modern improvements and how in the old days they had used wood blocks which they called printing in relief because part of the wood was inked and that was transferred to the paper so that it stood out in relief.

"Nowadays," he said proudly, "we use copper."

I was rather bored by the technicalities but Philip would ask innumerable questions about various processes while I stood by not really listening as I gazed at the maps on the walls. Most of them were copies of those which had been made in the sixteenth, fifteenth and even fourteenth centuries and I would be thinking of those intrepid explorers going to those places for the first time, discovering new lands.

Philip spent a lot of time in the shop and when he was twenty-one and had finished with his education, he was there all day, working with Benjamin, learning about the business. Granny M was delighted with him.

I hated to be left out and Benjamin sensed that. He, like Philip, seemed to be very sorry for me because I had been born a girl, which prevented me from taking an important part in this most fascinating business.

One day Benjamin was talking about the colouring of maps and he said that very soon he believed there would be a breakthrough and we should be putting coloured lithography on the market.

He showed me a print—not a map but a rather sentimental picture of a family scene. It was in colour.

"It was done by a man called George Baxter," said Benjamin. "Just look at those colours. If we could get those into our maps . . . "

"Why can't you?" I asked.

"He kept his method a great secret. But I have a notion how it was done. I think he used a series of blocks of different colours, but he would have to have had the correct register. It would be more difficult with maps. You see you cannot afford to be a fraction of an inch out. If you were you'd make a country miles bigger or smaller than it actually was. You see the difficulty."

"So you will go on colouring by hand?"

"For the time being, yes. Until we get the breakthrough."

"Benjamin, I could do that."

"You, Miss Annalice? Why, it's not an easy task."

"Now, why should you think because it is difficult I could not do it?"

"Well, you're a young lady."

"Young ladies are not all stupid, Mr. Darkin."

"Well, I wasn't saying that, Miss Annalice."

"Well then, let me try."

The outcome was that I was given a trial. I did well and after a while I was given a real map to colour. How I enjoyed it! That blue, blue sea . . . a colour I loved. As I worked I could hear the waves pounding on coral beaches. I could see dusky girls with flowers about their necks and ankles; I could see little dark children running naked into the sea, and long canoes cutting through the waves. I was there.

Those were afternoons of adventure. I climbed mountains and crossed rivers; and I wondered all the time what new lands had yet to be discovered.

Benjamin Darkin thought I should get tired of the work but he was wrong. The more I did, the more excited I became about it. Moreover I did it well. They could not afford to spoil those maps by careless colouring. Mine were examined by Benjamin himself and declared to be perfect.

I began to learn something about the art of map making. I studied those maps of the past and I became interested in the men who had made them. Benjamin showed me a copy of Ptolemy's map of the world which had been made round about 150 A.D. and he told me how even the great Ptolemy had learned from Hipparchus who had lived some three hundred years before. I became even more absorbed and spent those magic afternoons dreaming of far-off places and the men who had been there years ago and made their maps so that others could easily find their way.

Granny M came sometimes to watch me at work. There was speculation in her eyes. Her grandchildren were a credit to her—both of them
caught up in the fascinating world of maps. She could not have asked
anything better. She was a schemer by nature and there was nothing she
liked better than managing other people's lives because she was always
sure she could do it so much better than they could themselves.

At this time she had made up her mind that Philip should marry a
sensible girl who would come to the Manor and bear more Mallorys to
continue in the business of map making in Great Stanton and at the
same time making sure that squiral status was kept up in Little Stanton.
As for myself she was beginning to see that neither Gerald Galton nor
Charles Fenton was the man for me. She would wait until she found
someone who would fit more neatly into her ideas of suitability.

This was respite for me—to pursue my vicarious adventures in the
shop and enjoy life at the Manor.

The Manor was a house full of interest which one was apt to forget
having been born in it and lived one's life in it. For one thing it was said
to be haunted. There was one dark corner on the second floor where the
structure was rather unusual. It was at the end of a corridor which
seemed to come to an abrupt termination—almost as though the builder
had decided he had had enough of it and wanted to cut it short.

The servants did not like to go along that corridor after dark. They
were not sure why. It was just a feeling one had. There was a rumour that
someone had been walled up in the house years and years ago.

When I tried to find out something from Granny M, I was told:
"Nonsense. No Mallory would be so foolish. It would have been most
unhealthy."

"Nuns were walled up sometimes," I pointed out.

"They were nuns—nothing to do with the Mallorys."

"But this was long ago."

"My dear Annalice, it's nonsense. Now I want you to go over to Mrs.
Gow and take some of that calf's foot jelly. She's poorly again."

Mrs. Gow had been our housekeeper for many years, and was now
living with her son over the builder's yard which was situated between
Little and Great Stanton.

I could never fail to admire Granny M who dismissed walled-up
ancestors as decisively as she had Granny C.

But I used to wonder about that spot in the corridor. I would go up there after dark and I was sure I felt a sensation—a little frisson... something. Once I imagined that something touched me lightly on the shoulder and I heard a sibilant whisper.

I was trying to create something out of a long-ago rumour just as I dreamed of those coral beaches when I coloured my maps.

I used to go down to visit my mother's grave and make sure that the bushes there were well tended. I often thought about her. I had built up a picture of her from Granny C who had always wept a little when she talked of her Flora. Flora had been beautiful, too good for this world, said her mother. She had been a gentle, loving girl. She had been married at sixteen and Philip had been born a year afterwards so she had been only twenty-two when she died.

I had been able to tell Granny C how very sad I was because it was through me that she had died. That was the sort of thing one could never have said to Granny M who would have immediately retorted: "Nonsense. You knew nothing about it and therefore had no say in the matter. These things happened, and she was a weak creature."

Granny C was more sentimental. She had said that my mother would willingly have given her life for me. But that worried me even more. There is nothing that makes one feel worse than having great sacrifices made for one.

So I had not talked nearly as much as I had wanted to to Granny C about my mother.

However I did visit her grave. I planted a rose bush on it and a rosemary "for remembrance," and I used to go down rather secretly for I did not want even Philip to know of my remorse for having caused her death. Sometimes I would talk aloud to her and tell her that I hoped she was happy where she was and I was so sorry that she had died bringing me into the world.

One day when I was there I went to get some water for the bushes. There was an old pump some way off and a watering pot and jugs. As I turned away from my mother's grave I fell sprawling, for I had caught my foot in a jutting stone. I had grazed my knees a little, but nothing much, and as I was about to pick myself up I examined the stone which had been the cause of my fall, and I saw that it was part of a curb.

I delved beneath the weeds and discovered that it was part of a surround of a plot which must have been a grave. I wondered whose it was. I had always thought that piece of land was waste ground. Yet it was among the Mallory graves.

I set to work pulling up the tangled growth and there it was—a grave. There was no headstone, otherwise that would have betrayed its existence. But there was a plate on the grave. It was dirty and the letters were almost obliterated.

I went to the pump and brought back water. I had an old rag with me which I used to wipe my hands on after I had watered the plants, and with this I washed the grime from the plate.

I started back with dismay and I felt a shiver run down my spine for the name on the plate might have been my own.

"Ann Alice Mallory. Died the Sixth Day of February 1793. Aged eighteen years."

I was Annalice, it was true, and on the plate there was a division and a capital letter for Alice . . . but the similarity shocked me.

For a few seconds I had the uncanny feeling that I was looking at my own grave.

I stood for a few moments staring at it. Who was she—lying there silent for ever among the Mallory dead?

I went back to the Manor. Normality returned. Why should not one of my ancestors have a name like mine? Names continued through families. Ann Alice. And Annalice. Eighteen years. She had been just about my age when she had died.

At dinner that night I said to Granny M, "I saw a grave in the cemetery today which I hadn't seen before . . . "

She was not very interested.

I looked at Philip. "It was someone with my name . . . or as near as makes no difference."

"Oh," said Philip. "I thought you were the one and only Annalice."

"This one was Ann Alice Mallory. Who was she, Granny?"

"Ann is a name that has been used a great deal in the family. So is Alice."

"Why did you call me Annalice?"

"*I* chose it," said Granny M, as though it was therefore the best possible choice and that settled the matter. "It was because there were so many Anns and Alices in the family. I thought either name a little commonplace, but as you were a Mallory I combined the two and made something which you must admit is somewhat unusual."

"As I said," put in Philip, "the one and only."

"This grave has been neglected."

"Graves do become so after the occupant has been dead some time."

"Nearly a hundred years ago she was buried."

"That is a long time to be remembered," said Philip.

"It was a queer feeling . . . finding the name under all the weeds and then . . . my own almost . . . looking up at me."

"I must go and look for a Philip there," said my brother.

"There are Philips, several of them."

"You have this morbid fancy to read the gravestones, I know," said Philip.

"I like to think about them all . . . all the Mallorys . . . people who have lived in this house before us . . . people who are connected with us . . . in a way . . . a long line of our progenitors."

"It is pleasant to know you have such family feeling," said Granny M crisply and thereby dismissing the subject.

But I could not get Ann Alice Mallory out of my mind. I suppose because she had been more or less my age when she had died and she bore a name which was almost my own.

The next time I went to the cemetery to clear the grave of its weeds I asked one of the gardeners to give me a bush to plant there. He scratched his head and said that it wasn't the time for planting. But he gave me a rose bush and I said that I wanted rosemary as well.

"It'll never take," he said morosely.

If they didn't I would plant others, I told myself. I planted the bushes and cleaned the plate. The grave looked quite different now, as though someone cared about Ann Alice Mallory.

I thought about her often. She had probably been born in the Manor; she would no doubt have lived there for eighteen years; and she had my name. She might have been myself.

She intruded into my thoughts. It was rather uncanny.

She had died in 1793. That was not quite a hundred years ago. What would life have been like here then? Very much the same as now, probably. Life in country villages had not changed very much. Great events would be taking place in the outside world. The French Revolution would be in progress and the very year of Ann Alice's death the King and Queen of France would have been executed.

There would be nobody living now who knew Ann Alice. Even Mrs.

Terry would not have been born when she died—although she came into the world soon after. Mrs. Gow was seventy-nine; she might have heard some tale from her parents. They might have known her.

When I next visited Mrs. Gow I decided to bring up the subject.

Mrs. Gow had been our housekeeper for forty years. She had become a widow when she was twenty-eight and had taken the post then.

The Gows were, as Mrs. Gow herself would have said, "A cut above" the rest of our working community. They had been superior for a long time, owning their building and carpentering business, which served not only the needs of Little and Great Stanton but the surrounding neighbourhood as well.

There had always been an air of superiority about Mrs. Gow as there was about all the Gows. It was as though they must perpetually remind everyone that they were made of superior clay.

I remembered Mrs. Gow from my childhood—a stately, dignified figure in black bombazine, whom both Philip and I held in a certain awe.

Even later I felt I had to defer to her. Once I asked Granny M why even she treated Mrs. Gow with such respect.

"What is it about Mrs. Gow?" I asked. "Why do we have to be so careful with her?"

"She's a good housekeeper."

"She sometimes behaves as though she owns the Manor."

"Good servants feel this loyalty." Granny M was thoughtful for a few moments, then she said as though she had started to wonder herself: "The Gows have always been respected in this house. They've got money . . . We're lucky to have a woman like Mrs. Gow. We must remember that she does not depend on the post for her living as so many do."

There was evidently something about the Gows. Granny M always made sure that she gave Mrs. Gow little luxuries. She would not have accepted the ordinary gifts which came the way of the deserving poor— blankets and coal at Christmas and so on. For Mrs. Gow the brace of pheasants, the calf's foot jelly . . . the gifts of a friend . . . or almost. Mrs. Gow was not gentry; but nor was she of the servant class; she hovered confidently between the two. After all, her father-in-law and her husband— when they had been alive—had been master craftsmen. And William Gow, Mrs. Gow's only son, was now carrying on the flourishing business.

I decided I would call on Mrs. Gow and see if I could learn anything about Ann Alice.

Having delivered the marzipan fancies which I had prevailed upon cook to make and which I knew were special favourites with Mrs. Gow, I seated myself on a chair near the sofa where Mrs. Gow reclined, Récamier fashion, and began my interrogation.

I said: "I was in the cemetery the other day visiting my mother's grave."

"A dear sweet lady," commented Mrs. Gow. "I shall never forget the day she left us. How long ago was it?"

"Eighteen years," I said.

"I always said she'd never get through it. Too frail, she was. The prettiest thing you ever saw. He thought the world of her."

"You mean my father. You must remember a long way back, Mrs. Gow."

"I've always had a good memory."

"I found a grave in the cemetery. A very neglected one. I cleaned up the stone a little and it was someone who had almost my name. Ann Alice Mallory. She died in 1793 when she was eighteen years old."

Mrs. Gow puffed her lips. "That's going back a bit."

"Nearly a hundred years. I wonder if you ever heard anything about her?"

"I'm not a hundred yet, Miss Annalice."

"But you have such a good memory and perhaps someone told you something about her."

"I didn't come to these parts till I married Tom Gow."

"I wondered whether anyone in the family had ever mentioned anything."

"My Tom was older than me and he wasn't born till 1808 so that would be well after she was dead, wouldn't it? Funny you should mention that date. I've often heard it spoken of in the family."

"The date?"

"When did you say she died. 1793? Well, that was the year we started up our business. I've always noticed it. It's over the Gow yard. It says Founded 1793. That's it. So it was the same time."

I was disappointed. Mrs. Gow was far more interested in the achievements of Gow's, Builders and Carpenters, than in the occupant of my grave. She went on at length about how busy her son William was and that he was thinking of handing over a lot to his son Jack. "You have to give them responsibility. That's what William says. It just shows you,

Miss Annalice, what reliable good work can do for you. Everyone knows that it's Gow's for the best workmanship and I'd like to hear anyone contradict that."

I could see that I was unlikely to discover anything from Mrs. Gow; and I decided it was worth having a try with Mrs. Terry.

I found her in bed.

"Oh, it's you," she said, her greedy eyes looking into my basket to see what I had brought.

"This heat don't let up, does it?" She shook her head. "Well, they've brought it on themselves. Do you know they was dancing in the barn last Saturday . . . and carrying it on over midnight into the Sabbath. What can you expect? Then they ask me, What about the drought, eh? What about the cattle? What about the grass all being dried up?"

"Why should they ask you, Mrs. Terry?"

"Why indeed. They should look into their own souls, that they should. It's a judgement and there'll be worse to come if they don't stop their evil ways. Repent, I tell them, while there's time."

"Did you ever hear anything of an Ann Alice Mallory?"

"Ah? What? That's you, ain't it?"

"No. I'm Annalice. This is Ann Alice . . . two separate names."

"I always thought it was outlandish. Why couldn't they call you plain Ann or Alice like the rest. What did they want to muddle them up for and give you two in one. Ann was a name you heard a lot up at the Manor. So was Alice."

"I'm asking about the two together. Ann Alice."

"No, I can't say I ever heard that."

"You're ninety, Mrs. Terry. Isn't that wonderful."

"It's the godly life that does it."

She had the grace to lower her eyes. Her godliness had only been in existence for twenty years and I had heard it said that Mrs. Terry after the death of Jim Terry at sea—and even when he was alive during his absences—had not been averse to what was known in the locality as "A little bit of the best" on a Saturday night behind the bushes or even in her own cottage.

"It must be," I said, looking innocent as though I had never heard of these clandestine activities, for I was anxious to keep in her good graces. "I found a grave in the cemetery. Ann Alice Mallory. It looked like my name and it gave me a shiver to think that when I die my grave will be rather like that."

"Mind you're not took sharp with all your sins upon you."

"I wasn't thinking so much of that."

"That's the trouble nowadays. Young people—they don't think. I've made my Daisy promise that when I go, she'll have the parson there just to help me over . . . not that I'll need it."

"Oh no. You'll be certain of your place in heaven; and I bet you they'll send a company of angels to escort you there."

She closed her eyes nodding.

I felt very disappointed. Nobody seemed to know anything about Ann Alice. And yet Mrs. Terry must have been born soon after her death. She was a local girl who had lived in the neighbourhood all her life. Surely the name must have been mentioned. I had never yet known a villager who was not interested in what was going on at the Manor.

"Mrs. Terry," I said, "the lady in the grave must have died just before you were born. Did you never hear any mention of her?"

"No. It was something that wasn't spoken of."

"Wasn't spoken of? Do you mean it was a forbidden subject?"

"Oh. I don't know about that."

"Do you remember anyone talking about anything during your childhood?"

"Well, it was always the Gows. That's who they used to talk about. The Gows being stuck up and all that . . . and getting on and having their own business . . . That's what they used to talk about. My mother would say, 'Look at Mrs. Gow. Her and her purple bonnet . . . walking into church like a lady. Nobody would think that a few years back they was nothing . . . just like the rest of us.' "

"Oh yes," I said a trifle impatiently, "we know the Gows got on."

"Oh, it wasn't always like that . . . so I heard."

"They've been going for a long time. Since 1793 it says over their sheds. Founded 1793. I saw it the other day. That was the year this lady died."

"One goes to glory and one makes all the money and gets ideas about being better than the rest of us folks."

"So you don't remember . . . "

Mrs. Terry said: "There was talk . . . no, I can't remember. Something about one of the ladies up at the Manor. She died sudden, I think."

"Yes, Mrs. Terry, yes."

Mrs. Terry shrugged her shoulders.

I prompted: "You must have heard something."

"I don't know. People die. It's to be hoped they've had time to repent before they're taken."

She sighed and then was off on the subject of the Gows again.

" 'Tweren't right. There was a lot of talk about that. Couldn't do nothing wrong, them Gows. I remember way back . . . I couldn't have been much more than a nipper. Caught he was. What was his name? Dashed if I can remember. Tom I think. That was it. Tom Gow. Caught redhanded with the pheasant in his jacket . . . poaching. Brought up before the magistrate he was . . . and what happens? The Gows go to the master and before anyone can say Jack Robinson, there's Poacher Gow strutting about the place as proud as two peacocks. Got off scot free. What do you think of that? There's favouritism for you. Wasn't right. People don't like it. It seemed the master would do anything for them Gows."

"That must have been years ago," I said impatiently for I was not interested in the triumph of the Gows.

"Well," she went on, "as I said I wasn't no more than a nipper . . . But it was always like that. The Gows has always had the Manor behind them. That's what folks said."

"Well, they have done very well. I suppose they must be admired for that."

"Helped on . . . so it was said."

"It is also said that God helps those who help themselves. You should know being on somewhat more intimate terms with the Almighty than the rest of us."

Irony was lost on her. She nodded sagely and said: "That's so."

I took my leave of her then, realizing that I was not going to discover anything about Ann Alice Mallory from her.

I told Philip about it.

"Why the interest?" he asked. "Just because she has a name like yours?"

"It's a feeling I have."

Philip was always sceptical about my feelings. He laughed at me.

"What about going for a ride?" he asked.

I loved riding with him and I accepted the invitation with alacrity;

but I could not get Ann Alice out of my mind. I kept thinking of the mysterious young woman in the forgotten grave.

The heat intensified. There was a stillness in the air which seemed ominous.

Everyone said: It's too hot to work, too hot to move, too hot to breathe almost.

It will break soon, they said. My goodness we need the rain.

I felt frustrated out of all reason because my efforts to discover something about the woman who was haunting my dreams were proving to be so disappointing. Mrs. Gow was clearly too young to remember and Mrs. Terry was so obsessed by her envy of the Gows that she could not concentrate on the matter. Where else could I look?

Why did I care? Why should it seem so important just because I had found her grave and she had a name similar to mine and had been more or less the same age as I was when she had died? Why was she perpetually in my thoughts? It was almost as though she were a living presence. It was typical of me to concern myself with such a matter, Philip said. What could it matter what had happened to the girl now? She was dead, wasn't she?

She was unhappy, I thought. I sense it. It's in the house. It was round her grave.

Why was her grave neglected? The others were not. It was as though someone had buried her and wanted to forget.

That afternoon it was too hot to go out walking or riding. I stretched out on a chair in the garden in the shade, listening to the bees. The lavender was almost depleted now; the blooms had been gathered and made into sachets for drawers and cupboards so the busy little insects were at work on the purple blossoms of the veronica. Idly I watched a dragonfly flit across the pond over which Hermes was poised as though in flight. I caught a flash of gold as the fish swam round in the pond. There was a stillness everywhere as though all nature was tense . . . waiting for something to happen.

The quiet before the storm, I thought.

The heat continued through the afternoon. We sat about languidly after dinner. Granny M said it had been too hot for her to go into Great Stanton today. I agreed with her.

We retired early. The heat made sleep difficult, and it was about two o'clock in the morning when the storm broke. I was only half-asleep and was immediately startled into wakefulness by the violent crash of thunder which seemed right over my head. I sat up in bed. So the long-threatened storm was upon us.

A flash of lightning brightened the room to be followed immediately by another heavy clap of thunder.

The sky seemed ablaze. I had never seen such lightning. I heard movements in the house and I gathered that some of the servants were stirring.

Thunderstorms were not very frequent and when they came were usually soon over. This one was right overhead and the crashes were following fast on one another.

I got up and put on my dressing gown and slippers and as I did so I heard the loudest crash so far. I stood very still, my heart beating fast.

Then I heard it again . . . right upon us. I could hear the sound of falling masonry.

I ran out into the corridor. Philip was there.

"Something's been struck," he said.

"You mean . . . the house."

"I don't know."

Another crash, then another and another.

Granny M appeared.

"What's happened?" she demanded.

"We don't know yet," said Philip. "I thought the house had been struck."

"Well, we'd better find out."

Some of the servants had arrived.

"Mr. Philip thinks we may have been struck," said Granny M. "Don't panic. It can't be much. We'd soon know if it was. Oh!"

That was another clap right overhead.

"Philip . . . and you, Jennings." She indicated the butler who had just arrived on the scene. "You'd better go and look. Where do you think it could be?"

"I'd say the roof, Mrs. Mallory," said Jennings.

"The rain will be pouring in somewhere," said Philip. "Better find out quickly."

I could hear the rain lashing against the windows as Philip with Jennings and others went running up the stairs.

Granny M and I followed.

I heard a shout. It was Philip. "The roof's damaged," he said.

I could smell burning, but there was no fire. The rain would quickly have put that out. Water was pouring into the corridor.

Granny M was calm and in charge of the situation. Receptacles of all kinds were brought up to catch the rain. There was such a bustle and excitement that the storm was forgotten. It continued to thunder on.

One of the housemaids though was having hysterics.

"She always does, Miss, for thunder," one of the maids told me. "It's on account of her auntie shutting her in a cupboard when she was five and telling her it meant God was angry and punishing the world . . . "

Two of the maids went off to succour their hysterical companion.

Jennings was as calm as Granny M. He investigated the damage and said: "Nothing can be done till tomorrow, Mrs. Mallory. Then we'll have to call in Gow's."

The storm persisted for an hour and during that time we were emptying buckets of rainwater and doing our best to prevent further damage. It was a great relief when it stopped raining and the deluge in the receptacles was reduced to drips.

"What a night," said John Barton who had come in from his rooms over the stables to give a hand.

"Don't worry, Mrs. Mallory," said Jennings. "It's not as bad as I first thought. I'll go along to Gow's just as soon as they are opened."

"And now," said Granny M, "I think we should have something really warm. Some hot punch I think. Will you see to that, Jennings. For the family in my sitting room, please, and see that it is served in the kitchen too."

So we sat in Granny M's room listening to the faint rumbling of thunder in the distance, sipping hot punch, and telling each other that this was a night we should always remember.

In the morning William Gow came to assess the damage. One other house on the Green had been struck, he told us. People were saying it was the worst storm for a hundred years.

William Gow was up on the roof for some time and when he came down he looked grave.

"Worse than I thought," he said. "There'll be quite a bit of work to be done . . . apart from the roof repairs, and you know, Mrs. Mallory, how hard it is to find the right tiles for these old houses. They've got to be medieval and yet they've got to be sound. It's not only that, though. Some of the woodwork has been damaged. That will have to be replaced."

"Very well, Mr. Gow," said Granny M. "Just let me know what."

"Well, I wanted to look at the panelling in that part where the damage has been done. Some of it will have to be made good. Otherwise it's going to rot and break away."

"Make a thorough examination," said Granny. "And then we'll discuss it."

He spent the whole morning climbing about, tapping and examining.

I went out walking round the village. Many of the bushes had been beaten down but there was a smell of freshness in the air. There were puddles everywhere and the entire village seemed to be out and determined to hear the latest news.

I could not resist calling on Mrs. Terry. She was sitting up in bed with the air of an ancient prophet.

"What a storm, and can you wonder! I sat up in bed saying, 'Let them have it, O Lord. It's the only way of learning these here sinners.' "

I thought of the housemaid who at five had been shut in the cupboard and told the storm was due to God's anger and it occurred to me that the righteous could cause a great deal of trouble in the world.

"I am sure the Almighty was glad of the advice," I couldn't resist saying acidly.

"They say the Manor has been struck," went on Mrs. Terry, ignoring that remark. "The roof, wasn't it?" I fancied I detected a disappointment that the damage had not been greater. "And the Carters, too. Their place was hit. Well, they will go gadding about. And do you know they bought that Amelia of theirs a gold locket and chain. At her age."

"And the damage to their home is the wages of the sin of gadding about and buying a gold locket?"

"I don't know. People get their just deserts. That's what it says in the Bible."

"Does it? Where?"

"Never you mind where. It just does, that's it."

"Well, I'm glad you survived, Mrs. Terry."

"Oh, I knew I'd be all right."

"Special protection from Heaven. But the righteous don't always escape. Think of the saints and the martyrs."

But Mrs. Terry was not going to be drawn into a theological controversy.

She merely murmured: "This will be a lesson to them . . . perhaps."

When I arrived back at the house I went upstairs to see how William Gow and his assistant were getting on.

I met him in the corridor which I always called the haunted spot.

He said: "I've been looking at this wall, Miss Annalice. The damp got through here. Look at this." He touched it. "I don't reckon that's safe," he went on.

"What do you propose?"

"I reckon we should take down this wall. I can't understand what it's doing here. The panelling isn't quite the same quality as the rest of the corridor."

"I am sure my grandmother will agree that you should do what you think best."

He tapped the wall and shook his head.

"It's a bit odd," he said. "I'll speak to Mrs. Mallory."

There was a great deal of talk about the restoration necessary after the storm. The damage had not been so very great but, as in all such cases, more work was going to be required than I had at first thought. The roof was of paramount importance and that was dealt with immediately and then William Gow and his men started on the inside of the house.

I was interested in that wall which had to be taken down because it was in that corridor which some of the servants said was haunted, and which I myself had thought to have a strangeness about it; and on the day when the men started on it I contrived to be in the house.

I went up to watch them at work and that was how I happened to be the first one to step into that room.

None of us could believe our eyes.

There was a great deal of dust and plaster; in fact it made a kind of mist, but there it was . . . actually a room . . . looking as though someone had just left it expecting to return at any moment.

William Gow cried: "Well, I never did in all my born days."

His assistant murmured: "Holy Moses!"

I just stared and a great excitement possessed me.

I cried: "So it really was walled up. There is something extraordinary about this. There must be a reason."

I stepped in.

"Be careful," said William Gow. "This place must have been shut up for a good many years. The air will be none too good. Best wait a bit, Miss Annalice."

"What an extraordinary thing!" I cried. "It looks as though someone has just walked out and left it."

"I should keep away from all that dust, Miss Annalice. Could be nasty. Leave it for a while. Let the air get in. We'll take away the whole of this wall, Bill. It's the strangest thing I ever saw."

My impatience was so great that I had to get into that room, but I did curb my impatience for half an hour. I hung about waiting, every now and then asking if I could go in. At length William Gow said that the dust had settled and the fresh air had penetrated the place a little; and he and I went in together.

It was not a large room, which was the reason why it was possible to hide it, I supposed. It contained a bed. There were hangings on the bed of blue velvet—at least that was the colour they appeared to be, for it was hard to see under the layer of dust. The carpet on the floor was dark blue. There was a small chest of drawers, two chairs and a dressing table. Lying in a chair was a lace fichu and a pair of gloves. I stared at them in wonder. The impression was that someone had been living here right until the last moment when it was decided to shut it away and whoever had occupied the room had not had time to put her fichu away or pick up her gloves. It was a woman, that much was clear—providing of course the articles belonged to her. And it was a woman's room. I was sure of that. There was a certain femininity about it. The dressing table had a frilled flounce; and lying on it was a hand mirror ready to be picked up.

William Gow was beside me.

"There was a window there," he said.

"Of course. A window. There would have to be a window."

"Blocked in," he said. "Looks like a job that was done at top speed." I turned to stare at him.

"What a strange discovery," I said. "Who would want to block up a room like this?"

He shrugged his shoulders. He was not a very imaginative man.

I went on: "I should have thought they would have cleared out the furniture first."

He did not answer. His eyes had caught something in the wood he had just pulled down.

"What is it?" I asked.

"It's the mark."

"What mark?"

"Gow's mark."

"Where?"

He showed me. It was a tiny carving of a squirrel sitting up with a nut in its paws, its bushy tail sticking up behind.

I looked at him questioningly and he went on: "A Gow put up that panel that shut off the room. Must have been my grandfather. He always had that mark. We put it on our woodwork still. It's been passed down through the family."

"Well, I suppose that would have been the case. Your family have been doing carpentering here for generations."

"It gives you a bit of a shock like," said William Gow.

I thought that was a mild way of expressing it, but I was not interested in the carving. I was overcome by the adventure of finding the room, wondering whose room it had been, and why people had thought it necessary to shut it away. It was not easy to remove a room. There was only one way of doing it. Shut it in. Wall it in. Make it as though it had never been.

When Granny M heard what had happened she was amazed. I went up with her and William Gow to examine the room again. What struck her as so strange was that they should not have removed the furniture before walling up the room. "And why," she said to me, "did they not simply lock it up if they did not want to use it any more?

"The Mallorys could behave very extraordinarily at times," she went on, gently releasing herself from the family which she did very rarely. It was only when their actions were slightly less than exemplary that she disowned them temporarily.

"There must have been a reason," I said.

"That is something we shall never know," replied Granny M. "Now what's to be done. I think first we should examine the furniture. Did you say there was a window at one time? Well, we can put that back for a start. And this furniture . . . I should imagine it has been ruined after being shut up like this. For how long? Who can say? Certainly it has always been shut away in my time. We'll get them clearing it at once."

William Gow said: "Begging your pardon, Mrs. Mallory, but it should be left for a day or two. Let the air in. Could be unhealthy . . . if you see what I mean."

"Very good. Let the air in. All right. Let everyone know that they are not to go in here until they are given my permission. I expect there'll be a lot of talk about this. Tell them it is not an exhibition."

"That's right, Mrs. Mallory," said William Gow. "And anyone coming in should take a bit of care. I don't know what the woodwork and the floor will be like after all them years."

"We'll leave it till you say, Mr. Gow."

"I'd like to have a thorough examination first, Mrs. Mallory. I'd like to make sure it's quite safe before anything much is moved."

"It shall be so."

I went down with Granny M. Philip was there. He had to see the room and that evening we talked of little else but what had just been revealed.

I lay in bed. I could not sleep. The discovery had excited me more than any of them. Why? I kept asking myself. What an extraordinary thing to do. Why go to so much trouble to wall up a room? As Granny M had said, Why not simply lock it?

I could not get it out of my mind. Every detail seemed to be imprinted on my memory. The bed with its velvet curtains . . . grey with the years of dust. Cobwebs draped from the ceilings, I remembered. I kept seeing the dressing table with the mirror, the chair with the fichu and the gloves on it. Had she just taken them off or was she about to put them on? The chest of drawers . . . I wondered what might be in those drawers.

I tossed and turned. In the morning I would go and look. What harm could that do? I would be careful. What was William Gow suggesting? That the floor might give way? That I might be poisoned by foul air?

I was suddenly obsessed by the desire to go and see for myself. Why not? I looked up at the ceiling . . . up the stairs . . . along the corridor.

My heart started to beat uncomfortably fast. A little shiver ran through me. I half believed in the servants' talk that it was haunted, and now that this was revealed it seemed even more likely.

Wait till morning, said my cowardly self.

But of course it was a challenge. Besides, how could I sleep with my thoughts going round and round in my head, asking myself Why? Why?

Deliberately I got out of bed, thrust my feet into slippers and put on my dressing gown. My fingers were shaking a little as I lighted a candle.

I opened my door and listened. The house was very quiet.

I started to mount the stairs, pausing on each step, thankful because I knew the place so well that I was fully aware of the position of creaking boards.

I was in the corridor now. I could see there was still a haze of dust. I could smell the peculiar smell like nothing I had known before . . . the smell of age, of damp, of something not quite of this world.

I stepped over a broken piece of wood. I was in the room.

I let the light fall over the walls and ceiling. In candlelight the stains stood out more than they had before. Then I had seen the room through the daylight which came from a window in the corridor. What were the stains on the wall just by the bed . . . and on the other wall too? I lifted my candle. Yes, and on the ceiling?

I almost turned and ran.

I felt that this room held a terrible secret. Frightened as I was, the urge to remain was stronger than my fear, not exactly forcing me to stay, but begging me to.

Perhaps I imagined that afterwards. And yet I believed that something . . . someone . . . had called me up here on this night . . . that I was to be the one to discover.

I stood for what seemed like minutes but which could only have been seconds, looking about the room, and my eyes kept coming back to those stains on the walls and ceiling.

"What does it mean?" I whispered.

I was silent, listening, as though I expected an answer.

I took a cautious step forward. I was very much aware of the chest of drawers.

Some impulse led me over to it. I put my candle on the top of it and tried to open the top drawer. It was stiff and difficult to open, but I worked hard at it and suddenly it began to move.

There was something in it. I bent down. A small hat of grey chiffon with a little feather in the front held in place by a jewelled pin; and beside it another hat trimmed with marguerites.

I shut the drawer. I felt I was prying and it seemed to me that somewhere in this strange room in the dead of night, eyes were watching me and I had an uncanny feeling that they were willing me to go on.

I shut the drawer quickly and as I did so I noticed that from the second drawer something was protruding slightly—as though that drawer had been shut in a hurry. I tried to open it and after a little difficulty I succeeded. There were stockings, gloves and scarves. I put in my hand and touched them. They felt very cold and damp. They repelled me in a certain way. Go back to your bed, my common sense urged me. What do you think you are doing here in the middle of the night? Wait and explore with Philip and Granny M tomorrow. What would she say if she knew I had already been here. "You have disobeyed orders. William Gow said it might not be safe. The floor could give way at any moment."

I had taken out some of the things and as I was putting them back, my fingers touched something. It was a piece of parchment rolled up like a scroll. I unrolled it. It was a map. I glanced at it hastily. It looked like several islands in a vast sea.

I rolled it up and as I was putting it back my hand touched something else.

Now my heart was racing more wildly than ever. It was a large leatherbound book and on the cover was embossed the word *Journal.*

I put it on the top of the chest and opened it. I gave a little cry, for written on the flyleaf were the words Ann Alice Mallory for her sixteenth birthday May 1790.

I clutched the side of the chest feeling suddenly dizzy with the shock of my discovery.

This book belonged to the girl in the forgotten grave!

I don't know how long I stood there staring down at that open page. I was overwhelmed. I felt that some supernatural force was guiding me. I had been led to uncover the grave and now . . . the book.

With trembling fingers I turned the pages. They were full of small but legible handwriting.

I believed then that I had the key to the mystery in my hands. This was the girl who had been buried in the grave and forgotten, the possessor of the jaunty hats in the drawer, the fichu, the gloves. And she was Ann Alice Mallory—my namesake.

There was something significant in this. I had been led to this discovery. I had the feeling that she was watching me, this mysterious girl in her grave, that she wanted me to know the story of her life.

I picked up the journal and turned to leave the room. Then I remembered the map which I had put back in the drawer. I took it out, and picking up my candle walked cautiously from the room.

Reaching my bedroom, I caught a glimpse of my reflection in the dressing room mirror. My eyes looked wild and my face very pale. I was still trembling a little, but a great excitement possessed me.

I looked at the journal which I had placed on my dressing table. I unrolled the map. There was an expanse of sea and a group of islands to the north and then some distance away another island . . . all alone. There was some lettering close to it. I peered at it. It was small and not very clear. I made out the words Paradise Island.

I wondered where it was. I would show it to Philip and Benjamin Darkin. They would know.

But it was the journal which I was eager to read.

Somewhere a clock struck one. I would not sleep tonight I was sure. I would not rest until I knew what was in that journal.

I lighted another candle and taking off my dressing gown and slippers got into bed. Making a rest for my back with pillows, I opened the journal and began to read.

ANN ALICE'S JOURNAL

May 30th 1790   On my sixteenth birthday, among the gifts which were presented to me was this journal. I had never before thought of keeping a journal and when the idea first came to me I dismissed it. I should never be persistent enough. I should write in it enthusiastically for a week or so and then I would forget all about it. That is no way to keep a journal. But why not? If I write in it only the important things that would be the best way. Whoever would want to remember that it had been a fine day yesterday or I had worn my blue or my lavender gown. Such trivialities were of no importance even when they occurred.

Well, I have promised myself that I will write in it when the mood takes me or when there is something so momentous that I feel I must put it down when it happened so that if I want to refer to it later I shall have it here . . . exactly as it was, for I have noticed that events change in people's minds and when they look back they believe that what they might have wished to happen actually did. I want none of that. I shall strive for the truth.

Life here in the Manor goes on very much the same from one day to the next. Sometimes I think it always will. So what shall I write about? This morning I was with Miss Bray, my governess, as usual. She is gentle and pretty and in her early twenties and I have been very happy with her for the last six years. She is the daughter of a vicar and at first my father thought she was too young for the post, but I am glad he decided she might come in spite of that for ours has been a very happy relationship.

When I look at the date I am reminded that it is two years since my mother died. I don't want to write about that. It is too painful and everything changed then. I long for the days when I used to sit beside her and read to her. That used to be one of the happiest times of the day. Now she is dead I turn to Miss Bray for comfort. We read books together but it is not the same.

I wish I were not so much younger than my brother Charles. It makes me feel so much alone. I have heard the servants say I was "an afterthought," which is not a very significant thing to be. I do not think Papa is very interested in me. He does his duty by me, of course, which has always meant delegating the care of me to others.

I walk a little, I ride a little; I visit people in the village and take what are called "comforts" to them. And that is my life. So what sense is there in keeping a journal?

June 20th   How strange that I should have decided to write in this book. Something has happened at last. It is nearly a month since I wrote that first bit and I thought I never would write in this book again. And now this has happened and I believe there is some comfort in writing down what one feels when one is distraught.

It is my dearest Miss Bray. This morning she came to me looking prettier than ever. I should be happy, of course, for she undoubtedly is. It seems ironical that the same event should have such a diverse effect on two people who are so fond of each other.

She said to me as we were grappling with a rather turgid paragraph in the Sterne novel we were reading, "I have some news, Ann Alice. And I want you to be the first to know."

I was eager to stop and ready for a cosy chat.

"James has asked me to marry him."

James Eggerton, the vicar's son, was on one of his periodical visits to his father. He had a living of his own in a parish some fifty miles away and was therefore in a position to marry.

"But you will go away, Miss Bray!" I cried.

"I'm afraid so," she said, dimpling. "Never mind, you'll have another governess . . . much cleverer than I. You'll enjoy it."

"Of course I shan't." I felt my face set into apprehensive lines.

Miss Bray put her arms about me and cuddled me in that endearing way she has.

"I have thought for some time that he was going to ask me," she explained, "and when he didn't I thought I was mistaken. And all the time he was trying to pluck up courage."

"You'll go right away."

"I'll ask your father if you can come and stay."

"It won't be the same."

"When there is change, nothing is ever the same. Life would be rather dull if it went on in the same old way forever, wouldn't it?"

I said: "I want it to be dull. I don't want you to go."

"Oh come," said Miss Bray. "This is really a very happy event." ·

I looked into her face and saw how truly happy she was, and I thought how selfish it was of me not to rejoice with her.

July 4th   How the days fly! I have tried to be pleased for Miss Bray because she is undoubtedly happy and James Eggerton goes about looking as though life is a perpetual joke and he is living in some seventh heaven.

I saw my father on the stairs that morning. He patted my head in his rather awkward way and said: "We shall have to find another Miss Bray, shan't we?"

"Papa," I said, "I am sixteen. Perhaps . . . "

He shook his head. "Oh no . . . you need a governess for another year at least. We'll find someone as nice as Miss Bray. Never fear."

Miss Bray is busy getting her trousseau together. She is a little absent-minded. I fancy she does not always see me when I'm there because she is looking into a blissful future with the Reverend James Eggerton.

I feel a little lost and lonely. I walk a great deal on my own and I ride, but I am always supposed to take someone with me and one of the grooms can't take the place of Miss Bray.

August 1st   Miss Bray is leaving at the end of the month. She is going to her home in the Midlands and will be married from there. I am thinking about her less now because I am concerned for my own future. The new governess is arriving tomorrow. Papa called me into his study to tell me about her. He has met her. He went up to London to see her. I was a little resentful because I felt he should have taken me. After all, I am the one who will have to spend so much time with her. I do not hope for another Miss Bray but I do want someone like her.

"Miss Lois Gilmour will be arriving tomorrow," said Papa. "She will come before Miss Bray goes so that Miss Bray can initiate her into her duties. I am sure you will like Miss Gilmour. She seems to be a very efficient young woman."

I do not want an efficient young woman. I want Miss Bray or someone exactly like her; and I do not think Miss Bray could have ever been called efficient. She has always been a little absent-minded and is especially so now and her learning has been inclined to lean in one direction. Books, music and the like, which has always suited me. She is hopeless at mathematics.

Miss Gilmour sounds formidable.

I am full of apprehension.

August 2nd   Today was the great day. That is, the arrival of Miss Lois Gilmour.

I was watching from an upper window when she arrived. Miss Bray was with me. From the carriage stepped a tall slim young woman, quietly but very elegantly dressed.

"She does not look much like a governess," I said, and then I wondered whether I had hurt Miss Bray who for all her prettiness was scarcely elegant, being a little on the plump side and what is called "a little woman." She is cuddly, sweet and feminine—but never elegant.

The summons came very soon. I was wanted in the drawing room.

I went down in trepidation. Papa was there and with him the elegant young woman who I had seen alight from the carriage.

"This is Ann Alice," said Papa.

"How do you do, Ann Alice?"

As she took my hand I looked into her eyes which were large and deep blue. She was beautiful in a way. Her features were clear-cut, on classical lines; her nose was rather long but very straight; her lips inclined to be full. Warm lips and cold eyes, I thought.

But I am prejudiced against her for the unreasonable reason that she is not Miss Bray.

"And Ann Alice, this is Miss Gilmour who is so looking forward to teaching you."

"I am sure," said Miss Gilmour, "that you and I are going to get along very well."

I am not quite so sure.

"Miss Bray, as you know, has been with Ann Alice for . . . for . . . " began Papa.

"Six years," I said.

"And now she is leaving to get married."

Miss Gilmour smiled.

"I think you might take Miss Gilmour to her room," said my father. "And when you are ready perhaps you will take tea with my daughter and me, Miss Gilmour. And after that Ann Alice can introduce you to Miss Bray."

"That seems to me very satisfactory," said Miss Gilmour.

It has been a strange afternoon. I showed her her room. I felt she was assessing everything, the house, the furnishings and me. She has been too friendly too suddenly. She has said more than once that she is sure we are going to get along very well.

I fancied she was more at home taking tea with my father than with me alone. I wish I could rid myself of this uneasy feeling. I am sure it will be all right, for she seems eager to make it so, and if I am, too, how can we fail to be happy together?

Miss Gilmour talked a great deal over tea and I have been thinking how strange it was that my father, who was rarely at home at this hour, had gone to the trouble, not only of being here to receive her but of taking tea with her as well. In a way they had seemed to ignore me. Anyone would have thought she was coming to be governess to him instead of me, I remarked afterward to Miss Bray.

Miss Gilmour talked a great deal about herself. She came from Devonshire where her father had owned a small estate. He had been robbed by an unscrupulous agent who had escaped with the family's priceless possessions. Her father had never recovered from the shock and had had a stroke. She herself had been left almost penniless and forced to earn her living, and must do so in the only way open to a gentlewoman of some education.

My father was most sympathetic.

"But I must not burden you with my troubles," said Miss Gilmour. "In fact, I am sure they are now at an end. I feel I am going to be happy here with Ann Alice."

"We shall do our best to make you so," said my father, as though she were an honoured guest rather than someone in his employ.

Miss Gilmour might not be exactly beautiful but she has what I can only describe as an allure. My father seems to have recognized that.

I introduced her to Miss Bray as we had arranged. I was very eager to know what Miss Bray thought of her. But my dear governess is already living in the future and I can see that she is ready to accept

Miss Gilmour's own view of herself . . . just as my father appears to be.

I wish that I did not feel uneasy and I am glad I started writing in my journal because I can now capture what I actually feel at the time when it is happening. Perhaps I shall be laughing at my foolishness in a little while. I hope so. But I want to put on record that I felt it.

October 10th   It is some time since I wrote in my journal. That is because I have felt disinclined to do so. I have been very sad since Miss Bray's wedding. Why is it that one only appreciates people when one has lost them. I went to her wedding. It was a very happy affair and everyone—except myself—thinks it is an ideal outcome—so it may be for Miss Bray and her Reverend gentleman, but I can hardly say it is for me.

This is an entirely selfish point of view, I know, and I must be happy for Miss Bray—Mrs. Eggerton now. But how difficult it is to be happy for others when their happiness means one's own despair. Well, perhaps despair is too strong a word. I do write the most extraordinary things in this journal. It seems to have an odd effect on me. It is almost as though I am talking to myself. Perhaps that is the purpose of journals. That is why they are such a private matter and so useful in recording life as it is really lived and not suffused with a rosy glow or abject gloom—however one would want to represent the event after it has faded a little from the mind.

And Miss Gilmour? What is it about her? I do not know. She does not insist that I work hard. She is interesting. She is clever, knowledgeable. But she is not like a governess.

What makes me feel rather wistful is that there is no one in whom I can confide. My brother Charles was always at what they call the "Shop" in Great Stanton and was deeply involved in the business there. He went away some months ago on an expedition to some of the uncharted places of the Earth. I sometimes wish I were a man so that I could share in such adventures.

But I want to think about Miss Gilmour so I must write about her. I want to know about her and now that I am writing more in my journal I feel I am getting to know more about myself as well as other people. I have always been interested in people, always wanted to know about them. Usually one can draw them out. I can at any rate. I believe I have a special gift for it. But not with Miss Gilmour. I always feel that she has secrets. I imagine I can see secrets in her eyes. They are such strange eyes. They glitter. They are a deep shade of blue and her eyebrows and lashes are very black—so is her hair. I fancy she blackens her brows and lashes because sometimes they seem darker than others.

My father asked her to take a glass of sherry with him yesterday.

"He wants to hear of your progress," Miss Gilmour told me. "What am I going to say?" She looked at me rather archly. It did not fit her very well and I felt another of those odd twinges of uneasiness.

I said: "You must say what you think."

"I shall tell him what a wonderful pupil you are and that you make my task easy and me happy. How is that?"

"I don't believe it is true," I said.

"I want to make him happy. I want to make you happy. You wouldn't want me to say you were an idle pupil, would you?"

"No, because that wouldn't be true. But I do not believe for one moment that you think I am wonderful."

"You really are quite a clever little thing," she said. "There is no mistake about that."

Her face hardened a little. She was always a trifle cross when I did not respond to her offers of friendship.

October 14th   What is making me write in my journal tonight is something that happened this afternoon.

I am supposed to take someone with me when I go riding, but it is a rule which I am beginning to ignore more and more. Really! I am past sixteen. I shall be seventeen soon, well, in about seven months' time, and I really do think that a girl of my age should have a little freedom.

The stable people never mention it when I go alone and I always saddle my own horse in case there should be a fuss; so they are not involved.

Miss Gilmour rides with me now and then, but she is not one of those people who ride for pleasure. When she rides it is to get somewhere. She never notices the scenery as Miss Bray used to; and Miss Bray had a lot of funny stories to tell about animals and plants and people. Miss Gilmour has none of those. She is never interested in travelling—only in arriving. She is no fun to be with.

This afternoon I rode out alone and I had gone rather farther than usual, and as I came past the Royal Oak I saw one of our horses—the one Miss Gilmour usually rides—close to the block outside the inn.

There was another horse there. I wondered if I had been mistaken and was overcome with curiosity and eager to prove whether or not I had been.

I alighted and tethered my horse with the others and went into the inn.

No, I had not been mistaken. There was Miss Gilmour, sitting at one of the tables, a tankard before her, talking to a man. He was rather good-looking and his dark eyes were very noticeable because of his white wig—well powdered and fashionable. His long-tailed coat and broad hat were equally stylish.

Miss Gilmour looked strikingly handsome, wearing a dress which could be suitable either for riding or walking. It was very full skirted with a plain tightly fitted bodice and a frothy white cravat. On her head was a black top hat with a feather in it of the same shade of dark blue as her dress. I had never seen anyone look less like a governess. Nor had I seen anyone so overcome by surprise as when she lifted her eyes and saw me.

In fact I would say it was a great shock to her.

She half rose and said in a voice I have never heard her use before: "Ann Alice."

"Hello," I replied. "I was passing and I saw your horse outside. I thought I recognized him, and I came to see if I was right."

She recovered her calm very quickly. "Well, what a pleasant surprise! I came into the inn for refreshment and who should I find but an old friend of my family."

The man had risen. He was about Miss Gilmour's age—late twenties, I imagined. He bowed low.

"Oh yes," said Miss Gilmour. "I'm forgetting my manners. This is Mr. Desmond Featherstone. Mr. Featherstone, Miss Ann Alice Mallory, my dear little pupil." She turned to me. "Are you alone?" she asked quickly.

"Yes," I replied rather defiantly. "I saw no reason why I shouldn't . . . "

"No reason at all," she said in a most ungoverness-like manner.

It was as though we were all conspirators.

"Now Miss Mallory is here she might like a little refreshment," suggested Mr. Featherstone.

"Would you?" asked Miss Gilmour.

"Cider would be very welcome."

Mr. Featherstone called to one of the serving maids, a rather pretty girl in a cross-over laced bodice and a white mob cap.

Mr. Featherstone said, "Cider for the young lady, please."

The girl smiled at Mr. Featherstone in a rather special way as though she was delighted to serve him. I was beginning to notice those little signs which passed between members of opposite sexes.

Mr. Featherstone turned his attention to me. His glittering dark eyes seemed to be trying to penetrate my thoughts.

After the first few seconds Miss Gilmour had recovered her equilibrium. She said again: "This *is* a surprise. First Mr. Featherstone, and then Ann Alice . . . quite a little party."

She seemed so strongly to be stressing the fact that she had met Mr. Featherstone by chance that I wondered whether it was not so, and they had met by arrangement. She made the mistake a lot of people make of regarding me as a simple child when I was fast growing up and thinking like an adult quite often. And something was telling me that the attraction which I sometimes noticed between men and women was present between Mr. Featherstone and Miss Gilmour.

The cider came.

"I trust it is to your liking, Miss Mallory," said Mr. Featherstone.

"It is very good," I replied. "And I really was thirsty."

He leaned towards me. "I am so glad you decided to come in," he said. "I should have been quite desolate if you had not done so."

"If I had not done so you would not have known that the possibility of my coming in had arisen so how could you have been desolate?" I asked.

Miss Gilmour laughed. "My pupil is not a simple little girl," she said. "You will find it hard to fault her reasoning, I can assure you. Remember, she is taught by me."

"I must remember that," he said with mock seriousness.

He asked about the map-making shop and I told him that one of my ancestors had sailed with Drake and that ever since those days there had been great interest in maps in our family.

"Map making is not only interesting, it is profitable," added Miss Gilmour.

He asked me about the country and the Manor which had been my home since my birth. I told him that my mother was dead and that I still missed her very much.

He patted my hand in sympathy. He said: "But you have your father. I'll swear you are the apple of his eye."

"He is hardly aware of me."

"Oh come," protested Miss Gilmour, "he is the best of fathers. He talks a great deal about you to me."

"He did not talk much to Miss Bray."

Miss Gilmour smiled secretly.

"I think he is very eager that you should be well cared for," she said.

Mr. Featherstone had moved his chair nearer to mine. Every now and then he would reach out and touch my arm as though to emphasize a point. It made me feel uneasy and I wished he would not do it. Miss Gilmour did not seem to like his doing it either.

I said: "Are you staying in the neighbourhood, Mr. Featherstone?"

His eyes smiled into mine and he tried to hold my gaze but I looked away.

"I should like to think that was a matter of concern to you, Miss Ann Alice," he said.

"I should hope, of course, that you had comfortable lodgings."

"*I* hope I may meet you again when you take one of your country rides."

"Ann Alice is always breaking rules," said Miss Gilmour. "She is not supposed to ride alone. It is a good thing that we met. We can go back together and then it will be thought that we set out in each other's company."

"Do you often break the rules, Miss Ann Alice?" he asked.

"Some rules are really meant to be broken . . . if they don't make much sense. I shall soon be seventeen. That is quite old enough to ride alone."

"Indeed it is. Seventeen! A delectable age. I fancy you are something of a rebel."

"And I fancy," said Miss Gilmour, "that we should be returning to the Manor."

I rose. I felt that I wanted to get away from them both. I wanted to be in my room and write down every detail of that encounter in my journal before I forgot.

We came out of the inn and mounted our horses. Mr. Featherstone rode with us a little way and then with one of his exaggerated bows, he left us.

"What an extraordinary thing," said Miss Gilmour. "To run across an old friend of my family like that . . . quite by chance."

Yes, I thought, you are stressing that fact just a little too much, Miss Gilmour.

I do not trust Miss Gilmour.

I have come straight to my room to write it all down in my journal.

January 1st 1791   The first day of the New Year.

What a long time since I have last written in my journal. I seem to have developed a distaste for writing in it and I have only just thought of it because this is the first day of the year and of course because of Papa.

The journal has been lying at the back of the drawer where I keep it so that it is out of sight. I would not want anyone to read my innermost thoughts, which is how I like to think of what I write in my journal.

I have seen Mr. Featherstone on one or two occasions. He seems to make a habit of coming . . . "On business" he says. I wonder what his business is and where. If it is in London—as I suppose it is—he is rather far away. I know one can get there in not too long a time, but why not lodge up there?

Sometimes I wonder whether he is—as they say in the kitchen— "sweet on" Miss Gilmour. She is the sort of person men do seem to get "sweet on" rather easily.

I hope he is. Then perhaps he will marry her and carry her off as the Reverend James Eggerton did Miss Bray. Then I should be rid of them both and surely my father would say there is no need of another governess for such a mature person as his daughter has become.

It is Mr. Featherstone's attitude towards me that I find a little worrying. He always seems to try to get close to me; and his hands stray. That is the only way I can think of describing them. He gesticulates when he talks and his hands shoot out to rest on my shoulder, on my arm or sometimes on my hair. And they linger. His eyes glitter and they stare at me. I feel uncomfortable under the scrutiny.

I think he is a little sinister.

But I suppose as he is a friend of Miss Gilmour's family he would want to see her now and then. It is really quite natural and I suppose, as Miss Bray used to say, I am too imaginative.

Christmas was unlike last Christmas . . . or any other Christmas. We had a few guests as we always do, and my father suggested that Miss Gilmour join the party.

"Christmas is Christmas," he said to me—unusually communicative.

"And Miss Gilmour is here now. We can't leave her out. Perhaps you should suggest, Ann Alice, that she joins us like a member of the family. Coming from you that would show thoughtfulness and fine feeling."

Miss Gilmour started having her meals with us some time ago. My father had said it was time I gave up eating in the nursery. I was coming up to seventeen. So, with Miss Gilmour, I should join him. Miss Gilmour said she thought it was an excellent idea. In her opinion young people should not be kept too long in the nursery.

So now we sit at the table together. My father has changed quite a lot and this is due to the company of Miss Gilmour. She sparkles and he laughs a good deal at what she has to say. She displays a rather wonderful mixture of decorum and sophistication. She is modest yet bold. What is it? I cannot say except that it is Miss Gilmour and people of the opposite sex seem to find it very attractive.

Miss Gilmour looked embarrassed when the question of Christmas was raised. She was dubious when I asked her to join us and I did not press the point. She brought up the subject at dinner.

"I was so touched," she said. "But I thought it better not. You will have your friends . . . your special friends."

"But Ann Alice would very much like you to join us. Would you not, my dear?"

Why is it when people want something they like others to pretend they are really the ones who want it?

I hesitated for a moment and as I saw the look of horror begin to dawn in my father's face I said: "Oh . . . of course." And despised myself for lying. Why didn't I tell the truth and say, No, I don't want Miss Gilmour to be there at Christmas. Christmas will be quite different with her.

And I was right about that. Miss Gilmour took over Christmas.

One day, she said to my father: "I have a friend . . . a friend of my family . . . he is staying at an inn and can't get to his home for Christmas. I feel quite wretched thinking of him all alone for Christmas."

My father immediately said that she must invite him to the house.

I was not really surprised when the guest turned out to be Mr. Featherstone.

So he was there with her and if she had not spoilt our Christmas he would have done so.

He danced with me. His hands, his straying hands ... how I loathed them! They came to me in vague dreams from which I always awoke in a state of apprehension, though I was never quite sure why.

January 3rd · I am finding it very difficult to write this down because I really can't believe that it has happened. I want to write about other things because I know that when I see it written down in my journal I shall have to accept it. But what is the use of pretending.

My father called me into his study and said: "I want you to be the first to know."

I must have guessed for the impulse came to me to shout: "No. Don't say it. It can't be."

But I just stood there looking at him steadily and he had no notion of my longing to hear him say something other than what I feared he would.

"It has been a long time since your mother died, Ann Alice. A man gets lonely. You understand that?"

"Of course I understand," I said. "I wish people wouldn't keep hinting that I don't."

He looked surprised at my peevish retort but he went on: "I am going to be married again. Lois and I decided that you should be told right away ... before we make a formal announcement."

"Lois! Miss Gilmour."

"It has all worked out very happily. I was surprised when Lois agreed. She is considerably younger than I and very attractive."

I was staring at him wretchedly, trying to beg him to say it was all a joke.

"Tell me," he said, "isn't it a happy solution to everything?"

I stammered: "I ... don't know."

"It's a surprise to you. Ever since Lois came here as your governess the house has changed."

Yes, it has changed for me as well as for him.

"It seems brighter just as it used to when—"

"You mean when my mother was here."

"These tragedies come to us, Ann Alice. We have to accept them. They are God's will. But we should not nurse our grief. That is not what God intends. We should put sorrow behind us. We should try to reach for happiness."

I nodded and turned away.

"I am so pleased that you understand," he said. "I am doing this for you as well as for myself."

I wanted to shout at him: Don't think of me. It is not what I want. I want her to go right away . . . and take Mr. Featherstone with her.

"We shall give a dinner party on Twelfth Night," he was saying, "and then we shall announce it."

There was nothing I could say without betraying my feelings. I just nodded and escaped as soon as I could.

And now I sit here staring at the words in my journal. My father is going to marry Miss Gilmour.

Somewhere at the back of my mind I know that this is what I have been fearing for a long time.

March 1st   They were married today. The house is quiet now. It reminds me of a tiger . . . sleeping. But it will awaken and then it will pounce. It will destroy everything that was and make a new house of this.

I love my little room. I pull the blue curtains about my bed and shut myself in. This is my little sanctum. Here I can be private . . . all alone.

They left this afternoon for their honeymoon. They have gone to Italy.

"I always wanted to go," said Miss Gilmour.

They will do a grand tour. They can't go to France because of the troubles there. Terrible things are happening in France now. They say that the King and Queen are in great danger. Nobody in their right senses would want to visit France now, said Papa. So it is to be Italy — land of lakes, mountains and the finest art treasures in the world. Papa is very interested in these and Miss Gilmour — only she is not Miss Gilmour any more; she is my stepmother — is interested in everything that Papa is interested in.

She is the perfect companion.

It is such a short time ago that I was saying goodbye to dear Miss Bray. Oh, why did she have to go? She is now expecting a baby and she writes that she is the happiest woman in the world. It is selfish to wish that she had never gone to her Reverend James.

But how can I help it?

Just think, I say to myself, if Miss Bray had not left I should not now have a stepmother. Everything would be as it used to be. Dull perhaps, but cosy.

And now . . . it is so different. A new atmosphere is permeating the house. I wonder if anyone else feels it besides myself. I don't really think they do, so perhaps I am imagining it.

It is as though something evil has come into the house . . . silent, watchful, waiting to pounce.

March 2nd   I rode out alone today and I had not gone far when I met Mr. Featherstone.

It was quite a shock. A shiver went through me as he came up beside me. We were close to the woods and it was rather lonely. I could not help wondering whether he had followed me and waited for this moment to catch me up.

"What a delightful surprise!"

"Oh . . . good afternoon, Mr. Featherstone."

"I am going to be bold and ride with you."

"I hope your business is going satisfactorily."

"Couldn't be better."

"You must find it tiresome living in an inn. I expect you are longing for your business to be completed so that you can return to your home."

"I find the life here very diverting. After all, I have made some delightful acquaintances."

He brought his horse close to mine and I turned to look at him. He was gazing at me implying that I of course was among those delightful acquaintances. I was glad he could not reach me, for if he had been able to, his hand would be on my arm or my shoulder.

I said: "I like to gallop at this point." And I shot away. But of course he was pounding along beside me.

I was forced to slow down because we had come to the road.

"You must have a quiet house now that your father is on his honeymoon with his new wife," he said.

"I don't notice it."

"I thought you might be lonely."

"Not in the least."

"You have many friends, I don't doubt."

"I have enough to occupy me."

"No more lessons . . . not now you have lost a governess and gained a stepmother."

"I am getting a little old for lessons."

"Quite the young lady. I can see that."

"I turn off here, Mr. Featherstone."

"I was going that way."

"I am returning to the house."

"That was a short ride."

I did not answer. I was resisting the impulse to tell him I was going back to escape from him.

"Now that you are—alone—perhaps we could meet?"

"Oh, I have a great deal to do."

"Too busy to see friends?"

"Oh no. I have time for my *friends.*"

"Oh, Miss Ann Alice, I was hoping you would count me among them."

"You are Miss Gilmour's friend."

"Miss Gilmour? Oh . . . Mrs. Mallory, of course. It was so good of your father to invite me to his house. I expect now that the family friend has become his wife, I shall have more invitations."

"I daresay my father's wife will decide who is invited now."

"Then I should be assured of a welcome."

We had reached the Green. The house stood on the south side of it. I felt annoyed to have had to cut short my ride, but I was determined not to be with him.

"Well, goodbye, Mr. Featherstone."

I started to canter across the Green, but he was still beside me.

"Aren't you going to invite me in?"

"I am afraid I can't do that . . . now."

He looked rueful.

"Never mind. I shall call when you have more time."

He took off his hat and gave that ridiculously exaggerated bow which he must have learned in the set of the Prince of Wales of which he implied he was an associate.

I wish he would go back to London or Brighton or wherever they were and practice his fancy manners on them.

I came into the house—hot and angry.

Miss Gilmour—I refuse to call her anything else—had ruined my pleasant existence in every way.

March 6th   Is there no way of escaping that man? He called at the house yesterday. I was out and when I came in he was in the hall. If I had been told I could have sent the maid down to say that I was not at home. But I was caught.

He said he was thirsty in the hearing of the maid and she glanced questioningly at me so that all I could do was offer him some wine. Then I had to drink with him.

I took him into the small parlour which leads from the hall and where we entertain casual callers. I wondered how soon I could escape.

"This is most pleasant," he said.

I was silent, not being able to utter the blatant lie which even implied agreement would have been.

"I am so happy I came here," he went on. "It is such a delightful part of the world and London is within easy access."

"Wouldn't it be more convenient to be nearer?"

"Perhaps, but not so congenial. I can't tell you what a happy day that was for me when I discovered your stepmother, and she introduced me to your household."

Again I was silent. I was a most ungracious hostess but then I was a most unwilling one.

"When do you expect the happy couple to return?" he asked.

"I gather they will be away for a month. It is hardly worth travelling so far for a shorter stay."

"And a honeymoon!" His dark eyes tried to hold mine and strangely enough I found it hard to draw mine away. He had a certain effect on me. I wished I could be indifferent but he had a sort of horrible fascination for me. I suppose that is how a rabbit feels when face to face with a stoat. "Can you imagine it? Florence . . . Venice . . . Rome . . . I suppose they will visit all those places. How would you like to do that, Miss Ann Alice?"

"I am sure it would be most interesting."

"A great deal would depend on one's companion."

I looked at him pointedly. "That is always the case," I said, "whether one is in Venice or Venezuela."

"How do you know?" he asked laughing. "Have you ever visited Venezuela?"

"No. Nor Venice either."

"But you will one day, and when you do I hope it will be in the right company. I must confess never having been to Venezuela, but Venice . . . well, that beautiful city is not unknown to me. I should like to show you

Venice. You would enjoy that . . . drifting along the canals in a gondola
. . . or perhaps in Florence . . . shopping on the Ponte Vecchio."

"I suppose we all have our dreams of seeing the world."

"The great thing is to put those plans into action. Don't you agree?"

"Let me give you some more wine." I was sorry I had spoken for it
meant going near to him. His fingers touched mine as I gave him the glass.

"This is a very happy morning for me," he said.

I did not answer and he went on: "Will you ride with me tomorrow?
I know of a very pleasant inn not far away. They serve the most delicious
roast beef."

"It is out of the question," I replied. "I have commitments tomorrow."

"There is the next day."

"My time is fully occupied."

"What a busy young lady you are! I am determined to find some
time when you are free. I should like to see that establishment about
which I have heard so much."

"Oh, are you interested in maps?"

"Fascinated by them. There is so much I want explained to me."

"Then you have come to the wrong person," I replied triumphantly.
"I know little about them. You will have to go to the shop and ask them
there. If my brother were here he would talk to you about that."

"Oh, so you have a brother?" Did I imagine it, or was he a little
dismayed?

"Oh yes. He is away on some expedition. Exploring new territories.
That's an essential part of map making."

"I see."

"He could have told you all you want to know. He was always very
enthusiastic on the subject."

"He must be older than you."

"He is and he has never had much time to spare for his sister."

"Poor little lonely one!"

"Not lonely at all. I have so much to interest me. I don't really need
anyone."

"So self-sufficient. That's a very good thing to be."

"I think so."

"Well, what about our outing?"

He was so persistent that it was difficult to give him a definite
refusal without telling him the truth, which was that I did not like

his company and that he faintly alarmed me in a way which I did not fully understand. It was instinct, I suppose. So I prevaricated.

"This week is out of the question. I am not sure about the next."

He understood, of course. He regarded me sardonically.

"I am determined to catch you one day," he said.

And his words sounded ominous.

How glad I was when he left.

March 10th   He has proved himself right. He has caught me at last. I wish I had the courage to tell him that I want him to leave me alone. One has been brought up with such a respect for good manners—one might say a reverence—that one is never able to be absolutely sincere.

So I have gone on eluding him, escaping as gracefully as I could. I guess he is the sort of man who enjoys a challenge and the more I am determined to escape, the more determined he is to catch me.

Yesterday was a lovely day. The fields were white and gold with daisies, buttercups and dandelions; and the horse chestnuts and sycamores were showing their green leaves.

There was a fresh wind and that delicious tang in the air which is a herald of the spring. I love this time of the year when the birds seem to be going wild with joy.

Lovely springtime! And how good it is to gallop across the meadows and then slow down and trundle through the lanes and to look for wild flowers in the hedgerows and on the banks and try to remember the names Miss Bray had for them all.

It is ten days since my father and his new wife left for Italy. They will be back on the first of April. Then everything is going to be different. I am dreading their return. Sometimes I think I should be making plans. What will it be like when they come back? I should be prepared. But what can I do? There is no one whose advice I can ask. Unless it is Miss Bray . . . Mrs. Eggerton, mother-to-be. She will be absorbed in preparation for her baby and be quite unable to think of anything else. No, I cannot intrude on her blissful contentment. I must wait and see. Perhaps it will not be so bad. Perhaps I am exaggerating. After all, what harm has Miss Gilmour done to me? She has always been accommodating. She has never pressed me to study hard. She has been ready to be friendly. What is it? Why do I have this feeling of apprehension? It is the same with Mr. Featherstone.

I was not far from the inn where I had first seen him with Miss Gilmour when he came up to me.

"Hello," he said. "This is an unexpected pleasure."

"I am just on my way home."

"It seems to be your usual destination when we meet. In any case there is no hurry, is there?"

"I did not want to be late."

"I know you have many pressing engagements, but just once, eh? What about a little refreshment? It was in this very inn that we first met. So it is rather an occasion, is it not?"

I hesitated. Perhaps I was being rather foolish. I had been so curt with him and that was rather bad manners. And what harm could we do drinking a goblet of cider. Perhaps I could manage to convey to him subtly that I preferred to ride alone.

So I agreed; we dismounted and went into the inn.

We sat at the table where I had found him sitting with Miss Gilmour.

"Our honeymooners will soon be back," he said, when the cider was brought. "Your continued health and happiness, Miss Ann Alice."

"Thank you. And yours."

"I am glad you wish me well. For my future contentment, I have a feeling, will depend on you."

"You surprise me, Mr. Featherstone."

"You are surprised only because you are so adorably innocent. You are on the threshold of life."

"I find it rather irritating when people stress my youth. I am not so very young."

"Indeed not. You are, as I know, verging on seventeen. When is it? The glorious twenty-first of May?"

"How did you know?"

"What is it they say? A little bird . . ."

"The bird, I imagine, was not so little. It must have been Miss Gilmour."

"Miss Gilmour no longer. The happy Mrs. Mallory. And you should not be irritated by appreciation of your youth. Youth is the most precious gift the gods bestow. Unfortunately it does not last. Very sad, is it not?"

"I should not mind being a little older, I do assure you."

"We all want to be older when we are young and younger when we are old. It is the perversity of human nature. But why talk in generalizations. It is of you I want to talk."

"A not very interesting subject, I am afraid."

"An absorbing subject." His question startled me. "What do you think of me?"

I flushed. I could not tell him what I really thought of him. I sought the right words. "I think you are probably very . . . shrewd."

"Oh, thank you. What else?"

"Well, I suppose a man of the world."

"A shrewd man of the world. It does not sound too bad for a start. Anything else?"

"I cannot understand why you bother to pursue me."

He laughed. "Shall I tell you what I think of you?"

"I am not really interested."

"You are growing up, and you don't always tell the truth. Everybody wants to know what others think of them. I am going to tell you in any case. I think you are adorable."

I blushed to the roots of my hair I am sure.

"And," he went on, "*I* am speaking the truth."

I struggled for my composure.

"Now I will speak the truth," I said, "and I will say that I am sure you find many people of my sex . . . adorable."

"You are discerning. I will not deny it."

"It would be useless to."

"And quite out of the question, if this is to be an exchange of truths. But," he went on, "you are the most adorable of them all."

I looked at him cynically. "Well, the cider was good," I said. "Thank you for it. And I really must be going."

"We have only just come."

"It does not take very long to drink a goblet of cider."

"But look, I have not finished mine."

"I could leave you to finish it."

"I could not allow you to go back alone."

"I came out alone."

"I wonder what your father will have to say about your solitary wanderings when he returns."

"He will be too much engrossed with his new wife to think much about me."

His hand came out across the table and I was too late to elude it. He held mine tightly, fondling it.

"So you are a little—jealous?"

"Indeed I am not."

"Stepmothers have a reputation for being unacceptable."

"I would not judge beforehand. I have only had a stepmother for ten days and during those she has been absent."

"Marriages are in the air," he said. "They say they are catching."

I shrugged my shoulders and managed to free my hand. I stood up.

"Do you insist?" he asked.

"I do."

"Just as the conversation is getting interesting."

"Is it so interesting to you?"

"Enormously so. I am telling you how much I admire you. You are more than pretty. You are beautiful."

I looked at him scornfully. "I do have an excellent mirror, Mr. Featherstone. And even if it does not tell me what I would like to know, it tells me the truth."

I thought of dear Miss Bray comforting me. "You may not be exactly pretty, Ann Alice, but you have an interesting face. Yes, on the whole I think you may turn out to be quite attractive."

And now he was telling me I was beautiful!

"Your hair is a lovely shade of brown and your eyes . . . they show many colours. Which are they? Brown? Green? Grey?"

"Generally known as hazel," I said, "and really quite undistinguished."

"You have a pretty mouth."

"Thank you. That is a nice point on which to close this assessment of my appearance."

"I could go on talking of them endlessly."

"Then I am afraid I should have to leave you to talk to yourself. I find the subject rather boring."

He drained his goblet.

"Are you determined to cut short this pleasant tête-à-tête?"

He was standing beside me and taking my arm held it firmly. His face was very close to mine and for a moment I thought he was going to kiss me. I recoiled in horror.

"Do you not like me a little?" he asked almost pathetically.

I released my arm and started for the door.

"I hardly know you, Mr. Featherstone," I said over my shoulder. "I never make hasty judgements of people."

"I think when you really allow yourself to know me you might become rather fond of me."

He insisted on helping me into the saddle.

"Thank you," I said. He stood for a few moments looking up at me. Then he took my hand and kissed it. I felt as though I had been touched by a snake.

He looked at me pleadingly. "Give yourself a chance to know me," he said.

I turned my horse away and did not answer. Did I imagine it or did I detect an angry glint in his eyes. I was not sure but it sent a little shiver of alarm through me.

I walked my horse away from the inn and he was beside me.

We rode home in silence.

But my uneasiness is growing.

March 23rd   In a week they will return. I am almost eager for them to do so. This month has been a strange one for me and it seems to have been haunted by Mr. Featherstone.

I have not been riding so much because he is sure to be lying in wait for me. He is always trying to tell me that he is in love with me.

I don't believe him for one instant. As a matter of fact sometimes I think he dislikes me. I have caught an expression flitting across his face and he looks really angry. I think he has probably made easy conquests in the past and my aloofness does not please him at all.

There were times when I thought he was in love with Miss Gilmour. Oh, how I wish he had been and they had gone away together!

How different everything would have been then!

If Miss Bray were not in the process of having a baby I would go to her. I could never have explained my feelings to her though. It was better to do nothing but to continue with the cat-and-mouse game in which Mr. Featherstone seemed determined to indulge. I keep thinking of that analogy. What does the cat do when it catches the mouse? It teases it, pretending it is going to allow it to escape and catches it before it can do so, testing it, torturing it . . . until it finally kills it.

I am really working myself into a state of nervousness over Mr. Featherstone.

I sometimes wake in the night in a state of terror because I believe he is in the house. I have even risen from my bed, opened the door and looked into the corridor really expecting to see him lurking there. Sometimes, I stand at my window which is at the back of the house and does not look over the Green but onto the fields and the woods. I look for a figure hiding there.

Then I laugh at myself. "Silly dreams. Foolish imaginings," I say.

But it is the fear in my mind which produces these thoughts.

Why do I feel so intense about him? It is almost as though it is a premonition, a warning.

It will be better when they come home, I keep telling myself.

Just another week.

May 3rd   Today I remembered my journal. I could not find it at first and I had a horrible fear that I had lost it. I started to wonder what I had written in it and what my stepmother would think if it fell into her hands. I was sure I had written something unflattering about her.

Perhaps I should be careful what I write in it but what is the sense of having a journal if one does not write exactly what one feels at the time?

To my great joy I found it. It was where I had put it at the back of the drawer which seems to be a good place for it, behind the gloves and scarves, well hidden away.

It is some time now since they came back. I was there to greet them. I studied Papa carefully. He looked very happy. Miss Gilmour—I must remember to call her my stepmother—looked radiant. She had new clothes, very smart, "Continental" they call them in the kitchen. "That Frenchy touch." Though they hadn't been to France, of course.

I have begun to think that I may be mistaken about my stepmother. Everyone says what a good match it is and how pleased they are for Papa to have "found happiness again." He had been a widower too long, they all agree, and people have to learn not to mourn forever.

The same clichés are brought out over and over again and I have been thinking what a boon they are for they roll off the tongue in such an easy manner and people can always feel they have said the "right thing."

My stepmother has set about changing the house. There are new furnishings in several of the rooms. She does not interfere much with the servants and that makes her quite popular although there are certain members of the domestic staff who think it is not quite proper that one who had been more or less a servant in the house should now be elevated to the role of mistress.

However, they seem to be forgetting that and it is clear that my stepmother is enjoying her new position.

It has been decided that I could very well do without a new governess, though my stepmother has suggested that I do a certain amount of reading every day which she will supervise. My father listened to all this with approval and I have to admit that he seems more like a father than he has done since the death of my mother.

The supervising of my reading is dwindling and I believe that in due course it will cease. I am pleased about that.

There has been a little controversy about what I should call her. There have been one or two occasions when I have forgotten and the name Miss Gilmour has slipped out. That did not please her . . . nor my father.

It is amazing how one can manage for a long time without calling people anything—and that was what I did. One day, just as we were leaving the dining room, she put her arm round me and said in that cosy little voice which she uses now and then: "Wouldn't it be nice if you could call me Mother . . . or Mama . . . or something like that?"

"Oh . . . I couldn't," I blurted out.

"Why not?" Her voice was sharp and I could see that my father looked pained.

"Well," I stammered. "I remember my mother so well. There couldn't be anyone . . . "

My father looked impatient but she said, soothing now, "Of course . . . of course . . . " She sighed a little and then smiled sweetly. "Perhaps, Stepmamma. Could you manage that?"

"Yes, I suppose so," I said.

So I am to call her Stepmamma.

But I know that for quite a lot of the time I shall succeed in calling her nothing at all.

June 1st   Mr. Featherstone is still here. He waylays me just the same as ever, and I still avoid him when I can. I have decided not to be polite any more, and there are certain verbal battles between us which I find easier to handle than all that forced politeness.

When he said: "You were hoping to dodge me, weren't you?" I replied: "Yes, I was."

"Why?" he demanded.

"Because I want to be alone."

"A clash of wills! I want to be with you."

"I can't think why."

"I find you beautiful and stimulating. How do you find me?"

"Neither beautiful nor stimulating."

"I asked for that, did I not?"

"Indeed you did."

"What a forthright young lady you are!"

"I hope so."

"Very truthful."

"I try to be."

"Unkind."

"No, I don't agree."

"You cut me to the quick."

"You should not lay yourself open to cutting."

"What can a lovelorn fellow do?"

"Take himself off to more fruitful ground."

"But where would I find such beauty and wit?"

"Almost anywhere on Earth," I retorted.

"You are wrong. It is here . . . only here . . . and this is where my heart is."

I could laugh at him now. I was losing my fear of him. Everything seemed a little better since the return of my father and his wife. The pursuit of me was not quite so intense. I could ride out some days and never see him.

I wondered sometimes about the future. I was now seventeen. My stepmother said we should entertain more. "Don't forget," she told my father, "you have a marriageable daughter."

"I was lax in my duties until you came to look after me, my dear," he said.

"We have to think of Ann Alice," she insisted. "I'll invite people."

Desmond Featherstone came to the house to dine this evening. I was dreading it. I always hate to think of his being in the house. It is an odd creepy feeling, which is quite unaccountable, for what harm could he do? I wondered if I could plead a headache and not appear for dinner. I supposed that would be too obvious. Moreover it would not be so bad with others present.

I was right. It was not. I was aware when he looked at me across the table that it was different. He was now indulgent . . . as he would be to a very young person. He carefully addressed me as Miss Ann Alice, and he made it sound as though he thought I was just out of the schoolroom. I could hardly believe that this was the same man who had been trying to convince me that I was the young woman with whom he was in love. I could easily have convinced myself that he had been playing a game all the time.

I had the feeling that it was something to do with my stepmother and a strange quirk of fate enabled me to confirm this.

After the meal when they went into the drawing room, I said I would go up to bed. I often did this because they would drink port wine and usually stay up until very late, and although I dined with them as an adult, this part of the evening was considered to be a little unsuitable for my years.

I was very glad to escape so I came up to my room to write in my journal and to think about the strange behaviour of Desmond Featherstone and how different he seemed at some times when compared with others.

As I sat writing I heard sounds from below — the clopping of a horse's hoofs coming from the stables.

I went to my window and looked out. It was Desmond Featherstone coming from the stables on his way to his lodging. I dodged back quickly. I did not want him to see me.

Then I heard a voice and I recognized my stepmother's.

She spoke sharply and her voice was quite distinct.

"It has to stop," she said. "I won't have it."

Then his: "It is nothing . . . Only a game."

"I won't have it. You shall go straight back."

"I tell you it's a game. She is only a child."

"Sharper than you'd think. In any case, it is going to stop."

"Jealous?"

"You had better not forget . . . "

Their voices faded. I turned swiftly to the window. He was riding away and my stepmother was looking after him. He turned to wave and she waved back.

What did it mean? I knew they had been talking about me. So she was aware of his attempts at flirtation and she did not approve of them. She was warning him that it had to stop.

She had sounded angry.

I was glad.

But I think it is very strange that she should know and be so vehement.

When I have finished writing I shall put my journal away very carefully in future. I am glad I started it. It is so interesting to look back and remember.

June 5th   I have taken out my journal today because something astonishing has happened. Desmond Featherstone has gone away. It is so strange. He did not say goodbye. He just went.

I had seen him only once since that night when I overheard the conversation between him and my stepmother and then he seemed somewhat subdued. I think he really must have taken heed of her warning.

I have been thinking lately that perhaps I have misjudged her. I have disliked her without reason. One should always have a reason for liking or disliking people. Now I come to look back, I ask myself did I dislike Lois Gilmour simply because she was not Miss Bray to whom I had grown accustomed? People do unreasoning, illogical things like that.

She has been very pleasant to me always. She has gone out of her way to be kind and she really does seem concerned about getting eligible young men to the house as possible husbands for me. My father is delighted with his marriage so I suppose he has good reasons for being so.

A few days ago he was not very well. I did not hear about it until the afternoon because I do not normally see a great deal of him. He does not always come to breakfast, but then we take it at odd times and always help ourselves from the chafing dishes on the sideboard, so that if anyone is absent it can easily pass unnoticed.

But at lunch time my stepmother told me that he was spending the day in bed. She had insisted that he stay there because he was a little unwell. It was nothing to worry about she said. We must remember that he was not as young as he sometimes believed himself to be and she had insisted on his staying in bed.

She nurses him most assiduously. When I went to see him in the afternoon he was sitting up in bed looking, I thought, rather pleased with himself because my stepmother was fussing over him, wondering whether he was in a draught from an open window and whether he should have his dressing gown round his shoulders.

"You spoil me, my dear," he said.

"Get along with you. You're unspoilable."

"But you do fuss, you know, Lois."

"I worry about you, of course."

I watched them. He seemed so happy—and so did she.

Yes, perhaps I have misjudged her.

I will try to like her. I have promised myself to do so. It has been rather silly to dislike her just because I was so upset at losing Miss Bray and then again because she has taken the place of my mother.

I must be sensible. And really she has made my father very happy and everyone says what a wonderful solution it is for him.

September 2nd   I feel so ashamed because I have neglected my journal for so long. I really forgot about it. Then a little while ago I was searching for a pair of grey gloves to go with my new gown. I knew I had a pair and could not find them. And there they were caught in the back of the drawer and when I was trying to get them out I found my journal. I felt so ashamed—after all my resolutions to write in it more or less regularly. But I think this is a fairly common way people have with journals. They have—as I had—such good resolutions—and then they forget.

This is a good time to start again. I have read through what I wrote before. How it brings it all back! And how young I seemed when I wrote some of it.

I have come to live fairly peacefully under my stepmother's rule. I have tried very hard to like her but I can't really although I often think it is unfair of me not to. She is so good and kind to my father. She has looked after him so well when he has his turns. He has had about three in all and she insists on nursing him and he says she makes much more of them than they really are.

I have heard the servants talking about men who marry women so much younger than themselves. They whisper together mysteriously. "It's too much for them. They can't keep it up."

My stepmother insisted on his seeing the doctor. Dr. Brownless could find nothing really wrong. He merely said he must take life more slowly. My father is following his advice and does not go every day into Great Stanton as he used to. My stepmother is not very interested in the Shop, as we call it. I believe it is a very profitable business and highly respected throughout the country. Quite a number of people in the business of cartography come to Great Stanton to see my father and his manager. They are often entertained at the house and as far as that is concerned my stepmother is proving an excellent hostess.

I heard my father say to her: "It was the luckiest day of my life when you came to teach Ann Alice."

And she replied fervently: "And of mine."

So it is a very contented household and I am sure my father is quite happy to stay at home more so that he can be with my stepmother; and in any case there is an efficient manager at the Shop to deal with everything there.

We went to Bath during the season. My stepmother thought the baths might be good for my father; and he said that to humour her, he would try them.

My stepmother hinted that among the company there might be a suitable husband for me. It seemed hardly likely that I should find anyone among the gouty old gentlemen—mostly accompanied by their gossipy wives; and those exquisite young gentlemen, the beaux of Bath, could hardly be expected to notice me. More than once I had heard them declare in loud voices that they found the place devilish dull and that they felt inclined to desert the place and join H.R.H. without further delay. There were the fortune hunters, quizzing young women through their monocles, and doubtless comparing their charms with their alleged fortunes; there were simpering young girls and not-so-young ladies presumably looking for husbands.

I felt rather homesick for the fields and meadows and a life of freedom. I suffered emersion, which everyone seemed obliged to endure, and felt very ridiculous in my jacket and petticoat and most unattractive bonnet.

How long the days seemed! Drinking the water, taking the baths, going to the Abbey for the religious services, to concerts and the occasional ball at the Assembly Rooms.

My stepmother fitted perfectly into the life. Most people thought her charming. I noticed that quite a number of beaux ogled her, but although she was obviously aware of this and I thought I detected a secret satisfaction, she never strayed from my father's side.

She appeared to be interested in putting me forward, but I sometimes wondered whether she really was. That was how I constantly felt about her. I was never quite sure.

I did ride a little but always in the company of my father and stepmother and as she was not very keen on the exercise we did not do it often. But I could walk in the meadows and I did so every morning. There were people there so I was able to go alone and it was there that I encountered Desmond Featherstone. I was completely taken by surprise, not having seen him for so long.

He gave that exaggerated bow which always irritated me. "If it is not Miss Ann Alice herself! Well, who would have thought of meeting you here . . . and what a joy . . . alone! I am surprised that it is allowed."

"It is early morning, and I am older now, you know."

"And as beautiful as ever."

"Are you staying in Bath, Mr. Featherstone?"

"How formal! I had hoped I would be Desmond to you. Yes, a brief visit. And what do you think of Bath?"

"Very beautiful. I like the rocky wooded hills and the architecture is most elegant."

"And you like to mingle with the *beau monde?*"

"Not particularly."

"I wish I could see you alone. There is so much I want to say to you."

"I see nothing to prevent your saying it now."

"There is so much to prevent me. You for one thing."

"I have asked you to speak."

"If only you would like me a little!"

"Why should my likes or dislikes interfere with your powers of speech?"

"It is such fun to be with you."

"I daresay if you are staying here you will meet my family sooner or later. People here seem to get to know each other quickly and many know each other before they arrive."

"Ann Alice."

He had come close to me and gripped my arm. I shrank from his touch as I always do.

"Better not tell your stepmother . . . that we met like this, eh?"

"Why not?"

"She er . . . she might not approve."

"I don't have to get her approval before I speak to people, you know."

"I am sure of that, but on the other hand . . . just don't mention it."

"It wouldn't have occurred to me to. I shall probably have forgotten it by the time I see them again."

He looked at me reproachfully and then laughed.

"I don't think you forget me quite as easily as you pretend," he said.

I flushed, for he was right. Even now I have those odd dreams about him and they could easily fill me with disquiet. Now there, even in the open meadows, he could make me feel uneasy.

"I must go," I said. "Goodbye."

"Goodbye. I wish . . . "

But I did not give him time to say what he wished for I hurried off.

I think about him a great deal. He had been very earnest when he asked me not to tell my stepmother I had seen him.

I thought then: She does not want him to pester me. She really is trying to protect me.

That was another reason why I should try to like her.

I was glad when the visit to Bath was over.

Almost immediately after we returned my father had one of his attacks—a little worse than before. My stepmother wanted to call in the doctor, but my father said it was not necessary. He had been told it was due to overdoing things and it was obvious that the visit to Bath had been too strenuous for him.

However she did call the doctor, but that was after my father had recovered slightly. She said she was anxious and wanted him to see a physician. So to please her he agreed.

Apart from the visit to Bath and my encounter with Mr. Featherstone there seems to have been nothing worth recording, and I suppose that is why I did not think of my journal until today.

So now I sit here biting my pen and thinking back. Have I missed something important? Events should be recorded at the time they happen. That is the only way of getting the real truth. But looking back, I cannot see that there is anything of any great significance that I should remember.

February 1st 1792   Another long lapse. I am clearly not meant to be a diarist. I suppose my life is really so uneventful and it is only when something unusual happens that I remember my journal.

Something has happened. Today my stepmother told us about Freddy.

I have noticed that she has been preoccupied for some little time. My father noticed too because he said to me: "Do you think your stepmother is well?"

He was quite anxious.

"Why do you ask?" I said.

"She seems . . . a little worried."

I admitted I had noticed it.

"I have asked her and she says all is well."

"Perhaps we have imagined it."

Apparently we hadn't because today it came out.

I was having tea with them which my father liked me to do. He wanted continual confirmation that I was fond of my stepmother. I have heard him tell people that we get along splendidly. "It was the best thing for Ann Alice as well as for me," he says.

He deludes himself and as I don't want to disillusion him when he mentions this in my presence I just smile and say nothing.

I wonder why she decided to speak of it in front of me. After all this time I am still suspicious of her and at times I think I look for motives which don't exist.

Then suddenly when she had poured out the tea and I had taken my father's to him and accepted my own, she burst out: "There is something I want to tell you."

"Ah," said my father, "so there is something."

"It has been on my mind . . . for some time."

"My dear, you should have told me."

"I didn't want to worry you with my personal troubles."

"Lois! How can you say such a thing! You should know that I am here to share your troubles. When I think of how you have looked after me."

"Oh that," she said. "That was different. That was my duty and what I wanted to do more than anything."

We waited. She bit her lip and then she rushed on: "It's my sister-in-law . . . she died . . . a month ago."

"Your sister-in-law! You didn't say . . . I didn't know you had a family."

"Her death was rather sudden. I didn't hear until after the funeral."

"My dear, I am so sorry."

She was silent for a little while frowning slightly. My father looked at her tenderly, eager to give her time to explain as she wanted to.

"My brother quarrelled with my father and went off. He never came back and it was only when he died that we knew he had a wife. Now she is dead and she has left . . . a child."

"That's sad," said my father.

"You see this little boy is an orphan and . . . well, he is my nephew."

"You are going to see the child?"

"That is what I wanted to talk to you about. I'll have to go up there, you see. I'll have to do something about my nephew. I can't just leave him. Heavens knows what will happen."

My father was looking relieved. I don't know what he had been imagining was wrong.

"Why don't we both go. Where is it?"

"It's in Scotland. I think I should go alone."

"Very well, my dear. As you wish."

"I've got to find some solution for the boy." She lowered her head and crumbled the cake on her plate. "I have wanted to talk to you for some time . . . and I haven't really been able to bring myself to do it. It's worried me a great deal."

"I knew there was something," said my father triumphantly. "Well, what is it, Lois? You know I'll do everything possible to help."

"I—er—want to bring the boy here. You see, there is nowhere else. It might mean an orphanage . . . and I just can't bear the thought of that. He is, after all, my nephew."

"My dear Lois, is that all! You should have told me before. This is your home. Of course your nephew will be very welcome here."

She went over to my father and knelt at his side; then she took his hands and kissed them.

He was very moved. I saw the tears in his eyes.

I suppose I should have been moved too. It was a very touching scene. But all I could think of was: How theatrical!

I had the notion that I was watching a play.

March 1st   Little Freddy Gilmour arrived a week ago. He is a small pale boy, rather nervous and very much in awe of my stepmother. He looks at her with a kind of wonderment as though she is some sort of goddess. She has two worshippers in the household now.

I liked Freddy from the moment I saw him. He is eight years old but looks younger. I said I would teach him and my stepmother is very pleased. She has grown quite warm towards me and it is due, of course, to Freddy.

I feel I have another brother—although he is so much younger than I. Charles was never a real brother to me. He always looked down on me because I was so much younger. I don't feel in the least like that towards

Freddy. I am beginning to love him even though he has been here such a short time.

He seems to be very grateful to be in our house, so I imagine life was not very pleasant where he was before. When I speak to him about his mother he is noncommittal and clearly does not want to talk of the past. Perhaps it is because she is so recently dead. But when he mentions Aunt Lois he is really reverent.

Every morning when I awake I think of what I am going to teach him and it gives a zest to the day. He is very bright but I can see that few attempts have been made to educate him. He wants to learn and is always asking questions.

My father is absolutely delighted—with me, with Freddy, and of course, he is besotted about my stepmother.

He is glad Freddy has come because it has pleased Lois so much.

It seems we are a very happy family.

April 3rd   I have been too busy to think about my journal and it is only now that something really important has happened that I remember it.

This is the most exciting thing that has ever happened to me.

I have met Magnus Perrensen.

It all came about in a most casual way. Papa announced at dinner a little while ago that a fellow cartographer of Scandinavia had written to him about his son.

"A very enthusiastic young man according to his father. He has just returned from an expedition in the Pacific. It seems he is interested in the practical side of map making."

"I have always thought that must be the most interesting part," I said. "To discover new places and actually work out the distances between this and that point."

"You take the romantic view, my dear," said my father indulgently. He turned to my stepmother. "We shall have to entertain him. I daresay he will be a little lonely. Masters can find him a decent lodging in Great Stanton for his father would like him to stay for a while to study our methods. I have already spoken to Masters and he said that he has an extra room in his house and he thought Mrs. Masters might be glad of the extra money, in which case he could stay at their house. He may be with us for some little time."

Masters was the manager of the Shop—a very efficient person who always seemed to think there was nothing in the world to compare with the importance of making maps.

"Masters is quite excited at the prospect," went on my father. "Perrensens have quite a reputation. They are specialists in sea charts. He is very eager to meet the young man—particularly as he has just returned from this journey. We want to make sure that we give him every opportunity to study what we are doing here—and no doubt he will put us wise to the progress which is being made in his country."

"That is what is so pleasant about map makers," I said. "They all help each other. There does not seem to be the same rivalry that there is in other professions."

My father laughed at me.

"I wish your brother were here," he said.

I nodded. It was a long time since Charles had gone away. We knew, of course, that on voyages of discovery such as he was undertaking men could be away for years. But it did seem a very long time since he had gone.

"I daresay he will come home unexpectedly," said my stepmother. "I wonder what he will say to find me installed here."

"He'll delighted I'm sure," my father assured her. "He has plenty of good sense."

"I hope he makes lots of new discoveries," I put in. "Places hitherto unknown . . . great tracts of land on which no human foot has ever trod before."

"Ann Alice is very romantic," said my father smiling from me to my stepmother. "Let us hope that Charles will soon be with us."

"I hope so," I said. "Freddy is enormously interested in the maps. I took him into the Shop when we were in Great Stanton yesterday. Masters was quite impressed with him. He kept saying, 'Good lad. Good lad.' I have never seen Freddy so excited."

My father looked blissful.

"He is rather bright," murmured my stepmother with pride.

"He is indeed," I added.

"Ann Alice is very happy because she has a little brother," said my father.

I looked up. My stepmother's eyes were on me. They were very bright. There might have been tears there. And on the other hand one could not be sure.

I felt a little embarrassed and I said quickly: "Well, now we have to concern ourselves with . . . what is his name? This er—Magnus."

"Magnus Perrensen. Yes, we must give him a good welcome."

It is because I have seen him that I have to write in my journal. I want to recapture that moment when he bowed formally over my hand and his brilliantly blue eyes met mine and held them. I was immediately aware of a tremendous excitement and it has not left me since.

I cannot believe that I met him for the first time this night. I feel I have known him for a long time. I wish I had learned more about maps so that I could have taken a greater part in the conversation. No matter. I have decided to learn while he is here, for it is clear that he has a great interest in them. He glows when he speaks of them; and he has just returned from this map-making expedition to the Pacific Ocean. He talks knowledgeably about charts and islands and he makes me feel a great desire to see those places.

There is an intensity about him, a vitality; and I am sure that whatever he undertakes he will succeed in accomplishing.

He is very tall—very plainly dressed according to our standards, but then we have become a little dandified under the influence of the Prince of Wales and his cronies who I believe debate for hours on the cut of their coats and the manner in which a cravat should be worn.

Magnus Perrensen was in sober grey, his coat a slightly lighter shade than his knee breeches; his stockings were of the same grey as his coat, and his black shoes were buckled but the buckles were by no means elaborate. He was bewigged as all men are, but his wig was plain and tied at the back with a narrow black ribbon.

But it would not have mattered how he was dressed; it was his vibrant personality which one noticed.

He spoke English fluently but with the faintest of accents which I found most attractive.

My father asked him many questions about the expedition, and Magnus told us that he had been shipwrecked and thought he would never see his homeland again.

"How exciting!" I said. "You might have been drowned."

"I floated for a long time on a raft," he told me, "looking out for sharks and wondering how long I was going to last."

"And what happened?"

"I sighted land and came to an island." I don't know whether it was my imagination but I fancied there was something thrilling in his voice when he said that. As though the island meant something to him.

I said: "An island? What island was that? I'll look for it on the map."

"Sometime I'll tell you about it," he said. I was very happy because he was implying that we were going to spend time together.

"And eventually you were picked up and found your way home?"

"Yes."

"You must have lost your charts when you were shipwrecked," said my father. "What a terrible blow."

"Yes. But I shall go again."

"There are so many hazards," commented my father sadly and I guessed he was thinking of Charles. He went on: "I trust you will be comfortable with the Masters."

"I am sure I shall. Mr. Masters has so much knowledge. It is a pleasure and an honour to talk with him."

"I am sure you and he will have a great deal in common."

"And Mrs. Masters . . . she is so good. She tells me I am thin and she threatens to 'feed me up.' "

"She's a good soul," said my father. "I think her husband exasperates her at times because he is more interested in maps than in her cooking."

"She is a very good cook."

"And we hope to see you here . . . often."

He was smiling across the table at me. "That is an invitation which I shall delight in accepting."

When he took his leave I was so excited. I wanted to go straight to my room and write in my journal. Writing it down is like reliving it all again and I have a feeling that this night is important to me. I shall want to go over and over it again and again.

May 3rd   It has been a wonderful month. During it I have spent a great deal of time in the company of Magnus Perrensen. He is at the Shop all through the day but often I take the gig into Great Stanton—Freddy with me—and we visit the Shop. Sometimes I take a luncheon basket and we all go into the country and picnic. At others I sit with him in the Shop and we eat sandwiches and drink cider while we talk. It is what I call helping Magnus Perrensen to feel at home.

He is a fascinating talker and Freddy and I listen entranced. He will take one of our maps and point out the exotic places as he talks of them.

He will trace a journey over continents; but it is the sea which attracts him most.

The other day I said to him: "Show us the island on which you were shipwrecked."

He was silent for a moment and then suddenly he took my hand and pressed it. "One day," he said, "I'll tell you about it."

I was thrilled as I had been before when he mentioned the island. I knew there was something special about it and that he wanted to tell me . . . alone.

Freddy was there at the time. He was in a corner of the room with Masters, who was showing him one of the tools he used.

I heard Masters say: "This is a burin. Look at that sharp blade. It's made of steel. That's for cutting. Look at the handle. What does it remind you of? A mushroom? That's right. Now you hold this in the palm of your hand with your fingers curled round the mushroom. Now you press the blade into the copper. Like this. You must have even pressure."

I smiled. "He's initiating Freddy into the mysteries of map making."

"Freddy is an apt pupil."

I knew instinctively that it was impossible for him to tell me about his island here. He wanted us to be alone. Oddly enough, although I saw him frequently, we were never really alone. If I saw him at the Shop others were there. There was always Freddy to act as chaperon. And when he visited us at the house there were always several people there.

But his presence has made a great deal of difference to me. I arise every morning with a feeling of expectation. I think of him a great deal. I love the way his eyebrows turn up at the corners. There is a faint foreignness about him which I find immensely attractive. I like that very slight accent, the arrangement of words that is just a little quaint.

The fact is I am in love with Magnus Perrensen.

How does he feel about me?

He is interested, very interested. I have an idea that he is as exasperated as I am about this inability to be alone. But we shall overcome that one day.

My stepmother said a few days ago: "We must not forget your birthday. I think we should have a rather special celebration. You will be eighteen years old. I am going to speak to your father."

"I think he must know I am eighteen."

"He is a little unworldly about such matters. We should entertain more for you now."

I shrugged my shoulders. The purpose of entertaining would be to find me a husband. I did not want to search for one. In any case that, to my mind, would have been most undignified. But there is another point now. I have found the only one I could ever love and I have reason to believe that he is not indifferent to me.

However, this is to be a birthday party. My stepmother is getting out a list of guests. She is making arrangements in the kitchen.

"It is a good thing you have a May birthday," she said. "Such a lovely month! If the weather is good we can be in the garden—a sort of fête champêtre."

"You will enjoy arranging that, my dear," said my father indulgently. "What a good thing you are here to do what is right for Ann Alice."

I am having a special dress for the party. The village seamstress has been called in and my stepmother has been poring over patterns. We have decided on rose-coloured silk which she says will be most becoming for me. It is off the shoulders with short sleeves which are ruched and edged with lace. There is a wide lace collar; the bodice is tight-fitting, and the skirt very full with flounces, each one edged with lace. It is most elaborate. I am delighted because when I try it on and stand very still while our little seamstress kneels at my feet and gets to work with pins and tacking thread, I am imagining I am standing before Magnus. I believe he will think me beautiful in this dress.

I am grateful to my stepmother who has done so much to create it. It is almost as though she is grateful for my interest in Freddy.

Am I growing to like her? I am not sure. When one is in love the whole world looks different, and perhaps one is inclined to like everyone.

No . . . not everyone.

I had a shock today and I suppose that is the reason why I am writing my diary.

I was in the garden this afternoon. The house was quiet. My father was resting as he does most afternoons since he has had what we have come to call "his turns." I am sure they have weakened him considerably although he tries to pretend they have not.

My stepmother had taken the gig into Great Stanton to do some shopping she said; and she had taken Freddy with her. She was buying some clothes for him. He had been very short of them when he had come to us.

I liked to sit in the garden. From the front of the house we look out on the Green. A pleasant view it was true with the grass before us and the old church with its spire reaching to the sky and the row of six ancient cottages. In the centre of the Green was the duck pond with the wooden seat beside it. But I liked better the view from the back. I liked our lawn beyond which was the little copse of fir trees. When I sit in the garden I usually go to the small walled-in rose garden and sit on one of the wicker seats there.

That was where I was, pretending to read but in fact thinking of when I should next see Magnus Perrensen. I mean alone. He was dining with us tonight and that made me very happy. One always hoped there would be an opportunity to talk about the things which really mattered.

"Oh, Miss Ann Alice . . . " It was one of the maids. "A gentleman has called."

I sprang up.

Magnus was in my thoughts and foolishly I thought it was he, so I did not ask his name and it was a shock when I went into the hall and saw Desmond Featherstone.

I felt that sudden shiver of apprehension which he had so often inspired in me in the past.

"Miss Ann Alice. What a pleasure."

"Oh . . . Mr. Featherstone . . . It is a long time since we have seen you here."

"I have missed all this . . . sorely."

"So you are back again."

"For a brief visit, alas."

"You must er—come into the parlour . . . Perhaps you would like some refreshment."

"I have come to see you . . . nothing else is important."

"Come in." I took him to the small room which led from the hall and was used as a reception room for callers. "Pray sit down."

He had put his hat on the table.

"I will go and tell them to bring something. Would you like a dish of tea?"

"It sounds ideally refreshing."

"I will go and tell them."

"Oh . . . " He was protesting. He no doubt wondered why I did not pull the bell rope and summon a servant. I had a good reason for not doing so and I hurried out as quickly as I could.

I sped to my father's room. By good fortune he was up and sitting in his chair half-dozing.

I said: "Papa, we have a visitor. That friend of my stepmother. I do think you should come down."

"Certainly. Certainly." A friend of my stepmother must of course be treated with respect. "Who is it?"

"It's Mr. Featherstone."

"Why yes. Of course I remember."

"He's in the parlour. Will you go down to him. I'll see about getting some tea."

He followed me down and went to the parlour. When I returned Desmond Featherstone was chatting easily with my father.

I fancied the look he gave me was reproachful.

Tea was brought. They talked of the weather and Desmond Featherstone enquired solicitously about my father's health. My father said he never felt better. I don't think that was quite true but since his marriage he had always maintained that he was very well indeed.

"It is some time since I saw you. Miss Ann Alice has grown taller I swear."

"It's her eighteenth birthday soon, you know."

"Indeed! What a matter for celebration!"

I felt irritated. I hated their talking of me as though I were not there, as though I were some infant whose growth was to be commented on.

"Yes," said my father. "We are celebrating, of course. My wife is as excited as though it were her birthday."

"And when is the great day?"

"In a few days' time. The twenty-first to be precise. I don't know how many are coming. The list is continually being added to."

"I am going to be rather bold. As an old friend of Mrs. Mallory's family . . . I am going to ask for an invitation."

"Any friend of Mrs. Mallory is welcome, don't you agree, Ann Alice?"

I was glad he did not wait for an answer, although Desmond Featherstone was looking at me expectantly.

My father went on: "We are hoping that the gods will be kind and give us a warm evening. I am afraid we shall be rather crowded if we are forced to be indoors."

"I am sure the gods will be kind on such an auspicious occasion," said Desmond Featherstone.

I was sitting there exasperated. So he would be at the birthday party. I had an uneasy feeling that he was going to spoil it.

It had been so long since I had thought of him and now he is back again.

When my stepmother returned I could see she was as taken aback by the sight of him as I had been and I thought her greeting was distinctly cool.

"I am in the neighbourhood again," he said, "and I knew you would never forgive me if I did not call."

"For how long?" asked my stepmother, rather tactlessly for her, I thought.

"That depends on business."

My father said: "Mr. Featherstone has promised to come to the party."

"Oh," replied my stepmother quietly.

I was glad when he went.

But somehow I do not feel quite the same.

May 21st   My birthday and the most exciting day I have lived through! How wonderful that it should have happened on my birthday!

The day began rather cloudy and we were in a state of great anxiety lest it should rain. The servants kept running out to gaze at the sky.

I have looked at my dress hanging in the wardrobe at least twenty times during the day. It is the most beautiful dress I have ever had. I had pleaded with my stepmother to let Freddy stay up just for an hour or so and she has agreed, I think with assumed reluctance. She is really fond of Freddy and our affection has made a bond between us—in spite of my resistance.

During the afternoon the skies cleared and everyone was saying that it was going to be fine after all. The wind has dropped and as long as the rain keeps off, they kept saying, it will be perfect for our alfresco party.

My stepmother was in her element, organizing everything. My father looked on with amusement. How he has changed since his marriage! At least my stepmother has made him happy. I am sure he was never quite like this . . . even when my mother was alive.

The guests arrived. I, my father, my stepmother and Freddy, standing there like a small son of the house, received them.

And what a delight when Magnus arrived in the company of the Masters! He looked so elegant, I thought. How becoming was the more simple mode of dress. I heartily disliked all the affectations which had been introduced by the dandified fops.

The weather was perfect. There was even a moon to make the scene more enchanting and the company soon spilled out onto the lawns and gardens. The food would be served in the hall and dining room and people could take their food out to sit in the garden if they wished.

There was one thing which spoilt it: the presence of Desmond Featherstone. And it seemed to me that he was determined to seek me out.

How happy I was that Magnus was equally determined to stay at my side, and, for my fervent co-operation, we succeeded in foiling Desmond Featherstone's efforts and keeping together.

Freddy went off to bed when he was told to do so. He was a very meek little boy and I guessed was accustomed to doing what he was told without question. I found his gratitude rather pathetic and often wondered what sort of life he had had with my stepmother's sister-in-law. I never asked because I sensed a certain unhappiness in the boy when I did, and I guessed it was something he wanted to leave behind him.

Of course, as it was my birthday, I had certain duties to the other guests. I had to dance with one or two of my father's friends. Some of them were cartographers of good reputation who had come from some distance to be at the party.

I was able to talk to them about maps in a more knowledgeable way than I ever would have been before—and that was all due to Magnus.

Perhaps I was a little absent-minded, thinking all the time of how I could escape and get back to Magnus; and when I did, there he was waiting for me, as eager to be with me as I was with him.

Then came those magic moments in the rose garden. The scent of the roses was exquisite. I shall always think of that walled garden on the night of the twenty-first of May in the year 1792, for there was enchantment on that night. All through my life I shall remember.

We sat side by side on two of the wicker seats which were against the wall facing the wrought-iron gates into the garden, so that we could immediately be aware of intruders.

In the distance we could hear the sound of violins coming from the house and every now and then we would hear a burst of laughter. The air was soft and balmy.

He took my hands and kissed them.

He said: "As soon as I saw you, I knew."

"So did I."

"It was as though something passed between us . . . an understanding. Yes? You for me . . . and me for you?"

"That is exactly how it was."

"Life is good. It is rare I believe that there is such harmony."

"It's very precious."

"We will keep it so."

"Magnus," I said, "what is going to happen? It is not your home here."

"No," he answered. "I am here for a year . . . perhaps longer. Then I go home."

"A year," I said happily. "A year for us to be together."

"And then," he went on, "you will come home with me. We shall marry."

"And live happily ever after . . . It's like a fairy story."

"We shall have many children. They will work with us. They will explore the world. It is a good life."

"I am so happy," I said. "I don't think anyone could ever have had a happier eighteenth birthday."

He was silent for a while. Then he said: "We will go together to find my island."

"Oh yes. The island. I have often felt you wanted to tell me about that."

"Let me tell you now. This beautiful garden seems the place for it. I have wanted to talk to you about it for so long. It is like a dream sometimes. I could believe I had imagined it."

"Tell me. I long to know."

He hesitated for a moment and then began: "I had been with the expedition, charting the seas. We were sure there were many more islands than those known to us and we wanted to find them. I believe I found one. I am sure of it. But let me tell you. We were cruising in the Pacific . . . coming from the Sandwich Islands where Captain Cook had been clubbed to death by the natives just ten years or so before. How can

I describe to you what it is like to be at sea, perhaps sailing where men have never sailed before? Captain Cook had discovered so much that I used to be afraid that there was nothing more for me to find."

"Tell me about the island you discovered."

"Yes, I want you to know. I want us both to go in search of it. I shall never be completely content until I have found it again . . . and I want you to be with me when I do."

I put my hand out to touch his cheek and he caught it and kissed it again and again.

"You will feel as I do," he went on. "You will feel the call of the sea. It is here for mankind to explore . . . to tame, to use for himself. How fortunate we are to be born on this Earth. But I want to tell you about my island."

"Please do. Sometimes I think you are holding back . . . that you are reluctant to tell me. You say you will and then . . . you hesitate. What is it about this island?"

He was silent for a few seconds, then he said, "The sea was calm . . . so calm . . . you scarcely would think you were sailing. And then suddenly the storm blows up . . . storms such as you have never dreamed of, Ann Alice. You cannot imagine the fury of a hurricane. The wind is like a thousand demons, screeching, whipping up the waves so that the sea becomes a seething cauldron. The rain, caught in the wind, beats down horizontally. It seems as though the storm is intent on destroying everything in its path. What chance has a ship on such a sea, in such a storm. I knew it was going to happen. We prayed for a miracle but none thought one would come. We knew she could not stand up to all that fury—nor could she. I thought my last moment had come. Oddly enough, I felt calm and my great regret was that I was never going to discover all those tracts of land which yet were unknown. My name would die with me. My life was insignificant. Yet I had had grandiose dreams. Magellan, Henry the Navigator, Drake, Cook, Ptolemy, Mercator, Hondius . . . I had dreamed of being one of them. A man needs time to prove himself. I have often since then thought of all the men who were taken in their youth and never had a chance of doing what they dreamed of doing. I thought then, I shall be one of those.

"The sea took us up as though we were a cardboard box. It tossed us this way and that. The wind shrieked as though with demonical laughter at our plight and the rain, thunder and lightning did what they could to discomfort us. Right out there in that violent sea we broke up. The deck seemed to roll from under us . . . parts of our ship were flung out into the sea like debris. All hope was gone. We were a wreck.

"I found myself clinging to a spar of wood. Part of the deck, I imagine. I felt half-dead and believed the end was not far off. No one could survive in such a sea.

"I knew roughly where we were before the storm hit us, but could not calculate how far we had come and where the sea had thrown us. I could think of nothing but clinging to my piece of wood. The sea tossed it hither and thither. I was submerged . . . and then I was afloat again. I closed my eyes and waited for death.

"They say that when you are drowning your whole life comes back to you. You remember the details . . . childhood . . . schooldays. I don't know whether I was too numb to do so. I don't know how I clung to my raft. But I must have done and I remembered nothing of the past. There was only the need to cling to that piece of wood which was all I had to help me against that raging sea. I was exhausted by the battering I was receiving and I felt consciousness slipping away.

"When I opened my eyes everything had changed. I could hear the gentle swishing of waves against the sand. There was a scented breeze, very faint. I opened my eyes to a brilliant blue sky and a sea that was as gentle as a lake. How soft it was . . . translucent blue. Later I was to discover it could be a pellucid green. It was a sea which seemed different from any other sea I had known. But I had reached the island and everything was different there."

"So that is how you came to the island?"

"Yes, that is how I came to it. When I opened my eyes the first thing I noticed was . . . people. They were squatting some little distance from me—tall men and women and naked children watching me with great wondering dark eyes. Their skin was light brown colour, their hair dark and abundant. I noticed that they all wore ornaments which looked as though they had been made from gold and the women wore flowers round their necks and ankles.

"The biggest of the men—whom I took to be the chief—came to me and said something which I could not understand. I tried to explain . . . but little explanation was needed. My condition, the spar of wood which had carried me to those shores was enough.

"All the time I was there we communicated mainly by signs, gesticulation and mime. They brought pieces of wood held together by fibres and they laid me on this for I was too exhausted to walk. Two of the men carried me ... it was a sort of stretcher ... into one of their houses. I realized later that it was the house of the chief. It was round, with a roof of straw; the floor was earth and there were rough benches there. I was laid down gently and several of them came round to examine me. They brought me food ... fruit such as I had never tasted before ... mangoes and papaya, sweet bananas and nuts. They gave me something to drink which was fiery hot and made my head swim; and when I turned from it they brought me the milk of a coconut in its shell.

"I wondered what they would do with me. I had heard stories of the fierceness of the natives of some far-off lands. Captain Cook had been clubbed to death when he went to the Sandwich Islands to recover a stolen boat. I might have thought of a hideous fate which they were preparing for me—but I did not. Strangely enough I sensed the goodness of these people. They were tall and strong; they could have been warlike, but there was a gentleness about them and in spite of my position and the strangeness of it all, I felt no fear.

"I was completely exhausted and slept for a long time. When I awoke there was always at least one pair of dark eyes watching me. They gave me food—fruit milk and something which I had never tasted before but which I believe is known as breadfruit.

"I think I must have been at least four days and nights in their care before I was fully conscious.

"When I stood up they clapped their hands. They began to shout and one of the men ran out of the house and began beating with his hands on a drum which I learned later was the way in which they summoned the company. I shall never forget the hour or so which followed. They came in to look at me. They walked round me. They touched me, marvelling, I guessed, at my white skin. They looked with wonder into my light eyes; but it was my fair hair which intrigued them most.

"I had no fear of them. That was what was so wonderful. They stood around me, those tall men and women with their shining golden ornaments and their flowers. They could have tortured me, killed me in the most horrible manner ... and that did not occur to me. It was only after I left the island that I thought of it.

"They were happy people. They laughed continually. They squatted round me, touching my hair again and again, offering me fruit and coconut shells full of liquor.

"I sat beside the chief. I guessed he was the chief because he wore more gold ornaments than the others. Moreover he had an air of authority.

"Well . . . that was my island."

"And how long were you there?"

"I don't know. I lost count of time." He turned to me. "I have to find it. It was all so strange. I could at times believe that there is no such place . . . that I imagined it."

"How could you have done so?"

"No. It is impossible. I went there."

"Tell me more. Tell me everything. I want to share all your adventures."

"We talked to each other by signs. I learned one or two of their words. Go; Come. Words like that. It was a thriving community because they had all they wanted on the island. They had fish and fruit in abundance. They grew certain crops, the like of which I have never seen elsewhere. They cooked in earth ovens with pots made of gold buried in the ground with the sun's rays beating down on them . . . and sometimes in an apparatus like a haybox. They lived mainly on fish which abounded in the seas and could be caught with little effort. Any clothes they wore were woven from leaves and fibres of plants. They lived simply and I have never known harmony such as I found on that island. They had a simple faith in goodness . . . they worked together . . . one for all and all for each . . . It was paradise, Ann Alice.

"There was gold there—the metal which we call precious was as plentiful as the fish in the sea and the fruit on the trees. One could see it in the streams . . . on the surface of the earth. One picked up handfuls of earth and there was gold. They had learned how to weld it into necklaces and bangles. They polished it and held it up to the sun. I fancy they thought the gold had captured something of the sun itself and that was why they used it to such an extent. They worshipped the sun. The life giver. They watched it rise every morning and welcomed it with joy; and they were always very solemn when they watched it disappear at night. I remember standing there on the shore with them watching the great red ball drop below the horizon. It seemed to disappear suddenly. There is no twilight. Sunset is different there from how we know it. It is hard to believe that it is the same sun. But I shall go on talking for ever about my island."

"I love to hear of it."

"I lived with them . . . for how long? I really have no idea. I became almost one of them."

"Did you not want to come home . . . back to your family?"

"Oddly enough I did not think of them. I seemed to be in a different world. I had forgotten my ambition to sail the seas and discover new worlds. I was contented to live their life. I fished with them; with their help I built a house for myself. I lived as they lived; and I was aware of a great contentment. It is difficult to explain. I think it had something to do with the inborn goodness of these people. I would not have believed there could be such a place in the world."

"Why did you leave it? How did you leave it?"

"At times I think there is something mystic about my experience. That is why I am reluctant to talk of it. They lived on fish and as I told you, it abounded in the seas. We spent a great deal of the days in the boats. They were primitive craft . . . rather like canoes. I remember the day well. The canoes held two people and we used to fish in twos. I often went with one of them whose name sounded like Wamgum. He and I were special friends. He had taught me a few words of his language and I was able to make myself understood now and then. I taught him some of my words too.

"Well Wamgum and I went out. The sun was high in the sky, blazing down on us. We had a covering of straw on our heads for protection. We did not start to fish immediately. We just paddled along and after a while allowed ourselves to drift. I remember looking back at the island, lush, green and beautiful. I sang a song of my country which always delighted them. Wamgum closed his eyes as he listened. I dozed too.

"When I awoke heavy clouds obscured the sun. It was almost dark. I awoke Wamgum in some alarm. He looked about him in dismay. The island was no longer visible. A gust of wind suddenly shook the canoe.

"Storms spring up suddenly in tropical seas. The rain started to teem down, the wind to roar. It was happening again—and this time I was in a frail canoe. We could not fight against the elements. We were overboard, clinging to the canoe. Suddenly Wamgum was no longer there. A great wave seized the canoe and broke it in half flinging it high into the air. I found myself clinging to a piece of wood. It was as it had been before. Death was close to me. I thought, This must be the end. I clung to the wood. I was able to hoist myself onto it so that I was above the water. I hung on. I was tossed and shaken and it seemed like a miracle that I was able to keep my hold on the wood.

"It could not happen again, I thought, unless I was being saved for some special purpose. This time it must be the end.

"I do not know how long I clung there. It was all happening again . . . the numbness . . . the consciousness slipping away . . . the waiting for the sea to swallow me. I lost count of time. I did not know whether it was day or night. I could only cling to my spar and wonder whether the next gigantic wave would carry me off.

"The wind dropped suddenly. The sea was still rough but my broken piece of wood was riding the waves. The sky was bright; the sun so pitiless that I almost wished for the storm. I floated on these calm seas limp, exhausted for . . . I did not know how long.

"I was picked up by a passing ship but by that time I was not sure where I was or even who I was. I remember lying in the darkness of that ship, cool drinks passing my lips. I was delirious, I think. I talked of the island.

"Gradually I began to emerge from that state. The ship's doctor came to me. He said they were bound for Rotterdam and he told me that I had come through my ordeal miraculously. Rarely could anyone have come so near to death and escaped. I was suffering from acute sunstroke, starvation and exhaustion. But I was young and strong and before the journey was completed I had completely recovered."

"What an extraordinary adventure. Suppose it hadn't happened the way it did, you would not be here now."

I looked so forlorn that he laughed. "You would never have known me so you would not have grieved for me."

"I shall never let you go on voyages without me."

"We'll go together."

"Do you still want to go, after all that happened?"

"I must go. It is my life . . . I feel I must go and discover new lands. Besides, I have to go back to the island."

"Could you find it?"

"It won't be easy. I talked of it to the sailors. They thought I was delirious. An island where the savages are gentle, where love and amity reign, where the fish and fruit abound to supply all their needs; where one picks up gold and uses it for cooking pots. I was indeed in delirium. And do you know, Ann Alice, there were times when I believed I might have been, that I might have imagined the whole thing. You see, I had been shipwrecked. There was no doubt of that. I was picked up by the ship and brought home. Did I live in that fantasy world when I was half-conscious in my raft? Did it exist outside my imagination?"

"But you wouldn't have been all that time on the raft?"

"The time was short. I couldn't have been more than a couple of weeks on the island. It seemed a very long time . . . looking back. Sunrise merging into sunset. The days seemed long. I can't be sure. Sometimes I think they are right. That is why I must go back to find that island."

"I shall come with you."

"Oh, Ann Alice, I knew you would feel as I do. I knew it the moment we met . . . that first day. I have made a map. I want to show you. I have placed the island where I believe it to be. I know where we had sailed. I can roughly estimate where we were when the storm struck us . . . so I can't be far wrong."

"Oh yes, please show me the map."

"I will."

He put his arm round me and held me against him. Then he took my face in his hands and kissed me. We stayed thus for some minutes, our arms entwined.

Then vaguely in the distance I heard the sound of footsteps, but I wanted nothing more than to stay close to Magnus.

A voice broke in on the stillness. "I don't understand you. Why don't you do it? It's easy enough. What's happened to you? You've changed. Fallen in love with the easy life, eh? Edging out of the bargain."

It was the voice of Desmond Featherstone. It sounded harsh and angry. I had never heard that tone before. I wondered to whom he was talking. To whom could he be speaking? Only my stepmother. Surely not. I could not imagine anyone's daring to talk to her like that.

"What is it?" asked Magnus.

"I thought someone was coming. Listen."

The footsteps were dying away.

"They evidently changed their minds," said Magnus. "They have left us with this beautiful garden to ourselves."

"I think we ought to go back. I shall be missed." I sighed with reluctance. "I should like to stay here forever."

We kissed again.

"We will make plans," said Magnus. "Tomorrow I will show you the map of the island."

We went back to the house together.

So here I sit in my bedroom with my journal before me. I am so glad I started to write it. I want to capture every moment of this night and hold it forever. It is the happiest night of my life.

While I am thinking of it, though, every now and then I hear Desmond Featherstone's voice intruding. It spoils the perfection of the night. I wonder what he meant. It is there puzzling me, forcing its way into my happiness . . . bringing a faintly unpleasant whiff into perfection.

June 30th   Mr. James Cardew came this afternoon. It seems that I forget my journal except when something wonderful or disastrous happens. Perhaps that is as well. If I recorded everyday happenings it would become decidedly boring. As it is, when I read back I can relive the highlights—good or evil.

It is more than a month since Magnus and I revealed our love for each other. What a wonderful month! How we have talked! We have made so many plans. It was arranged that he was to stay in England for a year during which time he would study the methods which were used here. His family had thought that my brother might care to go into the Perrensen business to study their methods in exchange. And this would probably have happened if Charles had been here. My father had said that Charles would want to go when he returned home.

Magnus must stay his term here. He wants to. Much as he longs for our marriage he was completely absorbed in the making of maps and very interested in our methods. I wouldn't have wanted to disturb that for I had determined that I should never put anything in the way of his work.

So, we planned. Next year, early next year, we would be married, and I should go home with him.

He talked a great deal about Norway—the beautiful fjords and mountains. He showed me maps of his country and the place where his family had a country house. I was so happy. I was living in the future. I saw before me an idyllic life. I should see the midnight sun. I should lie in a boat in the fjords, I should fish and swim with him. We would ride through the forests; and then we would go in search of his island . . . together . . . always together.

He had shown me the map. There was the island. He had called it Paradise Island.

"It must be here," he said, pointing. "I have studied maps of the area but there is no mention of it. Here are the Solomon Islands, recently rediscovered. It could be miles south or to the north . . . I don't know. But it is there . . . somewhere. Of course the discovery of these islands is so recent and much of the seas are as yet uncharted. Isn't it exciting? To think of what we have to do? The discoveries we have to make? I am going to make another map, and when it is finished I shall give it to you. Then we shall both have a map on which is my Paradise Island. There will be no other such map in the world . . . as yet. Treasure yours, Ann Alice. Keep it in a safe place."

I have not yet received the map but when I do I shall certainly keep it in a safe place. I shall hide it in the drawer with my journal. Magnus does not want anyone to see it. I believe he is afraid that someone else might find the island before he does.

My father and stepmother know how things are between Magnus and me, although I do not think they realize how serious are our intentions. I have an idea that they believe it to be a boy and girl romance. Calf love, they call it. They seem to forget that I am eighteen years old and Magnus is three years my senior. We are not children, but I suppose parents find it hard to realize that their children have grown up. Oddly enough, only a short time ago my stepmother was talking of giving parties for me so that I could meet a prospective husband. I suppose they feel that only a marriage which they have arranged could be a serious one.

My father's health has deteriorated lately. Sometimes he looks very tired. My stepmother takes great care of him. She is always fussing over him—rushing up with a rug for his knees if he is sitting in the garden and a cold wind blows up, making sure that he has a cushion behind his head when he dozes off. He is always chiding her for treating him like an invalid. But how he revels in it!

I was very glad when Desmond Featherstone disappeared soon after my birthday. I had been afraid that he would be hanging about, waylaying me when I went out. It was a great relief to find that he had gone.

I am writing all this in order to put off the moment when I must write of this terrible thing which has happened.

Freddy and I had been into Great Stanton in the gig. We had had a wonderful afternoon, calling at the Shop and being with Magnus. I had driven the gig home in a haze of happiness and as we came out of the stables to walk across to the house, a rider came towards us.

He pulled up and bowed his head in greeting. "Am I right in thinking you are Miss Mallory?" he asked.

I was startled. I knew him vaguely but could not remember who he was. I said: "Yes."

"I thought I recognized you. You were much younger when we met."

"I remember you now. You are a friend of my brother." My voice trailed off. A terrible presentiment had come to me.

"I have to speak to you. May I leave my horse in your stables and come to the house."

"What is it?" I cried. "Tell me quickly. Is it my brother?"

He nodded gravely.

"We have been so anxious," I said. "Is he . . . dead?"

He said: "The ship was lost off the coast of Australia. I am, I believe, one of the few survivors."

I felt dizzy. I gripped Freddy's hand. I said: "Freddy, you'd better go and find your Aunt Lois. Tell her . . . we have a visitor."

I took James Cardew to the stables and we were silent while the groom took his horse.

We walked slowly to the house together.

"I cannot tell you how it grieves me to be the carrier of such news," he said at length. "But I had to come to see you . . . and your father."

"It was good of you," I told him. "He has not been very well lately. Let me break it to him first."

My father was dozing in the garden. I went to him and said: "We have a visitor. It is Mr. Cardew. Do you remember Mr. Cardew? He came to see Charles . . . just before he sailed. Oh, Papa, it is very sad news. Charles . . . "

I shall never forget my father's face. It was stricken. He looked old and tired.

My stepmother came down and sat by my father, holding his hand. James Cardew talked of the voyage, of the terrible night of shipwreck. It seemed to me that this was the fate of all who braved the sea. I had heard so much of the hazards from Magnus—and now it was like hearing the tragic story all over again. Only this one ended in death.

James Cardew did not stay long. I think he felt that the sight of him could only add to our sorrow.

Ours is a house of mourning tonight.

August 1st   The sadness persists. We cannot believe that we shall never see Charles again.

My stepmother has done everything she can to cheer my father. He had one of his turns the day after James Cardew left. My stepmother insisted that the doctor come. He said it was no surprise in view of the shock my father had received.

It was a particularly bad turn. He stayed in bed for a week. My stepmother read aloud to him from the Bible, which seemed to give him great comfort.

A few weeks after it happened my father seemed to arouse himself. He went into Great Stanton to see his lawyers.

He talked to me about it afterwards. "You see, Ann Alice, this makes a great difference. It means the end of our Mallory line. For centuries we have had Mallorys living in this house. Now the chain is broken."

"Do names matter?" I asked.

"Families do. People set great store by families. I have to think about this house and everything. If you marry and leave the country, what then? The family is scattered . . . the name is lost. Charles would have continued here."

"Yes, I do see," I said. "But when all is told is it so very important. People should be happy. They find happiness with other people, not houses and names."

"You talk like a girl in love. It is Magnus, is it not?"

"Yes, it is Magnus."

"A bright young man. He is much travelled. He is in love with the business of map making . . . as I never really was. Masters is like that. It absorbs some people. Masters says Magnus has a special talent for map making. He has adventure in his blood too. Your brother Charles was like that." He was silent for a moment then he went on: "I have had to see old Grampton."

Grampton Sons and Henderson are our solicitors.

"I have been thinking of the house. That should go to you. What would you do with it? I hope you would never sell it."

"No, Papa. I would not."

"I hope there would always be a home for your stepmother here for as long as she lives. I have provided for her. Of course, there is your cousin John. I haven't heard much of him for some time. But he is a Mallory ... so I suppose really the place should go to him ... if ... by any chance you do not want to live here ... That would not be while your stepmother was alive, of course."

"You talk as though you are going to die, Papa."

"I don't intend to for a long time yet. But I want to make sure that everything is in order ... and in view of what has happened to Charles ... " His voice faltered ...

I took his hand and held it. It was rarely that we were demonstrative with each other.

I do not like such talk. It is almost as though my father thinks he is going to die.

It has been a strange month. A terrible gloom hangs over the house and it is only when I escape to Magnus that it recedes a little.

To be so happy and to know tragedy is waiting to strike at any moment makes me pause to think. And in this contemplative mood I turn to my journal.

September 3rd   We are a house of mourning.

My father died in the night. My stepmother discovered him. She came to me, her face very white, her deep blue eyes enormous and her mouth quivering.

"Ann, Ann Alice, come with me ... and look at your father."

He was lying on his back, his face white and still. I touched his face. It was very cold.

I looked at my stepmother and said: "He's ... dead."

"He can't be," she insisted as though begging me to agree with her. "He's had these turns before."

"He has never had one like this," I said. "We must send for the doctor."

She sank into a chair and covered her face with her hands. "Oh, Ann Alice, it can't be. It can't be."

I felt amazingly calm. It was almost as though I was prepared. "I will send one of them for the doctor at once," I said.

I went out and left her there with him.

The housekeeper came back with me. She started to cry when she saw my father. My stepmother just sat still, her hands covering her face.

I went to her and put an arm about her shoulders. "You must compose yourself," I told her. "I am afraid he is dead."

She looked at me piteously. "He was so good to me," she said tremulously. "He . . . he has had these turns before. Perhaps . . . "

I shook my head. Somehow I could not stay in that room. I went out, leaving her. I went down to the front door and stood there facing the Green, waiting for the doctor.

It seemed hours before he came.

"What is it, Miss Mallory?" he asked.

"It's my father. He must have died in the night."

I took him to the death chamber. He examined my father but said very little.

As he came out of the room he said to me: "He has never recovered from the shock of your brother's death."

So here I sit with my journal before me, writing down the events of this sad day.

I keep thinking about him and how he had changed when he married my stepmother and through her it seemed we had become more of a family than we had ever been before.

His last years had been happy. She had made them so. I should be grateful to her. I wish I could be.

And now he is dead. I shall never see him dozing in his chair again, sitting at the head of the table, exuding contentment with his family life.

Gloom in the house. And soon we have to face the funeral. We shall be dressed in heavy black; we shall go to the churchyard, listen to the words of the preacher, watch them lower his coffin into the grave, and the bell will toll.

Then we shall return to the house . . . a different house. How can it be the same without him?

What will it be like? I find it hard to imagine.

My stepmother will be here. Freddy will be here. I have lost my father and my brother.

But in the Masters' house in Great Stanton, Magnus has his little room. He will be thinking of me as I am of him. There is nothing to fear because he is there . . .

Should I be afraid if it were not for Magnus?

I pause to consider that. Yes, I believe I should be. Of what? Of a gloomy house, a house of death? Of a life without my father?

Why should I feel so uneasy about that?

But there is nothing to fear. Magnus is there . . . waiting for the day when we shall be together.

September 10th   Today my father was buried. I seem to have lived through a long time since that day, only a week ago, when he died.

Immediately after my father's death my stepmother was prostrate. She was really ill. I had never seen her weep before but she did for my father. She must have really loved him. True, she had always behaved as though she did, but I never really believed her. I had taken such a dislike to her when she first came that nothing she did could eradicate that.

I thought she would be too ill to go to the funeral, but she roused herself and put on her widow's weeds, her black, black clothes. They did not suit her. She is a woman who needs colour.

The mournful sound of the tolling bell seemed to go on forever. The carriage, the black-plumed horses, the undertakers in their solemn tall hats and sombre coats, the cortège of death . . . they all accentuated our loss.

Why do people have to glorify death like this? I wonder. Would it not have been better if we had just laid him quietly in his grave?

I was on one side of my stepmother, Freddy on the other, holding her hand. She leaned on me a little, now and then putting her hand to her eyes.

A little group of the village people gathered to watch us leave. I heard one of them say: "Poor soul. She was so happy with him. It did you good to see them together. And now he's gone . . . gone forever."

My stepmother heard and seemed to be grappling with her emotion.

The service in the church had been brief and I was thankful for that. We walked out of the church following the pallbearers. I listened to the clods of earth falling on the coffin. My stepmother threw down a bunch of asters. She gripped my hand and pressed it.

Then I lifted my eyes. Standing a little apart from the group round the grave was Desmond Featherstone.

My heart started to beat faster. I felt a sudden fear. His eyes were fixed on my stepmother.

As we turned away from the grave, he joined us.

"My dear, dear ladies," he said. "I heard of this sad happening. I have come to offer my condolences . . . to you both."

I said nothing. Nor did my stepmother.

She had quickened her pace and I fancied she wanted him to fall behind.

He did not and when we reached the carriage which would take us back to the house he was still beside us. He helped us in and stood back, his expression solemn; but I noticed the glitter in his eyes as he bowed to us.

This dismal day is over and I cannot forget the sight of Desmond Featherstone standing there near the grave. For some reason, even now, the memory sends shivers down my spine.

November 1st   How everything has changed. I knew it would but not to this extent. I think I should be very much afraid if it were not for Magnus.

Magnus is my lifeline. He restores my spirits. He makes me happy, he makes me forget my fears. I go to him every day. We make plans. It won't be long now before we are married, he says. Then we shall go away together.

I sometimes have a strange feeling that forces are at work to destroy my happiness with Magnus and that something else . . . something terrible . . . is being planned for me.

When my father's will was read I discovered that he had been a comparatively wealthy man. The map-making business in itself was a flourishing concern. That could be run satisfactorily by Masters and his men. It was to remain in the family and would belong to me. I need have nothing to do with it, but my father did wish that it should continue. In the event of my marrying or wishing to be rid of it, it would go to that distant cousin John Mallory, to whom the house would also go on my death.

It was all very complicated. My stepmother had a very adequate income but the bulk of the wealth was in the business and the house and the land—and that was mine.

The clause which I found most hard to bear was my father's passing over my guardianship to my stepmother. He had stated in his will that he trusted his wife's judgement utterly so he was placing the care of his daughter in her hands until that daughter was twenty-one years of age or in the event of her marriage. He believed that was the best thing he could possibly do in the circumstances. His daughter had been without a mother's guidance until his second marriage. He therefore left her in the charge of one in whom he had complete trust—his dear wife, Lois.

I thought: He certainly was besotted about her—from the moment he set eyes on her to the end.

I was really annoyed by that injunction, but I did not think at first that it would make any difference to me.

Now things are starting to happen. It no longer seems like my home. There is something sinister about it . . . And I know what it is.

It was about three or four weeks after the funeral when Desmond Featherstone reappeared.

I was in the garden with Freddy when he walked in.

When I looked up and saw him my heart gave that little leap of apprehension which it always does at the sight of him.

"Hello," he said. "I have come to visit the bereaved."

"Oh. My stepmother is in. I will tell her you have called to see her."

"I have called to see you too, Miss Ann Alice."

"Thank you," I said. "But I am sure my stepmother will want to know that you have called."

I turned away and he caught my arm. "You are not still determined to be unfriendly, are you?"

I said: "Oh, Freddy, let us go and tell Aunt Lois that she has a visitor, shall we?"

Freddy was very quick and he had developed a rather touching way of looking after me. He must have sensed the appeal in my voice.

"Oh yes, come on."

He took my hand and pulled me away. We left Desmond Featherstone looking after us rather disconsolately.

That was the beginning.

He stayed to luncheon and then to dinner.

Then he said it was too late to leave that night.

And there he was. He stayed with us the next day and he is still with us.

I am not sure what my stepmother feels about his being in the house. Sometimes I think she wishes he would go. I wonder why she does not ask him to.

But what frightens me is his attitude to me. He has come here to pursue me.

If I am alone in a room it will not be long before he is there too.

Being in the house he can follow my movements. If I go out to ride he will be there beside me. I take Freddy with me a great deal. He acts as a miniature chaperon. He is very good at it and I believe has some inkling that he is there to protect me.

I often go to the Shop to see Magnus. Sometimes we ride out together to eat the picnic lunch which I have brought. Once Desmond Featherstone had the temerity to join us.

He has brought a new atmosphere into the house . . . an uneasiness . . . more than that . . . a kind of terror . . . for me. The truth is that I am afraid of him. Yes, I am really frightened of Desmond Featherstone.

November 6th I have an urge to write more in my journal now. I feel it is like a friend in whom I can confide. I still have this uneasy feeling that I cannot trust my stepmother, although she is gentle with me and so pathetic in her grief. I often wonder why she does not tell Desmond Featherstone to go, for I have a feeling that she does not want him here any more than I do. Yesterday I saw them together. I looked from my window and they were in the garden. She had a basket on her arm and was rather listlessly picking the last of the chrysanthemums. He was talking to her and she was replying with some vehemence. I wish I could have heard what they were saying.

Magnus has given me the copy of the map. I keep it at the back of my drawer with my journal. I wish I had a safe of some sort, a box I could lock, somewhere to keep my secret things. But perhaps the back of the drawer is the safest place. People wouldn't think of rummaging through my gloves and scarves, whereas if I locked things away they might think I had something to hide. This obsession with security has only come after my father's death.

I often take out the map and look at it. I dream of sailing in that sea, among those islands. How I should like to visit the Sandwich Islands, Tahiti . . . and those new discoveries.

Magnus and I will one day find our island. I shall look back on these days and laugh at myself. I am imagining things, building up something which is not there. I am endowing Desmond Featherstone with sinister intentions . . . just as I did long ago, my stepmother.

Desmond Featherstone went away for a few days and what a relief that was! I really am building up a case against that man. What has he done but forced himself upon us and made himself especially odious to me? But on the other hand he could not have stayed on at the house if my stepmother had not allowed him to. She could tell him to go, if she wanted to, and I would second her in that. Sometimes I fancy that she does want to. But then why doesn't she?

Of course he was soon back and is with us again.

He is there at meals. He appreciates the food that is served and particularly the wine from our cellars. I have seen him stretch his legs and look around the room with satisfaction, with an almost proprietorial air. It irritates me. Why does my stepmother not tell him to go?

Today I have been with Magnus, and although I have not mentioned this before, today I blurted it out.

I said: "I hate that man. He frightens me. He moves so silently. You are in a room . . . you look up . . . and find he is watching you there. Oh, Magnus, the house isn't the same."

Magnus said: "It wouldn't be . . . after your father's death. You were fond of him . . . and it is not as though you have your own mother."

"My brother is lost," I replied. "My father is dead. You see, in a way I am alone."

"How can you ever be alone while I am here," he answered.

"It's wonderful that you are. That makes me very happy. I just have this horrible feeling that something might happen . . . before . . . before I can be with you."

"What could happen?"

"I don't know. Just something . . . It seems so long to wait."

"Next April," he said, "we'll go to my home. We'll be there for a while and make our plans. We're going to explore together, be together for the rest of our lives."

"And find your island."

"What did you think of the map?"

"It doesn't tell me much. It is just those blue seas and the island . . . and the mainland and the other islands. I wish I could see pictures of the island."

He laughed at me. "We're going to find it."

"We shan't live there?"

"Oh no, I don't think we could do that. We'll visit them. We'll catch that contentment. Perhaps we'll help them market their gold."

"Wouldn't that change them? I thought their happiness came from simplicity and the idea of their going without their gold cooking pots so that they can sell to rich merchants somehow spoils the illusion."

"We'll go and discover together what we shall do. As long as we are together, I shall be happy."

"I wish it were next April."

"Perhaps we could make it earlier?"

"Oh . . . could we?"

"Ann Alice, you are not really frightened, are you?"

"N . . . no. I suppose not really. I expect I'm just so eager to start our new life together."

We laughed; we kissed; we embraced; and the times we spend together are always to me absolute happiness.

While I was writing that I heard footsteps on the stairs. I listened. There was a gentle tap on my door. I hastily thrust my journal into a drawer.

It was my stepmother.

"I knew you wouldn't be in bed yet," she said.

"You look pale," I told her. "Are you not feeling well?"

Even as I spoke I wondered whether she deliberately looked unwell. I knew there were mysterious-looking pots full of lotions and creams with which she treated her skin, and it occurred to me that she might be able to look pale or robust according to the mood she was in.

She touched her head. "I have headaches. It is since your father died. I should have guessed it couldn't have lasted. But he did seem better. I should have been prepared . . . but it was a great shock when it came. I sometimes feel I shall never get over it." She smiled at me ruefully. "It is a house of mourning . . . no place for a young girl."

"For me, you mean. But it is my home. He was my father."

"My dear Ann Alice, I know that when I first came here you resented me. You were so fond of Miss Bray, weren't you? It is always hard to follow on a favourite."

I was silent and she went on: "I have tried to do what I can. I think you also resented my marriage. It is understandable. Stepmothers are often not the most popular people, are they? How could they be—replacing a dearly loved mother? But I tried. Perhaps I failed."

I did not know what to say. I stammered: "You made my father very happy."

She smiled, looking like her old self. "Yes, I did that. And he has left me a sacred trust."

"Together with an adequate income, I believe."

She looked at me rather reproachfully. "I don't think of that. I think of you. I take this trust . . . very seriously."

"There is no need. I can't think why my father decided to make it. I am not a child any more."

"You are eighteen. It is not very old and you are a girl who has led a very sheltered life. He thought you were inclined to be impulsive, carried away."

"Oh, did he say that?"

"Oh yes. It was this sudden friendship with Magnus Perrensen which made him a little anxious."

"There was no need for him to be anxious," I said sharply.

"He was afraid that you might rush into something. After all you have met very few young men."

"I have met our neighbours frequently and some of them are young. Men have come to the house . . . "

"A young man who has sailed the seven seas . . . who has even been shipwrecked. That is very romantic. Your father used to talk to me a lot about it. He used to say the Perrensens are a good family . . . well-known map makers, known throughout Europe in fact, but Magnus is young . . . and so are you. Your father always said that if there was an engagement between you, it must be of long duration."

"That is absurd. We are not so young or stupid as not to know our own feelings."

"My dear Ann Alice, I think only of your good. You are so very young . . . both of you . . . "

"I am going to marry him. When he leaves, I shall go with him."

She was silent for a while, then she said: "Are you absolutely sure?"

"Absolutely."

She sighed. "I would rather see you married to someone more mature. You are high-spirited and need someone who can guide you . . . someone with a firm hand."

"I am not a horse, Stepmother."

"My dear, I did not mean that. You must understand that whatever I say, whatever I do, it is only for what I believe to be your good. So you must forgive me for being frank. But . . . how well do you know Magnus Perrensen?"

"Well enough to tell me all I want to know."

"Do you know that Mrs. Masters' niece is staying at her house?"

"Mrs. Masters' niece? What has she to do with us?"

"A young woman . . . living under the same roof. They would see a great deal of each other. And young men . . . well, they are only young men."

"You are suggesting that Magnus and Mrs. Masters' niece . . . "

"My dear Ann Alice, I am merely telling you that you should know what people are saying."

I was stunned. I did not believe her.

She lifted her shoulders. "I hope I haven't said anything to upset you. I was only doing what I thought to be my duty. My dear Ann Alice, you really are very young. I know someone who *is* devoted to you, and has been in love with you for a long time. A man who is older . . . and shall we say . . . more steady?"

"I really don't know what you are talking about," I said.

"I was thinking of Mr. Featherstone."

"Mr. Featherstone! You must be joking. I don't like him. I have never liked him."

"Sometimes great affection starts that way."

"Does it? It never would with me . . . and that man. I dislike him. And as you are being frank with me I will be equally so with you. What is he doing here? Living here . . . in this house. It is my house now. Why has he come to live here?"

"He is not living here. He is a guest. Your father was always hospitable and encouraged me to be the same. He said that all my friends would always be welcome in this house."

"Well, as he is a friend of yours, perhaps you can persuade him to confine his attentions to you. He always seems to be where I am and I do not like it."

"He is in love with you, Ann Alice."

"Please do not say that. I do not believe it. Nor do I want to discuss this man any more."

My stepmother put her hand to her eyes and shook her head.

"You must forgive me," she said. "I have spoken too freely. I am only thinking of your good."

"I am eighteen years old," I reminded her. "That is quite old enough to marry and to choose a husband for myself. Understand this, I shall choose whom I wish and no one . . . no one . . . is going to force me into marrying someone I do not want. I should never have allowed even my father to do that. Certainly no one else shall."

"My dear, forgive me. I see you are distraught. Remember, always remember, I only want to do the best for you."

"Then please do not speak of this matter again. It is distasteful to me . . ."

"I am forgiven?"

She came to me and put her arms about me. I laid my cheek against hers briefly. It was strange but I could never bring myself to kiss her wholeheartedly.

"Good night, my dear child, good night."

When she had gone I sat down by my bed and the words she had spoken kept ringing in my ears. Mrs. Masters' niece!

"It is not true," I said aloud.

I thought: She is trying to stop my marrying Magnus. She is trying to force me into marrying Desmond Featherstone.

That could almost make me laugh and I should have done so if I could have forgotten Mrs. Masters' niece.

Then I took my journal again and am writing this in it.

November 7th   All is well. I am happy again. I knew I should be as soon as I saw Magnus and talked with him.

He laughed at me when I told him what my stepmother had said about Mrs. Masters' niece. Yes, she had a niece and she was staying at the house. I should go with him now and meet her.

So I did. She is a plump and friendly woman. She must be at least thirty-five. She is a widow and has a son who is away at school. She is what is called homely. There is nothing of the *femme fatale* about her. She is fond of Magnus as all the Masters are. It is clear to me that my stepmother's hints are completely without foundation.

We laughed over it when we were alone. I said: "She talks about long engagements . . . and I told her that was out of the question as far as we were concerned."

"Perhaps March," he said. "How would that be? That gives you three months in which to prepare yourself."

"I don't need preparations," I told him. "I'm ready."

"I wonder what you'll think of my home."

"I shall love it."

"Do you always make your decisions before you have had time to test them?" he asked.

"Always where you are concerned," I retorted.

How happy we were and when I am with him I feel how foolish I am to entertain doubts.

It was different as soon as I went into the house. I dislike November. It is a gloomy month. I love the spring and the early summer, not so much because of the temperature but because of the light. In November it is almost dark by four o'clock. That is what I hate. It is such a long night.

It was about four-thirty when I came in and already I had to light a candle. They were kept in the hall and we took them as we came in. The servants collected them from wherever they found them and there was always a good supply waiting for use.

As I entered the corridor which led to my room that eerie feeling came over me. I soon knew why. Desmond Featherstone was standing at the end of the corridor.

I lifted up my candle as he came towards me and the light from my candle threw his elongated shadow on the walls. I felt my knees begin to tremble.

"Good evening," I said. I turned to my door but as I touched the handle, he was beside me.

I did not go into the room. The last thing I wanted was for him to come to my bedroom.

He came very close. "How nice to see you alone," he said softly.

"What did you want?" I asked curtly.

"Just the courtesy of a few words."

"Could you make them very few. I have much to do."

"Why are you so unkind to me?"

"I had no idea that I was. You are enjoying hospitality in my house."

"You are so beautiful . . . and so proud. Ann Alice, why won't you give me a chance?"

"A chance? A chance for what?"

"To make you love me."

"No amount of chances could make me do that."

"Are you determined to hate me?"

"It is not a matter of determination."

"Why are you so hard on me?"

"I did not think I was. I just have other things I must do."

Still I hesitated because I feared he would follow me in if I opened the door.

I said: "I must ask you to leave me now."

"Not until you have listened to me."

"I have asked you to say quickly what it is."

"You are very young."

"Oh, please, no more of that. I know how old I am and it is not so very young."

"And you know little of the world. I will teach you, my dearest child. I will make you very happy."

"I am happy, thank you. I don't need any lessons. Now, if you will go . . ."

He was watching me ironically. He knew that I was afraid to open the door lest he should follow me.

"You are heartless," he said. "Just one little moment . . . dearest Ann Alice."

He put his arms out to take me in them and I was so horrified that I pushed him back. He was taken off his guard for a moment and fell against the wall. I opened my door quickly and went inside, shutting it behind me.

I stood leaning against it, listening. My heart felt as though it were bursting; my breath was coming in short gasps and I was trembling violently.

How dared he! Here in my house at that! He must go. I would tell my stepmother that I would not allow him to stay under my roof.

I pressed myself against the door. I had a notion that he might try to come in. How vulnerable I was! There was no key to the door. I had never felt the need of one before. There must be a key. I would never sleep in peace while he was in the house and my bedroom door unlocked. I believed he would be capable of anything . . . just anything. I must be on my guard.

I listened. I could hear nothing. He was silent-footed. I had said to Magnus: "He walks like a cat." And so he did.

No sound at all. All was quiet in the corridor. Still. I stood there. I was afraid that if I opened the door, I should see him standing there.

In time my heart began to beat more normally, though I was still trembling. Cautiously I opened the door and peered out. The corridor was empty.

I came in and put a chair against the door.

It was time to dress for dinner. In a short time one of the maids would bring up my hot water.

I moved the chair away from the door. I did not know what construction the maid would put on that if she found it there, but I could be sure that she would report to the kitchen and there would be conjecture.

How far away April seemed! Perhaps it would be March though. Even so it was a long time to wait.

He seemed quite normal at dinner and made no reference to that scene in the corridor. But then I supposed he wouldn't.

When I retired to my room that night I barricaded myself in. I knew if I did not I should never sleep.

The last thing I said to myself before I went into an uneasy doze was: "Tomorrow I will have a key made."

November 8th   I feel triumphant. I study the key lovingly. It represents security.

The first thing I did this morning was to go down to see Thomas Gow. He has a small cottage on the Green which he uses as a workshop. He ekes out a small living by acting as carpenter and locksmith and doing odd jobs in Little Stanton. There is a firm of carpenters in Great Stanton and I have heard it said that they get the best jobs and poor Thomas Gow the unimportant ones.

I went to him and told him that I wanted a key and asked if he could make one. He said he could, and I told him I wanted it quickly and must have it today.

That could be done, he said.

He came to my room and before the end of the day he called at the house with my precious key. He came up to my room with me and we tried it in the door.

I cried: "Oh, thank you." And I paid him twice what he asked.

He could not know how much that key meant to me.

Now I am about to go to bed and the last thing I am doing is writing in my journal. From my chair I can see my blessed key in the lock. It is turned, shutting me in.

I feel peaceful and secure. I know I shall sleep well tonight to make up for the wakefulness of the last.

December 1st   Christmas will soon be here. Time is passing slowly. I am so relieved that Desmond Featherstone is not here all the time. He goes to London frequently, but when he returns he comes to the house just as though it is his home. I have spoken to my stepmother about it and she always shakes her head and says: "He was a great friend of my family. There is nothing I can do . . . really." And she invariably added: "Your father always said that any friends of mine were welcome here."

I console myself. It is only three months to March. Magnus says that we should make the wedding the beginning of March. So it is getting closer. The thought is a great comfort to me.

In a way Desmond Featherstone's absences—although it is such a relief to be rid of him—in themselves create a tension. One is never sure when he will return and every time I go upstairs I think of coming across him in the corridor or some unexpected place. It is like being haunted by a ghost; and that is almost as bad as the reality.

Sometimes I wake in the night and fancy my door handle is being slowly turned. How thankful I am for my key! I am very grateful to Thomas Gow and have tried to find one or two jobs for him, and I have decided that when we have something which needs to be done, I will not go to the big firm in Great Stanton but give Thomas Gow the chance to do it.

I believe he is quite ambitious and he certainly is prepared to work hard. Such people should be given a chance to get on.

I had an unpleasant surprise today.

I had thought that Christmas would be celebrated in the usual way. When I suggested to my stepmother that we ought to set about making the usual preparations she looked horrified.

"But, my dear, this is a house of mourning. We shall spend Christmas quietly. I could not agree to anything else."

"I was not suggesting that we should have a riotous feast . . . just a few friends."

"There cannot be any guests. It is such a short time since your father died."

I shrugged my shoulders. "Well, perhaps just Magnus Perrensen."

"Oh . . . but no guests at all."

"But my father said we must make him feel at home. He won't have any family of his own. We will just ask him."

I smiled to myself. That would be best of all. Just Magnus. We would ride in the morning and have a quiet day together.

"I had thought of that," said my stepmother. "And I have already spoken to Mrs. Masters about it. She said that naturally Mr. Perrensen will have his Christmas with them. He came in while we were discussing it and she suggested it to him there and then, and he was most agreeable."

I was angry. "It seems that plans are made without consulting me."

"Oh, I am sorry. But it was not exactly planned. It seemed just the only thing to do in the circumstances."

There is something about my stepmother. I suppose it is her worldliness. But in a situation like this one she has a gift for making one feel unreasonable, foolish, making a fuss about something quite trivial. She does it so well that she almost makes you believe it yourself.

December 27th   Christmas is over. I am glad. I am glad of everything that brings me nearer to March.

It went off reasonably well, except that we had the odious Desmond Featherstone with us.

He came to church with us in the morning. They stood on either side of me singing "O Come, All Ye Faithful." He has a deep loud bellowing sort of voice which can be heard above the rest of the congregation, and all the time we were standing singing he seemed to edge closer to me.

We walked across the Green home.

My stepmother was a little sad. She told me she could not help thinking of last Christmas when my father was there.

I saw Magnus in church, sitting with the Masters, and when he looked at me I was happy. His eyes were clearly saying: Not long now. This time next year, where shall we be?

I gave myself up to blissful wondering.

And so Christmas passed.

Soon we shall be into the New Year.

January 2nd 1793   What a strange beginning to the New Year.

I had been out with Freddy. He is beginning to ride quite well although when he came to us he had never sat on a horse. I often take him out with me.

As we came in one of the servants appeared and told me that two gentlemen had called and were asking either for Mrs. or Miss Mallory.

"Who are they?" I asked.

"They did not give a name, Miss Ann Alice. But they said it was important."

"Where is Mrs. Mallory?"

"She is out at the moment."

"I'll see them then. Are they in the parlour?"

She said they were so I told Freddy to go up to his room and I would see him later.

I went into the little sitting room which we call the parlour. It is a small room leading off the hall.

One of the men was familiar to me and as soon as he came forward I recognized him.

The last time he had come he had brought bad news.

"It's James Cardew, Miss Mallory," he said.

"Oh yes . . . yes . . . I remember."

"And this is Mr. Francis Graham."

We exchanged greetings.

"Mr. Graham has just arrived from Australia and in view of what he had to tell me I thought I should come to see you immediately. It concerns your brother, Miss Mallory. I am so sorry that you suffered such a shock on my last visit. It seems that your brother was not lost after all."

"Oh . . . " My voice sounded faint. I was filled with joy. Charles was alive! This was wonderful news. Mr. Cardew turned to his companion. "Mr. Graham will explain."

"Please sit down," I said faintly.

So we sat and Mr. Graham told me the story.

It appeared that Charles had been picked up after several days in the water. He was more dead than alive. The ship had been on its way to Sydney, and Charles had been in such a state of shock and exhaustion that he had been unaware of who he was.

"His memory had completely gone," said Mr. Graham. "He was in an emaciated state. It was thought he could not live. And even when he recovered a little, his memory was gone, which explains why you have heard nothing of him all this time. I was a passenger on that ship. I do business between England and the new colony. When we picked up your brother, I was very interested in his case and when we arrived in Sydney I said I would keep an eye on him. It was obvious that he was of good family and English, and when we were on the ship I had tried to help him recover his memory. He did remember enough to give me some indication of his background, and when we came to Sydney I took him to some friends of mine and asked if they would keep him there, which they did. When I returned to Sydney I was able to see him. Well, to get down to what really matters, I discovered that his name was Charles . . . Not an unusual name and we were looking at some maps recently and the name Mallory was mentioned. That set something working in his mind.

"I knew of Mallory's maps. Mr. Cardew was a friend of mine. It was some time before I could get in touch with him but finally I did and we are certain that this man is your brother. I did not want to bring him over until I had checked out a few facts with Mr. Cardew and yourselves—so he is still with my friends. But we are convinced now that this man is your brother. He will be sailing shortly and arriving in England perhaps in March."

I cried: "It's wonderful news. I only wish my father had lived for this."

"He died, did he?" asked James Cardew.

"Yes. He had been ill on and off for some time, but hearing of my brother's death seemed to undermine him completely . . . and he just succumbed to his illness."

"I wish I had never brought that news to you."

"It was good of you to come. We had to know. We were worried about that long silence before you came."

"I thought I must let you know as soon as I could. This is a happier visit than my last."

My stepmother came in then. She had heard we had visitors and that they were in the parlour.

"This is Mr. James Cardew and Mr. Francis Graham. They have brought wonderful news. Charles is alive!" I cried.

"Charles . . . "

"My brother whom we thought was lost at sea. He was picked up."

"Picked up . . . " She stared. "It can't be! After all this time."

I had an idea that she wanted to prove that the man who was picked up was not my brother.

"Strange things happen at sea," said Francis Graham. "I have heard of cases like this before. It is a fact that Mr. Charles Mallory was shipwrecked but picked up. He suffered from loss of memory among other things and was therefore unable to communicate with his family."

"It is so . . . incredible."

She was very pale. Of course, she had never known Charles. I could hardly expect her to share my joy.

"Won't it be wonderful when he comes home," I cried. "I can't thank you enough for bringing us this news. Now we are going to drink to the health of my brother, and to all those kind people who have looked after him."

My stepmother has recovered herself. She summoned one of the servants. She instructed them to bring wine and to set two more places at the table.

What a happy day this has been!

I feel so safe now. Charles will soon be home.

I suddenly realize that the house is no longer mine. I am glad. That is how it should be. I should have felt dreadful about going away and leaving it. And of course that is what I shall have to do when I marry Magnus . . .

Oh, happy day! A lovely beginning to the New Year.

January 4th   Desmond Featherstone arrived today. I came in and there he was coming down the stairs.

I stopped short and stared at him. "So you are back," I said.

"What a nice welcome! You make me feel so much at home."

"It seems," I said, "that you have made this house your home."

"You are all so hospitable."

I began to feel that shivery feeling, as though—as Miss Bray used to say—someone was walking over my grave.

Why should I feel this? It was broad daylight—a bright frosty day. We have turned the corner and the days are getting longer. It is still dark early, but every day there is a little change. And March will soon be here.

What am I afraid of?

He is shocked. I saw that at dinner. He is so angry about something that he cannot conceal it. I know what it is, of course. It is due to Charles. He is angry because Charles is alive!

Of course, he has some plans for me. He thought the house was mine, the business was mine. No wonder he wants to marry me.

All that is changed now. The true heir is alive. Charles will come back and when he does he will be master of this house. I am sure that then there will be no place in it for Mr. Desmond Featherstone.

Come home soon, Charles.

I am feeling happy today. The days have started to get longer. I have my key so that I may lock myself in. Charles is coming home. And very soon March will be here.

February 1st   I cannot believe this story. It is incredible. How could there possibly be plague in Great Stanton? When I think of the plague I am reminded of lessons with Miss Bray. A red cross on the door. The death cart and "Bring out your dead."

That could not happen nowadays.

I went to the Shop today. I love going there. I try always to go at midday when they are stopping work. Mrs. Masters often sends over a tray. She is only across the road, but Mr. Masters says he doesn't always want to leave the Shop. He is always busy on some project or other—so the food is sent over.

And I go in often and join them. It is such a happy hour, that.

The main topic of conversation for the last week has been the execution of the King of France. We were all shocked about that. It seems so terrible and we have long discussions about what effect this is going to have in France . . . and on England. Magnus is enormously interested, and coming from the Continent, he has a slightly different approach to every subject. He is a great talker and loves a discussion; and, I am discovering, so do I.

But now all that is forgotten. We have a local event which seems of greater importance.

The fact is that a certain Mr. Grant and his son Silas have just returned from Dalmatia bringing with them bales of cloth. They are tailors. A few days ago Mr. Grant senior developed a strange illness— severe fever, soaring temperature, sickness and delirium. The doctor was nonplussed, and when he was about to call in another opinion Mr. Grant developed dark spots and patches all over his skin. These turned into horrible sores and it seems that all these are the symptoms of bubonic plague, which has not been seen in England since the beginning of this century.

He died within a short time.

Perhaps the matter would have been forgotten but a very short time after the death of his father, Silas Grant began to show the same symptoms.

So now this has been definitely diagnosed as the Plague. There has been consternation everywhere, because when this sort of disease is brought into a country there is no knowing how far it will spread.

So we talked of this strange occurrence while we ate Mrs. Masters' excellent chicken.

Magnus as usual took charge of the conversation. He talked at length about the Great Plague of London in 1665 which quite devastated the country. We had suffered little from it since because, said Magnus, it had taught us a great lesson and that was that one of the main causes was a lack of cleanliness and bad drainage.

"Only twice in this century has it visited Western Europe," he said. "It was in Russia and Hungary and came as far as Prussia and Sweden; and when it arrives it is difficult to eradicate. Later there was an outbreak in Southern France . . . rather close, you might say. During the Russo-Turkish war there was another outbreak, and that little more than twenty years ago. Then it appeared again in Dalmatia."

"Well, that is where the Grants came from," I said.

"People are taking this very seriously," said Mr. Masters.

"And so they should," added Magnus.

While we were talking, John Dent, one of our workers, came in and said that he had just heard that Silas Grant had died.

"Two deaths," said Mr. Masters. "This is serious."

"They are saying the bales of cloth they brought back may be infected," said John Dent.

"That," said Mr. Masters, "is very likely."

"They should be burned," added Magnus.

"Nobody wants to touch them," explained John Dent. "They are all together in one room at the top of the shop. They are going to burn all the bedclothes, but nobody will touch the bales of cloth. They are going to board up the room. They think that is the thing to do."

"How strange!" I cried. "I thought it would have been better to burn them."

"The room itself might be infected," said Mr. Masters. "They've got a point."

"Well, if that finishes it, it will be proved they have done the right thing," commented Magnus.

I could not stop thinking of it.

Over dinner I told my stepmother. Desmond Featherstone was there. They did not display a great deal of interest. It seemed to me that they had something on their minds.

February 4th   This is such good news. Today when I went into the shop Magnus was anxious to talk to me alone. I was aware of this as I am of all his moods; there is a very special bond between us. I do believe we know what the other is thinking.

He whispered to me: "Tomorrow I am going to London. Mr. Masters wants to call on one or two people and he thinks it would be a good idea if I went with him. While I am there I shall make enquiries about our journey and get the tickets we shall need, so that everything will be in order."

"Oh Magnus, how wonderful!" I cried.

"Not long to wait now," he said and kissed me.

I could scarcely listen to anything that was said after that.

When I came back to the house I went straight to my room. I must be prepared. I still had the rest of the month to live through. February—mercifully—is the shortest month of the year. Only by a few days, it is true, but every day seems an age.

But very soon now . . .

I am so happy, so excited. I am even wondering if I betray my feelings and I realize that I do when Freddy said to me: "You're happy about something, Ann Alice."

"What makes you say that?" I asked.

"Your face says it," he told me.

I just squeezed his arm and he said: "Is it a secret?"

I said: "Yes. You'll know in time."

He hunched his shoulders and laughed. He loved secrets.

"When shall I know?"

"Oh . . . soon."

Then I remembered that I would be leaving him and I was sorry about that.

He did not say any more but during the day I caught him watching me; he smiled when his eyes met mine as though we shared a secret. We did in a way. The knowledge that there was a secret.

I was reckless. I should not have talked to anyone . . . not even Freddy.

Tomorrow morning, early, Magnus will set out.

After I had written that I put my journal away and prepared for bed. I was not in the least sleepy. I was full of plans, turning over in my mind what I should take with me. It was past midnight and still I could not sleep. Then suddenly I heard a board creak. Someone was walking about on the floor below. It must be my stepmother. Her room was down there.

I listened. Creeping footsteps. I looked at my treasured key. It jutted out from the door, promising security.

I rose, went to the door and listened.

Yes, someone was going stealthily along the corridor down there.

Very quietly I unlocked my door and looked out into the corridor. I tiptoed to the banister. Candlelight flickered on the wall and it came from the candle which Desmond Featherstone was carrying. His feet were bare and he had a bedgown flung loosely round him. I saw him open my stepmother's door and go in.

I stood back. This was significant.

I clutched the banister and thought what it meant. They were lovers.

Was it possible that he had to tell her something suddenly? Nonsense. He had walked in in the most casual fashion, as though it were a habit. He had not even knocked at the door. Besides, what would he want to talk about at midnight?

I stood there, shivering.

I felt I had to wait and see what happened, for I knew it was of importance.

I stood there until three o'clock. He had not emerged.

So there could be no doubt.

I crept back to my room and locked myself in.

They were indeed lovers. How long had they been? Obviously he had come down here to see her. Had they been lovers when my father was alive?

Those periodical visits . . . Did he come to make love to my stepmother? And the same time he was trying to court me! She knew about it. She was trying to help him. She had invented lies about Magnus and Mrs. Masters' niece.

What did it mean?

Sleep was impossible. I should have guessed. And yet my stepmother had almost won me over. I had believed in her grief. I had almost been ready to be her friend.

My thoughts are in a whirl.

And my father . . . what of him? He had loved her so deeply. Perhaps it was only since his death . . .

My thoughts alighted on a hundred possibilities.

So I am taking out my journal and writing it all down. It soothes me in a way. It calms me.

My first thoughts were: I shall tell Magnus what I have seen. But then he will not be back for a week. I am thankful that I shall soon be out of this house.

February 5th   I am spending the day in my room. I have pleaded a headache. I could not face either of them. I am not sure how I should act.

Sometimes I feel like confronting them. At others I feel I must keep silent.

The fact is, I am afraid of them. I am afraid of this house. All that uneasiness I felt, that instinct which insisted that I acquire a key and lock myself in, was a warning. Something within me saw more than my conscious self.

Everything had changed since Lois Gilmour came into the house. Before that how open and easy everything had been. She had brought that sinister atmosphere here—and of course she was the reason for it.

At midday she came to see me.

I lay on my bed and closed my eyes when I heard her coming.

"My dear child," she said, "you do look pale."

"It's just a headache. I'll stay in my room today I think."

"Yes, perhaps it is best. I'll have something sent up to you."

"I don't feel much like eating."

"A little soup, I should think."

I nodded and closed my eyes. Silently she went out.

Freddy was there.

"No dear," she said. "You can't go in. Ann Alice is feeling poorly today. Just let her rest."

I looked up and smiled at him as he stood in the doorway. He looked very sorry for me. He is such a nice little boy.

I took the soup and that was all I wanted. I lay on my bed thinking.

What does it mean? They are lovers . . . lovers since when? I thought of the first time I had seen Desmond Featherstone in the inn with her. Then, I suppose. Yet she had married my father, and my father had died. He had left her a comparatively wealthy woman. She had come merely as a governess and I imagined she had not had much then. And now her friend . . . her lover . . . was trying to marry me. I had been deeply shocked.

I did know that they had been shattered by the news that Charles was safe. Why? Because Charles would inherit. I should be provided for, of course, but I should not be the rich woman I should have been if my brother were dead.

It was all fitting into place.

"Conjecture," I said.

Look at it this way, I admonished myself. My father has been dead for some time. Perhaps she is the sort of woman who needs a lover. Perhaps it has only just started between them. Perhaps he no longer wants to marry me. Perhaps he will marry her now.

How could I be sure that the thoughts I had entertained about them were true? And if they were . . . ? Those turns of my father? What did they mean? He had never had them before his marriage.

What if she were a murderess? What if they plotted between them? What if they were plotting now. Would it be for him to marry me, and murder me as she had murdered . . .

It is helpful to write down my thoughts like this just as they come. They are a little incoherent perhaps, but it helps me to *think*.

The house has become a very sinister place.

I am afraid. Oh, Magnus, I wish you were here. If you were, I would say, Take me away, take me away tonight. I do not want to spend another in this place.

It frightens me. It is full of menace. What I have been thinking were childish imaginings are now taking on a sinister reality.

I must try to decide what I am going to do.

I have thought of something. I might try it out tonight. I will listen for him to go to her room. I know the house well, of course, and next to their room is another with a door leading into the corridor. Like most Tudor houses, some rooms lead into others. This one leads into hers, although it has that door into the corridor. The door between the two rooms is locked. If I were in that room I could listen to their conversation perhaps. I have decided that this afternoon when they are out, I will go down to that room and examine it to see if it is possible for me to secrete myself there and if I did I should be able to hear what was said.

It is now afternoon and I have found out what I want. I have been down to the floor below. The door between the two rooms is bolted on both sides.

I have made sure that it is locked. The door is ill-fitting. If I stand on a stool I can reach a crack at the top of the door and I am sure I should be able to hear what is being said on the other side.

I am going to try it tonight.

Of course I may hear nothing. I have already proved that he spends his nights with her. But I want to hear what they talk about.

I believe he is very partial to the port and likes to sit drinking after dinner. That would be the time perhaps to listen to what they say. But they might be more careful then. Servants have their ears everywhere.

So . . . tonight, I will try.

It is one o'clock. I am shaking so much I can scarcely hold my pen. But I must write it down while it is fresh in my memory. I heard them come up as before. It was past midnight. I fancied he was reeling a little. He must have drunk a great deal. I hoped not too much for that would probably make him sleepy and disinclined to talk.

I crept down very quietly into the room with the door wide open for my escape if necessary and my own door open so that I could run into it quickly.

My handwriting is shaking so much. I am so frightened.

It worked really better than I thought. He was in a quarrelsome mood.

Standing on the stool with my ear to the crack I could hear him distinctly.

"What's the matter with her?" he demanded.

My stepmother said: "She said a headache."

"That she-devil is up to something."

"You should give up. Let her go to her Swede or whatever he is."

"I'm surprised at you, Lo. You go so far and then you lose your nerve. You didn't want to get rid of the old man, did you? Look at the time you took over that! You liked the cosy life. I believe you even liked the old fellow."

She said quietly: "He was a good man. I didn't want to . . . "

"I know that. Tried to get out of it, didn't you?"

"Stop arguing and come to bed."

"You would have liked to stop there. Given up the plan. You brought our little bastard in, didn't you? That was a neat little job. Oh, it was nice and cosy. You're small-time, Lo. That's what you are. You come in, make a little nest for yourself and the boy and you want to keep it like that. So, what about me, eh?"

"You're shouting," she said.

"Who's to hear? And now the brother's coming back. What's that going to do to our little plan, eh?"

"Go away, Desmond. Leave things as they are."

"Very nice for you, eh? But what about me? I've got to marry the girl. You had the old man. It's only right. She's not as well padded as we thought . . . but she'll do very nicely."

"She won't have you."

"She's going to be made to."

"How?"

"That's what we have to fix."

"What do you plan . . . to seduce her . . . rape her. I wouldn't put that past you."

I was so overcome with rage that I moved. The stool jerked from under my feet. I leaped to the floor.

They would have heard the noise.

I dashed from the room to my own . . . and here I am.

I am so frightened. Tomorrow I shall leave the house. I will go to Mrs. Masters and tell her what I know. I will wait there for Magnus to come.

My handwriting is so shaky. It is scarcely legible. What was that? I thought I heard a noise. Footsteps . . .

I can hear voices . . . Something is going on down there.

They are coming . . .

RAYMOND

I lost count of time while I was reading Ann Alice's journal, and when I came to the end it was quite light for morning had come.

I had been there with her. I felt I knew her and her lover, her stepmother and the sinister Desmond Featherstone. I was completely frustrated by the abrupt ending and was filled with an intense longing to know what had happened on that night which I knew was the night of her death because of the date on her tombstone.

I could feel her fear . . . the steps on the stairs. I could see her hastily thrusting her journal into the drawer, not shutting it completely so that the telltale scarf was just visible.

And what had happened? Was the prized key in the door, or had she forgotten to lock it? Oh no, she never would do that. She had been so insistent about that key. Yet after what she had heard she would be in a state of extreme terror.

What had happened?

And how strange it was that I should be the first to read those words which had been written nearly a hundred years ago. It was almost as though they had been written for me. I was the one who had uncovered her grave, who had been the first to step into her room and find the journal.

I was impatient to tell my brother Philip what I had discovered. I even thought of going to wake him up, but I decided against that. I must be patient. He was an early riser and he would be at the breakfast table at half past seven.

I was there before him.

"Philip," I cried, "an extraordinary thing happened last night."

Then I told him and he was as excited as I was. But what interested him particularly was the map.

"Go and get it," he said. So I did.

He studied it intently.

"I know the area," he said. "These islands . . . well, we're aware of them . . . but this Paradise Island . . . It sounds rather fanciful."

"Well, we have the Solomon Islands. Why not the Paradise Island?"

"I'll show it to Benjamin. He's bound to know something."

Neither of us ate much. We were so excited. I suggested that we tell Granny M what I had found. She would be most put out if she were not informed.

We went to her room where she was having her usual tea and toast with marmalade on the special tray she used for her breakfasts in bed . . . her one concession to her years.

She listened intently and her first remark was a reproof for me.

I had been told not to enter the room. It might have been dangerous.

"I had an urge, Granny," I said. "It was irresistible."

"In the middle of the night!" added Philip.

"So I took the candle and went up."

"Very brave in view of all the talk of spectres," said my brother. "What would you have done if you had met a headless corpse with clanging chains?"

"When you have read the journal you will not talk so flippantly of the dead," I told him earnestly.

I went up to my room and brought down the journal for them to see. They were astonished.

"And you sat up all night reading that!" said Philip.

"Well, wouldn't you? In any case, once I had started I couldn't stop."

"I should have waited until morning."

"What do you think of the map, Philip?" asked Granny M.

"It's not done by an amateur. I know the area. That's clear enough. But I have never seen this Paradise Island before. I want Benjamin to have a look at it. We'll make some comparisons."

"It will be interesting to hear what he has to say," said Granny M. "Leave the journal with me. I shall read it."

It was a strange morning. I felt wide awake in spite of a night without sleep. I went up to the room again. It seemed different from last night. I suppose that was because the workmen were there. I could not settle to anything. I kept thinking of Ann Alice. It was almost as though

I were living her life and expected to see the wicked Desmond Featherstone appear at any moment.

Reading the journal had been a shattering experience for me.

At luncheon Granny M could talk of nothing else but the journal. She had stayed in bed all morning reading it.

"It's a terrible story," she said. "What do you think happened to that girl?"

"Do you think they came up and murdered her?"

"I think it very likely."

"And then walled up the room?"

"Why should they do that?"

"I don't know. They buried her . . . We know that. I was the one who found her grave."

"It is a mystery that we cannot hope to solve. I wonder what that map will reveal. This island the young man talked about . . . where is it? Perhaps it never existed. We don't know much about the young man. The girl was so besottedly in love with him, doubtless she didn't see him clearly."

"Oh, I am sure he loved her. He believed in that island. They were going to find it. I wonder what happened to him."

"Yes, so do I. Perhaps he went to the island after the girl died."

"Imagine his coming back and finding her dead!"

"Well, it will be interesting to hear what Benjamin has to say about the map."

I was so eager to know that I went over to the shop that afternoon. I found Philip and Benjamin surrounded by old maps.

Philip shook his head at me.

"There's no sign of it anywhere."

"If it existed it would have been discovered by now," said Benjamin. "These seas have been charted."

"It is possible, I suppose, that it could have been missed."

Benjamin shrugged his shoulders. "Just possible, I suppose." He tapped the map. "This has been made by someone who knows what he is doing."

"Yes. He was a professional."

"Mr. Mallory was telling me about the discovery of the journal. In my opinion, this young man made a mistake about the locality."

"But if it were somewhere in this area . . . "

"It is hardly likely. It would have been discovered by now. You say this map was made nearly a hundred years ago. We've made long strides since then." He shook his head. "One never knows. It could be wrong, of course. I imagine he drew it from memory."

"I should love to find that island," said Philip.

"If it exists," added Benjamin.

"It exists," retorted Philip. "I feel it in my bones."

We sat talking. To me it was like taking a journey through the ocean. I listened to them. I caught Philip's eagerness. I loved him dearly. He had such wonderful vitality and when he took an interest in something it was never half-hearted.

He was obsessed about that island as I was about Ann Alice. Our curiosity differed slightly. I yearned to know what had happened on that night. Philip's thoughts were all for the island.

Often later I thought back to that afternoon in the shop and many times I wished I had never found that map.

Philip could talk of nothing else. I would often find him with old maps stretched out before him.

"It could have been in an entirely different part of the world," he said.

"Listen," I replied. "He was a map maker. He would no more mistake the locality than you would."

"Everyone can make mistakes."

His intensely blue eyes looked into space. "Annalice," he said, "I want to find that island."

He wouldn't leave it alone. It was an obsession. Granny M noticed it and was disturbed.

Gow and his men had finished the roof and were working on the room. All the soft furnishings had been destroyed. They were in tatters. But some of the furniture was quite good and would be restored.

I went through her clothes. I wanted to do that myself. The gloves, the scarves, the hats and gowns . . . all her personal belongings. I instructed the servants to wash some of the dresses. Many of them were perished but those which were not I put into a trunk in the attic with her hats and shoes.

I treated them reverently. I felt very close to her and sometimes I had the extraordinary notion that she was watching me and thanking me.

I went up to the room before they started to mend the woodwork and paint the walls. Gow was there. I asked him about the stains on the walls.

He said it was hard to tell what had caused them after so long. It might have been damp . . . discolouration.

"It seems to be splashed," I pointed out. "Could it be . . . blood?"

"Blood, Miss Annalice? Well, it could be, I suppose . . . By the look of it . . . yes it could be. I wouldn't have thought of that though. Damp and time do odd things to buildings. Why should you think it was blood, Miss Annalice?"

"I just wondered."

"Well, whatever it was we'll soon have these walls looking like new. It'll be a nice room when we've seen to the window."

"And the window will be exactly where it was before?"

"Have to be. That was where it was walled in like. You'll be able to see it from outside now the creeper's cut away. I reckon that's why they let the creeper grow there. There's a difference in the bricks, you see. Oh, this will be a nice room when we've done with it."

Now they have done it. The restored furniture is there. The bed, the chest of drawers, the chairs. This is how it must have looked when Ann Alice sat in it and wrote her journal.

The servants still will not go there after dark. They say it is creepy.

But I often go and sit there in the early evening. Sometimes I speak to her. "Ann Alice," I say, "I wish you would come back and tell me."

Sometimes there seems to be a presence there. But maybe that is only my fancy.

The house and everything seem different since the revelations which came on that night of the storm. She comes into my mind so often and at odd moments I could almost feel that she is beside me. There is some special bond between us. We are of the same blood; we have almost the same name; we have lived in the same house. It is only time that separates us. I often think: What is time? Is it possible to bridge the gulf?

I never say such things. Granny M and Philip are far too practical. They would laugh at my fancies. But Philip has his fancies too.

Constantly he talked of that island. I can see plans forming in his mind. So can Granny M. And she is very uneasy.

One day at dinner Philip said: "I have always wanted to explore new areas, to chart right on the scene. I've always been intrigued by the practical side of the business."

I knew him so well that I was not surprised when he went on to explain that David Gutheridge, a botanist—this was a friend of his with whom he had been at school and who came of a seafaring family—was planning to go on an expedition to the South Seas. Philip went on: "He has suggested I go with him."

Granny M was silent but she expressed no surprise.

"It has always been what I wanted to do," said Philip. "There are some very sophisticated instruments in use now . . . some of which were never dreamed of a hundred years ago. I would like to check up on some of our charts. I think . . . and Benjamin agrees with me . . . that they might be a little in error here and there in these waters."

Granny M came to my room that night.

"He's determined to go," she said.

She looked rather pathetic suddenly—something I had thought she never could.

"I knew it had to come," she said. "It's natural."

"You won't try to stop him?"

She shook her head. "No. It wouldn't be right. It's his life . . . his profession. He's right in a way. We cannot stand still in one place. He should go out into the world. Benjamin should have done. If he had he would be right at the top now. Philip must go. I have always known it."

"We shall miss him . . . terribly."

"It will only be for a year or so. But he'll come back . . . enriched, fulfilled. Yes, I shall miss him. But I have you, my dear. I can't tell you what a comfort you two children have been to me."

I felt limp, frustrated. How *I* should love to go with Philip!

If I could have made plans with him, I should have been so happy, so excited.

I had been on the point of suggesting it to Philip. I had wondered what his reaction would be. But I could see now that I should have to stay with Granny M.

One day perhaps I would go out there to those secret waters. I longed to discover Magnus's Paradise Island.

That was what Ann Alice had wanted to do. And so did I.

I felt melancholy.

Life seemed frustrating.

On a bright day, at the beginning of October, Granny M and I travelled down to Southampton to wave our goodbyes.

Philip had gone on ahead with all his gear; he was to sleep on the ship for a night or two before it set out to carry him across the seas.

I felt very sad, and so did Granny M. But she was convinced that it was the right way to act and I suppose I agreed with her. It was the first time Philip had gone away—apart from school, of course. I remembered how desolate I used to be on those occasions. But how much worse was this!

I had helped him with his preparations and if anything we had been closer during the last weeks than ever before.

"I wish you were coming," he said. "What fun that would be!"

"Oh, how I wish it! It's going to be devastatingly dull without you."

Philip said: "Many times I've been about to say you should come. But we couldn't both leave the old lady, could we?"

"No, of course not."

"Never mind. When I've found the island we'll all go out and visit it. I'll bet Granny M would be game."

"Come back soon," I said.

He had suggested that I make a copy of the map. "So that you have one," he said. "In any case, it is better for there to be two."

"I think I could do it almost from memory."

"I want it to be exact."

"All right."

I made the map. I was rather proud of it.

I showed it to Philip who said: "Perfect. Exact in every detail. Put it in a safe place."

I said almost without thinking: "I'll put it at the back of one of my drawers." Then I had a strange feeling that that was what Ann Alice must have said—or thought—when the map had been given to her.

And now he was going.

Granny M looked pale and sad, as we stood there on the dock watching the ship glide out of the harbour while Philip stayed on deck waving to us.

We remained there until we could see him no more.

Life had become monotonous. The days seemed long and now that they were drawing in, rather depressing. When I was in the garden I often looked up at the new window which had been put in and sometimes I fancied I saw a face there. One gets fanciful on dark afternoons in a big house which has become full of shadows.

Christmas came. I was longing for it to be over. It wasn't the same without Philip and at such times it was brought home more vividly how we missed him.

We tried to be enthusiastic. We discussed presents and such things. The only Christmas present I wanted was to see Philip walk in.

The Fentons came to us and we visited the Galtons; we dined with the vicar and his ineffectual wife. We had the village children's Christmas party the day after Boxing Day in the Manor, all just as we always had had. We tried to make it a normal Christmas.

"Time is passing," said Granny M. "He'll be home soon. He just wants to look at the place . . . and satisfy himself that it is there . . . then he'll come home."

I wasn't sure. He had always wanted to go to sea. He would become fascinated sailing the ocean, hoping that he was going to make discoveries . . . just as I should if I had been with him.

In February we had a letter from him. What excitement that was! I read it. Granny M read it: I read it aloud to her and she read it aloud to me, for reading it was like having Philip with us.

"Dear Granny and Annalice,   *Sydney*

"Here I am! I can't believe I have really arrived and that you two are on the other side of the world.

"We had a fairly smooth journey—at least I was told it was smooth. It was hardly how I should have described it. There are some amusing fellows in the botanical party. They are here in Sydney at the moment and they are leaving tomorrow. I shall be on my own then.

"I am planning to explore the islands some hundreds of miles off the coast here. There is a ship that goes every Wednesday. That is the day after tomorrow . . . so I shall get this off to you before I leave.

"I hope it reaches you. It has a long way to go, but they assure me that letters do get safely home and four hundred mail bags leave Australia for England every week.

"I wish you were here. Then everything would be fine. I've seen several people in Sydney but none of them so far has given me any information about Paradise Island. I studied several maps but it is not marked on any of them. It really is rather mysterious.

"As soon as there are any developments, I'll write again.

"I am fit and well. Never felt better and am raring to go.

"Perhaps you will be seeing me soon.

"Your devoted grandson and brother,

"Philip."

"He seems as though he is finding the life amusing and interesting," said Granny M.

"Philip usually finds life amusing and interesting."

"He always had the urge to wander. Perhaps having had a taste of it he'll long for the comforts of home."

I wondered.

One day merged into another. Each day I watched for a letter from Philip.

"Of course mail coming from such a long way would be uncertain," said Granny M. "I daresay a number of letters get lost."

I agreed with her: but how I longed for news!

The shop had lost its charm for me. Every time I went in I thought of Philip. When I looked at the maps with those far-off seas, I would think of the terrible things that could happen on them. I remembered the account of storms in Ann Alice's journal. Where was Philip? and how would he be faring on those treacherous seas? He had talked of taking a boat to the islands. Was he still there?

Talking to Benjamin brought little comfort. He made a great effort to be cheerful and optimistic, but he was merely depressing.

Granny M was anxious to lift us out of our melancholy and with characteristic good sense made up her mind that we must stop torturing ourselves with possibilities. It would be wonderful to hear from Philip but if we did not, we must consider the difficulties of communication and not think the worst. In any event we must get on with our own lives.

When she heard there was to be a conference of cartographers in London she declared her intention of going. Benjamin and I should go with her. "It will be of the utmost interest," she declared.

My first thought was: How exciting it would have been if Philip were going with us. Then I tried to be sensible and gave myself up to preparations.

It was to last three days and Benjamin was instructed to book us in to Blake's Hotel, where the family had always stayed on its visits to London. It was highly respectable and what was called an "old-fashioned" hotel situated not far from Piccadilly. I had stayed there before and been impressed by the hushed atmosphere which I believed was created by the heavy curtains and thick carpets, by porters in liveries of dark blue lightened only by shining brass buttons, silent-footed waiters and discreet chambermaids.

There were to be several meetings and a ball at one of the more florid hotels.

Preparations ensued. We must have new ball dresses. There was bustle throughout the house, which in spite of myself I found exciting, and it did take our minds temporarily from our anxieties about Philip.

It was always thrilling to be in London and it was impossible for one's spirits not to be lifted a little to contemplate all that bustle and vitality which we lacked on our village Green. I was fascinated by the street traders and the German bands and the people dashing to and fro across the roads which they seemed to do so recklessly that I thought they were going right under the horses which were drawing the hansom cabs, the broughams and the landaus that filled the streets.

One could not help being caught up in the excitement. I liked the shops too and made up my mind that I was going to spend many an hour browsing through the goods displayed there before I returned home.

The conference was interesting. It was held in a big room at one of the grander hotels. There were lectures on various aspects, and coloured lithography was widely discussed.

Benjamin had gone on ahead of us because Granny M and I wanted to look in at one of the shops. Granny M had said: "Don't worry about us. We'll see you after the lecture. Don't attempt to save seats for us. We'll look after ourselves."

Our hansom was held up in the traffic and, as it happened, when Granny M and I arrived, the lecture was just about to start.

We were a little abashed when we entered the hall to find it full, and it seemed as though there were no seats available. I suppose we looked a little bewildered for a young man who was seated in the back row saw us and immediately rose and offered his seat to Granny M.

She was hesitating when an attendant came along with two extra chairs which were set down behind the back row, so the young man and I sat down behind Granny M.

I said: "Thank you very much. That was most kind of you."

"It was a pleasure," he replied with one of the most disarming smiles I have ever seen.

I found the lecture of great interest. So apparently did he, but I noticed that every now and then he was glancing sideways at me. I had to admit that I took a few looks at him too. He was of medium height— slightly taller than I, but then I was tall; he had light brown hair and eyes of a slightly darker brown, good, though undistinguished features, but what was so pleasant about him was his frank engaging smile.

The lecture over, Granny M turned to thank him again and he repeated that it was a pleasure. He added that he believed there was some sort of refreshment which was being served. Would we care to join him? He was alone.

Granny M said: "We have a friend here. He went on ahead. I daresay he is down at the front somewhere."

"Perhaps we could find him. I believe there are tables for four."

While we were talking Benjamin came up.

"This is Mr. Benjamin Darkin who is general manager of what we call our shop in Great Stanton."

"Don't tell me you are Mallory's Maps."

"We are indeed," said Granny M.

"This is a great honour to meet you. I'm Billington . . . Raymond Billington."

"It is indeed an honour to meet you, Sir," said Benjamin.

"What is so pleasant about gatherings like this," I said, "is that even though people haven't met before, they know of each other."

"And have a chance to get to know each other which is so much more satisfactory than knowing of," said Raymond Billington.

We all went along to the room where the refreshments were served and Granny M and I seated ourselves at a table for four while the men went off to get the refreshment.

That was an extremely fascinating encounter. We were all vitally interested in what had been said during the lecture and we discussed it with animation, exchanging views, agreeing, disagreeing, expounding our own ideas. The men took charge of the conversation because they were more deeply involved, but Granny M and I were knowledgeable enough to be able to take part and were by no means excluded.

We were reluctant to leave.

Raymond Billington said we should all go to the next lecture together because it was so interesting to exchange views afterwards.

There was to be some sort of forum later on during which he would be on the platform. He would get us tickets for the front row.

He had his own brougham for the Billingtons had their offices in the City of London and he told us that he lived just a little way out in Knightsbridge.

So he took us back to our hotel and we parted, having made arrangements to see him again.

Granny M was very taken with him.

"What a delightful young man," was her comment, and that said a good deal for she was inclined to be critical, particularly of the young.

Benjamin said that he had been rather overawed to meet one of the Billington family. "You know what a reputation they have, Mrs. Mallory."

"Very good indeed, but of course they are not of such long standing as the Mallorys."

"Oh no, Mrs. Mallory, of course not. They only go back about a hundred years."

"Not as long as that," Granny M corrected him. "About eighty at the most. However, credit where credit is due. They have a very good reputation in the world of maps."

"I liked that young man," repeated Granny M later.

So did I. He had helped me to forget Philip for quite a little time.

It turned out, during the next three days, that wherever we went we were accompanied by Mr. Raymond Billington.

He took us to his family's premises near the Strand and we had an interesting morning touring them. He introduced us to his father and to his young brother Basil, who was just coming into the business. They were very agreeable and, said Granny M, just what one would expect Raymond Billington's family to be.

Granny M said that Raymond must come to Great Stanton and we would show him how we worked.

We were all impressed by his performance at the forum and he gave straightforward and very knowledgeable answers to the questions which were asked.

We were all rather sorry as the conference was drawing to its close. It had been a stimulating three days.

He asked if he might conduct us to the ball which was to bring the proceedings to an end, and of course permission was gratefully granted.

It would have been false modesty on my part if I had not admitted that the assiduous attention he bestowed on us was largely due to his interest in me. And it would have been more than false if I had denied that I was pleased.

I liked him. I found him a great improvement on Charles Fenton and Gerald Galton. He was interesting, charming, sophisticated, in fact he was all that a young man should be.

He danced well and carried me along with him. I felt in complete harmony with him.

He said: "This has been an exciting conference . . . quite the best I ever attended."

"They have them every year, don't they? This is the first time I have been. Perhaps we shall meet next year."

"Oh . . . before that, I hope."

I laughed. "Well, a year is rather a long time."

"Your grandmother has invited me to see your premises in Great Stanton."

"She is very enthusiastic about them, although of course Mr. Darkin is the expert who runs the place."

"You are very knowledgeable too."

"Oh . . . I'm interested. They all say it is from the romantic angle. I look at the blue seas and see palm trees and natives in canoes."

"It's all part of it."

"But you are interested in sextants and the instruments you use for measuring distances . . . and so on. Far too practical for me. My brother is like that."

I paused. Philip had intruded and with him came sadness.

"Your brother? Where is he?"

"We don't know. We are very anxious. He went off on an expedition last October."

"And you haven't heard of him since?"

"One letter only."

"Well, that's not bad. Communication is difficult from so far off, you know."

"Yes, I suppose so."

We danced in silence.

"Now, you're sad," he said, after a long pause.

"I'm thinking of him."

"You must tell me more about him."

"Well, you know how it is. Two children . . . left to themselves. My mother died and my father went away and married again. He has another family in Holland. My grandmother brought us up."

"She seems a very charming lady but I fancy she could be formidable."

"That's true. Philip and I were a good deal together."

"You must tell me about it . . . about your childhood. I want to know everything about you."

"It's not very interesting. It could be told in a very short time."

"I believe I should find it of the utmost interest."

His arm tightened about me.

I said: "The music is coming to an end."

"Yes, alas. The dance is over."

We went back to Granny M and Benjamin.

"Shall we go and find some supper together?" asked Raymond.

He was very efficient looking after us. We secured one of the best tables in the room and he and Benjamin went off to bring the food from the buffet.

"What a pleasant conference this has been," said Granny M. "I never enjoyed one more, and a lot of it is due to that charming young man. Has it ever occurred to you, Annalice, how little incidents shape our lives. If we had not been late we might not have met him."

"He gave us his seat. That's hardly shaping our lives."

"Knowing him might well do so." She looked contented, rather complacent. I knew what she was thinking. Here was a young man who was attracted to me. She worried about my lack of opportunities for getting to know people and I think she realized that the Fentons and Galtons were not for me.

And myself? How did I feel? I liked him. I liked him very much. And how should I feel if I said goodbye to him forever? Sad . . . definitely sad. A little nostalgic?

Was that what was called falling in love? There was nothing violent about it. No breathtaking moments, no knowing without doubt that this was the one. It was just pleasant—well, rather delightful.

The men came back with salmon and little new potatoes and green peas. A waiter brought the champagne which Raymond had ordered.

And there we sat, on the last day of the conference, laughing, joking, reminiscing about the lectures, commenting on this and that.

"This is a wonderful finale," said Granny M. "And I want to thank you, Mr. Billington, for making it all so easy and pleasant for us."

"But I have done nothing."

"Nonsense. You, as they say, know your way about. And you have made it doubly enjoyable. Is that not so, Annalice? Benjamin?"

We declared that it was.

"Well, you are coming to see our little shop are you not?"

"I shall be there as soon as I am asked."

"Well, what about the week after next. That would fit in with your plans, Benjamin? Have you anything special to get in the way?"

"Nothing at all," said Benjamin.

"Perhaps you would like to think about it, Mr. Billington."

"I don't need to think about it. I am all eagerness to come whenever you suggest."

"Then that is settled. The Stantons are not very far from London. You will be our guest, of course. We are in the Manor House on Little Stanton Green."

"I shall be so happy to come," he said; and he was looking at me as he spoke.

Our anxiety over Philip did fade a little into the background as we prepared for Raymond Billington's visit.

"We shall have to entertain him," I said. "We had better arrange some dinner parties."

"We'll manage," said Granny M. "I expect he will want to see something of the countryside. I told him that you ride a good deal. He might like to ride with you."

Granny M was quite transparent. It was obvious that she regarded him as the ideal grandson-in-law. He was reasonably wealthy, of good appearance, had charm and good manners; moreover he was involved in the fascinating business of map making; and I think what influenced her a great deal was that he did not live too far away.

She visualized her granddaughter coming to stay at the Manor with her children. And Granny M herself visiting the happy family. I could see how her mind worked.

Dear Granny M, she suffered more than she would admit from

Philip's absence. She was always optimistic about his return but I wondered what went on in her secret thoughts.

I threw myself wholeheartedly into the preparations for Raymond's visit, partly because I did like him very much and was eager to see him again, but chiefly I think to turn away my thoughts of Philip, if that were possible, for with every passing day which brought no news of him, my anxiety must increase.

Raymond came and seemed more charming than ever. He was greatly intrigued by the Manor House and fascinated by the shop. He spent a long time in Benjamin's company examining the machinery as well as the maps.

I took him riding and I think he enjoyed that as much as anything. I showed him the countryside and we stopped at some of the smaller inns where we could drink cider and eat hot bread straight from the oven, with cheese or fruit or sometimes hot bacon and beef.

He told me a great deal about himself. This was usually while we sat in an inn parlour, or sometimes, if the weather was good, on a bench outside the inn.

He had been brought up with maps. It was in the family. They had not been involved as long as the Mallorys, of course, but his grandfather had founded the business, in the early years of the century. In the year 1820 to be precise. It seemed a long time ago, but compared with the Mallorys, it was hardly any time at all.

I talked to him a great deal about Philip, and talking I remembered so much about my brother which I had forgotten.

"I can see he is someone very special to you."

"Yes. He is wonderful."

"I think you would have liked to accompany him on his travels."

I nodded. "How I wish I had. But of course I could not have left my grandmother."

"It would be rather unusual for a young lady to go off to the South Seas. But you are an unusual young lady."

"I would have made him take me but for Granny M."

He understood immediately.

"I hope to meet your brother . . . one day."

"I hope you do."

"And I want you to meet my family."

"I should like that."

"We have a house in the country . . . in Buckinghamshire. The place in London is not really our home. We are there to be near the business, of course. I get down to the country when I can. I have a grandmother like yours. She is a wonderful old lady. I should like you to meet her. She is considerably older than Mrs. Mallory, but lively and bright mentally, though a little incapacitated with rheumatism. Will you come and meet her?"

"I should like to."

"Before the summer is out. I usually go in August. I am going to ask your grandmother to visit us then. Do you think she will agree?"

"I have no doubt whatsoever."

"I shall mention it to her this evening."

"Yes do. I am sure she will be delighted to accept."

We were in the inn when this conversation took place. A little light filtered through the small windows onto his face. It was very eager, tender, almost shining with affection. I felt drawn to him; he must have felt the same towards me for he put his hand across the table and took mine.

"I want us to get to know each other . . . well," he said.

"Yes," I answered. "I am sure that would be most . . . rewarding."

As we came out into the sunshine it seemed as though there was an understanding between us. For some reason I felt a trifle unsure. I liked him very much. His visit had been a great success and we should miss him when he had gone.

But perhaps I had dreamed too many romantic dreams. I had found his company very enjoyable, but it was not the intoxicating experience I had thought falling in love would be.

Our friendship with Raymond Billington ripened during the summer days. He would often come to us for the weekend; he and I would ride in the country and he spent some time at the shop with Benjamin. His visits helped to stop us brooding on Philip's absence.

I could see that I was moving towards an understanding. It was rather pleasant, like drifting downstream in a boat in the not-too-hot sunshine to the strains of a mandoline. Comforting without being breathtaking.

I heard one of the maids talking to another and she referred to Raymond as Miss Annalice's "intended."

I was now nineteen, a little older than Ann Alice had been when she

died. I could not help identifying myself with her, though since the
coming of Raymond she had grown a little remote. I was getting over the
shock of finding the diary and I was beginning to think of the days before
I had with a certain nostalgia, for if I had never found it, Philip would
still be here. He would not have gone off in search of an elusive island
which according to the map makers did not exist.

It was comforting to look to the future, to wait for Raymond's visits
and to allow myself a few discreet glimpses into the future.

Marriage with Raymond. I believed it could be for me . . . if I wanted
it. Did I want it? Partly . . . yes. Most people married and if they did not
they were often vaguely dissatisfied, constantly thinking with regret of
what they had missed. What had Granny once said? Something like: You
must choose and if you leave the choice too late there might not be any to
choose from.

I supposed most people accepted a compromise. Young girls dreamed
of romance . . . impossible dreams of knights on chargers, shining heroes
who in truth had no part in everyday life.

Raymond was what would be called highly eligible. I liked him very
much. I should be disappointed if he discontinued his visits or transferred his attentions to someone else. He had certainly made us all
happier and although we still looked for Philip's letters I am sure that
even Granny M did not mourn quite so much as she had before we went
to the conference. Raymond had done that for us and when he suggested
we should visit his family in Buckinghamshire, it seemed that my mind
was being made up for me.

"They all talk of the house in Buckinghamshire as home," Raymond
explained to us.

He told us that his grandfather had bought the house in 1820. It
was then an ancient mansion which had been damaged—though not
completely destroyed—by fire, and there was still much of the old building standing.

The family had lived in it ever since.

"You'll probably think it is a bit of a hotchpotch. Part of it is pure
Tudor and I think the architects made a mistake in not attempting to
restore it to what it was once. In the eighteen fifties a great deal of
building was done in the style of that period—flamboyant and ornate,
which really does not merge in very well. Still, for all its faults, we
love it."

Granny M and I travelled down by train and were met at the station by Raymond.

He was delighted to see us and we were soon bowling along those leafy lanes of Buckinghamshire. We turned into a drive and after we had gone for about a quarter of a mile, we rounded a bend and there was the house.

I saw at once how it fitted Raymond's description. It was solid and in its way magnificent. It was grey stone and very ornate—with twirls and coils at every conceivable spot. There was a great porch over which creeper climbed and a large glass conservatory stretching along the side of the house.

"We always say that everything that could be put into it, was," said Raymond. "It's an example of Victorian architecture, so I've been told. You might think it is a little flamboyant, but let me tell you one thing—it is comfortable."

"It looks most interesting," I cried. "I am longing to explore."

"And those members of the family who haven't already met you are longing to make your acquaintance."

Granny M was absolutely purring with satisfaction. I could sense she was liking everything about Raymond more and more.

The family was waiting for us. His father and Basil whom we already knew welcomed us like old friends and we were introduced to his mother, his sister Grace, and his youngest brother James.

Raymond's mother was a little woman with bright laughing eyes.

She said: "We've heard so much about you, not only from Raymond, but from Father and Basil. We're just longing to meet you."

I looked round at the smiling faces and I felt very happy to be received so warmly into such a family.

"Show them their rooms first," suggested Raymond. "Then we'll have tea and talk."

"You come with me, Grace," said Mrs. Billington. And to us: "We hope you'll be comfortable."

"I am sure we shall," I replied with conviction.

"It is so kind of you to ask us," added Granny M.

"We have wanted to do so for so long. Raymond has told us about your meeting at the conference. Maps . . . That's all they think of. The conversation in this house! It's maps, maps and more maps, isn't it, Grace?"

Grace said it was. "There was Raymond and Father," she added. "And now James is getting just as bad."

"It's in the family," said Mrs. Billington. She paused on the stairs, I guessed because she thought they might be a little too steep for Granny M. "You're on the second floor," she went on. "That's where the guest rooms are. It is a bit of a climb, but there is a nice view when you get there. The house is rather large and not very well planned, they say. You can get lost easily. But after a while it all slips into place. Oh, here we are. This is yours, Mrs. Mallory, and I've put Annalice . . . I hope you don't mind, my dear, but we always call you Annalice among ourselves . . . and it slips out."

"I'm glad," I told her. "It makes me feel at home right away."

"That's what we want. You're here. Right next to each other."

She opened a door. There were french windows onto a stone balcony on which stood pots of flowering shrubs. The room was light and lofty compared with our Tudor ones. I gave a gasp of admiration which clearly pleased our hostess.

"It's lovely," I said.

"These are the rooms in the front. They are a little bigger than those at the back."

"We wanted to make a good impression," said Grace.

"Grace!" said her mother in mock reproof.

"I daresay they would like to wash and tidy up before tea, Mother," said Grace.

"I'd thought of that. The hot water is coming. Here it is. Come in, Jane."

The maid bobbed a curtsey and I smiled at her.

"Put it down there, Jane," said Mrs. Billington. "About fifteen minutes, eh? Is that enough?"

"Quite enough, isn't it, Granny," I said, and Granny M agreed.

In ten minutes I was ready to go down and I went into Granny M's room. She was ready too.

"Charming," she said. "A lovely family. I am so pleased. I wish . . . "

I knew what she was wishing and said: "Perhaps it won't be long before we hear from him. Raymond says that mail is often delayed in these far-off places."

We went down to tea. Hot muffins and several kinds of cakes were laid out on the table.

The drawing room was large and lofty and the fireplace immense and very decorative with angels carved on either side of it as though supporting it. A large marble clock stood on the mantelpiece and on the walls were pictures of men in Victorian dress.

"The ancestors," said Grace, following my gaze. "We can't sport many so we make the most of what we have got. I hear it is different with the Mallorys. Raymond has described your house in detail."

"Don't give me away," said Raymond.

"He thinks your house is wonderful," Grace told me.

"I hope I shall get an invitation to see it," said Basil.

"You have it now," put in Granny M.

"Oh, thank you, Mrs. Mallory."

We talked about the country and the difference between our respective villages; and when in due course the conversation turned to map making that was natural enough.

"It's strange," said Mrs. Billington, "how this sort of thing runs in families."

Granny M agreed. "It is the same with ours. My grandson, Philip, was brought up to it and it was clear, from an early age, that there was nothing else for him."

"I hear he is away on an expedition."

"Yes, to the Pacific."

"That is what I should like to do," said James.

"Hark at him!" cried Basil. "They all want to go out to adventure. They think it is some pleasure cruise. It's quite different, I do assure you."

"You have been?" I asked.

"Yes, I went when I was sixteen."

"I thought it would be good for him," said Mr. Billington. "James will go in due course. It is a good way of introducing them to the realities. They soon realize it is not all that much of a pleasure cruise, as Basil says. There are certain discomforts."

"I'll second that," said Basil.

"My grandson has been away since last October," Granny M told them.

"You can't do much in a year," said Mr. Billington.

"We haven't heard from him for some time," I put in rather shakily.

"One doesn't. The mail is so very difficult. I don't think we heard from you, Basil, all the time you were away."

"I wasn't going to put all that effort into writing letters which might never arrive."

"From which," said Grace, "you gather our Basil is not the most energetic of mortals."

I met Raymond's eyes and he smiled at me. It was a warm and happy smile.

Tea over, Raymond and I went for a walk in the gardens surrounding the house while Mrs. Billington and Grace took Granny M on a tour of the house.

Raymond told me that he was so pleased I had come. "It is hard to believe," he added, "that it is only three months since that memorable day at the lecture."

"It has all gone very quickly to me. Has it seemed so long to you?"

He took my arm. "Both long and short. Not long enough . . . and short while it is happening, and yet I feel I have known you for years . . . and that makes it seem long." He paused to look at me earnestly and then he went on: "These gardens are my mother's joy. She does quite a lot of work in them. She has her garden and her stillroom. She'll want to show them to you."

"She is very charming," I said.

"I have been hoping that you two would get along."

"I should imagine no one could fail to get along with her."

"Nor with you."

"Oh, that is a different proposition, I am sure."

He laughed and pressed my arm.

We talked about the flowers but I don't believe that either of us was really thinking of them.

We dined that night in the big dining room with its massive fireplace and ornate ceiling. The woodwork was intricately carved and it gave the impression that everything that could be put in that space had been included.

It was a jolly company and even the servants gave the impression of enjoying the fun as they tripped round with the various dishes, supervised by the butler. I could sense a tremendous interest in me on all sides.

I remembered what our servants had said about Raymond's being my "intended." I rather felt that was what was being thought here.

How the conversation came back to maps! It was rather as it was in our house. We had constantly talked of them, and on those occasions when Benjamin Darkin came to dinner they were the sole topic.

This was like our family—only larger. The Billingtons gave me the impression that they were doing exactly what they wanted in life, achieving their goals and not forgetting to be grateful to fate for giving them so much.

I could easily become a member of this family—a Billington, spending my life here in this heavy, stone Victorian house—what a purist would call a monstrosity of architecture. Of course it lacked the fascination of antiquity, the elegance of an earlier age; but I liked it, with all its flamboyant carvings, its twists and its twirls, its stone lions and dragons; and I knew that the Billingtons would not have changed it for the finest mansion in the country. And I could understand that.

Our house would seem a little sad after this.

But we should stay for at least a week. I was looking forward to that and I need not think of leaving yet—nor of making any hasty decisions.

Coffee was served in the drawing room when the men joined us after sitting over the port while Granny M, Mrs. Billington, Grace and I chatted together.

"It is so pleasant to meet all the family," said Granny M.

Grace surprised me when she said: "Oh . . . you haven't met everybody yet."

"But I thought you were all here?" said Granny M.

"Well, all except Grandmother," said Grace.

"Grandmother," explained Raymond, "is eighty years old. She very much wants to meet you but she was a little unwell yesterday and the doctor says she must rest today. If she is better tomorrow we will take you to meet her."

"I look forward to that."

"She lives in the past a great deal," said Mrs. Billington.

"She can tell some good stories about the family when she gets going," added Basil.

The evening passed in pleasant conversation, and Granny M and I had a chat in her room before retiring.

"What a delightful family!" she said. "It makes you wish there were more of us. It's made me think of your father over there in Holland . . . with those children. We ought all to be together."

"Why don't you ask him to come over?"

"I don't know. There's been a rift. He knows I don't like his living over there and getting out of the business as he did. That was a big blow. What I should have done without Benjamin, I can't imagine. I envy these people. There are three sons . . . and the girl knows something about the business too."

"There is a fascination about map making. Our lives seem to revolve round it."

"Yes . . . But for it we should not be here. You would never have met Raymond. I like him, Annalice. I'm a good judge of people and I like him very much. I like the whole family. I should like to see a lot of them, be close to them."

"I know what you're saying, of course," I said.

"You are fond of him. And there is no doubt of his feelings for you."

"I like him very much."

"Feelings grow stronger, you know. Sometimes they need time. Oh, there's a lot of nonsense talked about taking one look and falling head over heels in love. You don't want to take too much notice of that. Sometimes . . . when all the surroundings are suitable . . . that's the best way. That's how it was with your grandfather and me. Everything fitted . . . and I was fond of him. I was fascinated by his enthusiasm for business. Well, you two start with that. I used to wish you were a boy, so that you could go into it thoroughly, make a career of it. It's difficult with girls. They don't have much chance. The only thing is marriage. Sometimes when you're very young, you don't think about it very much . . . You don't think of the future."

I put my arms round her and kissed her. "It's all right, Granny. You don't have to sell him to me. I liked him from the first moment I saw him and I am liking him more and more every day."

She smiled and returned my kiss warmly, which was rare with her, for she was not demonstrative by nature.

"You children mean a lot to me," she said. "I often think about Philip and wonder. Suppose he never comes back."

"Don't say that, Granny. Don't even think of it."

"That's not very wise. It's better to face all possibilities, however unpleasant they may be. You can handle them better if they become realities. I was saying suppose, just suppose, Philip never came back . . . one of those boys in Holland would have to inherit. Who knows, one of them might want to take up cartography as a career."

"Oh Granny, I don't want to talk like this. Not tonight, not here. I want to forget how worried we are."

"You're right, my dear. We're worrying about something that has never happened. I just want you to realize how good it is to have a family around you. Happiness does not just come to you, as young and romantic girls might think. You have to make it."

"You think Raymond is going to ask me to marry him, don't you?"

She nodded. "One little sign from you and he would."

"Granny, I have known him only three months."

"You've seen a great deal of him during that time."

"Yes, I have."

"And doesn't he improve on acquaintance?"

"I think perhaps he does."

Granny M nodded, well pleased.

The next day I was introduced to the grandmother. Grace took me up to her.

"She's a little deaf," Grace warned me. "She won't admit it, and often pretends she can hear when she can't."

I nodded.

"But she knows you are here and very much wants to see you."

I stood before her chair and she peered at me. Her eyebrows were grey and rather bushy, but her eyes beneath them were dark and alert.

"Ah. So you are the young lady I have been hearing so much about."

"Have you? I hope it was pleasant."

She gave a little laugh. "All very pleasant. Are you enjoying your stay here, my dear?"

"Very much, thank you."

"I am sorry I was in my room when you arrived. It was that young doctor. They order you about sometimes when you are getting on in years."

"Oh no, Grandmother," protested Grace. "You know you won't allow that."

"No, I don't, do I? I've got a will of my own. I expect they've told you. It's not a bad thing to have."

"I believe it is a very valuable asset."

"And I believe, young lady, that you don't merely believe that, but have one."

"Perhaps. I hadn't thought much about it."

"That proves you've got one. Well, sit down. Tell me about that Tudor Manor House. Your family has lived there for years, I believe."

"Oh yes, we've been there for ages. The family have been in possession from the time it was built."

"Very interesting. I wish we could go back so far."

"Grandmother always wants to delve back into the past, don't you, Grandmother?" said Grace.

"I like to think of those who have gone before. I hope you are going to stay for a while, my dear, and not run away as soon as you have come."

"We shall stay here until the end of the week."

"You'll come and see me again, won't you?"

"I shall be delighted if I may do so."

"We thought we would just pop in and say how do you do, Grandmother. Annalice will come again tomorrow."

"Will you, my dear? I shall look forward to that."

Grace led the way out of the room.

"She's a little tired today. Then she gets rather absent-minded. So I thought we'd make it a brief visit. You can go and see her tomorrow afternoon if you feel like it."

I said I should be delighted to do so.

There were local people who came to dine with the family that night and we had another delightful evening. The next morning Raymond and I went out together. James said he would come with us and as we were about to leave for the stables, his mother called him back and said she wanted him to go into the town to do an errand for her. She herself was going to show Granny M how she made a special posset and they were going into the herb garden to collect the ingredients.

I guessed James had been called back so that Raymond and I could be alone together.

It was a lovely day for late August. The fields were bright with the waving corn. Raymond said: "There will be a bumper harvest this year." I thought the wind rustling through the ripening ears reminded me of the rise and fall of waves on a sandy shore and I was momentarily sad, thinking of Philip.

But it was not a morning for sadness. I had almost made up my mind that when Raymond asked me to marry him I would accept. If I were not madly in love, at least I was reasonably involved. I wanted this visit to go on and on; and when we returned home I should miss him. I tried to imagine how I should feel, if he announced tonight that he was going to marry someone else. There had been two pretty girls at dinner last night. What had I felt when I had seen him laughing and chatting with them? Was that a faint twinge of jealousy?

Granny M was right. My life with him would be very pleasant. I should be foolish if I did not take the opportunity which was being offered to me. Deep, abiding love could grow out of affection—and I certainly felt that for him.

I visualized how pleased everyone would be if we announced our engagement. It was what they wanted and I had a notion that they expected us to announce it . . . perhaps on our last night. Then I should leave the house engaged to be married.

We should plunge into preparations. There would be so much to do that there would not be time to wonder where Philip was. I should forget now and then to look for a letter—only to have that hope dashed when there was none.

Yes, it seemed very likely that Raymond was going to ask me and that I was going to say Yes.

But he did not ask me that morning. Perhaps I had managed to convey my uncertainty to him.

The grandmother was not very well the next day so I did not go to see her as planned.

"Leave it for a day or so," said Grace. "She soon recovers and when she does she is very bright indeed. When you saw her she was not herself. She is usually very alert."

I said I thought she had been then, but Grace said: "Oh, but you don't know Grandmother. She can be very talkative when she is in form."

The days passed. There were rides with Raymond, Basil, and Grace. I very much enjoyed the evenings when we sat down to dinner with the family and sometimes their neighbours. They were rather given to entertaining. The conversation was always lively and when there were guests it diverged from cartography to politics. I listened avidly and as I had always taken an interest in affairs liked to contribute my own views.

One of the delightful aspects of life with the Billingtons was that if a subject was brought up it was always debated with some heat and not a little passion; but there was never any unpleasantness. It was in the nature of a debate rather than an argument.

The Irish question was, of course, on everyone's lips and the fate of

Charles Stewart Parnell was discussed at some length. The divorce in which Captain O'Shea had cited him as co-respondent had ruined his career and the question was whether a man who was undoubtedly a leader should be condemned and dismissed from office on account of his private life.

I declared warmly that his work and his private life were two separate matters. I was assailed by Granny and Mrs. Billington who thought that Mr. Parnell's lapse from morality had rightly caused his fall from grace. Raymond was on my side. Grace hovered between the two; and Basil and James were inclined to agree with him while Mr. Billington swayed towards the point of view of Granny M and Mrs. Billington.

I had rarely enjoyed a meal so much and I thought: This is how it will be when I become one of them. It was a most exciting debate and we sat long over the dinner table. And when the servants came to light the gas I was sure I wanted to stay here and become one of them.

I was enamoured of the entire family and the big rather ugly Victorian house which was so comfortable . . . as they were.

If I did not agree to marry Raymond I was beginning to believe that I would regret it all my life.

The next morning we went riding again. It was one of those lovely days towards the end of the month when the first whiff of autumn is in the air and you know that September is just round the corner, bringing with it a chill in the mornings and mists in the valleys.

We stopped at an inn for a glass of cider and as we sat there Raymond smiled across the table at me and said: "I believe you are getting quite fond of my family."

"Who could help it," I replied.

"I agree that they are rather nice to know."

"And I could not agree more."

"The more you know of them the more you will love them. You will have to put up with Grace's absent-mindedness, with Basil's assumption that he knows everything and James's determination to prove that he does too; with my father's preoccupation with maps and my mother's with her garden; and mine . . . Well, I am not going to tell you my failings. I just hope you won't discover them for a very long time."

"I refuse to believe that you have any shortcomings. You're a perfect family and you all fit so well together. Granny and I are going to be sorry to leave you."

He put his hand across the table and took mine.

"You'll come back," he said. "You'll come back . . . and stay for a long time."

"If we are asked," I said, "I think we might."

I believe he would have asked me to marry him then but just at that moment some rather noisy guests came into the inn parlour. They talked in very loud voices about the weather and the hunt ball which was to take place sometime . . . and they seemed to want to include us in their conversation.

It was as near as he had got to asking me. And I was certain he would do so before we left.

And at that moment I was sure of my answer. I was going to tell him that I wanted to marry him.

I should have done so but for one thing.

I had paid two visits to the grandmother. She seemed to like me to come. She would sit opposite me and watch me as she talked, her lively eyes beneath their bushy brows never leaving my face.

She told me she was very proud of her family and what they had achieved.

"They are a name to be reckoned with among people who make maps."

"Yes indeed," I agreed. "It is the same with my family. That was how we first met Raymond. At the conference . . . But you know that."

She nodded. "It was always the same. It was always the maps. Well, there is money in it. This house was built on maps, you might say."

"Oh yes indeed. It is quite a profitable business. Of course a great deal of risk and hard work goes into exploration behind and then the actual production of maps."

She smiled. "Your family too. They tell me you come from a family that can be traced right back to the days of the great Elizabeth."

"That's so. My grandmother always says that our ancestors were among those who sailed with Drake."

"I'd like to trace ours back. But there we are. We come to a full stop . . . and not far back either. The Billingtons are newcomers into the family. This house was built by my father. I was an only child and a girl. That meant the end of the family name. I married Joseph Billington, and that was the start of the Billingtons."

"I see."

"I thought of making a family tree. I started it . . . in embroidery. But my eyes weren't good enough. It was a strain; and then I came to a full stop. I couldn't go back beyond my father—so it would have been a very short family tree. I expect you have one with branches all over the place."

"I've never thought of it. There might be one somewhere in the house. I'll find out when I get back."

"Very interesting . . . I always find that sort of thing. I wish I knew of my father's father. His mother married twice . . . the second time after he was born, so we don't know much about what happened before that. I'll show you my bit of embroidery. That's if you would like to see it."

"I should very much like to see it."

"See that box over there . . . on the shelf. It's in there with all the coloured silks. I wrote the names in pencil and then embroidered them in whatever colour I thought best. I started at the bottom. I had to make it a tree . . . Start at the roots, you see."

"What a good idea."

"Yes, but there's so little. It only spans a hundred years or so."

"Nevertheless I am longing to see it."

I put the box on the table and reverently she took out a large piece of linen. "There you see: Frederick Gilmour. That's my father. Now I don't know who his father is . . . except that he must have been a Mr. Gilmour. His mother was Lois. She was Mrs. Gilmour first. Then she married a George Mallory."

I felt a little faint. I cried out: "What . . . Freddy Gilmour—"

"Frederick Gilmour, dear. He was my father. It was his father I don't know much about. If only I could find out . . . I might go farther back."

"Lois Gilmour," I repeated. "And she married a second time . . . a George Mallory . . . "

Words from the journal seemed to swim before my eyes. It was almost as though I were reading it again. It must be. The names explained it. It could not be pure coincidence that Raymond's great-grandfather was the Freddy of the diary. I made rapid calculations. How old had he been when he came to the Manor. Ann Alice wrote that he was eight. The grandmother must have been born about 1810, which would make her eighty now. Freddy would have been about twenty-five then. It fitted.

"What's the matter, my dear. You've gone suddenly silent as though you've had a shock."

I said: "I've just made a discovery. One of my ancestors married a Lois Gilmour. He was George Mallory."

"You mean you're one of the Mallorys?"

"Yes. Didn't you know?"

"Why, bless you, I don't think I ever heard your surname. They've always referred to you as Annalice."

"I'm Annalice Mallory. Our families must be connected in a way. What—er—happened to this Lois Gilmour . . . or Mallory as she became?"

"We don't know. It's a full stop. My father Frederick was a successful producer of maps and prints. He did well. He acquired this house. I was born here. Then when I married Joseph Billington he came to live here and I inherited the house and the business and everything when my father died. It was Billingtons from then onwards."

"It is so extraordinary," I said. "I feel quite shocked."

"Well, I suppose if we could go back far enough we would find we were all connected with each other. Think what the population was in the old days and what it is now. We must all have relations we have never even heard of. You'd heard of my father then, in your family?"

"Y-yes. I knew that there had been this marriage and Frederick Gilmour lived in our Manor House for some time. I don't know what happened later, where he went or whether his mother stayed there. I know nothing . . . except that he was there."

"Well, it seems there was a family connection between them. Look. You see I have worked him in. There is Lois . . . but I don't know anything about Lois' first husband, my father's father. I didn't put the second marriage in because I didn't think it had any relevance. There I am branching out from Frederick and Ann Grey, my mother. Then I married Thomas Billington and that is the real start."

I looked at the fine stitches and all the time words from the journal seemed to echo in my ears and dance before my eyes. "You brought our little bastard in . . . That was a neat little job."

I could tell old Mrs. Billington who her grandfather was; but she was so absorbed in her family tree, telling me stories of this one and that, that she did not notice my inattention.

When I left her I went to my room.

I thought: There is a connection between our families then. Raymond's great-great-grandmother was the wife of a Mallory.

I did not want to speak of it. How could I without explaining that I had found Ann Alice's diary. I could not tell Raymond about that. I could not say to him: Your great-great-grandfather was a criminal, a murderer, and so was your great-great-grandmother. How could I? Such things are best forgotten. If we start probing into the lives of our ancestors who knows what we should uncover. Oh indeed yes. Some things are best kept secret.

I did not mention the matter to anyone.

We were to leave the day after tomorrow. Mrs. Billington said that we should just have a family party for the last night. She felt we should all prefer it that way. I knew they were all waiting for an announcement. There was an expectancy throughout the house.

Raymond and I went off for one of our rides. He was a little more silent than usual.

We stopped at an inn for the usual glass of cider and while we were drinking it in the inn parlour he asked me to marry him.

I looked at his kindly face across the table and it seemed to me that there was a shadow behind him. I had visualized Desmond Featherstone so vividly from Ann Alice's journal that I had a clear picture of him in my mind; and as I sat there it seemed to me that I saw the evil face of Desmond Featherstone hovering over Raymond.

I felt a revulsion. I had lived with Ann Alice through that night when I had read her journal. I had felt I was there with her. Even now, when it grew dark, I imagined the presence of Desmond Featherstone in our house—and the more shadowy one of Lois. And the blood of these two was in Raymond; he had developed from their seed.

It was foolish, of course. Are we responsible for our ancestors? How far can any of us look back? But I could not help it. It was there.

Perhaps if I had been truly in love with him I should not have felt this. I should have laughed at it and asked myself what the past had to do with the present. Why should one person be responsible for the faults of another? To visit the sins of the fathers on the children had always seemed to me a most unfair doctrine.

And yet . . . because of that I could not promise to marry him . . . not yet anyway. Perhaps later my common sense would prevail.

Now I hesitated.

"What is it?" he asked gently.

"I'm not sure," I replied. "Marriage is such a big undertaking.

It's for life. I feel that we have known each other such a short time."

"Don't you think we know all we need to know? We're happy together, aren't we? Our families like each other."

"That is true," I answered. "But there is more to it than that."

"You mean you don't love me."

"I am very fond of you. I enjoy being with you. I have found everything here so—comforting and stimulating, but I am still not sure."

"I've rushed you into this."

"Perhaps."

"You want more time to think."

"Yes, I believe that is what I want."

He smiled gently. "I understand. We shall meet often. I shall come to you and you will come here. It is just that you feel you need more time."

It was more than that. If he had asked me a few days before I believe I should have said Yes. It was that revelation in the grandmother's room which had shaken me. I wanted to explain to him. But I could not tell him Ann Alice's story—and even if I did, it would not seem logical to allow the past to impinge on the present to such an extent.

I could not understand myself. I believe that when I was reading that journal I identified myself with Ann Alice; and I could not get out of my mind that this young man—pleasant as he seemed—was the result of a union between two murderers.

I would get over it. I did not want to lose Raymond's friendship. I liked his company. With him I had spent the happiest days I had known since Philip had gone. I was foolish to turn away from what could be great happiness.

I should let common sense prevail in time, but just at present I could not say a word.

There was disappointment in the house. I sensed it. And for that reason I was rather glad that we were leaving on the following day.

Granny M came into my room after we had retired that night.

I was brushing my hair when she came and going over the events of the day in my mind. I could hear the chatter at dinner, see the smiles, feel the expectancy.

Dinner over and there was no announcement—only talk of our departure next day. It was an anticlimax.

Granny M seated herself in a chair and characteristically came to the point.

"I thought Raymond was going to ask you to marry him."

"He did."

"And you refused!"

"Well, not exactly. I couldn't say Yes. I wonder if I ever shall."

"My dear girl, you must be crazy."

I shook my head. "I have really . . . asked for time."

"Time! You're not a child any more."

"Dear Granny, I am well aware of encroaching age."

"Don't talk nonsense. Tell me what happened."

"He asked me and I just said I couldn't. Granny, I want to tell you something. It's the journal."

"The journal! You mean Ann Alice's?"

"Yes. I have made a most extraordinary discovery. The grandmother was telling me about the family. She was a Miss Gilmour, and she married a Billington. That was when the family name changed."

"A Miss Gilmour!"

"You remember Lois Gilmour in the journal. She was Raymond's grandmother's grandmother. Her *father* was Freddy . . . the boy Lois Gilmour brought into the Manor."

"I can't believe it."

"It seemed an extraordinary coincidence at first. But when you think of it, you realize how easily it could have happened. Freddy was always interested in Mallory maps, wasn't he? Ann Alice mentioned it. He must have gone into the profession when he grew up. I daresay he was brought up away from the Mallorys. I have come to the conclusion that that must have been how it happened. Charles Mallory came back. He wasn't drowned after all. He must have settled in the Manor and taken over. What happened to Lois? We don't know. Perhaps she left when Charles came home. I wonder whether Freddy remained. In any case he became a cartographer, which was natural as he had seen so much of it during his childhood."

"And we have met . . . like this!"

"Well, that again is understandable. When you consider, you can see it has come about quite naturally. We are all in the same business. People come from all over the country to attend conferences. I daresay most of the leading cartographers in the country and elsewhere are present. It is not so surprising that we met. When you look at it like that it is not so much of a coincidence."

"No," said Granny slowly. "But all that happened long ago."

"I know, but . . . I have a strange feeling about Ann Alice. I have . . . ever since I discovered her grave. You see, I was the one destined to find it. I was the one to see the journal first. I sometimes feel that I am part of her, that she and I are one."

"I never heard such nonsense," said Granny M. "But I see what you mean about the gathering of map makers and how it is perfectly natural that as we attend these meetings we encounter people of our profession. Well, so you think Raymond has descended from that Lois Gilmour . . . "

"There isn't a doubt of it. It's all there. The family, the timing, and the fact that Lois Gilmour became Mrs. Mallory."

"What did you tell the grandmother?"

"That we were the Mallorys and Lois Gilmour's second marriage was to an ancestor of ours. I did not say that there was no first husband and that Freddy's father was a murderer."

"All this doesn't make Raymond our flesh and blood."

"Of course not. But the connection is there and Desmond Featherstone . . . that monster . . . was his ancestor."

"Did you mention what was in the journal?"

"No, indeed I did not."

"Don't. I daresay if we looked back into our histories we'd find rogues and scoundrels. And it is better not to know about them. That Featherstone was a most unpleasant villain—unless Ann Alice was romancing. How do we know that she didn't invent the whole thing?"

"But she died . . . that night. The room was walled up. I know she was telling the truth. She was writing down what she saw . . . and heard. That comes through very clearly. It is nonsense to suggest she was making it up."

"All right. It wouldn't be very pleasant to be confronted by the fact that your great-great-grandparents were murderers. I should say nothing to anyone about what you have read in the journal. It has nothing whatsoever to do with the present time."

"I know that's so, but I can't help thinking of that man Desmond Featherstone. When I look at Raymond, I see him. That is why I could not say I would marry him. I can't forget that those two were Raymond's great-great-grandparents."

Granny shook her head. "It's the shock," she said. "That's what it is. It was all so unexpected . . . discovering that. You'll get over it. It's disappointing to us all, but it will do no harm to wait awhile. You'll see what's right in time." She kissed me. "I'm glad you told me. Get a good night's sleep. We'll be off early in the morning."

But I could not sleep. I was haunted by strange, wild dreams. I was in that room . . . the room which had been shut for nearly a hundred years. My door was locked. There was an enormous key in the door. I heard footsteps on the stairs. Someone was trying the door. I kept my eyes on the key. The door was fast shut. But there was a loud noise and the door burst open. A man was coming in. It was Raymond. I cried out in joy and held out my arms to him, but as he came towards me, his face changed. It was the face of Desmond Featherstone. I screamed as he came close.

And my scream awakened me.

I stared into the darkness.

If I married him I should have dreams like that. I should be looking for that evil man in my husband.

I was afraid to sleep in case the dream came back. However, I dozed and when I awoke it was to find the maid in my room with hot water.

It was time to get up.

How different everything was by daylight! I remembered where I was and that this happy visit had come to an end. The thought saddened me. It ought to have been so different.

I was going to miss Raymond very much.

I had been foolish, I thought. In time I would see everything differently. Then all would be well, and I should banish my foolish imaginings forever.

AMSTERDAM

Arriving home was rather depressing. There was no news from Philip. The house seemed very quiet. Granny M remarked on it. "It's after that house full of family," she said. "They are a very happy group. There is something about a big family. I wish we could hear from Philip and I wish your father would come home."

I went to my room and unpacked my things and as I hung them up I thought of the occasions when I had worn them, sitting down to dinner, joining in the talk at the table.

Yes, our house did seem quiet, I wished I were back there. I had never before noticed how quiet we were. When Philip had been with us it had been more lively. Now we were back to the longing for him, very conscious of the void his absence made in our lives.

We were back with memories of him, with watching every day for the news which did not come.

I wished we were still with the Billingtons. I had been foolish. I should have agreed to marry Raymond. I must love him for I missed him so much. When I was in that house I had ceased to think continually of Philip and had been able to forget him for certain periods of time. Now all the longing to see him, the anxiety, had returned.

If I had said Yes to Raymond, I should now be thinking of my coming marriage. Granny and I would have been making excited plans.

I wished it were so. I was a fool.

I went up to Ann Alice's room and sat there.

"If I had never found your journal everything would have been different," I said to Ann Alice, as though she were there. I often felt as though she were. "Philip would not have become obsessed with the need to find the island. He would still be with us, I should be getting ready for my marriage to Raymond. You have changed everything for me, Ann Alice."

How silent it was. Nothing . . . but the gentle moaning of the wind rustling the leaves in the yew that was just outside the newly opened window. I could imagine I heard voices in the wind. But then I was always imaginative in this room.

Granny was right. The past was done with. It was folly to let it impinge on the present. It had been such a shock to discover that Raymond's ancestors had been involved with mine. Two of his had murdered Ann Alice, and Freddy . . . little Freddy of whom there was not much written but who seemed to have been a rather charming boy . . . was his great-grandfather. Raymond must have been rather like Freddy when he was a boy. Yet Freddy had been the child of murderers.

Again and again I wished I had never discovered the journal. I wished that I had never discovered the connection between our two families. There must be many things in life which it is better not to know.

I was sitting in that room close to the window thinking of Ann Alice on that night when suddenly I heard the sound of footsteps on the stairs. Slowly, laboriously, they were coming along the corridor.

In that moment I *was* Ann Alice. I sat there staring at the door. I saw the handle slowly turn. I was reliving it all again. Between me and that girl there was certainly some mystic bond.

Slowly the door opened. I was expecting him . . . that evil man. I had conjured up a picture of what he looked like—rather flashily handsome with thick sensual lips and dark fierce eyes, greedy eyes, who stretched out to take what he wanted and did not care whether he crushed anyone who stood in his way.

I gave a little gasp as Granny M stepped into the room.

"Up here again!" she said. "Why, you look quite white and scared out of your wits. You're as bad as the servants with their ghosts . . . only they do have the sense to keep away from the place."

She came in and sat on the bed and the room immediately assumed an air of normality.

"What are you doing up here? You're always up here. For two pins I'd have it closed up again."

"I have a sort of compulsion to come," I told her. "I heard your steps on the stairs and I thought for a moment . . . "

"You thought I was someone returned from the dead! Really, child, you've got to stop all this. It's a parcel of nonsense. You're working up something which is just a fantasy. If it hadn't been for that storm . . . "

"I often say that. If it hadn't been for the storm . . . "

"Well, it's no use saying that now. It happened and there is an end to it. Why do you come here? You're becoming obsessed by what you read in that journal."

"Well, you see Granny, first I found her grave . . . and then her journal, and now there is this discovery about Freddy's being Raymond's great-grandfather. It's like a pattern."

"It's all very logical, my dear. We agreed on that. Little Freddy went in for map making . . . naturally he would, having learned something about it in his childhood and become fascinated by it as so many do. What his parents got up to is no concern of ours. It's all long ago. People did all sorts of things then which we wouldn't do now. We met Raymond because he is in the business, and as there are not so many of us around, that's natural enough. There is nothing mystical about it at all. Get that out of your head. You've got a lot of imagination and sometimes that can be a bad thing. Stop thinking about it. It's over and done with. And when I think that you refused Raymond because of some fanciful ideas . . . it just makes me wonder how I brought you up. It does really. There's Philip goes off on some wild-goose chase . . . "

She was silent. We looked at each other. Then I went to her and for a moment we clung together.

She extricated herself almost immediately. She never believed in giving way to emotion.

"We have had a very pleasant visit," she said, "and now we've come home and we miss it all. I shall ask Raymond to come for the weekend. No use asking the brother and father. I daresay they will be expected to go down to Buckinghamshire. But I am sure everyone will understand if I ask Raymond. You'd like that, wouldn't you?"

I agreed that I would.

"You should see him more often. You should get away from all those morbid imaginings. Perhaps then you will come to your senses."

"I hope so, Granny."

"My dear child, so do I."

Raymond was at our house a good deal. Spending weekends with us had become quite a habit. He said his family would very much like it if we went to them for another visit.

Although I wanted to, I was still unsure, and I did not want to face that expectancy again until I could give a definite answer. It seemed unfair to Raymond, who was kind and understanding. Sometimes I almost said: "I'll marry you as soon as you want me to."

I could talk to him on any subject . . . except one, and that was my knowledge of the wickedness of his ancestors. That I could not speak of and until I did there must be a barrier between us. There were times when I thought of it in the clear light of day that it seemed quite nonsensical. I just had this horrible fear that I should look for traits of Desmond Featherstone in him . . . and find them. I had this uncanny feeling that Ann Alice was warning me.

It was nonsense, of course. I had just allowed myself to become obsessed by the discovery of the grave and the closed room—and the journal which had explained so much.

When I rode with Raymond, when he dined with Granny and me and some of our friends, everything seemed different. I was pleased when he excelled in discussion, when everyone said what a charming person he was, and when Benjamin Darkin and he talked together and the old man showed him such respect. Surely that was loving.

I think Granny was a little exasperated with me. A wedding prospect would have taken her mind off Philip. Marriage and, in time, babies. That was what she would have liked.

Sometimes I thought I could, and then would come those dreams . . . those rather fearful dreams, particularly that one which recurred, the one when I was in the room, heard the footsteps on the stairs, and the coming of Raymond who turned into Desmond Featherstone.

I seemed to hear a voice within me saying: "Not yet. Not yet." And in my more fanciful moments I imagined that it was Ann Alice who spoke to me.

October had come. It was a year since Philip had gone. Both Granny M and I were dreading the anniversary of his departure. She made sure that Raymond was with us on that day. I must say that that helped considerably.

We got through it and then it was November . . . dark gloomy days . . . the sort of days when memories came back.

We were invited to spend Christmas with the Billingtons and this we did.

We could not have had a more delightful Christmas although it was inevitable that we should think of past Christmases when Philip was with us. We neither of us mentioned him on Christmas Day. It was a sort of unspoken pact between us. As was to be expected, all the old customs were carried out. Great fires roared in the grates. There were quantities of seasonal food; and much merriment in which the whole neighbourhood seemed to join.

The younger members of the family all went riding on Boxing morning and Grace, Basil, and James followed their usual custom of losing themselves, so that Raymond and I were alone together.

I was as happy as I could be, considering my growing anxiety about Philip. Raymond understood and he talked of Philip. He did not try to soothe me. I believe he was beginning to think that some misadventure had befallen him and he wanted me to be prepared for bad news.

It was a bright day, with frost in the air—a sparkling sort of day which sets one's skin glowing. The horses were frisky and we let them gallop across a meadow, pulling up sharp as we came to the hedge.

Raymond said: "Ready for the glass of cider?"

I replied that I was. There would be the intimacy of the parlour with probably no one else there on Boxing Day. Perhaps he would ask me again. I hoped not, for although I was wavering, I was still unsure.

There was a big fire in the inn parlour and a Christmas tree set up in the window and sprigs of holly behind the pictures on the walls.

"They are determined we shan't forget it's Christmastime," said Raymond.

He ordered the cider. There was no one else in the parlour.

The host brought it. He said: "Not many people about this morning. It's the holiday. Most of them are at their own firesides."

Raymond lifted his glass and said: "To us, and in particular to you, Annalice. I hope you'll have some good news soon."

I felt sad because I knew he meant Philip.

"It is getting so long."

He nodded.

"It was a year last October. And only one letter since then. There must be something wrong. Philip would write because he would know how anxious we are."

Raymond was silent, staring into his glass.

"I wish I could go out there," I said. "To the South Pacific. I wish I could discover for myself . . ."

"Go out there!" He put down his glass. "You mean you . . . go out there alone!"

"Why not? I do hate these stupid conventions which seem to imply that because one is female one is half-witted."

"I know what you mean, but it could be a hazardous journey."

"Others have gone. We have had our intrepid lady explorers. Some of them have gone into the most dangerous country."

"Do you really mean you would go?"

"It is an idea which has been in my mind for some time."

"Is that why you won't marry me?"

"I am not sure. It isn't that I don't love you. I do. But I'm not sure about being in love, which is a different thing I suppose. I think loving is probably better than being in love."

"It can be more permanent. Being in love is often transient, I believe. People fall in love easily, so why shouldn't they fall out with equal ease?"

"Do you love me or are you in love with me?"

"Both."

"Raymond, you are so good, and I am so foolish."

"No. You want to be sure. I understand."

"You are the most understanding person I have ever met. You understand about Philip, don't you?"

"Yes, I believe I do."

"I can't settle. I want to know. If something terrible has happened to him I want to find out about it. Then I might accept the situation and perhaps in time put it behind me. What I cannot endure is this uncertainty."

"That is very understandable."

"And you don't think I am being foolish in hating this inactivity so much that I want to go out and do something about it?"

"I think it is perfectly natural. I should feel the same."

"Oh, I do love you. You are so sensible."

"Thank you."

"I think I shall marry you . . . in time. That is if you still want me to when I am ready."

"I shall be waiting."

I was so moved, I turned away.

He leaned towards me. "I think this stands between us," he said.

"This fear of what has happened to your brother. If he came home you would be at peace, and if you knew the worst you would come to me for comfort."

"It may be that is so. I think of him almost all the time. Sometimes I think I shall never know. We have been so long without word. And I'll never be able to go and search for him. There is my grandmother. I couldn't leave her, could I? You see, it would mean both of us gone."

"It is a pity there were only two of you. If there had been a big family . . . "

"I have two brothers and one sister. Half brothers and sister, of course. They are in Holland."

"Yes, I remember. Your father married again."

"Granny M is so angry because he gave up maps and went into the export business." I couldn't help smiling. "She gets really angry, but I think what hurts her is that she has grandchildren in Holland whom she doesn't know."

"When you marry me you will have to leave her."

"Yes, but that is different. She is hoping I will marry you. She thinks that would be very cosy. We wouldn't be far off and she hopes for great-grandchildren. She seems rather stern but she does love children. She likes the thought of carrying on the family and all that."

"It's a great pity that you can't at least meet the rest of the family."

"They are in Amsterdam. My father writes now and then and that is all. He is completely absorbed in his new family as I suppose he would be. They are there and we are far away, and as I cost my mother her life when I was born he might remember me with pain. I know exactly how he feels."

"It is a mistake for families to be apart unless of course they can't get on together. But this seems to be a sort of drifting."

"That describes it exactly. There is no feud . . . nothing like that, just a drifting."

"Now if these grandchildren were with your grandmother, your little jaunt might not be impossible."

"There would be great opposition but I could overcome that, if I thought there was someone there to comfort her."

"I am sure you would."

"Oh, I do wish Philip would come home."

"Let's drink to that," he said.

His eyes met mine over the glass, and I thought: Yes, I love him.

Where else would I find someone who was so kind, so tender, so loving, so understanding.

What a fool I am, I thought.

And yet the cruel memories came flooding back. It was in a place rather like this that Ann Alice had first seen Desmond Featherstone. He had been seated at such a table. I remembered the description vividly.

Perhaps I would eventually subdue these memories.

I believed I would . . . in time.

We were in February when Raymond made the announcement.

He was spending the weekend with us—a habit now for he always came except when he was at home in Buckinghamshire. He had just arrived and we were having tea in Granny M's small sitting room when he said: "I shall be going abroad in March. My father is going with me. We shall be on the Continent . . . France, Germany and Holland. It's a business trip which we make periodically."

"We shall miss you," said Granny M.

"How long will you be away?" I asked.

"About a month, I should think."

A month without him! I thought. Each day getting up, looking for news of Philip which did not come, wondering, asking ourselves again and again why we had not heard.

We were beginning to accept the fact that something must have happened to him, but that did not make it any easier. If only we could know, I used to think. Then we might begin to grow away from it.

Now the prospect of a month without Raymond's company was rather depressing.

"Grace wants to come with us," went on Raymond.

"Grace!" cried Granny M.

"We . . . the family . . . believe it is good for a girl as well as boys to see something of the world. I think she is getting round my father. He is rather susceptible to Grace's wiles. He thinks though that she might have to be left alone a good deal . . . while we are engaged on business, and she would get rather bored. Now . . . if she had someone with her . . . We thought if she had a companion . . . and we were wondering if Annalice would care to come with us."

I stared at him. I felt suddenly happy. To get away . . . to forget for a while . . . to travel. I had always wanted to see something of the world, to visit those countries which had hitherto been only a blob of pale green or brown on our maps . . .

Then I thought of Granny M. I looked at her. Her face expressed nothing.

"It would be pleasant for Grace . . . and for my father and me, of course. I think that if you agreed to go that would decide Grace's fate. She is very eager to hear your answer." He turned to Granny M. "You would miss Annalice very much, I know. My mother said, why don't you go and stay with them. She says it would be lovely for her to have you there. You know how she is with her garden and her recipes. She wants someone to talk to about them. She says none of us is interested."

There was silence. I dared not look at Granny M. I knew I was betraying my feelings.

"I doubt I could go away for a whole month," she said. "There is the business."

"We are leaving ours in the hands of managers," said Raymond. "Your Benjamin Darkin seems an absolute gem. I wish he were working for us. Sometimes I feel inclined to steal him."

Granny M said slowly: "I think it would be good for Annalice."

I went over to her and kissed her. I couldn't help it. "You are so good," I said. "So very good . . . "

"Nonsense," she said. "Gadding about on the Continent. I don't know whether it's right for a young girl."

"I should be in good hands," I said.

Granny M said: "Go and sit down, Annalice. What will Raymond think of us?"

I could see that her eyes were too bright. She was afraid she would shed a tear. I wanted to say: "Shed them, Granny. I love you for shedding them."

There was something very calm about Raymond. He met every situation with a complete lack of surprise.

"My father has travelled extensively," he said, as though our emotional scene had not taken place. "He's always felt that it is a necessary part of business. Is it settled then? May I relieve Grace's anxiety? May I tell her that she is to have Annalice's company on the trip?"

"I suppose so," said Granny M. "But we've not had much time to think about it. What do you feel, Annalice?"

"If you could do without me for a month . . . "

"What do you mean—do without you? I can manage on my own, I assure you."

"I know that, Granny. But I should worry about you."

"Why? I shall go to Buckinghamshire as I have been so kindly asked. I am sure I shall be very happy there . . . "

Raymond said: "I am going home tomorrow to tell them the good news. You will enjoy it so much, Annalice. Why don't you both come down next weekend and we will make plans."

So we decided to do that.

I was so excited at the prospect that my fears for Philip faded into the background. They would not disappear completely but the best way of preventing perpetual preoccupation with them was for something like this to happen.

We were leaving in the middle of March and would be back in April. There were conferences between the two families and I came to the conclusion that Granny M was as excited about the coming trip as I was. She knew that it was the best way of taking us out of our despondency and with her inherent common sense she knew we were doing no good at all by giving way to that.

I was determined that something was going to be done about Philip. More and more I thought of going out to look for him. I would start in Sydney. Someone must know something. But how could I ever get there? A woman alone! Even this trip to the Continent had to be in the company of the Billingtons.

Raymond and I went riding one morning. I felt so much better since we had been making plans for the trip and that must be obvious.

I could talk to Raymond freely about what was on my mind and I said: "I wonder if I shall ever be able to go out and look for Philip."

"You don't think he's gone native, do you? Perhaps he has married out there and decided he can't come home."

"You never knew Philip. He would realize how worried we would be. Whatever he had done he would tell us . . . me at any rate."

"I believe you are still dreaming of going out to look for him."

"He said in his letter that there were some islands off the coast of Australia and that there was a ship that went out to them every Wednesday. He must have taken that ship. I would like to go to Australia, get on that ship and go to the islands. I have a feeling that I might discover something there."

Raymond was looking at me intently.

I said: "I believe you think I ought to go. You don't regard this as an impossible dream."

"No, I don't regard it as impossible, and I know you will never be at peace until you have discovered where your brother is and why there has been this long silence. I want you to be at peace. I don't think you will be happy until you know. I want you to be happy. I want you to marry me."

"Oh, Raymond, I can't tell you how happy you make me. Everything has been different since we met. And now this trip. I do believe you thought of the idea of taking Grace so that you could ask me."

He smiled. "You need to get away. You need to stop brooding. You can do no good by that."

"I know. But how can I stop it?"

"By breaking away from routine . . . by making a new life. Whatever has happened to your brother, you cannot change it by fretting."

"That's why I can't sit at home thinking about it. You see we were such friends, closer than most brothers and sisters. It was probably due to the fact that our mother died. I never knew her, and he did. He remembered. Children of five do. And then there was the War of the Grannies. They both wanted us you see, my father's mother and my mother's mother. For some time Philip did not know what was to become of us. That has an effect. He thought he might be parted from me, and although I was too young to know of this, when he told me I felt all the horrors of it. There was a special bond between us. I know as sure as anything that if he were alive he would find some means of telling *me*. Yes, I must find him. I cannot settle to anything until I do."

"You'll have to go out there, I can see that."

"How?"

"As I said nothing is impossible."

"Granny . . ."

"Is getting old. She is lonely. She needs her grandchildren round her. But you are not the only one."

"No. There is Philip."

"I wasn't thinking of Philip."

"What do you mean?"

"Our first call will be Holland. We shall visit Amsterdam. I am going to suggest that you write to your father and tell him of your pending visit. Tell him you will come to stay. Get to know your half brothers and sister. Perhaps you could bring them back to England. Perhaps one of the grandchildren could become the compensation your grandmother needs. Perhaps you could have your freedom that way. After all if Philip does not return, one of those boys will inherit the Manor and the business, I presume. He should know something about them."

I stared at him. "Raymond, you're devious," I said. "I would never have believed you could make such machiavellian plans."

"People do all sorts of things when they are in love," he replied.

I wrote to my father and his reply was immediate. He was delighted. His wife, Margareta, his sons Jan and Charles and his little Wilhelmina were all overjoyed at the prospect of seeing me.

I showed the letter to Granny M.

"H'm," she said, sniffing: but I believe she was pleased.

Raymond was delighted.

He said: "It might be desirable for you to spend a month with them."

"A month! But I am so looking forward to France and Germany . . . "

"I thought you would want to look farther ahead than that."

I smiled at him and thought: I love you, Raymond Billington. Why do I hesitate? Perhaps when we are away . . .

But I went up to the room and sat there in solitude. It seemed very quiet, only the sound of the wind in the yew outside the window.

I looked at the bed, the chest of drawers in which I had found the journal . . . expecting, as I always did in this room, to receive some sign, perhaps to hear Ann Alice's voice coming to me over the years.

Nothing. I even found my thoughts straying to what I must pack; and I realized then that I had not had my nightmare since Raymond had suggested I should accompany him and his family on their trip to the Continent.

I was charmed by Amsterdam from the moment I saw it. I could not believe that there was another city like it in the world. I was sure of that even at this stage when I had seen few cities, and now when I have travelled farther afield, I still believe it.

There it stands on the dam or dike of the Amstel, on the arm of the

Zuider Zee—divided by the river and the canals into nearly a hundred small islands connected by three hundred bridges.

My father's house was large and imposing and situated in Prinszen Gracht where, with Kaizers and Heeren Grachts, most of the big houses were. There was about it an atmosphere which was decidedly Dutch; the steps from the front door to the street went up at right angles with a railing of highly polished brass; the gables at each end of the house were highly ornamental, and inside the house there was an air of spaciousness, but what struck me most was the polished brightness of everything. Cleanliness was the most striking feature of the place. The passages were marble and the walls tiled in delicate blues and whites. I presumed these were used so that they could be easily cleaned; the doors were elaborately carved; the windows were large and at these, mirrors had been placed so that what was going on in the streets could be easily observed. The furniture was far plainer than ours at home.

It might appear that there would be a feeling of coldness or austerity in such a house. This was not so; and the warmth of my welcome was instant.

My father embraced me and within seconds I knew that I had been right to come here. I liked my stepmother immediately. She was plump with a round face and a dazzlingly clear skin and light blue bright eyes. She was a little nervous at first, which I suppose was natural. I took her hands and kissed her. She flushed a little and looked so pleased that I knew I was going to like her. For a few seconds there flashed into my mind a scene from Ann Alice's journal when she had known Lois Gilmour was to be her stepmother. How strange that we both had stepmothers! But the resemblance between Margareta and Lois Gilmour ended there. I must not think continually of what happened to Ann Alice and compare my own life with hers.

I was introduced to my half brothers and sister.

What excitement to be presented with a ready-made family. My first thought was: How foolish we were not to have met years ago! And then how grateful I was to Raymond for having suggested that we should meet.

There was Jan aged fifteen, Charles aged twelve and Wilhelmina nine.

The children clustered round me and Jan said he thought it was the most wonderful thing imaginable to have a big sister whom he had never seen before. They spoke fluent English, although a certain amount of

Dutch was used in the household, so that all the children were bilingual and there was no language problem.

I liked them all very much and was thrilled to discover how pleased they were to see me. I was particularly taken by the eldest, Jan, because he reminded me of Philip. He might have been Philip at fifteen and I felt very emotional when he talked to me and called me Sister.

My father understood and I realized how deeply he regretted that Philip and I had spent our childhoods away from him.

They were very hospitable to the Billingtons and my father expressed his gratitude to them for including me in the trip to the Continent. I was to stay in the house in Prinszen Gracht, and Grace was invited to stay with me. The men would be in a nearby hotel during their stay in Amsterdam.

It was amazing how quickly we all came to know each other. Jan became my shadow. He wanted to show me everything. He came with us on our tours round the city and he thoroughly enjoyed being our guide. Proudly he showed us the landmarks of the city, taking us to the high bridge where the River Amstel enters the city, driving us through the grachts and showing us the fine houses, and taking us round the ramparts where we could see the windmills which were now used for grinding corn.

The Billingtons had arranged to stay only a week in Holland and although I longed to see other countries, I should be loth to leave my newly found family. I had several talks with Raymond about it.

He said: "You are so much at home with them. You are forging a link. If you go away now you will drift along more or less as before. You may be in communication. That much will have changed, but it is not what we had in mind."

"You think I should stay with them the whole month?"

He nodded, rather gloomily. "It seems to me that is the answer. You must make them feel that you want to be with them more than anything else. They must feel that they are indeed your family. You and Jan get on well together. There seems a very special feeling between you two. I think it would be a good idea . . . if this is possible . . . for you to take him back to England with you."

"Do you think they would let him go?"

"I don't know, but I don't see why not. Suppose he wants to. Why should he not visit his grandmother?" He gripped my hands. "Plans are beginning to mature. You want to set out on an adventure which means so much to you. When you have found the answer you seek, you and I will be married. But I know you well enough to understand that you will never settle to happiness until you have discovered what happened to your brother. I could say, Marry me and I will take you out there. That would be like a bribe, and much as I am tempted to, I don't want it that way. Moreover it would be very difficult for me to leave my father and the business for so long. It would be a great burden for them. But I suppose it could be done . . . as most things can if one makes up one's mind to it. No, it is because I want you to marry me for the right reason . . . Am I expressing myself badly?"

"No," I said. "It is very clear. You are a very rare person, Raymond."

"Does that mean you like me a little?"

"Not a little. A lot. Sometimes I think I am foolish not to jump at the chance of marrying you. Thank you . . . thank you for your help. You think I might be able to persuade them to let Jan come back with me to England. You think Granny would love him. I am sure you are right about that. And in your heart you think that Philip is never coming back and that Jan is going to take his place not only with my grandmother and me, but as heir to the house and everything."

"I'm afraid I am trying to work it out too neatly and life doesn't often oblige us so precisely, but yes . . . I was thinking along those lines, and even if you had to abandon your dream—which, forgive me, is a little wild—of going out to search for your brother, I am sure that Jan could help you a great deal, not to forget . . . but to mourn your brother less."

I said: "Grace would not want to stay in Amsterdam."

"I don't know how she would feel."

"I shall envy you travelling all over Europe."

"You can't decide anything yet. Wait a few days and see how everything turns out."

I did have a talk with my father. I somehow felt he had been waiting for this.

It was after dinner one night. The children had gone to bed; Margareta was busy somewhere and I found myself alone with him.

He spoke very earnestly and was eager to explain his neglect of the past years.

"I always wanted to see you and Philip. I thought about you a great deal. But your grandmother is a somewhat formidable lady. She was furious when she knew I was going to marry again and live in Holland."

I smiled. "That was largely because you deserted maps for export."

"Margareta wanted to live in her native land with her own family. I would have had you children here. But your grandmother was fiercely against that. She said on no account were you coming here. I had to let it go. I felt I had upset her enough without demanding that she give you up."

"You're happy, Father?"

"As near as one can be. I missed you and Philip . . . and now there is this trouble about him. Why did he have to go off to these far-off places? They are full of danger."

"He had to go. The urge was so strong. He couldn't resist it. He wasn't like you, Father. He loved the business of map making. It was romantic and exciting to him. I am a little like that, too."

"It's in the blood, I think. It passes over some of us. I never had it, but would you believe it, Jan has. He is always talking about maps and plying me with questions."

My heart began to beat fast. Jan interested. This seemed too good to be true.

"I like Jan very much, Father."

"Yes, I can see there is something special between you two. I'm glad. That pleases me a great deal."

"Father, would you like me to stay the whole month here with you and the family?"

"My dear Annalice, nothing would please me more. But would that not be a sacrifice for you? I gathered there was so much you were looking forward to seeing."

"It's true. But how could anything compare with discovering one's own family?"

"You are welcome, my dear. We should love to have you."

"I feel I want to get to know Jan . . . absolutely. I am sure Granny would love him. And he is so interested in maps you tell me. Are you going to let him take it up as a profession?"

"If he persists in his enthusiasm, of course."

"You still have Charles to follow you in the export business."

"I never believe in forcing people. It is their own choice. That is something your grandmother and I did not agree about."

"I know. She mourns Philip terribly."

"But there is hope . . . ."

"It seems to grow less as time passes. I was wondering . . . would you allow Jan to come and visit us?"

"Do you think your grandmother would want that? She was very much against the marriage."

"I know she wants it very much indeed. It might be difficult to get her to say so, but I am sure she does. *I* want it very much."

"Well, we could ask Jan."

"So I have your permission to do so?"

"Shouldn't you ask your grandmother first?"

I shook my head. "I know her well. If I returned home with Jan she would be delighted. She would love him on the spot. He is so like Philip . . . his enthusiasms . . . his ardour about map making. It would help her so much. It would help us both so much. Jan too . . . Perhaps he could stay with us for a while and go to the shop and meet old Benjamin Darkin. Philip was constantly at the shop, so was I. It seems that Jan is one of us."

"Sound him out . . . gradually. Make sure it is what he really wants."

I did not think there was any doubt that Jan would seize the opportunity with alacrity, but I would, as my father said, approach it gradually.

When I told Raymond he was delighted.

"Fate is on our side," he said. "I have another idea. Why don't we ask Jan to be a member of our party. I am sure he would like to see something of the world. Then . . . we should not have to lose your company."

"Raymond," I cried, "you have the most wonderful ideas!"

Raymond smiled modestly. "Am I moving too fast?"

"Certainly not. It is always an advantage to move fast."

"Almost always perhaps," he said with a smile.

When I asked my father about Jan's joining us, he was hesitant. He said he would talk to Margareta.

I wondered whether she would want to let her son go because I was sure she was wise enough to see the way events were moving. I suppose she knew that Jan would want to come to England. I was a little unsure of Margareta. My father I understood. He was a man devoted to his children but his greater affection was for his wife. That was how he had been with my mother and was the reason why he was able to leave his children with our grandmother. Although he loved his children and wanted the best for them, it was Margareta who had his great love. Much would depend on her.

Margareta was a home-builder, I could see that and whether she would allow her eldest son to leave home, even for a short time, was doubtful.

I believe she grappled with herself and came to the conclusion that as Jan was so set on a career with maps it was better for him to go into the family business if that were possible. And she must have decided that it would be excellent experience for him to travel a little. Permission was given and when I suggested that he should come with us on the trip his excitement was intense.

He had been sad because he had thought I was going away soon and was wondering when he would see me again—which was immensely gratifying. But to hear he was coming with us, to see the forests of Germany, the castles of the Rhine, the lakes of Switzerland and the big cities of other countries dazzled him.

He left with us. We were seen off by the whole family. "See you soon," they cried, for it was arranged that on our return journey I should spend another three days with them before leaving for England.

It was wonderful to watch Jan's excitement, to have long talks with him, to drift across lakes, to climb grassy slopes round the chalet in the Black Forest where we spent two nights.

Sitting on the hillside in the mountains, listening to the occasional tinkle of a cowbell, deeply aware of the resinous smell of the pines, I felt almost content. If only it were Philip beside me. I pulled myself up sharply and I said suddenly: "Jan, how would you like to come to England?"

"To England? Do you mean that, Annalice?"

"Yes, I do. You could come back with us. You could stay awhile and see if you liked it. I could show you the shop, as we call it. It is quite fascinating with all the maps and the printing presses. We have a wonderful man in charge called Benjamin Darkin. He is reckoned to be one of the finest cartographers in England. He would show you how maps are made. It really is fascinating."

Jan was silent. I held my breath watching him.

Then he turned to me and his eyes were blazing with excitement.

"My parents would not let me go," he said.

"I think they would."

"My father might."

"Your mother would too."

"You don't know her, Annalice."

"Yes, I do. As a matter of fact I have spoken to them. I thought I should before I spoke to you. They are agreeable. So it is up to you."

He remained silent. But I realized that the wonder of my suggestion completely bewildered him.

They were exciting days. I shall never forget the magnificence of the Swiss mountains and the beauty of the lakes, the excitement of sailing down the Rhine and looking up at the fairy-tale castles perched high above the river. We stayed in small towns in which one could expect the Pied Piper to appear at any moment; we passed through forests where characters from the stories of the Grimm brothers would have fitted so perfectly.

The men had certain business to attend to and Grace, Jan and I would go out together. We explored cathedrals, markets, narrow cobbled streets and broad highways and as I watched Jan's enthusiasm for everything I could almost believe I was young again, and this was Philip who was with me.

Once he said to me as we raced down a hill slope together and came level with each other: "The nicest thing that could ever happen to anyone is to find a grown-up sister."

"No," I retorted. "The nicest thing is to find a brother."

We laughed at each other but I was very much afraid that I would betray my emotion.

He meant so much to me, because I suppose he had come into my life at a time when I was obsessed by Philip's disappearance. I needed help at this time—and it was help which he alone could give me.

We returned to the house in Prinszen Gracht and there was great rejoicing.

"Margareta has cooked the fatted calf," said my father; and we spent the evening talking of our adventures. We sat up late and I think Father and Margareta were a little sad contemplating Jan's departure.

I said: "It is so good of you to let him come. Remember the distance between us is not so very far. It is not as though we were on the other side of the world."

Margareta said: "It is sad for us that he is going, but like little birds they must leave the nest and learn to fly on their own. And when they do it is natural that sometimes they fly far away."

"He is quite passionate in his desire to become a cartographer," I said.

My father agreed. "I recognize the passion," he said.

"Granny will love him. Believe me, she needs him. I need him. And he needs to be where he can learn what he longs to."

"You are right, of course," said my father. He looked at Margareta and she nodded, smiling rather sadly at him.

"You are so fortunate," I told them. "Being here I have felt the harmony, the happiness, in this home. You have each other, Charles and Wilhelmina. And Jan is there too . . . just across a little stretch of water."

"That is true," said my father. "To tell the truth we have often wondered about Jan. I was going to see someone in this town about what he wants to do. He is fifteen so it is time to be thinking about that."

"And when he has a desire which is undoubtedly born in him it cannot be ignored," added Margareta.

"You want the best for him," I said.

"Yes. We must put aside our selfish feelings," Margareta said. "I have wanted to keep the children round me . . . "

"Alas, time passes. Perhaps you will come and see us . . . all of you. Granny would be delighted. It is just a matter of breaking the ice, of forgetting these foolish differences."

"Well, it seems you have done that, Annalice," said my father.

"We must make sure that I have."

"And you are leaving tomorrow," said Margareta. "Your friends are charming people."

My father smiled and looked at her. I knew what they were thinking. They had already decided that I was going to marry Raymond.

I said nothing. But seeing their joy in each other made me wonder if I was being very foolish indeed to hold back.

I kept thinking of all Raymond had done for me. He had even brought this about. But for him I should now be at the Manor, watching for the news which never came.

Everyone thought I was lucky to be loved by Raymond Billington. Surely everyone could not be wrong.

The experiment was successful as I knew it would be. When I arrived home with my half brother, Granny was astounded and a little piqued I think because it had all been arranged without her knowledge; but her joy very soon overcame all other feelings.

In a very short time Jan had won her heart. His likeness to Philip was both saddening and heart-warming. "He is a Mallory from head to toe," she told me. "There doesn't seem to be anything Dutch about him."

I said: "You would like his mother, Granny. She is a sweet, homely and loving person."

"I can see that you have been completely bewitched by them all."

She was deeply moved and in spite of herself could not help showing it.

"You're quite audacious, Annalice," she said almost angrily. "Slyly going over there and arranging all this. I think you had it in mind right from the first."

"Well, Granny, it has always seemed a little silly to me. Family feuds always are. It is my family, don't forget . . . as well as yours."

"I can see I shall have to be watchful or you will be managing us all before long."

But she was delighted; and I think she admired me for what I had done.

I said: "Let us ask them all over for Christmas. Wouldn't that be fun?"

"I'm not sure. We'll see how Jan feels about it here."

"He loves it. Benjamin says he reminds him so much of—"

"I know. I can tell. He's got it in him. Heaven knows what happened to his father."

"Jan can't get to the shop quickly enough. He is into everything. Benjamin says it is What's this? What's that? all the time."

"I know. And he is certainly fond of you. I don't think he exactly dislikes his old grandmother either."

"He told me he had always wanted to come to England and that his father had talked about us and the Manor, and he thought about England as his home."

"He is a sensible boy."

He was good for us. We had to hide our grief from him and we did not talk of Philip in his presence.

It was the beginning of May when we visited the Billingtons again. Jan went with us. He had settled in amazingly well. It was true he spoke rather nostalgically now and then of his family but when I asked if he would like to go back, he was emphatic in his assurances that he wanted to stay.

He spent most afternoons at the shop.

Granny had been in correspondence with my father and they were writing regularly to each other now. He wanted to hear about Jan's progress, and she was happy to be on friendly terms again. Jan's education had given some anxiety but Granny had engaged the curate, who was a scholar and eager to earn a little extra money, to take Jan in the mornings until other arrangements could be made and we knew how long he was going to stay with us. Granny said that if he was going to make maps his career, he could not start too early and surely the ideal opportunity was in the family business.

My father agreed with that but it was decided that, for the time being, Jan should study with the curate.

"You see," said Granny to me, "when people make arrangements so hastily, they are inclined to forget the practical details."

"Which," I reminded her, "can always be worked out later."

She nodded, looking at me with that mingling of affection and grudging admiration.

But she thought I was very foolish to continue to refuse Raymond Billington.

I still went up to the room and would sit there thinking of Ann Alice. I was almost twenty now, and I still had the uncanny feeling that our lives were linked. I could not talk to anyone about it. Granny would have thought the notion quite ridiculous and would not have hesitated to say so. Raymond might too, but he would try to understand.

It was a great pleasure to arrive at the station and be greeted by Raymond and Grace.

"We have visitors," Raymond told us. "Old friends of the family. Miss Felicity Derring and her aunt, Miss Cartwright. You'll like them."

He asked Jan how he was getting on and Jan enthusiastically told him.

"Jan's days are full," I said. "Shop in the afternoon and Mr. Gleeson the curate in the mornings."

Jan grimaced.

"A necessary evil," I reminded him.

"I'd like to be at the shop all day," he said.

"There's enthusiasm for you," I commented.

"So all goes well. I'm glad of that."

When Raymond helped me down from the carriage which had brought us from the station, he whispered: "Our little plan worked."

"You should have been a general."

"Wars are more difficult to manage than family reconciliations."

We went into the house to be greeted by the family and introduced to Miss Felicity Derring and her aunt.

Felicity was pretty—about my age, I imagined. She had soft brown hair and big brown eyes. She was small-boned and not very tall, very dainty and completely feminine. I felt quite large and a little clumsy beside her. The aunt was small too, with a rather fussy manner.

"Felicity and Miss Cartwright are very old friends of the family," said Mrs. Billington. "I've heard all about your adventures on the Continent. And this is Jan. Jan, it is good to meet you. I am so glad you came to visit us."

It was the same warm atmosphere which always made me feel cosily content.

But there was a difference this time because of the visitors, and I learned something about them at dinner.

"Is there any news about your going out to join your fiancé?" asked Mrs. Billington of Felicity.

"Oh yes," replied Felicity. "I am planning to go in September. If I go early in the month I should escape the worst of the weather. It takes a long time to get there and it will be their summer by the time I do."

"How thrilling," said Grace.

"I'd love to go to Australia," added Basil. "You are lucky, Felicity."

"Oh yes, I am," she agreed, casting her eyes down.

Raymond said to me: "Felicity's fiancé is in Australia and she is going out to join him."

"How exciting!" I said.

"I'm a little frightened," Felicity confessed. "The thought of all that sea which has to be crossed, and then going to a new country . . . "

"I shall go with you, niece," said Miss Cartwright, as though her presence would be a guarantee that all would be well. She was that sort of woman.

"One has to have a chaperone," said Grace. "Why can men go off on their own and not women?"

"Well, my dear," replied her mother, "a man can protect himself better than a woman."

"Some men are rather weak," commented Grace. "Some women are quite strong." She looked at Miss Cartwright and me.

I said: "Women in our society are treated as of secondary importance."

"Oh no," declared Raymond. "If we are oversolicitous that is because we prize you so much that we are determined that no ill shall befall you."

"I still think we are denied opportunities."

Everybody was getting interested and I could see this becoming a discussion on the rights of women in our modern society—and that was typical of dinner at the Billingtons.

I was right. It did; and the talk became lively and controversial. Granny M joined in wholeheartedly and so did I. Felicity said little. I came to the conclusion that she was rather a timid little creature.

Later I asked Raymond to tell me about her.

"It was a whirlwind courtship," he said. "William Granville came over for a few months, looking for a wife I believe, and he found Felicity. She is hardly the type to go off to the outback. It would have been different if William had been in Sydney or Melbourne or one of the towns. But I don't believe he is. I can't imagine Felicity on some vast property coping with droughts and forest fires and all the disasters one hears about."

"No. She hardly seems fitted for that. And she is going out in September?"

"So she says. Miss Cartwright will go with her. Felicity is an orphan and has been with her aunt since she lost her father some years ago. Miss Cartwright is a bit of a dragon as you have no doubt seen. It is a good thing that Felicity has her to go out with."

"I take it Miss Cartwright approves of the match."

"William Granville is a very forceful man. He's not so young. I should think he is a good fifteen years older than Felicity. He swept her off her feet, though. And I suppose it seemed very romantic. I hope she will like it out there . . . I can see that Jan is doing a good job with your grandmother."

"She is very proud of him. Benjamin is full of praise for him and you can guess how that delights her. I heard her talking about 'my grandson' to someone the other day, and you should have heard the pride in her voice. It was a wonderful idea to bring him over."

"When you leave home she would have been so lonely. When are you going to, Annalice? My people are waiting to know. They think it is inevitable and they can't understand why we delay."

"Do they know . . . about Philip?"

"Of course."

"And they don't understand?"

He shook his head. "They think that I should be with you to comfort you if . . . "

"You say if. It seems like a certainty now. Where is he? Why do we hear nothing?"

"I don't know."

"It torments me."

"Marry me . . . and I'll take you out there. I'll give up everything and we'll go together."

For a moment I was tempted. It was what I wanted. The idea of going there, to the place where Philip had gone, dazzled me.

I don't know why I hesitated. It was almost as though I could hear Ann Alice's voice saying: No. It is not the way. When the time comes for you to marry Raymond, you will know.

"Why not, Annalice?" He put his arms round me and held me close to him. It was so comforting to be held thus. I turned my face and buried it in his coat.

"We'll tell them tonight," he said.

I withdrew myself. "No, Raymond. I don't think it is the way. You can't leave your business . . . just like that. I might have to stay there a long time. Think of the journey out . . . "

"It could be a honeymoon."

"A honeymoon which could perhaps reveal a tragedy. I just know it is not the way."

"Think about it."

"Yes," I said. "I will think."

I don't know where I got the notion that Felicity was in love with Raymond. Was it the manner in which she looked at him? The way her voice changed when she spoke to him?

Raymond was of course a very distinguished man. Anyone would be proud of him. I realized what a fool I was to hesitate about marrying him. I did not always know why I did. It was something to do with the journal. I still kept it in a drawer at the back of my gloves and scarves, following in her footsteps. It was some impulse, some instinct, almost as though she were guiding me.

And now that same instinct would not let me say Yes to Raymond.

I thought a great deal about Felicity. I sought her company. She was not easy to talk to. She seemed to have firmly closed herself in, which could indicate that she had something she wished to hide.

I learned that her family had been friends of the Billingtons for years. Felicity's mother had died of a fever when Felicity was three years old, and Miss Cartwright, her mother's sister, had come to keep house for them. She had the care of Felicity from an early age and when her father had died had taken over completely.

Felicity, I began to believe, was rather frightened by the prospect of going overseas. She confessed to this.

"But it is so exciting," I said. "It is so romantic. A whirlwind courtship . . . engagement and then going out to join your husband."

"He's not my husband yet," said Felicity, and the tone of her voice gave me a clue to her feelings.

I asked how long she had known Mr. Granville and she said only a month before they were engaged.

"Not very long," I commented.

"It all happened so quickly and it seemed right at the time."

"I think it will be most exciting."

"I'm not sure it will."

"But you'll have Miss Cartwright with you. So you'll have someone from home."

She nodded. "And you . . . " she said. "I suppose you will marry Raymond."

"Oh, nothing has been settled yet."

"But he wants to and surely you . . . "

"I do not think one should rush into these things."

She flushed a little and I realized the tactlessness of my remark. " . . . unless," I added, "one is very sure."

"Oh yes," she agreed, "unless one is sure."

There was a good deal I should like to have asked about Miss Felicity Derring, but her feelings were tightly shut away and she kept a firm hold on them, as though she were afraid for them to be known.

Raymond said to me: "I have an idea. Why should you not go out with Felicity and Miss Cartwright?"

"What?" I cried.

"It's a way. They'll never agree to your going alone. You could get out to Australia. You might find out something there. Miss Cartwright will be in charge. She will stay for a while and then you and she can come back together."

"Oh Raymond," I said, "you do get the most wonderful ideas!"

"I know you will never settle until you know what happened to your brother. It is possible that you can find out something on the spot. He went to Australia. I daresay someone might have heard something of him in Sydney. You could try to contact that young man he went out with. David Gutheridge, wasn't it? He might still be around if he went on an expedition in that country. You'd be on the spot. You'd be company for Felicity too. I think she is getting a little uneasy and it would be good for her to have a friend with her. She wouldn't feel quite so lost in a new land."

"It is an amazing idea. I wonder what Felicity would say to it. She hardly knows me."

"She would love to have a friend with her. So would Miss Cartwright. She would enjoy having someone to come home with."

"As I said before, you are devious, Raymond."

"I might get out there for a spell and give you a hand with the sleuthing."

"Would you?"

"The only way we could go out together is if you married me. We could not defy the conventions all that much by going out without being married."

"I don't know what I should do without you, Raymond. When I think how everything has changed since you appeared in the conference hall, I just marvel."

"It was fate," he said, and lightly kissed my forehead.

"And what of Granny, what is she going to say to this suggestion?"

"It might not be easy to persuade her."

I laughed. "We can be sure of that."

"You must work gently towards it. She knows you well and she loves you dearly. She wants to see you happy and she knows how your brother's disappearance weighs heavily upon you. She does give you credit for being able to take care of yourself. A few hints here and there . . . get her used to the idea . . . Make it seem quite natural that you should go out to Australia with Felicity. And when Miss Cartwright has seen her niece settled, you come back together. It seems perfectly plausible to me."

"It is becoming more and more reasonable," I said. "I thought it quite outrageous when you first suggested it."

"We'll work gradually towards it."

"Oh, Raymond, I do love you."

"Let's change the plans then. We'll go together."

I shook my head.

"When I have found the answer to Philip's disappearance I'll come back and marry you."

"That's a promise," he said.

ON THE
HIGH SEAS

On a bright September day in the company of Felicity Derring and Miss Cartwright I boarded the *Southern Cross*. The weeks had been so busy that I had hardly had time to think of all that was happening. It seemed incredible when I looked back—the coming of Jan and now my departure. A year ago I would not have believed this could possibly have happened.

My emotions were mixed. I was doing what I wanted to do, what I had to do if I was ever going to know peace of mind; on the other hand I was setting out on what might well be a disappointing enterprise.

Granny M had been hard to convince.

"A wild-goose chase," she called it. "What are you going to do when you get there?"

I replied: "I shall have to wait and see what I find. But I feel in my heart that I am going to find the truth."

"I'm surprised at Raymond. He's encouraged you in this. I should have thought he would have done all he could to keep you here."

"Raymond understands me. He knows I can't be happy until I know. Philip is part of me. You must understand that, Granny. We were always together. I can't just let him go out of my life and not know why and where he is."

"Don't you think I feel the same? Are you the only one with any feelings?"

"I know, Granny," I said. "But I'll find out and I'll come back and when I do, I'll marry Raymond. He understands. That is why he is helping me to go."

"I don't want to lose both of you, you know."

"You won't, Granny. I'll come back. Perhaps I'll bring Philip with me."

"Where do you think he is then? Hiding away from us?"

"I don't know, Granny. But I am going to find out. Try to understand. You have Jan with you now . . . "

"H'm. I expect he'll be wanting to go off to Australia next. How shall I know what's happening to *you*?"

"Granny, it is only a trip. Lots of people take them. I shall be with Felicity and Miss Cartwright, and I shall have to come back when she does."

I cannot say that she was agreeable to the project but she was resigned.

I had seen a little more of Felicity and Miss Cartwright since I first met them, and I felt I knew Miss Cartwright well. She was one of those forthright, self-righteous women—of whom there are so many about that they have become stock characters. I even used to guess what she was going to say before she said it.

It was different with Felicity. On the surface she seemed meek, rather insipid. But I was not sure that this was truly so. I felt she was hiding secrets. I wondered what.

I thought of what I should do when I reached Sydney. I supposed I should have to accompany them out to this place which they referred to as "a property" and which I learned was in New South Wales, some miles out of Sydney. Then I supposed I should be expected to stay there for a while until Miss Cartwright was ready to return. But what should I find out there? It was hardly likely that Felicity's prospective bridegroom would have known Philip. That would be asking too much of coincidence.

Still, I was on my way, and I had an unshakable belief that something would come to guide me. I was still thinking of Ann Alice and I had the strange feeling that she was watching, helping me along the way she wanted me to go.

Granny came to Tilbury to see us off, in the company of Raymond and Jan. It was gratifying to see the way in which Jan put his arm round Granny as though to comfort her. Her mouth was tight with disapproval and suppressed emotion. But in my heart I knew she understood and that had she been my age and the opportunity had arisen, she would have acted just as I was doing.

I don't think for a moment she believed I was going to solve the mystery, but she did realize that I had to *do* something. I could not remain inactive. I had to try and if I failed I would come back and if I could not exactly put it all out of my mind I could at least convince myself that I could do no more and must accept what was.

I was rather glad when the last farewells had been said. Such moments are always rather agonizing. One is aware of the emotional atmosphere all around one—parents, sons, daughters, lovers . . . parting. One senses the apprehension of those who were leaving home to go into the unknown—even though they had chosen to do so.

Raymond held my hands tightly and said: "When you come back . . . "

"Yes," I repeated, "when I come back."

"It won't be long."

"Perhaps not."

"I shall be here to meet you."

"Yes . . . please do. And thank you, Raymond. Thank you for all you have done for me."

I clung to him for a moment. Then I kissed Granny and Jan once more and without turning back went on board.

What a noise! What a bustle everywhere! People seemed to be running about in confusion. Orders were shouted; sirens blew.

Felicity and Miss Cartwright shared a cabin. Mine was next to theirs and I shared with a young Australian girl who was travelling with her parents.

I looked round the small space which was to be my home for the next weeks and wondered how I should manage. There were two bunks, a dressing table with a few drawers and a cupboard. I had not been there long when my travelling companion arrived.

She was a big girl of about my age—sun-tanned with thick wiry fair hair and a breezy manner.

She said: "Hello. So we're stable mates, are we? Bit of a tight squeeze, but we'll have to make the best of it, won't we? Would you mind if I have the top bunk? I don't like the idea of people climbing over me."

I said I did not mind in the least.

"I hope you haven't much gear," she said. "Space a bit limited, isn't it? My name is Maisie Winchell. Pa and Ma are a few cabins along. We're in wool. What are you going out for? Let me guess. Going out to get married, are you? Some Aussie came over looking for a wife and found you."

"Quite wrong," I told her. "Though I am travelling with a friend who is going out for that purpose, and my name is Annalice Mallory."

"Oh, I say! I like that. Annalice, eh? Call me Maisie. Everyone does. And you'll have to learn to be free and easy out there."

"I am ready to be, Maisie," I said.

She nodded with approval and we divided up the cupboard and the drawer space.

After that I went to the cabin next door to see how Felicity and Miss Cartwright were faring.

Miss Cartwright was complaining about the lack of space and Felicity said it was a good thing that her trunks, full of the things she was taking with her, were in the hold.

We went into the dining room together.

There were few people there. The Captain was not present, naturally, for I supposed he was on the bridge taking the ship out of the harbour. We were too excited to eat though the soup was good and appetizing.

I noticed a man seated close to us who appeared to be watching us intently. He was very striking-looking because of his height. He must have been well over six feet tall and correspondingly broad. There was a boldness about him which I rather resented because he did seem to be particularly interested in our party. He was very fair and his hair had a bleached look as though he spent a great deal of time in the open air. He had deep blue eyes which looked startling in his sun-tanned face. When I caught his eyes—which I could not help doing because every time I looked up he appeared to be staring at me—he smiled.

I lowered my gaze and looked away.

Miss Cartwright said the soup was not hot enough and she hoped the food was going to be edible. She had heard that shipboard fare was very poor.

Felicity said little. She looked pale. No doubt her preparations had been particularly strenuous and she was taking a big step in leaving her home for a man whom she had only known a month before she decided to marry him.

When we left the dining room the big man was still sitting there. We had to pass close to him.

He said: "Good evening."

There was nothing to do but respond so I said: "Good evening."

"I think we are in for a rough night," he added.

I nodded and went on quickly.

Miss Cartwright said: "What impertinence! To speak to us like that! And to say it was going to be a rough night! He seemed quite pleased about it."

"Perhaps he was just trying to be friendly," I said.

"I daresay we shall be introduced by the Captain or officers to those people we ought to know."

"I doubt it will be as formal as that," I replied. "We shall have to wait and see."

I bade good night to them, saying I would go to my cabin and unpack.

This I did. Maisie came in while I was thus engaged.

She confirmed the stranger's view that the sea was going to be rough. "Wait till we get in the Bay." She grinned.

"You're a seasoned traveller, I imagine."

"Pa comes over every two years or so. We're in wool, as I said. Property north of Melbourne. Ma comes with him and I don't let them leave me behind. I like to have a squint at the Old Country."

"Do you enjoy that?"

"Oh yes. Nice to get back home though . . . to feel free and easy."

"You find us rather formal?"

She just looked at me and laughed. "Well, what do you think?" Then she started to tell me about the property near Melbourne.

I said: "I must introduce you to Miss Derring. I am travelling with her and her aunt and she is going out to marry a man who has one of these properties not far from Sydney."

"Oh, New South Wales. We're Victoria, you know."

I laughed with her. "Quite clearly," I said, "there is no place like home."

I thought I should get on with her very well.

They were right about the rough night. I awoke to find myself almost pitched out of my bunk.

"It's nothing yet," said Maisie from above, almost gleefully. "It's a pity it couldn't have waited awhile. Just to let first-timers get their sea legs."

"Oh, they come in time, do they . . . sea legs?"

"To some they do. To others never. You're either a good sailor or you're not. I hope you are going to be a good one. Try to forget about it. That's the secret. Fresh air too . . . that's a help. I'm tired. Good night. We won't need rocking tonight."

I lay awake for a little while listening to the creaking of the wood and the whistling of the wind as the waves pounded against the sides of the ship. Maisie was right. Finally the rocking sent me to sleep.

The next morning, when I awoke, it was to find that the wind had not abated. It was difficult to stand up in the cabin but I managed to stagger along to the bathroom and dress. I felt quite well but these operations took some time because of the movement of the ship.

Maisie said from the top bunk: "I'll get up when you've gone. We'll make that arrangement. There's not room for two to dress at the same time. Do you feel like breakfast?"

"Just a cup of coffee and bread and butter perhaps."

"That's good. Then I'd get some fresh air if I were you. If you can take food, that's the best thing. Food and fresh air."

I went to the next cabin to see how Felicity and Miss Cartwright were.

They were both feeling ill and wanted nothing more than to be left alone. So I went to the dining room. There was hardly anyone there. I had coffee and bread and butter and, taking Maisie's advice, went on deck.

The waves were washing over it and I could scarcely stand. I found a dry spot under the lifeboats, and, wrapping myself in a rug which I found in a locker, I sat down and contemplated the raging sea.

I thought of arriving in Sydney. A wild-goose chase. I could hear Granny's voice. Was that what it was going to be.

Someone was staggering along the deck. I saw at once that it was the big man I had seen in the dining room and I felt faintly irritated but a little intrigued. It would not have surprised me if I discovered he had followed me up here. He took a seat beside me.

"Why, hello," he said. "You're a bold young lady, braving the elements."

"I am told it is the best thing."

"If you have the nerve for it. Ninety per cent of our passengers are groaning in their bunks. Do you know that?"

"I didn't and I am not sure that the percentage is accurate."

"How many did you see in the dining room? How many are here? Fortunately only two which is far more interesting than a crowd."

"Do you think so?"

"I do, indeed. But I am lacking in courtesy. I should, of course, have asked permission to sit down with you."

"Isn't it a little late to do so now?"

"It is a *fait accompli,* as they say. Where else is there to sit? It is the only dry spot . . . here under the lifeboats. Permission granted?"

"What would you do if it were denied?"

"I should sit here just the same."

"Then to ask is rather superfluous, isn't it?"

"I can see you are a very logical young lady. Let me introduce myself. I am Milton Harrington. A noble name you think. Milton. 'Thou shouldst be living at this hour . . .' and all that. I'll tell you how it came about. My mother was a very beautiful lady—as you may well imagine from my inherited charms—and before I arrived in the world I gave her a wretched time. She was unable to indulge in her social activities which were the meaning of life to her. Paradise Lost, you see. And as soon as I —the most delightful cherub you could ever imagine—was laid in her arms, she cried: 'Paradise Regained.' So after that I just had to be Milton."

I was laughing. I had forgotten the uneasiness the wild weather had created in me. I had forgotten my seemingly hopeless mission. I was just amused. He was so sure of himself, so persistent in his determination to drum up an acquaintance.

"Now," he said, "it is your turn."

"Annalice Mallory," I said. "Ann Alice were two names which were used a great deal in our family for generations. Well, my grandmother, who had the task of naming me, decided to ring the changes, join them together and she came up with Annalice."

"Annalice," he said. "I like it. It's unusual. It suits you."

"Thank you for the compliment . . . if it is a compliment. Unusual, I suppose, could mean unusually unpleasant."

"In this case it means quite the reverse."

"Then I will renew my thanks. How long will this weather last? Do you travel often?"

"One can never be sure about the weather. It could be a rough passage or a smooth one. It's in the lap of the gods. The answer to your second question is Yes. I do the journey frequently. I go home on average once a year."

"To England?"

"Yes. I own a sugar plantation. I come to London periodically on marketing matters. Why are you going to Australia?"

"I'm travelling with a friend and her aunt. She is going out to get married."

"I don't think I have ever made a crossing yet when there was not at least one young lady who was going out to get married. Men get lonely away from home. Then they go home to find a bride and bring her out to share their solitude. At first I thought you must surely be going to join some lonely man."

"Well, you are quite wrong."

"I'm glad of that."

"Indeed?"

He laughed. "Oh yes, indeed I am. I could not bear to think of such a young lady grappling with all that has to be done on a property in the outback. The beautiful English skin would become ravaged by the pitiless sun. You don't know how lucky you are in your rainy home where the sun doesn't dry up the crops and kill off the stock and hurricanes don't blow away the work of years, where you don't have plagues of locusts . . . "

"You make it sound like the plagues of ancient Egypt."

"That's exactly what it *is* like."

"Then why do people stay there?"

"It is not easy to pack up and walk to the Promised Land."

"Is that why you are there?"

"I don't live in the outback of Australia. I live on Cariba. That's an island more than a hundred miles off the coast of Australia. My father was out there and from him I inherited a sugar plantation. Sugar grows well in Cariba. But one day I am going to sell the plantation and I'm coming home to acquire a manor house with a large estate . . . farms, the lot . . . and I'm going to be an English squire."

"Squires have usually been on their land for generations."

"I'll get round that," he said. "Tell me, what are you going to do when you get to Australia?"

"I am going to attend the wedding of my friend. Stay for a while and then I suppose go back with her aunt."

"I come to Sydney quite frequently. Shall we be friends?"

"How can we say? Friendship is not something which is decided at a brief meeting. It has to be nurtured. It has to grow."

"We'll nurture it then."

"That is a hasty decision," I told him. "We only boarded the ship yesterday. We saw each other for the first time in the dining room."

"When I was rather bold. You will discover, when the nurturing begins, that that is a trait of mine. Do you like it?"

"So much would depend on when it occurred."

"You and I are going to get along well. We're two of a kind, you know."

"So you find me bold?"

"Boldness lurks beneath the refined manners of the perfect lady. I can see it peeping out. For instance, what are you doing, sitting out here on deck with someone to whom you have not been formally introduced?"

"I would call it extenuating circumstances. The weather drove me to sit here and as it was the only place where a traveller could be seated, it was inevitable that you should sit here too. I don't own the ship, so can't order you to leave me."

"Logical reasoning. But I still think I was right about the boldness. Time will show whether I was right or wrong, I daresay."

"I think the wind is abating a little."

"Perhaps . . . just a little."

"And I shall go in and see how my fellow travellers are faring."

"They are prostrate, are they?"

"I'm afraid so."

"It will be some time before they recover."

"Nevertheless I shall go to see them."

I stood up and almost fell, reeling against the deck rail. He was beside me, holding me, his face close to mine. He was the most disturbing man I had ever met.

"Be careful," he said, "one wild wave could carry you overboard. You should not come too near this rail. Allow me to escort you down."

He put his arm about me and held me tightly against him. We rolled rather than walked along the deck. I felt breathless and rather glad of his strong arm.

"When I left England, I thought Ah, Paradise Lost," he said. "Now I am thinking Paradise Regained. I was not called Milton for nothing."

I laughed again. It had been a stimulating encounter.

I staggered down to the cabins. Miss Cartwright looked very wan and Felicity was not much better.

She said: "This is terrible. How much of this do we have to endure? I thought I was going to die."

"It is getting better, I think."

"Thank Heaven for that."

"Where have you been?" asked Miss Cartwright.

"On deck. My cabin mate said it was the best thing to do."

"You look so rosy," said Felicity. "Almost as though you enjoyed it."

I smiled and thought: Yes, I believe I did.

After two days the weather improved. Miss Cartwright was shaken. She had suffered more than Felicity and I was sure she was wishing she had never come on such a hazardous journey. Here we were, only three days out and the whole voyage stretched before her. She was really quite perturbed at the prospect.

By this time I had become well acquainted with Milton Harrington, who seemed to appear like the genie of the lamp wherever I happened to be.

I shall not pretend that I did not enjoy being sought after, particularly by a man who was treated with such respect throughout the ship. He appeared to be a friend of the Captain and well known to other members of the crew; and I believed that special privileges were accorded to him.

When we arrived at Madeira, our first port of call, he asked if we were going ashore. I said, Yes, of course. But Miss Cartwright put in very firmly that she was not at all sure that it was right for ladies to go unaccompanied.

He regarded her gravely and said: "Indeed, Madam, how wise you are! It would be unseemly for ladies to go alone and I am going to beg you to allow me to escort them."

"Oh but Mr. Harrington, I could not allow that. Our acquaintance is so brief."

"But, Madam, you and I between us could make sure that no harm befell the young ladies."

He gave me a mischievous glance for he knew me well enough to realize how infuriated such a conversation would make me.

Miss Cartwright, however, I noticed with some amazement, was rather fascinated by him. That surprised me. I should have thought such boldness, such arrogant masculinity, would not have found favour in her spinster's heart. Quite the contrary. She thought he was what she called "A real man," and she respected him for it.

She appeared to hesitate but the prospect of such a jaunt in his company was irresistible. "Well, Mr. Harrington, if we were both there ..."

"Leave it to me. I will show you the island. It is ideal as a first port of call. It is so beautiful. Always a favourite port of mine. Now I shall share my appreciation."

It was a happy day. He took charge of us and was so courtly to Miss Cartwright, always considering her comfort first, that she blossomed and I believe thought her days of prostration were worth while since they had brought her to this.

He hired one of the bullock carts and we drove round the town. We went into the market to admire the magnificent flowers for sale there; we explored the dark red, stone Cathedral; we drove past the Governor's palace, the old fortress of São Lourenço and on to the site of the old Franciscan monastery where beautiful gardens had been made.

Milton Harrington wanted to look at the sugar canes which grew in profusion. So we drove out of the town.

He talked knowledgeably and told us a great deal about the production of sugar and how the juice from the plants was distilled in mills and boiling houses. He made me feel that I wanted to see his island.

"The canes were brought here from Sicily, Cyprus and Crete during the fifteenth century and at that time became the main industry of the island. Nowadays it is the wine for which they are famous. Who has not heard of Madeira wine? I tell you what, Miss Cartwright, I am going to be very daring. May I?"

"Oh Mr. Harrington," replied Miss Cartwright with a little laugh, "if you insist, how could *I* stop you?"

"I would obey your instructions, of course. But I was going to say that I have a good friend here. He has a wine cellar. He would like to show you how his wine is made and preserved. He might even invite you to try a glass."

"Oh dear, Mr. Harrington, that sounds almost improper."

"You have your protector here, Miss Cartwright, and nothing to fear."

So we left our bullock cart outside the wine lodge and went into the cellar where we were greeted by a swarthy man in a big leather apron who talked in Portuguese at a great speed. Every now and then he would break into broken English. He was clearly pleased to see Milton Harrington.

When we had made a tour of the cellars we were invited to sit down on stools which were in the shape of barrels. These were placed at a round table and glasses of Madeira wine were brought to us.

We declared it delicious. Perhaps it was the effect of the wine but

Felicity became quite talkative. She was obviously enjoying the outing. She said she was quite taken with the island and would like to spend some time here.

"Ah, but that would delay your arrival in Australia," Milton Harrington pointed out. "I am sure you are all eagerness to get there."

The moment's hesitation told me—and, I was sure, Milton Harrington —a good deal. I knew now what Felicity's secret was. She was a very frightened young woman and now that she was getting nearer to her new life she was beginning to wonder whether she had made a mistake.

"Oh yes . . . yes, of course," she said, too vehemently for conviction. But I could not forget the stricken look in her eyes.

"Where is the property?" asked Milton Harrington.

"It's a few miles out of Sydney."

"What is the name of it? Perhaps I know it."

"Granville's. That is the name of my fiancé. The place is named after him."

"William Granville?" Milton Harrington spoke rather bleakly.

"Yes. I am going out to him."

"Do you know him?" I asked quickly.

"You might say I am on nodding acquaintance. I call in at Sydney on average about once a month. In the hotel there one meets up with graziers and people from around. I have met him."

"What a strange coincidence," cried Miss Cartwright.

"It is not really," Milton Harrington told her. "You see it is not like London. In fact the population of Australia can't come anywhere near that of London, nor Birmingham and Manchester . . . or any of the big cities. It's sparsely populated. People come in from miles round and congregate in one hotel. It is not so strange that one comes across people."

"No, of course not," I said.

But I began to feel uneasy.

Miss Cartwright was persuaded to try a second glass of wine and after that she began to laugh a great deal.

We went back to the bullock cart and to the ship.

My uneasiness persisted. I was sure that Milton Harrington knew something about William Granville and that he had been somewhat reticent in the wine lodge because what he knew was unpleasant.

I determined that when I was alone with him I would ask him outright. It was better to know the worst. I was beginning to feel rather protective towards Felicity. It was that quality of helplessness in her which made me want to look after her and I felt that if there was something which was not quite what we expected we should know about it.

It was not difficult to waylay him and I did so.

I said: "I should like to speak to you . . . somewhere where we can be alone."

He raised his eyebrows in surprise and said: "I shall, of course, be delighted."

We found a secluded spot on the deck and sat down.

"It was not exactly what you said but the way in which you said it," I began. "I am referring to the conversation in the wine lodge when William Granville's name was mentioned. You know something about him, don't you?"

"I know a little of him."

"What do you know?"

"That he has a property not far from Sydney."

"We all know that. What do you know especially about him?"

"What do you want? Height? Colour of eyes? Hair?"

"You are being flippant. Miss Derring is going out to marry him. If there is anything wrong, I think we ought to be prepared. Please tell me."

"What would you do about anything that you considered wrong?"

"I could break it to her. We could decide . . . "

"One is always wary of giving an opinion of another person. One could be quite wrong."

"Why did you say then . . . ?"

"My dear Miss Annalice, I said nothing."

"No, you didn't. But you implied. You know him, but you seem to be holding something back . . . something that you did not talk about."

"I don't know the man very well personally. I have only heard gossip . . . comment. People talk about each other in small communities and not always charitably."

"Will you stop beating about the bush and tell me frankly what these rumours are?"

"Nothing much. He is a good deal older than Miss Derring."

"She knows that. Sometimes marriages are quite successful when there is a disparity in ages. It is more than that, isn't it?"

"You are so persistent. I'll tell you that I heard he takes too much drink. People do, you know, in these lonely places."

"I see. And that was what made you act as you did?"

"I was not aware of any acting."

"It was your silence which said so much."

"I'm sorry if I caused Miss Derring anxiety."

"She didn't notice. But she does seem to be a little uncertain. I wish she would confide in me. I might be able to help."

"She knew him in England."

"Yes, when he came over looking for a wife."

"Well, she agreed to marry him. She was not forced into it."

"I feel quite anxious about her."

He put his hand over mine.

"You're very nice," he said.

I withdrew it at once.

"What else do you know about him?"

He shrugged his shoulders but he would say no more. Yet he gave me the impression that he knew something and was holding it back.

I rose and he was beside me. "Would you like to take a turn round the deck or join me in an aperitif?"

"No, thank you. I am going back to my cabin."

He had done nothing to diminish my uneasiness. Rather had he increased it.

After we left Madeira we ran into bad weather again. Felicity seemed to be much better able to cope with conditions than she had before. But Miss Cartwright was very ill. She was confined to bed for two days and after that, when the sea was calm, she was very weak and continued to be ill.

We were now in warm waters, along the west coast of Africa and it was very pleasant to sit on deck. Miss Cartwright came up and sat in a deck chair, but she looked very wan and Felicity confided in me that she was very worried about her.

"I am sure nothing would have induced her to come—not even her duty towards me—if she had known how rough seas would affect her," she said. "If we have another bout of bad weather I shall really fear for her."

She did not stay long on deck and wished to retire to her cabin.

Felicity and I took her down and would have stayed with her, but she wanted to sleep if possible.

When we went back on deck Milton Harrington came and sat down beside us.

"Miss Cartwright looks very poorly," he said, and Felicity admitted that she was anxious about her. She thought she might be really ill, she said.

"We could run into bad weather round the Cape," he said. "It's called the Cape of Storms, you know."

"Oh dear," said Felicity.

"There are some who can't take the sea and Miss Cartwright is, I am afraid, one of them. And when she gets to Australia . . . she will have the prospect of the journey back."

"I wish she could go home," said Felicity.

"That would be easy enough."

"How?"

"She could go back from Cape Town."

"Alone!" said Felicity.

"Unless we went back with her," I added. I looked at Felicity. "We could hardly do that."

"Seeing how ill she was, made me think," said Milton Harrington. "I know Cape Town well. I have friends there."

"You seem to have friends everywhere," I commented.

"I travel a great deal. I call in at these places. One collects people."

"Like souvenirs?" I suggested.

"Well, you could call it like that. I could arrange something . . . "

Felicity was staring out to sea. Was she wishing that she could go back from Cape Town?

"I'll talk to Miss Cartwright," said Milton Harrington.

"You?" I cried.

"Yes, why not? I am sure she would listen to me."

"I am sure she would think a man's opinion so much more valuable than that of someone of her own sex."

"Yes. I always thought she was a wise woman." He was looking at me and laughing. "I wish, Miss Annalice, that you shared her opinion."

"Could we be serious?"

"Indeed we can. She should go back. I have no doubt of that. I could arrange it quite easily. I could get her a passage on another ship. I might even know someone who is going back who could keep an eye on her. It is better for people in her state of health to be in their own homes."

I looked at Felicity. She nodded.

She said: "She would never agree to leave us to travel alone."

"I will tell her that I will keep an eye on you."

"You!" I cried. "She would think that most unconventional. Why we didn't even know you until we came on board."

"Friendship matures quickly when people live in close proximity. She would have to face the passage back, of course; but all the time she would be getting nearer home. You have no idea how helpful that can be."

"At home," I told him, "they only agreed that we could come because Miss Cartwright was with us. They would have thought it most improper to allow young women to go to the other side of the world alone."

"It only shows how mistaken people can be. Here are you two, taking care of Miss Cartwright. Leave it to me. The next time I see her I will gently hint at the suggestion."

He did.

The next day the weather was fine and Miss Cartwright came on deck again. Felicity sat on one side of her, I on the other. She certainly looked ill and the bright sunlight made her skin look yellow.

It was not long before Milton Harrington strolled past and came to speak to us.

"Miss Cartwright, what a pleasure to see you!" He drew up a chair. "May I join you?"

"If you wish," said Miss Cartwright well pleased.

"I was so sorry to hear that you were ill," he said. "The sea can do that to people. There are some who should never go to sea."

"And I am one of them," said Miss Cartwright. "I can tell you, Mr. Harrington, that when I have finished with this I shall never never make a sea voyage again."

"Nor should you. What a pity there is more to come, and then you will have the long journey home."

"Don't speak of it, I beg you. I dread it."

"You could, of course, cut the journey short."

"Cut it short? How?"

"By returning home from Cape Town."

I saw the gleam in her eyes; then it faded. "But, Mr. Harrington, I have to deliver my niece to her future husband. I am in charge of her and Miss Mallory."

"And you have carried out those duties with excellence. But, Miss Cartwright, if you become ill, how can you continue to do so?"

"I must overcome this weakness."

"Even a lady as dedicated and determined as yourself cannot overcome the sea."

"Well, I have to do my best."

"If you decide to return home from Cape Town, I can arrange it easily."

"What? Do you mean that?"

"I could fix a passage on a ship going home. I have friends who constantly make these trips. I could give you an introduction to one of them so that you did not make the journey alone."

"Mr. Harrington, you are so kind, but I have come out here to look after my niece."

"Her future husband will be waiting for her at Sydney. He will look after her from then on."

She was silent. She looked a little better already. There was a touch of colour in her cheeks. It was the pleasure of the prospect of soon being on English soil.

She gave a little laugh. "So good of you . . . but, of course, impossible."

"It would need a little arranging, certainly. But impossible, no. It could be done and without a great deal of trouble. Quite easily in fact."

"But these two . . . "

"They are both very capable young ladies. I would be there to make sure no harm could come to them. You could safely leave them in my hands."

I was amazed at the man's audacity. He was really urging her to go. Why? I wondered a great deal about him. His pursuit of me for one thing was intriguing. There was a certain intensity about him. He was very different from Raymond. He was the sort of man who would be capable of everything. I was realizing more and more how predictable, how reliable Raymond was.

"Oh, but Mr. Harrington . . . " murmured Miss Cartwright.

"I know you are thinking of our brief friendship. But we have seen each other daily in this short time as often as one sees friends of years' standing. The span is unimportant. It is the time we have spent together.

Just think about it, Miss Cartwright. The long expanse of ocean has to be traversed. True, you have to make the journey back from Cape Town, but you would be home by the time we reach Australia. And then your health would recover rapidly."

"You make it all sound so simple, Mr. Harrington."

"Well, remember that it is not impossible."

He then began to talk of other matters such as the places he had visited on his journeys. Always, he said, he wanted to return to England. One day he would settle there.

He said no more about Cape Town; but he had sown the seed.

I could see that Miss Cartwright thought of his suggestion continually, wrestling with herself. Could she come to terms with her conscience if she left us to make the journey alone? I imagined conscience had played a big part in Miss Cartwright's life. The prospect was so inviting. I knew from what she said that she sadly missed her home and garden. She found the heat almost as trying as the buffeting winds. She was not intended to travel the world.

A few days passed. Every now and then Milton Harrington—our constant companion now—would drop a little more of his honied suggestions into her ears. I was amazed at the skill he used. He never persuaded; but almost everything he said pointed to the advisability of her returning. Nothing could be done until we reached Cape Town, but he would have to know her decision by then. We were staying there for three days and we would need all of that time to make the arrangements.

I was thinking a great deal about him. He was a man who would have a motive for what he did and his pursuit of me could mean only one thing. I was not so simple as not to understand that. He had not mentioned a wife, and I did not know whether he was married. He gave an impression of virility and I gathered he was a man who would not consider it necessary to deny himself anything he desired; I was sure he must have known many women. There was an air of worldliness about him. I was very intrigued by him and wondered how far our friendship would have gone if I had responded to his advances.

He was returning to his plantation from England and he had mentioned that people went home to look for wives. Did he mean that that was what he had done? And if he had, he appeared to have failed to find one; and I could not imagine his failing in anything—least of all in the pursuit of a wife.

There was a great deal I had to learn about him.

At the moment I believed I should keep him at arm's length, which was not easy for he was constantly there. I knew that the passengers were beginning to speculate about us, and as it was known that Felicity was going out to be married, they would assume that I was the target for Milton Harrington's attentions.

I have to admit that I was rather pleased to be at the centre of such a romantic intrigue. It certainly gave a spice to the day.

As he had predicted we were in rough seas again approaching the Cape and this time Miss Cartwright made her decision. She was, she confessed, a little anxious about me, for while Felicity would be in her husband's care, I should have to make the journey back to England alone.

Milton Harrington assured her that he would arrange for my passage home when the time came and would make sure that I should travel in the company of friends of his, who would surely be returning to England. Indeed she had nothing to fear; and his assurances, combined with the weather, helped her to make up her mind.

If it could be arranged, she would go home for in her present state she could be no guardian at all—only an encumbrance.

Milton Harrington said that as soon as we docked he would set about making the arrangements.

Our stay in Cape Town was given over to the departure of Miss Cartwright. Constantly we had to reassure her that we should be perfectly safe without her.

We should be met in Sydney by William Granville. I should stay with Felicity until after the marriage; and then Mr. Harrington would help me to arrange a passage home, introduce me to the Captain of the vessel and some of his numerous friends who would surely be sailing because he knew so many people who made the journey often.

It would all work out satisfactorily in his capable hands.

And they were indeed capable. He took charge of everything. Miss Cartwright was to stay for a week in one of the best hotels. He introduced her to some of his friends who would be sailing to England. They would all be together and there was nothing to fear.

As for her charges, she could trust Mr. Harrington to do the same for them as he had done for her.

I was amazed that she was prepared to put so much trust in a man she had not known a few weeks before. I put it down to the power of his personality. Power was the word. He exuded power, and while that power was benevolent, that was very comforting. But I was wondering how one would feel if one were in conflict with it.

I felt there was so much I had to learn about this man.

Those days in Cape Town passed quickly. We had only a short time for sightseeing of perhaps the most beautiful of all the places we should visit. I shall never forget the sight of Table Mountain with what they call the tablecloth over it. There it was reaching to the sky and over the plateau frothy white clouds looking very like a tablecloth. The weather was warm, but not too hot; the flowers were colourful and the scenery majestic.

Miss Cartwright was in a state of nerves at the parting. I thought at the last minute she was going to change her mind and return to the ship. She kept talking about abandoning her duty and I knew her conscience was having a fearful battle with her dread of the sea. Conscience was defeated; and when we sailed out of Cape Town we left Miss Cartwright behind.

I had the impression that Milton Harrington was pleased that she had gone. Indeed, sometimes I thought he had skilfully manoeuvred her departure. Why?

He would have his motives. He was a man of motives. He was also occupying my thoughts far too much. I thought, He is a little brash; he is rather arrogant; he is certainly bold.

Felicity was impressed by him. I noticed that she was a little nervous in his presence. He had an effect on her too.

Now that Miss Cartwright had left, it seemed reasonable that I should move in with Felicity and leave my Australian companion with the cabin to herself.

This I did, and sharing a cabin brought us into closer contact. Consequently, our relationship changed a little.

We used to lie in our bunks, she above, me below, and talk until we fell asleep. I found that a certain drowsiness and the gentle rocking of the ship was more prone to bring out confidences than sitting on deck in the sunlight.

At length Felicity spoke of her fears.

"I wish this voyage would go on and on," she said.

"Oh, you are enjoying it then?"

"Yes . . . once I got used to the sea. The first part was dreadful. I just wanted to die."

"Like poor Miss Cartwright."

"I was so amazed that she went. I never thought she would. She's always been so strict about watching over me."

"I think Milton Harrington persuaded her."

"She was very taken with him. Annalice, what do you think of him?"

"Oh, I don't make hasty judgements."

"But you must have some idea."

"Well, I find him interesting . . . stimulating in a way. The sort of person it is quite amusing to meet . . . briefly . . . on a ship. We reach Sydney . . . we say goodbye to him . . . and in a few months' time we shall be saying, 'What was the name of that man we met on the ship . . . ?' "

"You can't really believe that. Why, he has promised my aunt that he will make sure you have a safe passage home."

"Well, perhaps not a few months . . . a few years, say."

"I don't think I shall ever forget him. It was the way he got rid of my aunt."

"Got rid of her?"

"Oh yes . . . He wanted her to go, didn't he?"

"Why should he?"

"Chaperones can be rather restricting."

I laughed. "Since she spent most of her time prone in her cabin she could hardly have been restricting."

"Her very presence was restricting. Now we are two young females all alone."

"Felicity, you're not scared?"

She was silent for a moment, and I went on: "You are, aren't you? Why don't you tell me?"

"I should have liked to go back with my aunt."

"Felicity! But you are going to the man you love." She was silent again and I went on: "I guessed you were worried. Wouldn't you like to talk about it?"

"It all happened so quickly."

"You were, as they say, swept off your feet."

"Well, I think I wanted something to happen . . . because . . . "

"Because what?"

"Oh nothing . . . William was there. I met him when we went to tea at a neighbour's. He talked to me and was clearly interested. Then I saw him quite a lot after that and he asked me to marry him. It seemed the best thing . . . "

"And now you are wondering."

"I'm thinking that I don't know him very well. And I'm all those miles from home. It's like going to strangers."

I was silent, trying to find the right words to comfort her. I was thinking of what Milton Harrington had said about his drinking habits. Poor Felicity! She was too weak, too helpless to cope with this situation into which she had thrust herself.

"It's my own fault," she said. "That doesn't help. It makes it worse really if it is something that you could have avoided. It serves you right . . . "

"No," I agreed, "it doesn't help. But you are imagining the worst. You'll probably find when you get there that you will like it very much. He must have fallen in love with you, otherwise he wouldn't have asked you to marry him . . . and you must have liked him."

"I don't think it was quite like that. He came to look for a wife. Quite a lot of people would have been suitable. He just happened to meet me."

"That's life. It is a matter of being in a certain place at a certain time. That is how we meet our fate."

"You don't understand. I was flattered to be taken notice of. I was pleased because someone wanted to marry me. I see now how stupid I was. You see, there was someone else. I love him, you see. I always have."

"And he?"

"He's in love with someone . . . not me."

"Oh, Felicity, I'm so sorry."

"My aunt thought I should marry him. They all thought I should, but when he fell in love with this other one, that was the end. Ever since I was fourteen I thought . . . Well, we were friends, our families I mean, great friends. We saw each other often . . . and when he was in love with someone else . . . and it was so obvious . . . I just felt lost and lonely and terribly hurt and when William said, 'Will you marry me and come back to Australia with me,' I thought it was a good way out . . . till I realized what it meant."

"I understand so much now, Felicity," I said. "I knew something was troubling you."

"And soon I shall be there . . . all alone."

"You'll have your husband."

"That . . . is what I am afraid of."

I tried to comfort her. "I think a lot of brides feel like this on the eve of their weddings."

"Do you?"

"I'm sure of it."

"I'm glad you came with me, Annalice."

"You know why I wanted to come."

"Yes, because of your brother."

We were silent for a while.

Then I said: "Felicity, are you asleep?"

"No."

"It will be all right," I told her.

She did not answer.

There were hot days while we crossed the Indian Ocean and our constant companion was Milton Harrington.

"Don't forget I have promised Miss Cartwright to keep a wary eye on you," he said. "She will almost be home by now, poor lady. I am glad I was able to alleviate her sufferings."

"You were most assiduous in your care for her," I told him.

"I am a very humane man."

"You are certainly not a modest one."

"I deplore modesty. It is almost always false, you know. I prefer to come out into the open. If I had a poor opinion of myself I should expect others to have the same."

"Because in your case you think you must always be right. Therefore if you were modest—which it is almost impossible to conceive—there would have to be a reason for it. And as that is equally impossible, you could never be modest."

"It seems a little involved but I imagine your reasoning is correct, Miss Annalice. When we reach Sydney, which we shall do very shortly, I shall want you to come to Cariba to visit me."

"Oh, but I am going to stay with Felicity for a while."

"You know I promised the estimable Miss Cartwright to look after you. I am to book your passage home and to see that you are accompanied by suitable companions."

"There was no mention of a trip to Cariba."

"I want to show you the plantation. Why are you so remote? An ice queen, that is what you are. I believe I have the means of melting the ice, and as queens are women, stripped of their regality they are quite human really."

"I am surprised I seem icy to you. I thought I was being rather friendly."

"You did express gratitude for what I did for Miss Cartwright certainly. Sometimes when I catch you on the deck or elsewhere I fancy I see a little gleam of warmth in your eyes . . . as though they are glad to see me."

"I find you entertaining."

"Indeed? Shall I tell you what I find you?"

"I am sure you are going to, whether I give my permission or not."

"Right again. I find you enchanting."

I was silent and he leaned towards me and taking my hand, kissed it.

"I want you to come to Cariba and stay awhile," he said. "I am not going to lose you. I am determined in that."

"What do you mean?"

"I mean that I am obsessed by you. I am delighted by everything about you. The way you look, the way you talk . . . even your cool manner towards me . . . everything enchants me. This is the most delightful and exciting voyage I have ever made—and I have made many. And why? The answer is clear. It is due to Miss Annalice Mallory."

"I think I should tell you that I am contemplating marriage with someone in England."

"Then the contemplation must cease."

I couldn't help laughing. "You are the most arrogant man."

"It is what you admire so much."

"Who said I admire you?"

"You do. In a hundred ways. Words are not always necessary. You and I . . . together . . . That is how it should be. I'll take you out to the plantation. We'll have a wonderful time together. Never mind this man in England. How can he love you? If he did, he would never allow you to take a trip to the other side of the world without him. Where is he? *I* would not let you out of my sight."

"You are very vehement, Mr. Harrington. I expect you have a wife at home on your island and this is a prelude to some planned seduction."

"I have no wife . . . as yet. But I intend to remedy that."

"Is this a proposal of marriage?"

"You don't imagine I would suggest anything else to a lady of your breeding and character?"

"You are absurd."

"It is maddening on this ship. There are people everywhere. I want to be alone with you. There is nowhere to go. I want to show you what it is like to be really loved."

"I have already told you that I know very well what it is like to be loved. I have been surrounded by loved ones all my life. And now I have already told you that I have an understanding with someone at home who is very dear to me. When I go back I am going to be married."

"I don't believe it," he said.

I shrugged my shoulders. "Your belief or disbelief does not alter the facts."

"I shall not let you go, you know. I am not the man to meet the one person in the world I want to marry and then let her slip away from me."

"You are a very forceful man who is in the habit of getting his own way. I don't doubt that. But this is one occasion when you will not. In view of what you have just said, I think it would be better if you and I saw less of each other."

He laughed. "You are the perfect English Miss at times. I love it. But it is not you really."

He turned to me suddenly and took me into his arms and kissed me violently on the lips. I had never been so kissed before. I tried to push him away and was immediately aware of his immense strength. I was breathless, angry and yet excited.

At length he released me.

"There," he said. "I wish we could be somewhere alone."

"Can you not understand that there are some people in this world who are determined to resist what you think of as your irresistible charms?"

"It strains my understanding too far," he said.

And I found myself laughing with him. I should be angry, I knew, so I tried to simulate anger.

If I were honest I would admit that I was enjoying this. I could not help being flattered that he had singled me out for this attention. Instinct told me he would have had numerous love affairs and I could not—or should not—deceive myself into thinking that he found me different from his conquests. What he was implying now was no doubt a well-tried method.

But although I did not believe in his sincerity, I was attracted in a way in which I had never been to anyone else before. It was purely physical, something I had never felt for Raymond. Though I was perfectly aware that Raymond was the better man.

I said: "I hope you will not repeat this conduct."

"You cannot know me very well if you hope that—but of course you don't hope that. Perhaps you really hope that I will."

"Mr. Harrington, I must ask you to stop this nonsense."

"You sound so formal."

"I want to be formal."

"I admit it has its charms. When you finally admit to your true feelings I shall hear you say, 'I love you, Mr. Harrington.'"

"That is something you will never hear."

"Never is a word it is not wise to use. Often people have to retract. As you will."

"You must be very optimistic to think that."

"You are very sharp with me. But that is what I love."

"You have strange tastes."

"I have the best taste in the world. I have chosen the queen of women, the ice maiden whom I shall melt, to discover beneath the ice the perfect passionate woman—the only one in the world who is worthy to be my mate."

I was laughing again.

"You do find me amusing," he said. "At least that is a start."

"If you were not I should find your conduct most distasteful."

"You don't, my love. You find it very much to your taste."

I saw Felicity coming along the deck towards us.

He said: "The magic moments are over. Never mind. There will be more."

Everything had changed. I could not help thinking about him. He was outrageous, of course. A wise woman would not believe a word of what he said. This was what is called a shipboard romance.

It meant nothing. Did he expect that I was the sort of person who would indulge in a passionate love affair of a few weeks and then say goodbye when we came into port?

But he had talked of marriage. And I could not stop myself contemplating marrying him and going out to his plantation. We should return to England once a year. We should visit Sydney regularly. But it was not that which was important. I thought of him . . . the big man with the overpowering presence; his way of talking; the manner in which he had bewitched Miss Cartwright. There was no other word for it. She had meekly allowed herself to be sent home and had left her niece in the care of a strange man . . . him.

Nothing but a spell could have done that. Yet he had done it.

And now sometimes I felt he had laid a spell on me. I used to lie in my bunk and pretend to be asleep so that Felicity would not intrude on my dreams . . . and they were mostly about him. It was the manner in which he had kissed me and held me to him; it had made me wonder what it would be like to make love with such a man.

I tried to think of Raymond—so calm, so gentle, so chaste. There was nothing chaste about this man. He was the complete opposite of Raymond. I was being disloyal to Raymond by thinking of Milton Harrington. But I could not help it. Continually he intruded into my thoughts.

Soon we should be in Sydney. Should I say goodbye to him then forever? This interlude on the ship would be nothing but a brief incident. It was only because we were on a ship and real life seemed remote that it could have happened. Normality seemed far away. That was it. He had a strong personality; he had an air of authority; and from the first he had singled me out for his attention, which had flattered me, for after all, I was only human. I liked attention, to think that I was attractive. It was all very understandable. So . . . I must stop thinking of him and remember the purpose of my journey which Raymond had so kindly helped me to arrange.

Raymond! I must keep Raymond in mind. I must do what I had come out to do. Leave no stone unturned to discover what had happened to Philip; and when I had the answer I would return to Raymond.

We were fast approaching the end of our voyage. Within two days we should be in Sydney.

Felicity was now in a state of extreme nervousness.

She said: "Promise me you'll stay with me for a little while."

I wanted to remind her that the purpose of my journey was to find out what had happened to my brother; but in a weak moment, feeling sorry for her, I promised I would stay awhile.

I did remind her that while I was in Sydney I intended to contact the botanist in whose expedition Philip had gone out—if that were possible. He might be able to throw some light on Philip's activities and if the trail led somewhere I must follow it. But at least I would stay for a while. I would go out with her, after her marriage, to her new home . . . perhaps for a week or so. She seemed content with that.

The days now seemed long. Everyone was impatient to get ashore. There was the bustle of preparation on board with its air of expectancy.

I was alone with Milton Harrington the night before the last. It was a warm velvety evening with no wind and the stars, among which I could see the Southern Cross, standing out clearly against the darkness of the midnight blue sky.

"A very short time now," he said.

"Everyone is longing to get ashore."

"Not I," he said. "I should like to sail on with you forever."

"That is a very romantic sentiment and hardly credible."

"You make me feel romantic."

"I should have thought nothing could have done that."

"You think I am too earthy for romance?"

"Perhaps."

"There is so much you have to learn about me."

"There is so much to learn about everybody."

"And sometimes the lessons can be boring. It would be different with us."

"Are you ready to leave? Packed and so on?"

"I am not ready to leave you."

"The sky is so beautiful. The stars look very near."

"We have wonderful skies in Cariba. You will enjoy them. In fact, you will enjoy a great deal about Cariba."

"You must be longing to get back to your paradise."

"No paradise on earth is perfect. Something is always needed to make it so. I have found that someone . . . "

"And has she agreed to go with you?"

"Not in so many words. But I read her thoughts."

"You are clairvoyant then? Another of your accomplishments?"

He took my hand. "She really does want to be with me as much as I want to be with her . . . or almost. She is rather prim at times. Her upbringing. You know these old English families. But she doesn't deceive me."

"But perhaps you deceive yourself. Unless of course you are talking of someone whom I don't know."

"You know of whom I speak. There could only be one."

"I am surprised that you consider her worthy of you."

"I never thought I should find one who was."

"But you don't accept the impossible."

"No never. How well you have summed me up!"

"Do let us be sensible."

"I'm never anything else."

"This senseless pursuit of me . . . The voyage is nearly over. It was to be an amusing interlude, wasn't it? To pass the monotonous days at sea? Well, it is nearly over. You did not succeed in seducing me, which I believe was your motive. Admit it."

"I won't deny it."

"You are shameless."

"The seduction was to have been a prelude to a lifelong love affair."

"Your conversation is as extravagant as your ideas."

"Shall we be serious for a while?"

"I should prefer that."

"Then I will speak with the utmost seriousness. I cannot say goodbye to you in Sydney. I want you to come and visit my island. Cariba is a beautiful place. You have no doubt pictured it as a desert island with palm trees, sandy beaches and natives in canoes. It is all of that but also a flourishing community. We have made it that with the exportation of sugar. We have utilized the natural resources of the island. It is not small—quite large in fact, as such islands go. It is the largest in a group of four. We have our docks and a reasonably good hotel. Sugar has made the island rich and the people there are sensible enough to know it. I want you to come and visit us."

I hesitated.

"I have a large house on the plantation. I should like you to stay there. But if that would not be agreeable to you, there is, as I said, a reasonably good hotel. Promise me you will come."

"I can't make any promises."

"What a stubborn woman you are."

"You see how undesirable I really am."

"No. I even love your stubbornness. I am so besottedly in love with you that I think everything about you is perfect."

"I have promised to stay with Felicity for a while."

He nodded. "You won't want to stay long, I imagine. Do you know, you haven't told me very much about yourself . . . about your family. All I know is that you are travelling out with Miss Felicity to keep her company on the voyage."

"Nor have you told me of yourself."

"I will tell you when you come to Cariba. I do know that you live with your grandmother and I presume your parents are dead."

"My mother is. My father married again and settled in Holland."

"I want to know all about you. I always think of you as Annalice. My Annalice . . . the unusual girl with the unusual name. Annalice Mallory. There is a well-known firm of map makers with the name of Mallory."

"That is my family."

"Well then, you must be . . . ."

"Yes?"

"A young man from that family came out to Cariba . . . I've just remembered . . . It must have been about two years ago. Now what was his name . . . ? I am almost sure it was Mallory and he was connected with maps."

My heart was beating very fast. I could scarcely speak. "Philip . . . Was it Philip?"

"Philip Mallory . . . Yes, I believe it was."

"And he went to Cariba?"

"Yes . . . he was there some time, I think."

My throat was dry. I was at a loss for words. To think that he had seen Philip more recently than I had; and all this time when we had been indulging in frivolous conversation he might have given me this vital information.

"What happened to him?" I asked.

"I don't know. He was just there . . . and then he must have gone."

"He was my brother," I said.

"Your brother. Of course. Mallory . . . I had forgotten all about him until this moment."

"Please tell me all you know about him."

"You surely know more than I do."

"What happened to him? He never came home. What did he do? What was he doing on the island?"

"Wait a minute. It's coming back . . . I believe he had a map and was trying to find a certain place which no one seemed to know anything about. I only remember vaguely. I was not much interested in him. We get so many people on the island with plans for this and that."

"Please try to remember everything you can about him. It's very important to me."

"I only met him on one occasion. It was in the hotel. He was staying there, I suppose. I didn't see him again. That's all I know."

"So he was at Cariba!"

"Yes, he was definitely there."

I was stunned. Here was a clue, though a flimsy one. And to think that Milton Harrington, with whom I had been in close contact over the last weeks, should have been able to tell me this and I had not discovered it until now, was astounding.

So Philip had stayed in the hotel on Cariba. There might be hotel staff who remembered him, who could perhaps tell me something.

I felt a great excitement. I had not yet arrived at Sydney and already I had made this discovery.

"You will come to Cariba," said Milton Harrington.

"Yes," I said firmly, "I shall come to Cariba."

I was leaning over the rail with many others as we came into the harbour. What a magnificent sight it was! I could well believe it was what its first governor had declared it to be: "the finest harbour in the world." On one side of me was Felicity, on the other Milton Harrington. He had taken my arm and held it against his side. I wanted to protest but I felt I could not call attention to ourselves with so many people looking on. I was sure he was aware of this and that it amused him.

Felicity was looking nervous, and I myself was not thinking so much of the coves and beaches and the luxuriant foliage as of Philip's arrival here with the botanical party; and I was wondering what the next weeks were going to reveal to me.

I had already decided that there must be people in the Cariba hotel who would remember him. I must meet them and talk to them. As soon as Felicity was married and I had honoured my promise to stay with her for a week or so, I would go to Cariba.

I understood that a ship left for the island every Wednesday and when I arrived I could be sure of being welcomed by Milton Harrington. Certainly I should not accept the offer to stay in his house, but there was the hotel; and it was the hotel in which I was interested because Philip had stayed there.

We were coming into dock now. Very soon we should land.

"What a sight!" whispered Milton. "Are you impressed?"

"Who could fail to be?"

"Wait until you see Cariba. I shall be looking out for you."

"There is a hotel, you tell me."

"You will be more comfortable in Harrington Hall. Do you like the sound of that?"

" 'Apt alliteration's artful aid,' " I quoted.

"Indeed yes. And does it not sound like an old English country mansion? When we finally go home and choose our estate, let's name it that."

A group of people had gathered on the dockside. They were clearly waiting for arrivals.

I looked at Felicity. "Is your William there?"

Anxiously she was peering at the crowd.

She said: "It's too far away yet. I can't see."

"He'll be there I expect."

She shivered.

People were now returning to their cabins, ready to collect their hand luggage and leave.

"We had better go," I said.

Milton Harrington released my arm and we all left the deck.

A man was coming towards us, his hat in his hand, a smile on his face.

Felicity said in a small voice: "It's William."

"Felicity at last!" He embraced her. "I thought you'd never get here."

Felicity said: "William, this is Miss Annalice Mallory."

He gripped my hand so hard that it hurt. "I've heard all about you. Welcome to Sydney."

There were pouches under his faintly bloodshot eyes. He looked at me as though he were assessing me for a purpose which made me feel slightly uncomfortable. He was rather fleshy but of a fair height; he looked to me like a man who might be given to self-indulgence.

Felicity explained: "Aunt Emily left at Cape Town. She became so ill, she had to go home."

"Poor old lady!"

"And this is Mr. Milton Harrington who has been so kind and helpful to us."

"We've met before," said Milton.

"Of course. In the hotel . . . among the graziers. From the islands, aren't you? Sugar?"

"That's right. I've been to England on business and had the pleasure of meeting the ladies on board ship. I suppose you'll be leaving Sydney soon for the property?"

"We shall be here for a short time. We'll get married here. It's simpler. I've booked us into the Crown. I thought that was most suitable."

"Yes, indeed."

"What about our baggage?" asked Felicity.

"I expect you have trunks?"

"Naturally there was a great deal to bring with me."

"Naturally. Don't worry. I'll arrange for it to be sent direct to the property when it is unloaded. You'll manage with what you have with you while we're in Sydney, and when you get to your new home you'll find it all waiting for you." He turned to Milton. "I suppose you will have to wait until Wednesday. It is Wednesday, isn't it, for the Cariba boat?"

"That's so. But I might stay a little longer in Sydney." He smiled at me. "I have things to do."

"We'll take a buggy to the hotel," said William Granville. "It's not very far."

I was too excited to take much notice of the city then. I felt very unsettled. I could not imagine what could have possessed Felicity to accept this gross man. It was clear to me that she was not in love with him—far from it. But it was her decision and no concern of mine. She had agreed to it so presumably it was what she wanted. I was thinking that I should soon have to say goodbye to Milton Harrington and I was not quite sure how I should feel about that. I should miss not having to avoid him, not indulging in those verbal battles—which I believe were quite a pleasure to us both. It was all going to be rather strange.

But I would come back to Sydney and get on that Wednesday boat out to Cariba, and I expected that while I was there, making enquiries about Philip, I should see something of Milton Harrington. I might as well admit that I should look forward to that.

But I could not curb my anxiety concerning Felicity. She was on the verge of marriage with a man for whom she did not care; and now I had seen him I could understand why. What on earth had possessed her to agree to marry him? Why did she feel that just because she had been jilted by this other man, she had to take the very next one who came along? Was she afraid of growing into a spinster and becoming like Miss Cartwright? It was madness and I had a very strong notion that she was regretting it now. But even at this hour it was not too late. She was not married yet.

We went through narrow winding streets into a busy thoroughfare and in due course arrived at the hotel. It was spacious with red velvet curtains and rich red carpets and a great deal of brass.

I noticed that Milton Harrington was treated with great respect by the staff of the hotel who seemed to know him well. He whispered to me: "I'm a good customer. I always stay here when I am in Sydney." He went on in a louder tone: "Shall we all meet before dinner for an aperitif?"

William Granville said that would be an excellent idea.

So it was arranged and we were taken to our rooms. Mine and Felicity's were next door to each other.

I looked round mine. The furniture was large, the ceiling was high and there was a window which looked out on the street. The furnishings were similar to those in the reception hall—heavy red velvet curtains caught back by thick bands of brass. There was an air of cleanliness about the place which was pleasant.

I felt a little bewildered. Here I was, miles from home, bent on carrying out a rather vague mission and very much aware of moving towards a climax for which I had not bargained. First there was Felicity. Her wedding was imminent, and I could not help feeling alarmed at the prospect of what was going to happen to her. I had taken an instant dislike to her bridegroom. There was much about him that I did not trust. He looked . . . what was the word . . . ? Debauched? No, that was a little too strong, but somewhere near it. I thought his glance at me had been offensively bold . . . but only slightly. He had been pleasant enough outwardly. He had seemed to be delighted to greet Felicity. Was I seeing him clearly? How unwise it was to judge people on one meeting! So there was Felicity to stir up my apprehension; and of course, Milton Harrington. I was annoyed because that man kept coming into my thoughts. He was a born intruder, always where he was not wanted. Or was he wanted? Why did I feel faintly depressed because soon he would be taking that Wednesday boat?

I must forget these side issues and remember my mission. I was here to find out what had happened to Philip; and when I had the answer I would go home and marry Raymond and live in peace.

I unpacked my small case, washed and changed, and when I had done that, Felicity was knocking on my door.

"Oh . . . are you ready?"

"Yes, come in. How is your room?"

"Just like this one."

"It seems very comfortable."

This was small talk because we were afraid of saying what was on our minds.

"William seemed very pleased to see you here," I said, banally.

"Yes," she answered.

"You're going to find it all very exciting."

She nodded unconvincingly.

I put my arm round her and kissed her. She clung to me for a moment.

"You're coming out to the property with us, aren't you?"

"If you want me to . . . for a little while. But I dare say William won't want an intruder on his honeymoon."

"You promised to come."

"I know and I will . . . for a week or so. You'll be settled in by then."

That seemed to comfort her.

There was a knock on the door. It was a maid who said she had come to take us down to the gentlemen.

I awoke next morning to brilliant sunshine streaming into my room.

I lay still for a few moments reminding myself that I was in Sydney and my quest had begun. This morning I would see if I could find David Gutheridge. I remembered that there had been talk of an Australian Botanical Association. David would certainly have been in communication with them. Who knew, I might have the astounding good luck to find him there now.

In any case it would be a start.

My thoughts drifted back to the evening. We had had our aperitif and then dined off great steaks which seemed to have been enjoyed by the men; both Felicity and I found them far too much.

"We have big appetites in Australia," said William Granville. "It is due to being so much out of doors."

I noticed he drank with relish and as he did so there was a change in him. He took Felicity's hand, patting it and placing it on his thigh. Felicity looked decidedly uncomfortable.

Milton Harrington took charge of the conversation and talked about Australia at great length and I learned that William Granville had been here for twenty years. I gathered that he was about thirty-eight although he looked much older.

"The first thing you ladies must do tomorrow," said Milton, "is to buy big shady hats. That is so, is it not, Granville? We can't have them ruining their delicate skins. I tell you, this Australian sun will wreak havoc with your complexions."

"We'll go shopping tomorrow, Annalice," said Felicity.

I found the evening embarrassing and Milton Harrington knew that I did. I was very glad to get to my room. I thought Felicity might come in after we retired but she did not. I was glad. I wanted to comfort her, of course, but there was really nothing I could do except advise her to go back to England with me.

But how could I? The decision was hers.

However, here I was in Sydney where I had dreamed of being. I chided myself for almost forgetting the reason why I was here because I was getting myself involved in side issues.

When I was dressed, I knocked at Felicity's door.

She was still in bed. "I've got a headache," she said. "I'll stay in bed a little while, I think."

"You could have something sent up. I'll go down and see about it."

She looked at me appealingly and I thought she was going to say something about changing her mind. I did not prompt her. I believed I must leave her to confide when she wished to.

I went downstairs and asked them to send some coffee and bread and butter up to her, and I sat down and had the same myself. The waiter seemed disappointed that I did not order steaks—which quite a number of people were eating.

When I had finished I asked at the desk if they could give me the address of the Australian Botanical Association and was told without hesitation that it was in George Street.

How could I get there? I asked. Did I need a conveyance? No, I was told, it was only about ten minutes' walk from the hotel.

I was given instructions how to get there. I went back to my room hoping that I would not meet either William Granville or Milton Harrington on the way. I did not want to explain my intentions; and now that I was on the trail I was all eagerness to begin.

The morning air was invigorating. It would be hot later I did not doubt. I thought about Milton's advice to get big hats to protect us. Our town ones would certainly be inadequate.

Later, I thought. First David Gutheridge.

I found the Botanical Association with the utmost ease. There was a brass plate on the door. I went in. A man at a desk looked at me brightly.

"Good morning," I said. "I wonder if you could help me. I want to get into touch with Mr. David Gutheridge."

He looked puzzled. "I don't think we have anyone here of that name."

"No, you wouldn't have. He came out from England almost two years ago. He is a botanist and I think he must have been in touch with this office at some time. I wonder if you could give me an idea of where I might find him."

"In connection with an expedition which came out from England some two years ago, you say. If you wait a moment, I will see if there is anyone who can help you. Do sit down."

I sat down and waited, feeling rather sick with excitement, wondering if I were on the verge of discovery.

After a while the young man came back.

"Will you come this way?"

I rose and followed him. He paused before a glass door, opened it and stood aside for me to enter.

A man rose from a desk.

"Good morning."

We shook hands.

"I understand you are enquiring about Mr. David Gutheridge."

"Yes. I know that he came out here on an expedition some time ago."

"It is about two years."

"Yes, that's so. I thought this might be his headquarters and I was wondering if you could give me his address."

"He does have his mail sent here, but at the moment he is not in Sydney."

"You know where he is?" I asked excitedly.

"We never know where people are when they are on these expeditions. They plan to go to some place and get side-tracked and decide to go off in another direction. I know that he was going to Queensland at one time and from there to the Barrier Reef. Some of those islands have flora that you find nowhere else."

"Oh." I was disappointed.

"He has been gone some six months," he said. "We did hear recently that he was on the mainland . . . so it may well be that he will be here before long."

"What do you mean by before long? A week . . . two weeks . . . ?"

"Oh I should hardly think so. I imagine a month at the earliest."

"A month!" I felt deflated. But at least they knew him. It was a little step forward.

"When he does come will you tell him that I called. And will you ask him to get into touch with me. I may be at this property . . . If not I will give you a change of address. The property is some miles out of Sydney and I shall be staying there with friends."

"Certainly I will."

"My name is Miss Mallory."

"Oh . . . any relation to the map people?"

"It is my family."

"We had a Mallory out here from England . . . Yes . . . he came, of course, with David Gutheridge."

"That was my brother. It is he with whom I am trying to get into touch. Do you know whether he stayed in Sydney or when he left?"

"I'm afraid I don't. He did come in here once or twice with Mr. Gutheridge. And then we didn't see him any more."

"Thank you," I said. "You have been very kind."

"I'll make sure Mr. Gutheridge knows you called . . . just as soon as he gets back. And that's the address. Goodo. I'll make a note of it. Don't worry. As soon as he comes in he'll get the message."

I came out into the sunshine.

A start. Not a very propitious one. But a start.

When I returned to the hotel the first person I met was Milton Harrington.

"You've been out," he cried. "You've stolen a march on us."

"It is pleasant in the early morning. It will be hot later."

He looked at me intently. "You've got something on your mind," he said.

I shrugged my shoulders.

"Tell me. Perhaps I can help."

I shook my head. "It's nothing. Where are the others?"

"The bridegroom, I imagine, is sleeping a little late. The bride-to-be likewise. That leaves us free. I suggest a little ride round the city. I'm rather proud of it. It's come a long way since the first fleet came out here, I can tell you. Come on. We'll take a buggy."

I allowed myself to be hustled into one. I was still thinking of David Gutheridge who might provide the key to the mystery.

It was a happy morning. Milton showed me the harbour as we drove in and out of the coves; he took me through narrow winding streets which had once been tracks, and he told me something of the city's history, and I was wondering how those people who had arrived here with the first fleet had felt when they stepped ashore on the land which was to be their home for the rest of their lives.

I forgot my disappointment at not finding David Gutheridge. He would return and perhaps have something to tell me. I realized that when I was in the company of Milton Harrington I became an optimist. I caught his belief that everything was possible; something of his ebullient nature was passed on to me.

We stopped at a store and bought a sun hat for me, and I chose one for Felicity in a shade of pale lavender which I thought would suit her.

"Now," said Milton, "I can quieten my fears. The beautiful complexion is safe from the enemy."

"It seems an odd way of describing the sun—the life-giver to us all on this planet."

"Ah. A good friend but a bad enemy. That is the nature of life. The sea. Fire. Great friends and at times implacable enemies."

"It doesn't say much for friendship if it can turn like that."

"Why is it, Miss Annalice Mallory, that whenever I am with you you turn the lightest discourse into a psychological discussion?"

"I'm sorry," I said. "I suppose I can be rather pedantic."

"You can never be anything but fascinating. How soon shall I see you in Cariba?"

"I don't know. I shall not stay long on this Granville property."

"No. I am sure you will not want to do that."

"I am a little uneasy about Felicity. If you know anything against this man I think she ought to know."

He was silent for a moment as though grappling with himself, which was unusual for him. He was usually so sure.

"She sees him for herself," he said at length.

"He drank quite a lot last night, but he was sober."

"He is accustomed to it and he can, as they say, take his drink. What effect it has, I don't know. I doubt that he stopped drinking when we left him. He would continue in the privacy of his own bedroom, I imagine."

"Don't you think Felicity should be told?"

"It is always difficult in such circumstances to know whether one should tell or not. I think Felicity is able to see for herself. It may be that she is in love with the fellow. Love is blind. We all have to work out our own lives, you know."

"When they are married it will be too late. I can't help feeling she is making a mess of her life."

"My dear Annalice, that is for her to decide."

"You don't think . . . "

"I think you should stop worrying. Let her make her own decisions. Everyone has a right to do that. Go with her and see her settled in. Think a little more about yourself . . . about us. And as soon as possible come to Cariba. Every Wednesday the boat sails. I shall be watching . . . and waiting . . . "

I laughed at him. But oddly enough those words gave me comfort.

INTERLUDE
IN A DARK HOUSE

We were on our way to the Granville property. Events had moved quickly, and now I sat in one of the much publicized coaches of Cobb and Company which was carrying me away from the city and into what I learned was the "outback."

Felicity was now Mrs. Granville; she seemed to have shut herself away since her marriage, which was only of a few days' duration. It was hard to understand what she was feeling. Moreover Milton Harrington had gone back to his sugar island and had left an emptiness behind. While he had been around my uneasiness had abated a little. It came back in full force after the Wednesday boat had sailed.

The wedding had been quiet and brief. There were many such weddings in Sydney; brides coming out to join husbands, and the object was to get the ceremony over as quickly as possible.

There was an absence of family for one thing; and usually only a few friends attended. The sort of wedding with white dresses, orange blossom and bouquets would have been out of place here.

So now here I was, jolting along in the coach with Mr. Granville and his new bride and six other passengers, for the coach carried nine. Our driver was a cheery little man.

We had left the city and the magnificent harbour behind and were now in the open country. The roads were rough and I was struck by the tall eucalyptus trees with which I was now becoming familiar, and I wondered how long they had stood there. Perhaps even before the coming of Captain Cook. The coach rocked dangerously, but the other passengers, with the exception of Felicity, seemed to take that for granted.

Felicity wore an expression of resignation, as though she could no longer be surprised by anything. I pondered what that meant. I rather wished she would talk to me as she had before her marriage because that would be good for her.

The Granville property was a day's coach ride from Sydney and it was still light when we arrived at Lalong Creek. They called it a township. It was a road with an earth pavement, an inn, a few shops and a scattering of houses. The coach pulled up at the inn where the horses were to be changed—and here was our journey's end.

My heart sank. This was our nearest town, and I could not imagine that we should want to come here frequently.

As the coach approached the inn, a man in a straw hat and corduroy trousers and a brown shirt rose lazily from the bench outside the inn and spat out a quid of tobacco.

I glanced at Felicity. She looked impassive with that air of resignation which implied that she must accept everything, however unpalatable.

"Oh, there is Slim," said William Granville. "Got the buggy there, Slim?"

"Yes, Master. Been waiting here the last hour."

"Good. We'll get away at once."

We dismounted, rather stiff from our long ride.

Slim had left us and when he came back he was driving one of those conveyances they called buggies—a light, four-wheeled vehicle, drawn by a grey horse.

"We shall not be long now," said William Granville. "We have about five miles to go."

He helped us into the buggy and stowed in the hand luggage we had brought with us. He seated himself on one side of the buggy, beside Felicity. I sat opposite. I found it embarrassing because every time I looked up his eyes were on me. I noticed a certain sardonic expression in them. I expected I had conveyed my disapproval of him.

Then we left the township for the drive to the Granville property.

The country seemed stark and so alien from home. In comparison our trees and meadows looked as though they had been tended by gardeners; this was wild country. Some of the tall trees had grey barks which gave them a ghostly look.

"They look like ghosts," I said, feeling some comment was needed.

"We call them ghost gums," William Granville told me. "The abos won't go past them after dark. They think they are the ghosts of men who have died violently and can't rest. You're thinking how different it is from home, eh?" He put his arm round Felicity and pressed her to him. I was not sure whether she winced or not.

"You girls are good horsewomen, I hope," he said.

"I enjoy riding," I said. "I believe Felicity does too."

Felicity nodded.

"You'll find horses to ride in the stables. You'll have to take care not to get lost. You get out there and you can go round and round in circles. One of the easiest things you can do here is get lost."

He subsided into silence. I looked at the scenery, at the clumps of bushes; here and there feathery wattle bloomed; I could smell its fragrance. We called it mimosa at home and ever after when I smelt that unusual haunting perfume I was reminded of that drive.

"Better speed up a bit, Slim," said William Granville. "Want to get there before nightfall."

"Yes, Master," replied Slim, and put the horse into a gallop.

I was thrown forward and William Granville put out his arms to catch me. For a few seconds he held me so that my face was close to his. I could smell the whisky and found the contact most repulsive.

I hastily disengaged myself.

"It's a rough ride," he said. "Better slow down a bit, Slim. You're making the ladies uncomfortable."

He grinned at me. I was silent.

The horse went splashing through a creek. Some of the dirty water was on my coat. I brushed it off with a handkerchief.

"Steady, Slim. You're splashing the lady, now."

I felt he was laughing at me, that he disliked me in a special sort of way and enjoyed humiliating me; and I thought, As soon as I can leave here, I will.

It would soon be dark. The sun was low on the horizon and I understood that in this part of the world there would not be our long twilight. Darkness came swift and sudden.

There was a grandeur about the landscape which I should have enjoyed in different circumstances, but the farther I went from Sydney, the more uneasy I became.

He said: "We're on my land now. All this is mine. And there are acres and acres of it. One thing that is cheap here is land . . . well land and labour. People came out to make their fortunes. There was the gold rush. There is wool . . . all this grazing land. They come out here and they don't always make it. Then they've got to do something. That's where we get our cheap labour."

We jogged on. It was almost dark now and we were there.

"Here it is. Your new home, my bride. What do you think of it? Not like your old homestead, is it? No fancy mansion which has stood for hundreds of years. No mullioned windows, Palladian columns and the like. Here they build houses to live in for a while . . . not to last five hundred years. You'll get used to it."

We had drawn up before the house. He helped us alight and we stood there looking at Felicity's new home.

It had two storeys with several outhouses attached and the wood was a dirty grey colour. The paint was peeling off the door and there were dark patches on the wood. Above the porch there was a balcony, and I noticed at once that some of the staves were broken away. There were glass doors leading onto this balcony.

The door opened and a woman stood there. I imagined she was in her early thirties. She had very thick dark hair which she wore piled up high on her head in a rather elaborate knot; her eyes were long, narrow and slanting, which gave her an almost oriental look. She was tall with large hips and bust and a small waist. She was very striking but in some way I felt repelled. Her eyes were on me and with a flash of intuition I realized that she thought I was the new Mrs. Granville, and there was a certain malevolence in her gaze.

I felt an urgent need to correct her.

"Here we are at last, Mrs. Maken," said William Granville. "This is Mrs. Granville and her friend, Miss Mallory. Mrs. Maken helps to keep things in order here, don't you Millie? She sees to all my comforts."

I felt the phrase was significant and because of what I was rapidly discovering about Felicity's husband, something in their manner towards each other suggested to me that he was on very intimate terms with his housekeeper.

"Well, come on in," he said.

Mrs. Maken said: "Welcome to Granville's."

"Thank you," I replied. Felicity nodded; she seemed unable to speak. It was now Felicity who had Mrs. Maken's attention, so I was sure my instincts were founded on fact.

We went into a small hall. A door was open. I could see a large kitchen where a big fire was blazing in spite of the heat.

"Food is the first necessity," said William Granville. "We're starving. We've been in that coach all day. It gave us a shaking. The ladies are not used to roughing it, Millie. Straight from the Old Country, they are."

I said: "We had something of a buffeting on the ship coming out."

"Preparation for what was to come," said Mr. Granville. "Well, what about that food, Millie?"

"It's all ready."

"Perhaps we could wash first," I suggested.

"There we are, Millie. The ladies want to wash."

"They'll want hot water," she said. "I'll get Sal to bring it. Shall I take them up?"

"I'll do that. You see to the food."

We went into a room which was large and rather sparsely furnished. There was a lack of comfort perhaps because of the wooden floors and rush mats. William Granville lighted an oil lamp and its light flickered round the already darkening room.

"You're seeing your new home for the first time in the dark," he said. "You're silent, my love."

Felicity said: "I'm very tired."

"Of course, of course. Never mind. You're home now."

We went up a staircase to the next floor.

"This room is the nuptial chamber," he said. I saw the french windows which opened onto the balcony. "Have to keep the windows shut up. Mosquitoes can be a plague. Them . . . and other things. There's a lot you have to get used to in the outback. Well, I'll show you Miss Annalice's room."

It was at the end of the passage. I was glad to be as far away from them as possible.

It was a smallish room, with bare boards, rush mats and a brass bedstead. There was a wash-basin, a cupboard and a chair—and very little else.

"There," he said. "This is where you sleep while you honour us with your presence."

"Thank you," I replied dismissively.

He hesitated, giving me one of those looks which I dreaded and hated.

I looked out of the small window. It was too dark to see much but I could make out some of the outhouses and the bushes in the distance.

A young girl came in with hot water. She could not have been more than fourteen; she was very small and rather scared to see William Granville there—for I was sure she was not frightened of me.

"Thank you," I said to her. I took the water and turned my back on William Granville. I was relieved when he had gone. And I was thinking: How soon can I get away?

Then the thought of leaving Felicity made me very uncertain. I argued with myself: How could she? Surely she could see what he was like. Or had he been different in England? I had the impression that he was a devious man.

When I had washed I went into the passage. I could hear the sound of voices below. I went swiftly to the room which he had called the nuptial chamber. I tapped on the door.

"Who's there?" That was Felicity in a high nervous tone.

"It is I . . . Annalice."

"Oh, come in."

I went in. She looked at me for a moment and I thought she was going to burst into tears.

She came to me suddenly and I put my arms round her and held her close to me.

"It's all right," I said. "It'll be all right. It's dark. Places always look different in the dark. It will be all right in the morning."

"I'm so glad you're here," she said.

I wanted to cry out: "I'm going. I can't stay here. There is something about the place . . ."

I said nothing. I realized how much more strongly she must feel. She was trapped.

I patted her gently and was relieved to see that she was not crying. I wondered how he would have reacted to tears. She must be remembering that she had to face him and that woman downstairs.

We descended together.

Mrs. Maken was standing in the hall. She led us into the kitchen. "This is where we eat," she said. "Though sometimes we eat out of doors . . . Cook out there, too."

On the fire were saucepans and a kettle. William Granville was already seated at a long wooden table which was set at one end of the room, as far away from the fire as possible.

Mrs. Maken ladled out soup for us. It tasted good and we evidently needed it for I felt my spirits reviving a little. Cold beef followed. William Granville ate voraciously. He was rather scornful of what he called our "ladylike appetites."

"The outback will change all that," he said with a look at Felicity.

It was a relief when the meal was over.

"Well," said William Granville. "To bed, I think. We can all do with that."

He put his hand on Felicity's shoulder and smiled at me.

"Off we go."

I lay in my bed from where I could see the window. It was dark, but the stars were bright and they threw a little light into my bedroom.

I thought longingly of the comfort of home, and wished I could rid myself of this increasing uneasiness.

But I could not get Felicity out of my mind. What was happening to her now? I shuddered. She had changed. I kept thinking of her when I had first met her at the Billingtons'. She had appeared to look forward to her marriage then. I supposed the prospect of travelling to the other side of the world had appealed to her, and had seemed adventurous as it would to any girl. And now the reality had to be faced. She seemed to have lost all her spirit. Perhaps the only way she could endure the ordeal of being married to William Granville was to numb her sensibilities. I could well imagine that was necessary.

But what was I doing here? If only Miss Cartwright had remained with us she would have brought a certain normality with her. I wondered what she would have thought of this place, the meal in the kitchen, the voluptuous housekeeper . . .

I must get away. It was easy for me. I could ride into the township and discover at what time the next Cobb's coach left for Sydney. I would go and stay at that hotel for a night or so and on the first Wednesday . . .

How happy I should be to see Milton Harrington again! There was nothing in the world I wanted so much at this moment.

I thought I should never sleep, but I must have been very tired because I did.

I awoke early and for a moment I could not remember where I was. As I looked round the room memories came back and with them that feeling of dread.

But everything seemed easier in daylight.

There was a horse to ride, he had told us. I could explore the countryside. There was a sameness about it and one could get lost easily. I could well imagine that. But one could pick out landmarks. It would be pleasant to ride again.

Perhaps I could talk to Felicity. Perhaps she, too, would decide that she wanted to get away and we could escape together.

I noticed that some of the water which had been brought last night was still in the jug, so I washed with that. I could see that here I should have to dispense with the niceties of comfortable living. I dressed and went downstairs. It was quiet down there. I opened the door and stepped out. The morning freshness was very pleasant. I walked round the house, looking back at it. My eyes went to that wooden balcony with the broken staves; and I tried not to think of what it must be like married to such a man.

As I stood there, I was aware of someone standing close to me.

I turned sharply. It was Mrs. Maken. She must have seen me leave the house and had come up to me very quietly.

"Taking the air?" she said.

"Yes, it's lovely this morning."

"Before the heat," she said, her eyes going all over me, assessing me as it were.

She looked up at the balcony and then gazed sideways at me enigmatically.

Then I heard a laugh such as I had never heard before. It was jeering, almost uncanny.

I looked about me, startled.

Mrs. Maken grinned. "Kookaburras," she said. "Birds, you know. There they go again. There's two of them. They're often in twos."

"It sounds as though they are laughing at us."

"Perhaps they are. Come in and I'll give you some breakfast. There's coffee, if you like it. And I've got some dampers all ready."

I sat at the table in the kitchen.

"It's like a furnace in here when the fire's going," she said. "But we've got to cook though. Mr. Granville likes his food."

"The heat must be unbearable."

"Not much hotter here than outside. We cook out there sometimes . . . just before sundown. That's the best time. The flies aren't such a pest then . . . but the food brings them."

She sat down and, leaning her arms on the table, watched me.

"You'll find it a bit rough going out here. Bit different from the Old Country, I should reckon."

She was smiling at me maliciously.

I thought: Yes, I'll go into that township and find out what time the first coach calls.

During the day I felt a little better. I went for a walk after leaving Mrs. Maken and when I went back, which was about three quarters of an hour later, Felicity was up and William Granville was just about to leave. He would be away all day, he said. "You ladies will have a little time to get your bearings. Millie will show you what you want to know, won't you, Millie?"

Mrs. Maken said it would be a pleasure.

As soon as William Granville had ridden off Felicity's spirits rose a little. The prospect of a day without him must have been a tremendous relief to her.

I suggested that we go and look at what horses were available and perhaps take a ride.

Felicity seemed pleased at the suggestion.

We found horses and were very soon riding from the house. I thought that in other circumstances I should enjoy exploring the country. There was an undoubted grandeur about it. I loved the wattle and the great eucalyptus trees fascinated me, and the wildness had a strong appeal.

"I'd like to ride on and on," I told Felicity.

"You mean as far from this place as possible."

I looked at her swiftly. "You'll get used to it," I said. "It's just that it is strange at first. Shall we see if we can find that township?"

"You mean the place with the inn?"

"Yes. It can't be so very far."

"Do you think you can find it?"

"Yes, I think so. There is a road of sorts. We might follow that and try to remember the way we came last night. I remember one tree which seemed bigger than all the others. There were some grey ones clustered together. Let's try, and hope we don't lose our way."

Felicity looked as though she did not care if we did.

I had meant to broach the subject of my departure but decided I would wait awhile.

"There must be quite a number of people working on the property," I said.

"Yes, I think so. It's so vast. Some of them live in places quite a long way from here. It takes several days to ride all round it."

"I suppose your husband will have to do that, after being away for so long."

She was silent.

I wished she would talk to me. I felt I could be so much more helpful if she did.

A man came riding by.

He said: "Hello there."

I recognized Slim.

I said: "Good morning, Slim. Is this the way to the township?"

"Right. Go straight on, past the clump of ghost gums."

"I remember those from last night's drive. Thanks."

He rode on.

"He was quite pleasant," I said. "They are probably all right when you get to know them."

Felicity said nothing.

"Look!" I cried. "There it is."

"What should we do there?" she asked.

"Explore."

We came to the inn. There was a post outside to which people could tether their horses.

"Are you going in?" asked Felicity.

"Yes."

"Why, do you want some refreshments?"

"No. But I want to make some enquiries."

I opened the door. There were several men sitting about drinking out of tankards. They all looked up as I entered with Felicity behind me.

I ignored them and went up to the man at the bar.

"Could you tell me what time the coach calls here on its way to Sydney?" I asked.

"Can't be sure of times on the road, Miss."

One of the men shouted: "Ten if it's early . . . could be eleven . . . or midday. You never know on the roads."

The men laughed. "Wheels come off," said one of them. "They might have met Ned Kelly's ghost."

They all seemed to think this was a great joke and laughed among themselves.

"No use coming on a Sunday," said one of them. "There's no coach on Sundays. Nor ain't there one on Tuesdays. Mondays there is and Wednesdays and Saturdays. That's the little lot."

"Thank you. You are very helpful."

Again they seemed to find the situation very amusing.

We came out to our horses. Felicity was silent until we were riding away when she said: "You're going, aren't you?"

"Well, I wasn't supposed to stay, was I?"

"I did not think you would go so soon."

"I haven't gone yet. I just wanted to know about the time of the coaches."

"They would have known at the house."

"I just thought I should like to enquire for myself."

"Those horrible men . . . " she began.

"They weren't so bad really. They did tell us what we wanted to know. I expect you get used to them in time. It is just their manners that are different."

"I don't think I shall ever get used to it here."

"Oh, you will."

"Annalice, you won't go home, will you, just yet?"

I hesitated. "It may be that I shall not be wanted. After all, I am only a visitor."

"I think . . . my husband . . . quite likes you."

"Oh, I hadn't noticed that. I expect he won't want me to overstay my welcome."

"Promise you won't go . . . yet."

I was silent. "You know I came out here because I wanted to find out about my brother."

"Yes, I know."

"I'll never find out anything here."

"Just for a little while . . . And you won't go without telling me, will you? I couldn't bear it if I woke up one morning and found myself— alone."

"I promise I won't go without telling you."

We left it at that. She had confirmed the fact that she was very frightened.

A few days had passed. I was beginning to know something about my surroundings, and the more I discovered, the more I longed to get away.

Many times I was on the point of telling Felicity that I must go. Then I remembered that I had been glad enough to use her journey out as a means of getting away. Now I could not desert her when she needed me. Only what I could do to save her from the man she had married, I did not know. It was just that I was company during the day.

I was growing accustomed to the hot midday sun; the swarms of flies which came from everywhere to pester us; the smell of cooking steaks. They seemed to live on steaks. They were part of the scene with the heat of the fire, the cooking dampers—a sort of leavened scone which they baked in the ashes—the hungry-looking dogs which prowled about and looked so ferocious until they got to know us. I was always taking scraps out to them so that after a while they positively fawned on me. There were lots of men about; they all had sunburned faces and wore straw hats—some of them with corks attached to them to keep off the ever-present flies. Sometimes the men would come to the house; or they would sit about outside or in the kitchen playing cards and drinking ale. There was much coming and going. There were sheep on the property—millions of them it seemed, because William Granville was "in wool."

Often, as Mrs. Maken had said, they cooked out of doors. They had great pails stuffed with paper and the meat was cooked on a grill over this; the fat from the meat kept the paper continually burning—and in any case they ate their steaks half raw. They sang songs: "Botany Bay" and something about a kangaroo; and when they saw us they assumed a somewhat jeering attitude which I believe was half resentment, half admiration.

William Granville was often with them. They would sit outside in the evenings and I could hear them from my room. They would laugh and talk in loud voices, often breaking into song—and drinking all the time.

I would lie in bed listening to them, telling myself that I was going to catch the next coach to Sydney. I would stay at the hotel till Wednesday and then I would take the ship to Cariba.

But when the morning came and I saw Felicity I knew I could not leave her just yet.

I had been here a week. It seemed like a month. I went out riding a great deal. Felicity always came with me. Often I thought she was on the verge of confiding in me; but she never did. I had made up my mind that I would tell her I must go and if she hated it so much she must come with me.

I was not sure of the wisdom of advising a wife to leave her husband.

Meanwhile I was rather fascinated by the country. It was one of contrasts. There was so much that was beautiful. I gasped with pleasure when I saw the flame trees with their bright coral-coloured flowers and a flight of the grey rose-crested cockatoos which they called galahs. That was sheer beauty. Then there were the miles and miles of scrub land and the swarms of insects unlike anything we had ever encountered at home, like the hairy nannies, little centipedes which came into the house—and the interminable flies. Millie Maken went about watchfully, silent-footed and resentful of us, I believed; but what I disliked most was the presence of William Granville.

It was a night when I had completed my week. The men were outside drinking and talking. I could hear the sudden bursts of laughter. It was almost midnight.

I always felt uneasy until I heard William Granville go to the room he shared with Felicity, and it was only some little time after the door shut on him that I felt safe to sleep. There was no key to my door and I was afraid that he might come into my room.

He lumbered up the stairs, muttering to himself, so I guessed that he had been drinking more than usual.

I heard the bedroom door shut behind him. I lay there telling myself again that surely now I could begin to plan my departure and I came to the decision that I would speak to Felicity in the morning.

As I lay there, thinking of what I would say, I heard a door open. I was alert immediately. I got out of bed, waiting.

The doors were ill-fitting and there was a crack at the side through which I could see into the passage. My heart missed a beat. Coming along the passage was William Granville clad in a nightshirt which reached to his knees. I shivered with apprehension. I was ready to defend myself and I thought: Now I shall go in the morning.

He had paused and was opening a door halfway down the passage. It was Mrs. Maken's.

He went in.

I leaned against the door breathing heavily with relief. It was

confirming only what I had guessed already. At least he was not attempting
to come to my room.

So . . . Mrs. Maken was his mistress; hence her resentment at the
intrusion of his wife. This was monstrous. Under the very roof and only
a few doors from that room in which his wife lay!

"The man is a monster," I said to myself.

It was no use trying to sleep. I wrapped a dressing gown round me
and sat by the window.

The bright starlight gave a weird look to the country. I could see
grey eucalypts in the distance—like ghostly sentinels.

I must do something, I thought. I have to go, but I can't leave
Felicity unprotected.

Then suddenly I had an idea.

I took out writing paper and pen. It was just light enough for me to
be able to see.

I wrote:

"Dear Raymond,

"I am very anxious. There is something very wrong here. This marriage was a great mistake. It is not just a matter of fitting into a new way
of life and a new country. Felicity is frightened. And I understand why.

"Life here is crude. Felicity would find it very difficult to adjust
herself even if she had a good husband. But William Granville is a
monster. I know that sounds exaggerated but I do believe it to be so. He is
unfaithful to her. There is a housekeeper here who, I am sure, has been
his mistress and still is. She resents Felicity and at the moment I am
writing this, which must be one o'clock in the morning here, he is with
the housekeeper. I want to leave, but Felicity begs me not to. I don't see
how I can stay here but when I talk of leaving she is almost hysterical.
She has changed a great deal.

"I think something must be done. Raymond, you have been so good.
You have helped me in so many ways. What can be done? Unfortunately
Miss Cartwright had to go home. You will know that by now and Felicity
has no one to protect her from this man she has married. Please help her.
She needs someone to look after her.

"I will stay as long as I can, but life is very awkward here for me in
this house. I am ill at ease with her husband and I find him most
offensive.

"Please Raymond, this is a *cri de coeur.* Advise me what to do. I want her to leave but she has a strong sense of duty. He is, after all, her husband.

"I am writing this in my room, in the dark more or less. There is just enough light from the stars—they are brilliant here—to write.

"I feel desperate. Perhaps I shall feel differently in the morning, but I think I shall post this letter however I feel for I know when night comes I shall wish I had. I want you to know what it is like here.

"Writing to you has made me feel much better. It is like talking to you.

"I have made a little progress in my search. I think I mentioned to you in my letter which I posted in Sydney, that we had met a man named Milton Harrington. Miss Cartwright will have told you about him, I expect. He helped her to get a passage to England from Cape Town. Well, he remembered Philip's staying in a hotel on the island where he has a sugar plantation. It's a place called Cariba. I thought I would go there when I get away from here, but I want first to see David Gutheridge if possible. He is the botanist with whom Philip came out. I called at the Botanical Association's headquarters when I was in Sydney and they knew approximately where he was and when he will be back . . . say in a month. I would really like to talk to him before I go to Cariba. Philip stayed at the hotel there according to Mr. Harrington. There is a hotel on the island. Some of the people there must have known him. So I am making progress . . . but slowly.

"My main worry is Felicity. I wish you were here. You would know what ought to be done.

"It would be wonderful to see you and talk to you. Then everything would seem sane and normal.

"I hope this doesn't sound hysterical. But I really am worried.

"Your loving Annalice."

I sealed the letter.

Tomorrow was Wednesday. One of the days the coach called, and the coach would take the mail to Sydney—and from there it would be shipped to England.

It would be a long time before that letter reached Raymond; but it must go tomorrow and I must be at the inn before ten o'clock. I must not miss the coach.

One of the stockmen took the letters into the township when he collected any that might have come. But I was not going to trust this one to him. William Granville might be curious to see what I was writing about. I could suspect him of opening letters and reading them. I was sure he would stop at nothing.

I went back to bed. There had been no sound in the passage all the time I had been writing and I had been alert, listening. It was clear that William Granville was spending the night with his housekeeper.

Finally I slept.

I awakened early for the events of last night must have been on my mind.

I went downstairs. Mrs. Maken was not there, as she usually was. The fire was out. There was a spirit stove, so I made some coffee and taking one of yesterday's dampers spread a little butter on it.

That would suffice.

Felicity joined me. She looked a little better, I thought. She had been spared the attentions of her husband last night which must have been a great relief. I imagined she would be delighted if he spent his nights with an obliging housekeeper.

I said: "I have a fancy for an early morning ride. I've written a letter and I want to take it into the township. It's Wednesday, so I can catch the coach."

"I'll come with you," she said.

"All right. Be quick and change."

When she came down ready, we set out.

"Why don't you let one of the men take your letter in."

"I want to catch the coach. Goodness knows when it will get there."

"It would only have to wait until Saturday."

"I want it to go at once."

She came into the inn with me. There was a small section of the counter where they collected and dispensed mail. Felicity glanced at the letter as I handed it in. So she knew I was writing to Raymond. Well, there was nothing unusual in that. After all I was engaged to him . . . unofficially, so it was the most natural thing in the world for me to write to him. I wondered what she would have said if she had known what the letter contained.

I felt better when the letter had gone off. The responsibility seemed to have lifted a little, although it would be weeks before Raymond received the letter and more weeks before I could have a reply. But still, I had done something. I had taken action—and that always made me feel better.

We had a stroke of luck that day. One of the jackeroos came to the house at midday. He was one of the young apprentices who was learning the way sheep farming was carried out in Australia and one of his tasks had been to ride round the estate to make sure all was well with the sheep, for these were numerous and the grazing land so extensive that there had to be these occasional round trips to make sure all was in order.

He was a fresh-faced young man—recently out from England—and very eager to learn the business, I should imagine with a hope of owning his own property one day. He had gone off before we arrived in the company of Walloo, an aborigine whose duty it was to instruct the young man. Walloo, I heard later, had been one of the more trusted workers and had been on the property for three years which was a long time for an aborigine. It was said that they all had an inborn urge to wander. They called it "Walkabout"; and suddenly they would leave whatever they were doing and without a moment's notice, wander off and not be seen again for months . . . perhaps never.

Walloo had gone off with this young apprentice and suddenly decided to "walk about." He had left the young man to fend for himself in unknown territory. That was why he had been delayed in getting back.

William Granville was deeply concerned by what he had to tell. The young jackeroo might not know the country but he certainly knew sheep. He had found some of them in urgent need of attention if they were not to perish; moreover more repairs were required to certain fences than he had been able to give them.

Our good luck grew out of this for the result was that William Granville was going off with three of the men and the young jackeroo and he reckoned he would be away for at least a week.

My spirits rose. A week without him! I would be able to put off that agonizing decision for a little while. Meanwhile my letter would be on its way to Raymond.

William Granville had to leave that day and I watched the party set out with joy in my heart.

The change in Felicity was miraculous. She seemed to come alive and I realized how cowed she had been. I dreaded to contemplate what she had to submit to in her marriage.

That night I slept peacefully. No apprehension. No waiting until he was safe in his room.

The next morning we went riding. It was a beautiful day. We skirted the township and made our way to a creek which we had discovered. It was a beautiful spot—an oasis among the scrub. The trickling stream glistened silver in the sunlight and in the distance I could see the clump of ghost gums, looking quite uncanny in the shimmering light.

"I could enjoy all this," I said, "if . . . "

I had spoken without thinking. Felicity went on: "You mean if it were in different circumstances."

I was silent.

"I'd like to explore," I went on. "I should like to find the Blue Mountains and explore them. Bathurst is on the other side. I heard that years ago they used to believe there were evil spirits in the mountains who would never allow people to cross them. And on the other side is Bathurst . . . and wonderful sheep country."

"Yes," said Felicity, "I should like to explore them too."

She was looking wistfully towards the horizon. I had meant to broach the subject of my departure to her when she was a little calmer, but somehow I could not spoil this day . . . our first of freedom. And we had the whole week.

"Perhaps we shall one day," I said.

"You're planning to go though, aren't you?"

She had brought up the subject so we must talk of it.

"Well, I shall have to, shan't I? This is not my home."

"I suppose you'll go back to England and marry Raymond. I think you are the luckiest person in the world."

"You never know how things are going to turn out."

"Annalice, what can I do?"

"About what?"

"About everything. About my life. I can't endure it here. I can't endure . . . him. I didn't know married life was like this. The things that are done . . . I had no idea."

"Do you want to talk about it?" I asked gently.

"I can't bring myself to speak of it. It's unspeakable . . . every night."

"Last night . . . " I began.

"Last night?" she said quickly.

I said: "I know. I heard him come out of your room. He went to Mrs. Maken."

She nodded. "I was glad. I thanked God. Annalice, you have no idea."

"I think I have."

"I never thought . . ."

"It was a rough awakening."

"If I had known. I thought it was beautiful . . . romantic . . . But I never wanted William."

"I know. You told me there was someone else you loved."

"He would never have done these things. Sometimes I think I shall go mad. I just can't endure it."

"Try to be calm. There's a week's respite. Let's think what we can do. We could go into the township tomorrow. The coach leaves for Sydney. We could get on it . . . get out of this place."

"He is my husband, Annalice. I'm married to him."

"That does not mean you have to endure the humiliation he subjects you to."

"But I am married to him."

"Well, what are you going to do? Stay here and endure it?"

"I'll have to. Sometimes I think I'll get used to it . . . and there is Mrs. Maken."

"You would accept that!"

"I have to."

"I wouldn't. I'd walk out. I wouldn't stay another night."

"He would never let me go."

"I would not say that he is besottedly in love."

"He despises me. I think he has from the first."

"Then why . . . ?"

"He came to England to find a wife. He wanted one who was meek and had some money. I suppose I fitted into that."

"Money!" I cried.

"Well, my father left me well provided for. I never thought much about money before. William wants my money, he has plans for improving the property. All this land belongs to him. I am not sure of the boundaries. He wants to clear the scrub. He thinks he might have gold on the land. He wants to prospect for it. You see, I am very useful in a way . . . although in others I am such an ignoramus."

"Oh, my poor Felicity. Now I am sure. You've got to get away. You've got to get help."

I was thankful that I had sent that letter to Raymond. It would be a start. I wished I had known this before. I could have mentioned it to him. I would write another letter—even more urgent than the first.

"Look. There is one thing to do. We'll ride into the township now and book our places on that coach."

"I couldn't go, Annalice. I know he would find me. It would be worse then. He would never forgive me for running away. He'd make sure that I didn't do it again. I'd be a prisoner."

"You're not quite as helpless as that. I can help you. We'll go together."

"It's all very well for you. He can't harm you. Oh, Annalice, you've no idea. When he comes into that bedroom I pray that something awful will happen. Fire perhaps . . . anything to save me from him."

"My dear Felicity, this is terrible. You must be sensible. I'll get you away. You can stay with me and when I find what I want we can go home together."

"You make it all sound easy. Life is easy for you. You are so fortunate. Raymond loves you . . . "

There was something about the manner in which she said his name which told me.

I said: "It is Raymond isn't it, whom you love?"

She was silent for a few moments, then she said: "It was more or less understood. Everyone said that he was just waiting until I grew up. We were always together. There was something special between us. It would all have turned out as they expected, but . . . he met you. He fell in love with you. You are so different from what I am. You are clever and I am rather stupid. But . . . Raymond seemed to like me the way I was. He was always so tender, so protective. It seemed as though it was all working out and then . . . he met you."

I stared straight ahead. I was seeing it all. It fitted in naturally. Poor, poor Felicity! And I was responsible for her unhappiness.

"Oh, Felicity," I said, "I'm sorry . . . so very sorry."

I saw the tears glistening on her cheeks.

"It was not your fault," she said. "I suppose his feelings for me weren't strong enough. It was a sort of habit . . . and he only had to meet you to realize this. If only . . . It would have been so different. And then it all went wrong and now there is . . . William."

"You married him because of Raymond and me," I said. "Oh, Felicity, how could you?"

"I thought I would get right away. If I had stayed there would have been times when I should have had to see you and Raymond together. I don't think I could have endured that."

"What a mess," I said. "An unholy mess!"

"You have been so good to me. I don't think I could have lived through all this without you. I should have taken a horse and ridden off and lost myself . . . or perhaps drowned myself in one of the creeks . . . anything to get away."

"I am more convinced than ever that we should leave here."

"He would find me."

"He wouldn't. The world is a big place. And when we get back to England we can get help. Raymond will help."

"I can't face Raymond."

"What nonsense! He is your friend. He cares a great deal about you."

"He loves you."

"He loves you, too. There is a great deal for you at home. You have suffered a terrible experience, but it is not the end. You're young. You've got the whole of your life before you."

"Annalice, stay with me. I couldn't go on without you."

"Look here. Let us be calm. We have a week to plan. We should not delay. Let us go to the inn and book our places on the first available coach. We'll get to Sydney. We'll go to Cariba on the next ship. Milton Harrington would help us, I am sure. He would know what we should do."

"He is another who is in love with you."

"You talk too lightly of love, Felicity. Milton Harrington is in love with himself—and I imagine it is an abiding passion which would not let anyone else in."

"I think he is in love with you."

"He has been helpful. He wants to help. He would know how best to deal with your case. One thing I know is that if it is horrible for you, you don't have to endure it."

"It's a comfort talking to you."

"It would be more comforting to take some action. Let's go to the inn."

"Not today. Please, Annalice, leave it for today. Perhaps tomorrow . . ."

"I think we should book soon. We might not be able to leave on the first coach. After all they only take nine passengers. What if they were fully booked?"

"I can't decide. Annalice . . . please give me until tomorrow."

"Till tomorrow then. Come on. Let's ride. We have a week. Let's enjoy our freedom."

I might have known that she would continue to hesitate. She was always pleading for time. There was no doubt that she was terrified of her husband; her resigned acceptance of his bestiality amazed me. I pictured myself in her circumstances. I would not have endured it for another day. But then I should never have married him in the first place, for I had been aware of his gross sensuality from the moment I met him. I had no doubt that in England he had been on his best behaviour. He had probably been born and bred in a similar environment to that of Felicity and would know what was expected of him. But he would never have deceived me, I was sure.

His absence had lulled Felicity into a sense of security. She was sleeping well at night and that made a great difference. She no longer lay trembling, waiting for his arrival. But she seemed numbed and unable to act.

I realized that he would not easily relinquish her. He had brought her out here for a purpose—to bear sons and provide the means for developing his land; and he was determined that she should fulfil that purpose.

Perhaps in her mind was the thought that if she became pregnant he would desert her for a while. The housekeeper was waiting to supply his comforts, as he called it. Others too, probably. I had seen one or two women about the place.

It was an insupportable situation and Felicity was a fool to go on enduring it.

I talked to her constantly. Again and again I pointed out how simple it would be to go to Sydney, take the boat to Cariba, and ask the advice of Milton Harrington. He would know what was best to be done. If she wished we might put her on a ship to England. Then she would be perfectly safe. I was here to pursue my enquiries about my brother and would stay. But I had nothing to fear from William Granville.

At one moment she might appear to listen. But always she came up with the excuse: "But he would find me."

And so the days began to pass. Three . . . four . . . five . . . and then I was certain that she would not agree to come. I would eagerly have gone myself but she implored me so earnestly to stay and in view of what she had told me about Raymond, I felt impelled to do so.

He returned late one afternoon. Mrs. Maken had cooked a leg of mutton and made many pies pending his return. The entire household changed. Menace had come back into it.

Many of the workers were at the house that evening. They sat outside eating and drinking.

I went to my room and sat there watching . . . waiting for him to come up.

It was past midnight when he did.

I heard him lumber up the stairs and burst into the bedroom with the balcony.

I could not sleep, thinking of Felicity who had not had the courage to escape when she had the chance.

What would become of her, I wondered.

I thought that one day she might really go out and lose herself or drown herself in a creek.

It could come to that. But she was more likely to fall into the role of acceptance, to bear child after child, to lose her prettiness, to become drab, worn out, without spirit, just accepting, taking for granted the cruel life which had been thrust upon her.

Another week went by. I had been in the house three weeks. It seemed incredible that I could have stayed so long. I wondered whether David Gutheridge had returned to Sydney. Whatever happened I would go soon. I would insist. I would tell Felicity that either she came with me or we must say goodbye.

One Sunday afternoon I heard a great commotion below. I looked out of my window and saw a group of men talking excitedly together.

William Granville came out to them. I heard snatches of the conversation. "Over at Pickering's . . . Bushrangers . . . That's it . . . Only the women there. All the men out working . . . Mrs. Pickering and her two daughters . . ."

"They're only girls . . . Thirteen and fifteen, I reckon."

"The devils," said one man.

"They say there were five of them."

"Five and three women . . . my God."

"Robbed the place . . . took every penny . . . and other things too. They don't know whether Mrs. Pickering will survive. Poor woman . . . seeing her daughters handled . . . by that scum."

"Who are they? Anyone know?"

"Not a clue. Except that it's a gang they think are ranging the country. No woman's safe. That's about it."

I drew back.

What an awful story. I would tell Felicity that we must make plans to leave without delay.

Everyone was talking about the terrible affair over at Pickering's. William Granville rode into the township. When he came back he shouted to Felicity and me to come into the parlour.

The parlour was the big room near the kitchen where the men sat and played cards in the evening . . . when they did not use the kitchen.

On the table were several pistols.

He looked at me sardonically.

"How good a shot are you?"

"Me? I have never had a gun."

"Well, you have something to learn."

He put his hand on Felicity's shoulder. I noticed her suppress the desire to wince. So did he, I think, for he put his fingers inside the neck of her bodice as though to punish her. She stood impassive.

"And you, my love, how good are you with a gun?"

"I'm no good at all."

"Now it may surprise you, but I didn't think you would be!" He shouted: "Well, you're going to learn. You heard what's happened over at Pickering's. There are wicked men around. Bushrangers. They are on the look-out for what they can steal and they have a fondness for people like you. You wouldn't like that . . . You wouldn't like it at all. So you are going to learn to shoot . . . and if any of them come near you you'll have to use your guns. No good being squeamish out here. They would come during the day. There are men around at night. They wouldn't come then. They come when they think there are only women in the place. You show your guns . . . and you shoot if necessary. You understand?"

"Yes," I said. "I understand."

He nodded and grinned at me.

"That's the ticket," he said. "Now what I'm going to do right away is give you some practice. I am going to teach you how to use a gun. I know my dear wife will never learn. She's more likely to be turning it on herself. That, my love, is the barrel of the gun . . . that's where you shoot out from."

Felicity stood impassive.

"Now we are going to practise. Right now . . . without delay. Take one of these each. Now those are yours. They go with you everywhere. When you go out riding or when you're at home. You'll have to have belts to put them in. Never let your gun leave your side till they catch these fellows. And even then there could be more. You have to be ready. Now out. We're going to have a lesson right away."

A piece of metal had been attached to a bush not far from the house and there the shooting began.

Mrs. Maken was with us. She was quite a good shot. All the women were given guns.

I mastered the art fairly quickly, and although I might not be able to hit a bull's-eye at least my shots went into the metal.

William Granville said to me: "Not bad. Not bad at all. Hold it like this. More firmly." His fingers closed over mine. He knew I hated the contact and I was sure that made him enjoy it. There was a sadistic streak in him.

Felicity was aiming wide of the mark. He said sarcastically: "We shall all have to beware when my dear wife has a gun in her hands."

When the first lesson was over, at least I knew how to load and handle a gun.

"You can practise every day," said William Granville to me. "Then you should be quite a good shot."

"Thank you," I said coldly.

And we went into the house. Poor Felicity looked humiliated. He took a delight in making her feel so, and I was sure she was more afraid of him than of bushrangers.

I had become interested and enjoyed practising. I slept with the gun beside my bed so that all I had to do was reach for it. When I went riding I wore it in my belt. It was amazing what a sense of security that gave.

I felt I was becoming quite adequate. I could draw the pistol from my belt and shoot with speed taking aim in a matter of seconds. Felicity was hopeless. She was afraid of the gun as she was of everything else here.

Two days after we had had our first lesson I was practising. The house was quiet. Felicity was sleeping, I thought. She was often exhausted —more due to William Granville, I believed, than the heat.

Someone had come up to stand beside me. I knew it was William Granville and went on shooting.

"Good," he said. "Goodo. You're quite a shot. But then, of course, you would be."

I put my pistol in my belt and turned away.

"You're a fine woman, Miss Annalice," he said. "You'd be more suited to the life out here."

"I do not agree," I replied.

"I thought you were settling in nicely."

"Indeed not. I shall be leaving soon."

"My dear wife implores you to stay, does she not?"

"She has been most hospitable."

"I hope I have been, too. It's my property, you know. I have no desire for you to leave. I like to have you around."

"Thank you," I said, and took a step towards the house.

He stood in front of me, barring my way.

"I wish I had seen you first," he said.

I raised my eyebrows pretending to misunderstand.

"Before my dear wife," he said. "I should have asked you."

"It would have been of no avail."

"Oh, I don't know. We've got a lot in common."

"Nothing at all, I should imagine."

"I like you. You've got spirit."

I took another step towards the house but he caught my arm, and brought his face close to mine. The overpowering smell of whisky sickened me.

I must have shown my feelings, for he squeezed my arm so hard that it was painful.

"Please release me," I said coldly.

He slackened his grip but did not let go.

"You and I could have a lot of fun together," he said.

"I despise you," I retorted. "And I shall take the earliest opportunity of leaving your house."

He laughed. "You won't, you know," he said. "When little Felicity comes crying to you, you'll stay . . . just a day longer . . . then another day . . . I don't mind. It suits me. I think a lot about you. There are a lot of things I should like to show you."

"Keep them for your friends," I said.

I wrenched my arm away and walked into the house. In spite of my outward calm I was very shaken.

Tomorrow, I promised myself, I will ride into the township and book a place on the coach.

I was very uneasy. I had known for some time that he had cast lascivious eyes on me but this was the first time that he had spoken of his feelings.

It was certainly the time to get out.

That night I waited in my bedroom for him to go up to his room. I had my gun ready. It should never leave my side.

I heard his footsteps; and then the door open and shut with a bang.

I breathed with relief. Then I put a chair behind my door so that I should be immediately awakened if he made any attempt to come into my room. I should at least be warned and . . . there was the gun. I decided that I would shoot him in the leg. I should be ready.

I heard the door open. I picked up the pistol, leaped out of bed and peered through the crack in the door.

Someone was in the passage. No. It was not William Granville. It was Mrs. Maken. She went quietly along the passage to the room with the balcony. She opened the door and went in.

What did that mean?

I waited. Five minutes passed. Ten minutes.

Then I understood. She was in there . . . with him and Felicity. This was monstrous. It could not be endured. What sort of orgies was he planning? The man was lascivious, sexually perverted and insatiable.

I must leave. And Felicity must come with me.

I had scarcely any sleep that night. Whatever happened I was going off next day to book my seat on the coach.

The next morning Felicity looked remote—as though she did not belong to this world. I think she was dazed. My imagination failed me. I could not conjecture what might have happened in that bedroom on the previous night.

She could not go on living with such a man. She must see that.

I said to her: "I am going to ride. Will you come with me?"

She nodded.

When we were riding out together, I said: "Felicity, I am definitely going. I cannot stay here any longer."

"I understand how you feel."

"Are you coming with me?"

"I can't, Annalice. I daren't."

"You know I have to go. I can't bear to leave you here."

"I have to stay. I have made my bed, as they say, and I have to lie on it."

"But you don't have to. You could get out of this marriage."

"I can't. I'm caught. I'm trapped."

"There is always a way out. Come with me. I'll book our places this morning, and as soon as we can get out, we'll go."

"I can't."

"I know what's going on here. I'll be frank. It's no time for pretence. I have seen him go into Mrs. Maken's room and last night . . ."

"Oh, Annalice . . ."

"Yes, last night, I saw. She came in to you. She stayed. Oh, Felicity, this is terrible. You don't have to endure that. There could be a divorce. I'm going to ask Milton Harrington what to do. Come with me."

"He'd follow us."

"He wouldn't."

"He would . . . because of the money . . ."

"We could try. If we go to Sydney, we could get that ship to Cariba. Milton Harrington will help us, I know. He is very worldly. He would know what could be done. No one has to go on enduring what you have. It's monstrous. Everyone would agree with that."

"I can't bear to face anyone," she said piteously. "I can't bear to talk about it . . . even to you."

"It's got to stop," I said. "I don't trust him. I'm frightened of him myself. I can't stay under that roof any more nights than are necessary. I'm going to book my place on that coach. Be sensible, Felicity. Let me book for you, too."

"I can't. I daren't. He'd kill me."

"He wouldn't dare."

"He would dare a great deal for money."

"Are you condemning yourself to a lifetime of what you have already tasted? Milton Harrington half warned me against him. He must have an evil reputation for people as far off as that to have heard about him."

"I'm terribly frightened, but I should be more so if he found out I had booked on the coach."

"Why should he find out?"

"People might tell him."

"It's a risk you have to take if you want to get away."

"I can't. I can't."

"Then, Felicity, I shall have to go without you."

"Oh, Annalice, please . . . "

"I have stayed so long. It has to be now. I can't stay any longer. I have to get away."

She closed her eyes. I saw that resigned look come into her face. I found it irritating. I suppose because it was so alien to my nature. I should never accept what was so repugnant to me. I should fight.

Felicity was no fighter.

But I could not give way again. I kept thinking of that man . . . his bloodshot eyes, his whisky-tainted breath. I knew that sooner or later he would turn his attention to me. I was agile; I was quick-thinking. I was strong. But he was stronger.

Resolutely I rode into the township.

I did not look at Felicity for fear I should weaken. We tethered the horses and went into the inn.

At the counter I asked about the bookings.

The Saturday coach was fully booked. There were places on the Monday one.

"What would that be, Miss? Two?"

I looked at Felicity but she shook her head.

"One," I said. "One place on the Monday coach."

I came out into the sunshine, experiencing a great sense of relief, but it was tempered with a sadness and a deep anxiety, because although escape for myself was close at hand, I was leaving Felicity behind.

Two more days and I should be free! Saturday and Sunday—and then Monday. I would get down to the township early so that I should be there in time.

I should have to get Slim to drive me in because of my luggage. He could not refuse.

Felicity looked desperately unhappy. I tried to comfort her but she could only say: "You're going. What will it be like without you?"

"It's not too late," I told her. "There might still be room on the coach."

But she refused.

I was getting my things together. I asked Slim if he would take me into the township early on Monday morning and he said he would do so.

Mrs. Maken said: "So you're leaving us?"

I felt I could scarcely speak to her since I had seen her go into that room with the balcony. I did not blame her so much when I had seen him going into her room, for I had long realized the relationship between those two. But that she should actually go into the room with him when Felicity was there disgusted me.

I said coolly: "Yes, I did not mean to stay long."

"Mrs. Granville persuaded you, no doubt."

"Well, I stayed to be with her, of course."

"What a timid creature she is."

"Everything here is very different from what she has been brought up to," I said.

"Well, the outback is no place for you ladies."

I went up to my room to continue with my packing. After tonight only one more to get through, I kept telling myself. I was longing to get to Sydney. I should arrive in the evening. On Tuesday I would go to the Botanical Association and then I should book myself in on the Wednesday boat for Cariba.

I had to admit the prospect of seeing Milton Harrington again excited me. I should be able to tell him about what was happening here. I was not going to abandon Felicity. I had to help her even if she would not help herself and I believed that Milton Harrington might have some suggestion to make.

It was just like any other Saturday night, though the merrymaking out of doors seemed more riotous than usual. It was midnight when they dispersed and went off to their own quarters. I heard William Granville come up to bed.

I waited, listening. He went into his room and shut the door.

I breathed more freely. I would give him a little time to settle down and then I would go to bed, not forgetting to put the chair against the door.

Ten minutes passed.

I got into bed.

It must have been about fifteen minutes later when I heard stealthy footsteps in the passage. I sat up in bed and felt for the pistol. I held it securely and waited.

My heart was hammering. The footsteps had stopped outside my door.

The chair moved a little. There was a scraping sound and it fell backwards. He had stepped into my room. The starlight showed me his grinning face—horrible, lustful and determined.

I leaped out of the bed and stood on the other side of it, holding the pistol ready in my hand.

"If you take a step towards me, I'll fire," I said.

He looked amazed and stared at me.

"By God," he said, "you were ready and waiting for me."

"I know too much about you," I retorted. "Get out . . . unless you want a bullet through you."

"You wildcat," he said.

"Yes. Remember it. You will be sorry if you take another step into this room."

"You couldn't shoot me, could you?"

"I could and I would."

"Murder me in my home . . . in cold blood."

"In your home but in hot blood. I am seething with anger against you. I loathe you. I despise you. I distrust you. You are not a man. You are the lowest form of animal. Do you think I don't know what goes on here. I wanted to take Felicity back with me but she would not come. Some misguided sense of duty. Duty to what? You! Who call yourself a man! Stand back. I shall fire if you move."

He was recovering from the shock of seeing me facing him with the pistol in my hand.

"Now . . . now," he said. "I only came in to see if you were all right. I thought I heard a noise . . . Someone prowling about."

"Perhaps it was your mistress coming to visit you."

"I thought it might be the bushrangers . . . "

"Well, it isn't. Go away, and if you set foot in this room again while I'm here I shan't warn you. I shall shoot."

"Spitfire! Wildcat! You're a tigress, you are. I wouldn't hurt you. I like you. I could get very fond of you. I like women with a bit of spirit. If you'd only take the trouble to get to know me . . . "

"I know all I need to know and the more I know the more I despise you."

"Give me a chance."

"Go away."

"You don't mean that, do you?"

He was trying to sidle round the bed.

"I do. One step nearer and I shall fire. I shan't miss. You yourself said I was a fair shot."

"That's murder, you know."

"I shall shoot you in the leg. And it will be in self-defence. I shall tell everyone that you came into my room intending to rape me. I shall tell them that you take your housekeeper to bed with your wife. You wouldn't be very welcome, even in this wild land, after I had told all I know about you."

Suddenly I knew that he was defeated. He looked at me with something like hatred.

He said: "All right, you bitch, you she-wolf. You think you are so precious, do you? Get out of my house. Get out now."

"I shall leave first thing in the morning."

"And where will you go? Sleep rough? That would hardly suit her ladyship."

"I shall go to the inn. I am leaving in the Sydney coach on Monday. If I can't get a room there, I will sleep anywhere . . . in their parlour . . . I shall not mind. All I want is to get away from this place."

"Go," he said, "and good riddance."

With that he went out of the room kicking the chair aside and banging the door after him. I sank onto the bed. My knees felt as though they were giving way, and now that I no longer had to steel myself to face him, my hands were trembling so much that I could not hold the pistol. My teeth chattered. I thought if he were to come back what good would I be in the fight against him?

I lay still, all senses alert. I heard him go downstairs. I waited, listening for the time of his return, trying to control my trembling limbs. I must go tomorrow. I would ride out and ask if I could stay the night at the inn. Surely someone would give me shelter just for one night—and on

Monday morning I would be off. The hideous nightmare would be over.

What was he doing. I could hear nothing.

An hour passed. My limbs had ceased to tremble. I kept the pistol in my hand.

Then I heard him. He was coming up the stairs. I put my eyes to the crack in the door. I could hear him muttering to himself and I could just make out his tall figure. He was reeling a little. He must be very drunk.

I watched him hesitate at the top of the stairs. Then he turned and went into the bedroom with the balcony.

It could only have been five minutes later, and I was still waiting tensely, when I heard the shot.

I knew where it came from and carrying my pistol in my hand I went along the passage and opened the door of their bedroom.

The door to the balcony was wide open. I saw Felicity. She was on the balcony, clinging to the broken wood.

"Felicity!" I cried. "What happened?"

She tried to speak but no words came. She shook her head and pointed to the balcony.

I saw that several more of the staves were broken away and the front of it had collapsed almost in its entirety. I went forward and looked down. Sprawled on the ground below was William Granville. Some distance from him was the gun.

He lay inert like a big puppet and there was something unnatural about his position.

My instinct told me that he was dead.

I did not ride on the coach that Monday. I stayed in the house with Felicity. I took her out of that room of many evil memories and made her lie on my bed. It was wide enough for the two of us and she was in no state to be left alone.

She was numb; she stared ahead of her and there was a glazed look in her eyes. I began to fear for her reason.

The days that followed now seem rather vague in my mind. There was much coming and going. The body of William Granville was taken away. He was shot through the head.

Officials rode out from Sydney and a great many questions were asked. How had he fallen? they wanted to know.

He had leaned against the balcony and it had given way.

I felt calm. Felicity had not told me what had happened and I was afraid to ask her. I felt she would break into hysteria and I did not know what she would say if she did. I had a niggling fear in my mind that she had come to the end of her endurance and possibly had fired the fatal shot. I could well understand that. I had been ready to shoot him myself. There is a limit beyond which even the meekest person cannot be goaded.

What I wanted more than anything was to get away from this place. And I wanted to take Felicity with me. Whatever had happened was over. I wanted to soothe her, comfort her. I understood so clearly what she had suffered.

The theory was that the bushrangers had been prowling around. The Pickering story was discussed in great detail, and the bushrangers were in everyone's mind.

I said that the dead man had come to my room earlier that evening and had said he thought he had heard prowlers whom he suspected might be bushrangers.

That was true enough.

It was confirmed that he had been constantly watchful for bush-rangers after the Pickering affair. Everybody was.

It was believed that he had heard strangers outside and had taken the gun and gone to the balcony. It was a fact that the balcony was in need of repair. One stave had been missing for months. It was easy to see how it happened. He had dashed out with his gun, forgetting the wood of the balcony was rotting; he had leaned against it and in falling had shot himself. Then the gun had been knocked out of his hand and so was found a few feet away from him.

It was another tragedy of the outback.

I believed that at home there would have been more enquiries into the matter. Here life was cheaper. People were pioneering, making a new country, and the risks that entailed were numerous. Death was not such a rare occurrence.

Mrs. Maken told how we had all been given guns after the bush-ranging outrage at the Pickerings'. Mr. Granville, she knew, was very anxious not to leave the women unprotected.

"The bushrangers have a lot to answer for," said one of the officials.

But I was not sure that they had to answer for William Granville's death.

I said I wanted to get away as soon as possible. Mrs. Granville was in a state of shock, from which I feared she would not recover until we left this house of tragedy.

But first there was the ordeal of the funeral to be faced.

There was a small cemetery just outside the township and his grave was close to that of Mrs. Pickering, who had died after her ordeal with the bushrangers.

We stood round it—Felicity, Mrs. Maken, myself and several of the men. A number of people came in from miles around to witness the burial. Much sympathy was shown to Felicity, and I watched her anxiously, wondering whether she was going to lose that calm and betray her real feelings.

It was quite unlike the funerals at home—no glorious trappings, no ceremonial black-clad undertakers, and elaborately caparisoned horses. We had tried to find as much black as we could but there was no way we could get new clothes.

"Poor soul," said one of the women spectators. "I'd like to murder those bushrangers. When they find them they'll be lynched, I can tell you. That poor Mrs. Pickering . . . what she suffered! And now Mr. Granville."

Our silence was construed as grief, and we went back to the house in the buggy, with Slim driving us, as he did on our arrival.

It transpired that William Granville had borrowed heavily on the strength of having married a woman of fortune. His debts would have to be met, and this could only be done by the sale of his property after which there would be very little left. Felicity agreed listlessly to all that was suggested and was glad that the matter could pass out of her hands. She told me she wanted nothing of her late husband's estate. All she wanted to do was get away, and for things to be as though this had never happened.

I had packed our things and made the arrangements.

Felicity would not stay in the house alone; nor would she go to the township. When I went in I had to leave her some little way off. She could not bear the condolences which were offered her. She was in a highly nervous state.

I made the bookings on the coach for a Wednesday which was eleven days after the death of William Granville.

Felicity was exhausted and for that I was grateful because it meant she slept heavily at night. I used to sit by the window watching her and trying not to imagine all that she must have endured in that room.

The balcony had been repaired. I went into the room once. It seemed evil to me because I knew something of what had happened there. I shuddered as I looked at the brownish curtains at the french windows which opened onto the balcony, the big cupboard, the dressing table and the two chairs. My eyes came to rest on the bed and I shivered again.

I stepped out onto the balcony and looked down. The new staves shone brightly among the old ones.

How had it happened? I wondered. Perhaps Felicity would tell me one day.

I should never ask her.

There was a menace in this place and it was centred in this room. This was where Felicity had suffered her ultimate humiliation.

I felt myself turn cold. There was a tingling sensation in my scalp. Was this what was called one's hair standing on end?

I was not alone.

I swung round, clutching the balcony just as he may have done. I fully expected to see him standing there with that lustful grin on his face.

I was looking into the enigmatic eyes of Mrs. Maken.

"Oh," she said, "taking a last look at the place?"

I replied: "The balcony looks firm now." My voice sounded high-pitched and unnatural.

"It was a terrible thing to happen," she said. "Those bushrangers have a lot to answer for."

I nodded.

"It will make changes round here."

"I daresay. What plans have you, Mrs. Maken?"

"I'm to stay till it's all cleared up. The solicitors have asked me to. There's got to be someone here . . . and as things are with Mrs. Granville . . . "

"It seems an excellent arrangement. I was thinking of after that."

"I've had an offer from a very nice gentleman in Sydney. House-keeper and all that."

She was smiling at me complacently.

"I'm glad," I said.

"And you'll go off. Well, it's the best thing for Mrs. Granville. She never took to our ways out here."

She was looking round the room reminiscently, but I could see she was already making plans for her life at the establishment of the nice gentleman in Sydney.

"They'll catch those men," she said. "There's an outcry about it. This makes them more determined than ever. Just think, if Mr. Granville hadn't heard them prowling about he'd be here now. Well, you'll soon be off. You were going on that Monday . . . well, then you had to stay for a bit when all this happened. But if it hadn't been for those men . . . "

I said: "Yes, indeed." I had come back into the room from the balcony and I had to walk past her to get to the door. I kept seeing images of her in that room with Felicity and William Granville.

She looked at me sardonically and I wondered if she read my thoughts.

She was an uncomfortable woman. But on Wednesday we should be on our way.

Our last night. Felicity lay in bed, but she was not asleep.

I sat on a chair watching her. The bed was not really big enough for two and I usually lay on the edge so as not to disturb her.

She had always been fast asleep by the time I retired. I think she was really worn out with fear and emotion. Sometimes I would sit at the window until past midnight looking out and thinking over the time I had spent here. Since the death of William Granville a touch of unreality had crept into everything. When I finally left here I hoped it would become vague in my memory—a nightmare, grotesque, terrifying while it lasted but which faded from memory in daylight and the return to normal life.

That was what I hoped at least.

Felicity's trunks had already gone to Sydney where they would be stored at the docks until her departure for England. My baggage and Felicity's lighter possessions had already gone to the township to be put into the coach when it arrived. All that was left for us to take was one capacious piece of hand luggage each.

I went to the window and sat there. I had no inclination for sleep. I should make up for that when I had left this place.

Felicity spoke to me then. "Why are you sitting at the window, Annalice?"

"I don't feel sleepy. Our last night, Felicity. I feel so relieved that we are going together."

"Oh, Annalice, it was dreadful when you were going without me."

"I know. I had to do it though."

"I understand that."

There was silence for a while, then she said: "It's all over. I can't believe it."

"There is only tomorrow morning. We will leave in good time for the coach."

"And then we shall say goodbye to this place forever."

"Forever. We shall put it right out of our minds."

"Do you think we shall ever be able to do that."

"I'm going to have a jolly good try."

"It's easy for you."

"In time it will be for you."

"I shall never forget, Annalice."

"I suppose the memories will come back. But they will get fainter . . . more remote . . , "

"I don't think they ever will . . . not of that night."

"Well, for a time of course . . . But when you are away from this place, it'll fade. It will, I promise you."

"Not that night. It is there forever . . . stamped on my mind. I shall never forget that."

I was silent and she went on: "It wasn't as they said, Annalice."

"No," I replied.

"It wasn't the truth. I have to tell someone. I can't keep it to myself."

"If you have to tell someone it had better be me."

"That night . . . he came up . . . he was laughing to himself. He had drunk a lot of whisky but he was not drunk . . . not like he was later. He went out . . . I thought he was going to Mrs. Maken. He did, you know, often."

"Yes, I know."

"He was always saying how much better she was than I was . . . things I can't talk about."

"Then don't."

"I've got to tell you. I think once I have told you I may be able to stop thinking about it . . . at least not so much."

"Tell me then."

"He was away a long time. I thought he would stay the night. He usually did. I liked that. It was wonderful when he was away. I was grateful to Mrs. Maken for being so much better . . . at that sort of thing . . . than I was."

"Oh, Felicity," I cried, "I don't care what brought you out of this . . . but I'm glad it happened."

"I'm glad, too. It's wicked, but I'm glad he's dead."

"The world is a better place without him and his kind. Let's rejoice he is no longer in it."

She shivered and sat up suddenly, her eyes coming to rest on the door.

I said: "He can't come in. He's dead. You're not afraid of his ghost, are you?"

"I would be in this place. I think one of the eucalyptus trees will turn grey and he'll be in it."

"I wouldn't worry about that. You'll be far away. In time you'll forget this place ever existed."

"Home," she said. "It's like a different world."

"It won't be long now. You could get on a ship and be home very soon. I shall not go yet. I have things to do."

"I know. And I stopped you, didn't I? I want to stay with you, Annalice."

"All right then. We'll be together. It will be exciting. We shall go to Cariba."

"Yes . . . yes . . . as long as I am with you. And in time we'll go home together."

She was lying down now, smiling.

Then she said: "But I have to tell you about that night."

"Go on then . . . tell me."

"I shan't rest until I have told you. I want you to tell me that I am not wicked."

"Of course you are not wicked. Whatever happened, he deserved it."

"Well, he came back into the room. I was sleeping. I was so tired, Annalice. I was always tired. Those fearful nights . . . "

"Don't think of them. Just tell me."

"He came back. It was a long time after . . . It must have been more than an hour. He was very drunk. He looked awful. He shouted: 'Wake up. I suppose I'll have to make do with you.' Yes . . . that's what he said. It flashed into my mind that he might have quarrelled with Mrs. Maken. Then something seemed to snap in me. I couldn't endure any more. I pushed him away. It was only because he was so drunk that I was able to do it. I jumped out of bed and picked up the pistol, the one we were supposed to carry round with us. I said, 'If you touch me I will shoot myself.' "

"Oh no, Felicity!"

"Yes . . . yes . . . He laughed at me. I wasn't sure what I was going to do. I would have killed myself. I could not stand any more of him. It was too degrading, too humiliating. It was everything that I hated. I hated him and that made me hate myself. I felt unclean . . . unworthy to live. He came after me and I ran onto the balcony. He caught me. He was trying to get the gun away from me. He was laughing. He was very drunk. Then suddenly . . . I may have pushed him. I don't know. I can't remember clearly. The balcony gave way . . . the gun went off . . . it spun out of our hands and fell clattering below . . . and there he was lying beside it . . . with blood all over him. I screamed . . . and that was when you came in."

"I see," I said.

"Do you? I think I may have fired the shot that killed him."

"It was a struggle, the gun went off. Stop thinking about it. It's over. Whatever happened wasn't your fault."

"Oh, it wasn't, was it?"

"No, no. You must remember that."

"I will. I feel so much better now I've told. Perhaps I should have told those men, but how could I without explaining things that I didn't want to talk about?"

"It was better as it was. He's gone. That's the end of it. You're free, Felicity, gloriously free. That's what you have to think about."

"Thank you, Annalice. I'm so glad you're here."

"Well, we shall be together . . . and in time we'll go home."

"That would be wonderful. Home. I wish I had never left it."

"You'll love it all the more when you get back. Just think; tomorrow we shall walk out of this place and leave it all behind us forever."

"It's wonderful. I shall think of that. I shall try to forget. Talking did help."

She was silent and after a while she slept.

I did not go to bed. I sat in the chair and dozed. I saw the dawn come into the sky, the glorious dawn of the day of departure.

The next day we were jolting across the roads to Sydney, and with every passing minute my spirits lifted. The nightmare is over, I thought. Now we can go on from here.

We arrived in the evening and I was relieved to find they had a room at the Crown. We both had a good meal and a good night's sleep; and in the morning we were greatly refreshed.

My first task was to call at the Botanical Association. I left Felicity in the hotel while I set out.

There was good news. David Gutheridge had returned from the expedition and was at this time in Sydney.

They had informed him of my previous visit and he had asked them to give me his address if I called again. This was great progress and I was delighted.

He was staying at a small hotel not far from the Crown and I went there immediately. Another stroke of good luck awaited me. He was in.

He received me warmly. I had met him when he and Philip were making their preparations, so we were not entirely strangers.

He took me into a small room and we settled down to talk.

I said: "We have had no news of Philip . . . for a very long time."

"It is strange," he said. "I heard nothing of him. I did make enquiries at the time and no one could tell me anything."

"Where did you make enquiries?"

"It was at a hotel on one of the islands . . . the biggest of the group. Cariba actually."

"Oh yes . . . I did hear he was there."

"Apparently he made it his headquarters for a while."

"Yes?" I said eagerly.

"He was determined to find some island, wasn't he? I remember he had a map and the mysterious thing was that the island did not appear where it should have been . . . according to the map. It wasn't on any other map either. But Philip was certain this island existed somewhere . . . and he was going to find it."

"What was the last you heard of him?"

"It was in Cariba actually. There is a sugar plantation on it . . . and on one of the others too, I believe. Yes, he was there when I heard the last of him. They said he left suddenly."

"Left the hotel, you mean?"

"Yes . . . the hotel. That's all I can tell you. He was staying there. It was his headquarters for a while because he was sure the island was in that vicinity. Apparently he just left . . . and no one heard of him after that."

"I see."

He looked at me ruefully. "I'm afraid I'm not much help. It is all I can tell you though. It is a long time now, isn't it?"

"It is more than two years."

"All that time since he disappeared!"

"Yes. He did write once . . . and that was all we heard. I decided I just had to come out here and find out."

"And you are not getting very far."

"No. The only thing I have discovered is that he had been to Cariba. A man whom I met coming over told me that."

"I was a little while in Cariba. It's practically owned by the man who has the sugar plantation. He's a sort of big white chief."

"That would be the man I met. Milton Harrington."

"That's the man."

"He was quite helpful to me and to the ladies I was travelling with."

"Cariba would appear to be the last place he was seen."

"And you have no idea where he might have gone from there?"

"I'm afraid I haven't. Unless he went off in a boat somewhere. Squalls blow up pretty fast in this part of the world and small boats . . . well, they don't have much chance."

"It seems strange—if that were the case—that he told no one he was going."

"He may have done so."

"I thought someone at the hotel might be able to throw some light on his disappearance."

"That might be so. If I hear anything, Miss Mallory, I'll contact you. You're going to Cariba, are you? You'll be at the hotel. It's the only one actually. If I should hear of anything . . . or something occurs to me, I'll write to you."

"That is kind of you."

He looked at me quizzically. "You've got a hard task ahead of you, I'm afraid."

"I'm prepared for that. But I am determined to find out what has happened to my brother."

"Best of luck," he said warmly.

He clasped my hand, and said he would escort me back to the Crown, which he did.

On the following Wednesday, Felicity and I left for Cariba.

THE ISLAND
OF CARIBA

It was early on the Thursday morning when we came into Cariba.

Felicity and I had been sitting on deck dozing through the night. I felt more at peace than I had since what I called the nightmare had begun. The sea was smooth; now and then I saw a phosphorescent gleam on the waters—weirdly beautiful; the Southern Cross above, with its myriads of companion stars, reminded me how far from home we were— but we were going to Cariba, and there I hoped I should discover some news of Philip and . . . I should see Milton Harrington.

Life had become full of adventure—sometimes terrifying—but I believed that nothing which lay in store for me could be more fearful than that horrific experience through which I had just passed.

I looked at Felicity; her eyes were closed. There was a change in her since she had confessed to me what had really happened on that night. It was as though she felt she had shifted her burden a little. Poor Felicity! What she had suffered was beyond endurance. I could only be thankful that it was at an end—by whatever means we had reached that end.

And now before us . . . Cariba and Milton Harrington.

The sun rose as suddenly as it set and the water lost its mysterious darkness and was opalescent in the morning light.

And then I saw the islands. There was a group of them. I made out four . . . and yes, another one some distance away, separated from the others. It is an exciting moment when one catches sight of land and I could well imagine the exhilaration which those early explorers must have experienced when they sailed the uncharted seas.

As we drew nearer I awakened Felicity.

"Look, Felicity. We are nearly there."

We stood together leaning over the rail. I turned to look at her. She was smiling. I put my hand over hers. "You look so much better," I said.

"I feel more at peace. I didn't dream at all as I sat there dozing. It was . . . well, peace."

"That is how it is going to be from now on."

"Thank you," she said. "I'll never forget all you have done for me."

I was thoughtful for a moment, thinking: But for me it would never have happened. You would have married Raymond if I hadn't come along. And that episode would never have taken place.

What a difference that would have made to Felicity! I could see her married to Raymond, becoming a good wife and mother, living uneventfully, never dreaming that there could be men in the world like William Granville.

For the first time it occurred to me how suited they were—she and Raymond, and how but for me they would have drifted into marriage. Raymond would make the perfect husband . . . to any woman he married.

It was strange that I who had contemplated marrying him myself— and had made excuses for delaying fulfilment—should be thinking of his marrying someone else.

But here was Cariba. A new adventure was beginning and I promised myself that this was going to be wonderful. I should achieve what I had come out for.

The islands were green and lush; a heat haze hung over them at the moment.

Felicity was shading her eyes. "That one seems a little apart," she said.

"Yes. The others are very close together. What would you think? No more than half a mile between them. Except that one. I wonder what it is called and if there are people on it."

We were approaching the largest of the islands—Cariba itself and our destination. There were several boats in the small harbour, which was alive with activity. We had weighed anchor. As I had expected the water was too shallow for the ship to go right in and we should go ashore in small boats.

Now little boats were rowing out to us. In them were small boys who grinned up at us and called to us in pidgin English to throw down coins which they would dive for. So we threw pennies into the water which was so clear that the sea bed was visible.

We hastily searched our purses and found more coins. We laughed as we watched the lithe brown bodies dive and squirm in the water like little fishes. When they found a coin they held it up to us triumphantly, threw it into their boat and called: "More. More."

This continued for some time before we were told to assemble below for the journey ashore.

We climbed rather perilously down a rope ladder to the boat below and in a short time we were being rowed to the island.

My excitement was intense. This was the last place where Philip had been known to be. Someone here must know something.

The sun was getting higher in the sky and it was perceptibly warmer. It glinted on white houses. I picked out a large building which I took to be the hotel.

It was not the desert island I had imagined. There must be a thriving community here. The dock was littered with large cases; of course it would be, for it was the day the ship came in from Sydney, and those cases would be loaded and taken for distribution probably to various ports in the world. I saw crates of green bananas, and fruits, the names of which I did not know. There were people of all colours—black, brown and some white. Everyone seemed to be dashing about and making a great deal of noise.

I said to Felicity: "We will go straight to the hotel. Some of these people will tell us how to get there."

The boat was almost there. One of the two big black men who had rowed us leaped into the water and secured it.

Then he lifted us out so that we did not get our feet wet.

I heard a shout—and there he was pushing his way through the crowd. I noticed the flash of his white teeth in his sunburned face.

"I thought you were never coming," he said.

I felt ridiculously emotional and the absurd idea came to me that my troubles were at an end.

He was shouting orders. Where was our baggage? He would see to that. Everyone seemed to stand to attention at the sound of his voice.

I laughed, feeling deliriously happy. I said: "You really are the big white chief."

"It is the only thing to be out here."

He took my arm and that of Felicity.

"You poor girls must be worn out. It's an exhausting journey, I know, and a night without sleep."

"We dozed, didn't we, Felicity?"

"It was so peaceful on deck and such a lovely night."

"You were lucky. It can be quite the reverse. Now I'll have your baggage seen to and sent up to the house."

"What house?"

"My house, of course. You are my guests."

"No, no," I said. "We are staying at the hotel."

"I won't hear of it."

"I insist. It is good of you to be so hospitable, but we must be in the hotel. I have so much to do and I want to be in the hotel."

"Every time the ship has come in from Sydney I have been here waiting. I have your room prepared. I did not know you would be here, Mrs. Granville."

"That is a long story which must wait," I said. "We shall stay at the hotel."

He looked at me sardonically.

"Short of taking you to my house by force, I see there is nothing I can do but take you to the hotel."

"Absolutely nothing."

"Perhaps I can persuade you to visit me later."

"Thank you. And please don't think I am ungrateful. I do appreciate all your kindness and the help you gave us before . . . But I must be in the hotel. We don't want to be in a house again for a while. Something awful happened to Mr. Granville."

He was taken aback. So the news had not reached Cariba yet. I supposed it would in due course, but there had hardly been time yet.

"It was an accident," I said, willing him with my eyes to say no more in Felicity's presence.

"I'm sorry," he said to Felicity.

"It would be nice if you would help us get into the hotel," I put in quickly. "I dare say a word from you would ensure our getting the best treatment."

"Come along," he said. "This is your light baggage, is it?" He shouted to one of the men. "Have this brought to the hotel."

"Yes, Master," said the man.

"Now, let us go. It is here . . . right on the waterfront."

I said: "The big white building with the balconies?" I stopped suddenly and looked at Felicity who had turned pale.

"That's it," he said. "It's moderately comfortable. You'll find it cooler inside. I'll see that you get good rooms."

He took me on one arm and Felicity on the other. It was almost like a royal progress. People stood aside respectfully to let us pass.

"It seems you are the king of the island," I commented.

"Monarch of all I survey." He looked sideways at me and grimaced. "Well, not quite all."

We mounted three steps to the door. A little black boy rushed to open it for us, and we stepped into a reception hall.

A woman who was almost white sat behind the desk; she was a quadrocn, I guessed.

"Good morning, Master," she said.

"I've brought you two guests, Rosa," he said. "I want the best rooms in the hotel for them . . . in the front with balconies overlooking the harbour." He turned to us. "You'll find that interesting. It's a busy harbour . . . always something going on."

"There's only one vacant at the moment, Master."

"Then we'll have that and the one next to it."

"There's no balcony to that one."

I said to Felicity: "You'd like that, wouldn't you?"

"Yes, yes," she said quickly.

"You'll like the balcony in the cool of the evening," Milton told me. "The temperature changes quite a bit at sundown."

"Well, Felicity can share mine if she wants to. Let us have those two rooms."

"That's settled then," he said. "You two ladies will be dining at my house tonight. I'm going to give you the whole day to rest. You'll need it after your journey. I shall be calling for you at seven o'clock. In the meantime, rest. Now, I'll see the rooms, to make sure they are satisfactory."

"Yes, Master," said the quadroon girl, and signed to a man in livery.

"Morning, Master," he said.

"Good morning, Jacko."

As we went up the stairs I said: "It seems you manage everything on the island."

"On such an auspicious occasion, yes."

"It is really rather awe-inspiring."

"That's what I like to do . . . inspire awe. It makes me very happy . . . but what makes me happier is that you have come at last."

We were taken to the rooms. They were large with big double beds, blinds to shut out the sun and small rush mats on polished floors. There were nets over the beds.

"Never forget to use these," Milton Harrington warned us. "You'll be eaten alive by morning if you don't. You'll be delighted with the flora but the fauna can be quite another matter. And you'll want to keep the blinds down during the heat of the day."

He opened the french windows onto the balcony. "There. You see, it's a fine view of the harbour. It is interesting in the evening when the sun's gone down. Then you can sit out here. You'll enjoy that."

I stepped out and looked. Felicity hesitated. I took her arm and drew her out.

I put my hand on the ironwork of the balcony. It was firm and strong. I felt her tremble a little and we went back into the room.

"You'd better get something to eat," said Milton. "I'll tell them to send something up."

"You think of everything," I told him.

"I've been waiting for this day so long so I have had plenty of time to think about it. What kept you?"

"I'll tell you sometime," I said significantly.

And he understood.

"Now," he said, "I shall leave you. I will come for you at seven o'clock and take you up to my house. If there is anything you need just ask for it. I've instructed them to look after you."

"It is very comforting to have such a powerful friend."

"I intend that you shall enjoy your stay on my island."

"Thank you. You are very kind."

He took my hand and pressed it firmly. His eyes were gleaming. There was no doubt that he was delighted because I had come.

When he had gone I looked at Felicity. "Well, here we are at last," I said.

"He is so good to us."

"He helped us when we were on the ship, didn't he? Do you remember how he made all the arrangements for your aunt?"

She nodded. "I always thought he wanted to be rid of her."

"Why should he?"

"So that he could have more chance of seeing you. Aunt Emily was always there . . . a chaperone, wasn't she?"

"She wanted to go."

"I sometimes think he helped to make her believe she did."

I laughed. "He is a very forceful man."

"It is good to have him on our side. I should not like to have him against me."

While I was preparing a remark a tall negress came in with a tray. On it were little rolls of bread and a plate of fruit—mangoes, bananas and pineapples. There was some milk which turned out to be from a coconut.

It was very appetizing and just what we needed.

When we had eaten I asked Felicity if she would like to unpack her bags which had by now been brought to our rooms. "Unpack," I said, "and sleep a little."

She said she would like to do that.

I went with her into her room. The blinds were drawn to shut out the sun. I was glad there was no balcony to remind her.

"I'm really tired," she said.

"Sleep first," I advised. "You can unpack later."

"And you will be in the next room."

"Of course."

"You won't go out without telling me?"

"I promise. All you have to do if you want me is to come next door."

I kissed her and left her.

I went into my own room and stepped out onto the balcony. People seemed to be running all over the place. The ship lay out there. It would stay there for some days while the loading of cargo took place and it would be ready to leave for Sydney in time for the next Wednesday's sailing.

I listened to the noise and bustle, watching the brilliantly clad women in their long flowing gowns. Many of them wore flowers round their necks and most of them had long black hair. They were beautiful and moved with the utmost grace. The men were scantily dressed and less attractive; many of them wore only a loin cloth. They were busy unloading crates and shouting as they did so.

It was a colourful, fascinating scene.

I went back to my room and unpacked a little. But I realized I was indeed tired. I lay on my bed and in a very short time was asleep.

It was about five o'clock when I awoke and I remembered that Milton Harrington was coming at seven to take us to his house.

I rose and knocked on Felicity's door. She was still sleeping and I was struck by the tranquillity of her face. I felt suddenly happy. She would forget now, I told myself. This island is the best place for forgetting.

I sat by her bed and called her name gently. "It is Annalice. Do you know what the time is?"

She opened her eyes and I saw the horror dawn on her face. For a brief moment she must have thought she was back in that bedroom she had shared with her husband.

"It's all right," I said quickly. "We're in Cariba. You've had a good sleep. So have I. We needed it."

She sat up.

"What time is it?"

"Fivish."

"He's coming at seven."

"Yes, we shall have to get ready. Did you think to hang out one of your dresses?"

"Yes, I did. The blue. I never wore it at . . . "

"It wouldn't have been suitable. But you are not there now . . . "

"I left behind most of what I wore there. I don't ever want to see it again."

"Where is the blue dress? Oh, I see. That will be lovely."

"He won't look at me. He'll be looking at you all the time."

"I think he takes everything in."

"He seems very important here."

"It's his island. He owns the plantation and I imagine that is the main business, so they are all depending on him."

"What are you going to wear?"

"My red."

"It's very colourful. They do wear colourful clothes here."

"It fits in with the flowers and everything."

"How long shall we stay here, Annalice?"

"Are you longing to go home?"

"I don't think I shall ever feel really safe until I am home."

"You know why I came. I am going to find out about my brother. As soon as I have, I'll be ready to go. But if you want to go before . . . "

"No. I couldn't face going back to Sydney, getting on a ship . . . "

"You see how Mr. Harrington works. I daresay he could arrange everything for you and make it all smooth and easy."

"No, no. I want to be with you . . . and I think I am going to like it here. I do believe I ought to have a little time . . . time away from all that . . . time to recover a little . . . before I go home."

"Well, there is the long sea trip."

"I'd like you to be with me. I shall stay with you, and I hope you soon find out about your brother."

"So do I. Now I must go and get ready, and so must you. We could ask for hot water to be sent up. I'll see what I can do."

"Annalice."

"Yes."

"It's wonderful to be away . . . to have escaped from all that."

I agreed that it was.

He came for us at seven and drove us up to his house in a carriage rather like the buggies we had seen in Sydney, but his was much more grand. It was highly polished and he drove two magnificent horses.

"I use this very little," he told us. "It is easier to go around on horseback. You'll want horses to ride. I'll have two sent up to the hotel for you."

"You overwhelm us," I told him.

"I'm so honoured to have you visit my island."

The day was drawing to an end for the sun set at half past seven. It was like that all the year, I gathered. There were not the seasons which we had at home. No winter; no summer; just the dry and the rainy season; I was glad we were not yet into the latter.

We came to some iron gates which were wide open and then we were in an avenue with high stalks of cane on either side. This was the plantation. I saw the house then. It was large, white and impressive and the scene was touched by the red glow of the setting sun. Everywhere I looked I could see sugar cane.

I caught my breath in wonder.

"You like it?" he asked.

"It's quite . . . splendid."

"What were you expecting?"

"Something grand . . . but not like this. I've never seen anything like it before."

"You've never been on a sugar plantation. I am glad the mill and the boiler houses are out of sight. They are slightly less beautiful."

We had come to a halt on a gravel path.

"Here we are." He leaped out of the vehicle and as if by magic a man appeared to take charge of the horses; and putting an arm through mine and one through Felicity's, he led us into the house.

We stood in a lofty hall built in the style of an English manor house. It reminded me a little of our own. There were light silk curtains at the windows; heavy velvet would have been out of place in such a climate. There was a long table with elegant chairs round it. It looked eighteenth-century.

"I hope you like my house," he said. "Shall we sit here and have a cooling drink before we go in to dinner?"

"It's just like being at home," said Felicity.

He smiled, well pleased.

Drinks were brought by a silent-footed girl in a long loose-fitting cotton gown with red and white roses patterned on a blue background; about her neck and arms were red beads.

"It's a cooling native drink," Milton explained. "Not intoxicating, or not very. It's designed for a hot climate."

It tasted delicious.

He asked about the journey and he told us that he had now heard of the tragedy for the news had been brought in by way of the ship.

"The coming of the ship means news from the outside world and there are always plenty to bring it, and here there are those to make sure it is well circulated. It must have been a terrible shock. The bushranger menace is growing, I believe. You need have no fears here. We are a law-abiding island. The penalties for misdeeds are so great that no one is going to risk incurring them."

"It would be easier to catch criminals here than it would in Australia," I commented.

"It's true. So you can put your fears at rest."

He told us a great deal about the island and how the sugar was grown and marketed.

He took us to a very pleasant dining room, very much like ours at home. He even had a large tapestry on one of the walls. There were french windows which opened onto a courtyard. He said: "After we have eaten we can sit out there. It is rather pleasant after sundown. I'll give you a fan so that you can ward off the insects. You'll need one in the heat of the day."

The food was unusual. There was a great deal of fish such as I had never tasted before. I had my first introduction to baked breadfruit.

"It's an acquired taste," he said. "You'll find it palatable and get to like it very much in time." There were all sorts of fruit and the special drink of the island.

It was certainly the best meal I had had since leaving home.

After we had finished eating we went into the courtyard where our fans were brought to us. They were beautiful, made of ivory and painted in rich colours. Mine was blue and green—Felicity's red and white.

We exclaimed with pleasure when we saw them.

"Something to remember me by when you find the heat unbearable," he said.

So we sat out there in the scented evening. There were flowers in abundance in the courtyard; red hibiscus, pink jasmine and gladioli.

Sitting there I felt intoxicated with the perfume and the drink which I felt was more potent than he had admitted.

But perhaps I felt this dreamy contentment because I had escaped from the nightmare of William Granville's house, because I was starting on my quest, because it was all so strange and beautiful and because I did enjoy the company of this man.

That night I lay in bed drowsily going over the events of the evening. I could still smell the heavy scent of frangipani, hear the sudden whirring of an insect as it fell against one of the lamps.

"The flying beetle," he had said. "Nothing to worry about. They come in often. They're quite harmless and you get used to them. There are lots of strange things you get to know out here."

And we had sat on in that scented velvety night and I could savour nothing but a deep contentment.

He had brought us back to the hotel at ten o'clock. He said we needed a good night's sleep.

I told him we had slept most of the afternoon.

"A good night's sleep is what you want," he said firmly. So he took us home, along the drive with the cane on either side, down to the harbour. I could hear the clop clop of the horses' hoofs as we came down the slight incline; and I could see the little boats rocking on the water, and the ship, which would sail tomorrow, was still lying there in the bay.

And when I went to bed I tried to ward off sleep because I wanted to go on remembering.

I awoke feeling greatly refreshed. I threw aside my mosquito net, jumped out of bed and drew up the blind. I stepped out onto the balcony. Below me the harbour was already stirring to life. Carts drawn by bullocks were coming in—I presumed from the hills beyond. People with produce to sell were arranging their stalls.

There were several boats on the water—fishing I guessed.

Water was brought to my room and I washed and dressed. Then I knocked on Felicity's door. There was no answer so I went in.

She was lying on her back staring at the ceiling. As I came close I saw the tears on her cheeks.

"Felicity!" I cried in alarm. "What's wrong?"

She said: "He came . . . he came in the night . . . He came back . . . He was here . . . just as in that dreadful room."

"You've been dreaming," I told her. "It was nothing but a dream. You're here in Cariba. You loved it yesterday. The harbour is just down there. It looks so exciting."

She began to shiver. "I shall never get away from him," she murmured.

"Listen, Felicity, he's dead. He can't touch you now. That's all over. We're starting again."

She shook her head; her teeth began to chatter and there was a blankness in her eyes. I realized she was not listening to me.

I was horrified and bewildered and uncertain what to do.

My first thoughts had been that she had had a nightmare which, although it left unpleasant effects, could be dispersed with the coming of daylight. It was more than that. She just lay there inert and when I spoke to her she did not seem to hear.

I grew more and more worried. I was realizing that I had been simplifying matters when I thought I could just take her away from the scene of horror and she would forget. She had gone through several ordeals, culminating in the violent death of her husband. I could not expect her to recover from that merely by removing her from the place where she had endured her misery.

I immediately thought of Milton. I needed help and he was the one to give it.

I went downstairs and spoke to the quadroon at the desk.

I said: "My friend is ill. I am very anxious about her. Could a message be sent to Mr. Harrington?"

"But certainly. I will send someone immediately."

"Thank you very much."

She summoned one of the men and he set off without delay.

"The poor lady is sick," said the quadroon. "She seems not very strong."

"Yes," I agreed. "She has had rather a bad time."

"The doctor will soon make her well."

The dark eyes surveyed me with some curiosity. I supposed it was partly Milton Harrington's interest which made us special objects of curiosity. Moreover if they knew of William Granville's sudden death they would know that Felicity was his widow. They would not, therefore, be very surprised to find that her health had suffered.

I went back to Felicity. She was still lying there staring into nothing.

I sat down by her bed and took her hand. I said: "It's all right, Felicity. I'm here to take care of you."

She did not speak but the pressure of her fingers told me that she was reassured.

It was not long before Milton arrived.

He came straight up to my room. I heard his approach and went out to meet him.

"It's Felicity," I said. "She's acting rather strangely. She doesn't seem to be aware— She had a bad night . . . dreams . . . nightmares . . . But it is more than that."

"Shall I see her?" he asked.

She looked up fearfully when he came in.

I said: "It's all right. It's Mr. Harrington. He's come to help."

She clenched her teeth together: "He didn't die . . . " she whispered. "He's here . . . "

I looked at Milton.

"I'll send for Dr. Norton," he said. "I know him well. I'll explain."

"Oh, thank you."

He went out of the room. Felicity just lay there as though unaware of anything that was going on.

I heard him coming back and I went out into the corridor to meet him.

"She's suffering from delayed shock," he said. "It was a terrible ordeal she went through. It's beginning to show now what an effect it has had on her."

"I thought she was getting on so well."

"She left Australia, she came here . . . the effort all that entailed could have sustained her. Now that she has arrived it's quiet and the accumulated effect of all that tension begins to show. I daresay all she needs is rest and careful treatment. Norton is a good fellow. He's been out here some years. He came out for a bit of experience five years ago . . . and stayed. He'll do the best possible for her."

"I'm very worried about her."

He put his hand on my shoulder. "I'm here. You know you can trust me to look after you . . . both."

I turned away. I felt too moved to speak. I was desperately worried about Felicity.

The doctor arrived and examined her. He gave her something to make her sleep. Milton and I, with the doctor, went downstairs and sat at one of the tables outside the hotel to talk.

Dr. Norton said: "She's in a highly nervous state. We'll have to be careful. She has had some terrible experience."

"Yes," I said. "Her husband died violently and she was with him when it happened."

"The Granville case," explained Milton.

"Oh, I see. That explains a great deal. Poor lady, she seems to be of a rather nervous disposition. It must have been a great grief as well as a shock."

"It was not a happy marriage," I said. "Mrs. Granville could not fit into the life to which she had gone. She had lived quietly in England and had no idea to what she was going."

"I see. We will restore her to health but it may take time. I shall keep her sedated for a few days. After that we will see that she does not have too much excitement. Your room is next to hers. Good. I think she is going to rely on you a great deal."

"I shall be there when she wants me."

"Quiet and rest . . . and then she should be all right."

"Thank you," I said.

"I've given her something to quieten her. It will make her sleep. I'll send some pills to the hotel at once, and I'll look in tomorrow to see how she is. I think you will find rest is what she needs more than anything. That will restore her peace of mind. You should take charge of the pills I shall send. One each night before retiring. Two might be injurious—

more than that fatal. So you should take care of them. Make sure that she cannot get at them. She appears to have a lack of interest in anything at the moment. Give her one pill tonight and that should ensure a good night's rest."

When the doctor left I went in to Felicity. She was lying still, her eyes closed, so I left her and went downstairs. Milton was still there.

"Well?" he asked.

"She's quiet. But I'm terribly worried about her. She looked so wild."

"She looked to me as though she could break down completely. But don't worry. Norton knows what he is about. We're lucky to have him on the island. He keeps talking about going home and we keep persuading him to stay. He's doing an excellent job here. Even the natives regard him as a very special witch doctor with extraordinary powers."

"Thank you for coming."

"My dear Annalice, I am always at your service."

I smiled at him. He seemed different, tender, gentle almost. I warmed towards him—not with that heady excitement which I had felt on some occasions but with something deeper.

"Sit down for a moment," he said. "You must not let this make *you* ill, you know. You have to be the strong woman, the comforter, the healer, the good nurse. It would be an excellent idea if you moved up to my place."

"I must stay here."

"You would be more comfortable there . . . and so would Felicity."

"No. I must be here."

"You say that with such finality that I know you are determined. You are an obstinate woman."

"I suppose I am and I'm sorry to be so ungracious."

"We should allow ourselves to be frank. I know why you won't come. You want to pursue your enquiries, for one thing, and the other is that it might not be *comme il faut.* Conventions are not so rigid here as they are in Merrie England. You think I am not to be trusted, and I'll tell you a secret as we are being frank. I'm not."

I laughed and I realized it was the first time I had done so since I had gone into Felicity's room and found her lying there lost and bewildered.

"Sit down here," he said. "Watch the harbour . . . its very bustle will make you feel sleepy."

"Yes," I agreed. "It has that effect. I am sorry for calling you in. I could have sent for the doctor. I must have called you away from your work."

"It would always be a pleasure to be called by you."

I shrugged the remark aside. I felt this was no time for light flirtation.

He was serious at once. "Know always that if you are in difficulties I am here to help."

"I am grateful."

"One day," he said, "I shall want more than your gratitude."

"Please . . . not now . . . "

"I was merely stating a fact. I can see how worried you are. Whatever happens I'll look after you."

"Thank you," I said.

"All this is understandable. She was actually present when he fell and killed himself."

I nodded. Then I burst out: "It was not only that. That was just the climax. It was before . . . "

He was looking at me wonderingly.

Then because I was overwrought, because I felt I must make him understand, I found myself blurting out everything . . . the arrival at the house, the presence of Mrs. Maken, those terrible nights which Felicity had had to endure in the room with the balcony, the participation of Mrs. Maken, the stolid acceptance of Felicity, her pent-up emotions about matters of which she could not even talk to me.

"He had an evil reputation. Drink and women. But one does not always pay a great deal of attention to scandal and rumours."

"In his case no rumour could have been bad enough."

I told him about the guns and how one night he had come into my room and I had threatened to shoot him.

"Good God!" he ejaculated.

"I should have done so, too," I said. "I never thought I could kill anyone, but I believe I would have killed him. I said I would shoot him in the leg . . . cripple him . . . and that frightened him. He knew that I meant it and that I was a fairly good shot."

"If I had known . . . "

"What could you have done?"

"I should never have let you go with him."

"How could I have left Felicity? She is frail and gentle. She couldn't take care of herself and yet . . . "

He said: "That night . . . on the balcony . . . "

"They said he was about to take aim at what he thought were bush-rangers."

"And there were no bushrangers?"

"I don't know. I think she had come to the end of her endurance. There was a struggle and the gun went off and he fell."

"No wonder she is in this state. I'm glad you brought her here. We'll take care of her together."

My lips trembled a little. I said: "I'm glad we're here . . . with you. How can I thank you."

"You just have," he said, "in a way which means more to me than anything."

We sat there in silence for some minutes looking out over the harbour. I hardly saw it. I was back in that house. I was reliving it all again. I would never forget. How much more deeply had it affected Felicity!

The doctor's assistant came with the pills. I took them to my room and hid them at the back of one of my drawers beside the map.

Then I went to Felicity. I sat beside her for some little time. She was sleeping peacefully.

When I went downstairs Milton was still there.

"She's asleep," I said.

He nodded. "That's what she needs. We'll have lunch together and then I shall send you to rest. Siesta is the order of the day here. In the afternoon it is too hot to do anything else but sleep. Everything is silent from two o'clock until four. This evening I shall come to see how you both are."

"Thanks—again thank you," I said.

I could eat nothing more than a little fruit. I was very shaken by Felicity's state. That blank look in her eyes had worried me more than anything.

Milton seemed to understand my mood. He tried to divert my attention by telling me stories of the island, the plantation, the habits and customs of the people. Sometimes he made me smile faintly; and all the time I was overwhelmed by my gratitude towards him.

I kept asking myself what I should have done had he not been here.

After he had left I went to my room, first looking in on Felicity. She was lying on her back with her eyes closed, and there was a look of tranquillity on her face.

I could not sleep. I kept turning over and over in my mind all sorts of possibilities. What if she were really ill? What if she lost her reason? What should I do? She was my responsibility. I thought comfortingly: He is there. He will help.

And thinking of him I was able to doze a little.

Felicity slept through the day. At sundown I went in and sat up by her bed. She opened her eyes and smiled at me.

"I feel tired . . . so tired," she said.

"You need rest," I told her. "Sleep all you can."

She smiled and closed her eyes.

I went downstairs. Milton was there. He asked about Felicity and I told him she was sleeping all the time.

"It's what she needs," he said.

We dined together in the hotel. I was rather silent but he talked cheerfully and somehow I got through the evening. When he said good night, he took my hands and kissed me tenderly on the cheek.

"Don't forget, if you are frightened, you only have to send for me."

I went up to my room and from the balcony watched him ride away. He turned to wave, putting his fingers to his lips and then blowing a kiss towards me.

I smiled and waved. Then he was gone.

I went to Felicity's room.

"Is it night now?" she asked.

"Yes."

"I'm afraid of the night."

"There's no need to be now you are here in Cariba."

"I dream . . . nightmares."

"Remember I'm next door. The walls are thin. Just knock if you wake . . . and I'll come in."

"Oh yes . . . I will. You are so kind to me, Annalice."

"Nonsense. I'm looking after you and I fancy I am rather good at that."

I settled her down and adjusted the net over her bed.

"I feel shut in," she said. "Just like . . . "

"You're miles away from there. That's all behind you. This is quite different and remember I am on the other side of the wall."

I kissed her lightly and sat beside her till she slept and then went to my room. I was really very tired.

It must have been about two o'clock when I was awakened by the knocking on the wall. I hastily rose and putting on my dressing gown went into Felicity's room.

She was sitting up and wildly staring about her.

"No, no," she was moaning.

"It's all right," I cried. "I heard the knock. I'm here. Was it a dream?"

"He came in . . . " she stammered. "The whisky . . . I could smell it. I hate whisky because . . . because . . . "

"Listen to me," I said. "It's all over now. You've got to forget it. As soon as you can you'll be all right. There's so much to do here. It's such a lot of fun really. Milton is ready to help us. All you have to do is get well. I'll give you a pill," I went on. "The doctor said you might have one . . . only one . . . each night. Perhaps I should have given you one before I went to bed but you were sleeping so peacefully. However, I'll give you one now. It will make you sleep and give you pleasant dreams."

I went to my room and brought the pill to her. She took it obediently.

"I'm here . . . in Cariba, aren't I. You're with me and he's dead . . . dead. He was lying there with all the blood round him . . . "

"He's dead," I said, "and buried. That is the end of him. He can never torment you again. He's gone and we are here; and that is all that matters."

She said: "Yes."

"Now lie still, close your eyes. I shall stay here until you are asleep."

"Will you promise to?"

"I promise and if you have a bad dream all you have to say is: 'This is only a dream.' And if you need me, all you have to do is knock on the wall."

"Yes . . . yes . . . that's all. It's all right, isn't it? It's all right."

"It's all right," I repeated.

She lay still murmuring: "It's all right . . . "

The pill took effect quickly and soon she was breathing easily. She would soon be asleep.

Then I heard her say something. "Raymond . . . why . . . if only . . . Oh, Raymond . . . "

I sat there looking at her.

I thought: If I had never gone to the conference . . . If I had never met Raymond . . . none of this would have happened.

She was fast asleep and I rose and went to my room.

I could not sleep. I was thinking what a tangle we had got ourselves into. She loved Raymond. What she needed more than anything now was Raymond to come and say that he loved her.

Fervently I wished he would because it was becoming increasingly clear to me that if I said goodbye and sailed away from Cariba—and by that I meant Milton Harrington—I should never be completely happy again.

Next morning, as soon as I was up, I went to see Felicity. She looked blank but at least she was quiet in her mind.

I went downstairs and ate breakfast in the courtyard at the back of the hotel. It consisted of yams with fresh bread and coconut milk. While I was eating it the quadroon girl came out and asked about Felicity.

I told her the doctor would be coming later, and that Felicity seemed a little better but was still very tired.

"If you need anything, ask me," said the girl. "I'm Rosa. I know people here."

"Yes, I suppose so. In your job you see everyone who comes into the hotel."

"Poor Mrs. Granville. She looks so ill."

"She'll soon be better, we hope."

"Mr. Harrington is really concerned for her . . . and for you."

"He has been very kind and helpful to us."

"He is a very important man. The island depends on him. We don't forget that . . . nor does he."

Was that a faint criticism? I wondered.

I merely nodded.

"The plantation is good for the island. All this prosperity . . . " She waved her hand.

"Yes, that must be true."

"So many people want sugar . . . so many people. Our plantation is bigger than Manuel's on Second Island."

"That's the island closest to this is it? The next biggest of the group?"

She nodded. "Mr. Manuel . . . he died not long ago. Mr. Harrington was in England then. Mrs. Magda . . . she manage it now. She very clever lady."

"How interesting. I want to see the other islands while I am here."

"Perhaps Mr. Harrington will take you to Second Island, yes? Perhaps not."

She seemed to find the situation amusing, then she said suddenly: "Forgive me . . . I have work."

I sat back thinking about the other island and wondering what was significant about Mrs. Magda Manuel which had seemed to provide Rosa with some amusement.

I finished breakfast and then went to take another look at Felicity. She opened her eyes as I entered and I asked if she would like a little breakfast. To my joy she said she would and I went down and asked them to bring up some milk, fruit and bread.

I sat with her while she ate it. She seemed much better and did not refer to my visit during the night; and indeed appeared to have forgotten it. She said she still felt tired and I told her that was probably due to the medicine and she clearly needed sleep.

I sat with her until she slept and then went down. I came out to the front of the hotel and stood for a moment looking at the harbour. Several people were seated on chairs on the raised terrace in front of the hotel. Sunshades had been put up over the tables which gave the place the look of a Continental café. People were sipping liquid from glasses—the cool drink of the island, I supposed—or perhaps the hotel had other wines to offer. But it seemed odd to be drinking wine so early in the morning. Other lands, other customs, I murmured to myself.

I sat down in one of the chairs and a waiter came up to me and asked if I wanted anything. I told him I did not.

I said: "What a lovely morning," and he replied that it would be very hot later. "When you see the mist over the island you know what is to come."

He was like most of the people on the island, very responsive to a show of friendliness. They all seemed to enjoy talking and laughing.

I asked him what his name was and he told me it was Obadiah.

"A good biblical name," I commented.

"Oh . . . we're Christian, Mistress. We've been to the Mission School."

"On this island?"

"Oh yes. It's here for the little ones. They go to Mission School. They learn about God and how to add up. They're educated."

"Have you been in the island long, Obadiah?"

He burst out laughing as though that were a huge joke.

"Why, Missie Lady, you must be joking. I was born here. People don't come to Cariba . . . not unless they is ladies like yourself or here for business . . . or holiday . . . Our sort, we gets born here."

"And you have worked in this hotel for some time, I gather."

"Why, bless you, Missie Lady, I was working here when I was no higher than that." He indicated the height of a boy about ten years old. "Opening doors, I were, all dressed up in my fancy clothes. I was proud and happy all the day. Master he said to me: 'You work hard, Obadiah, and there's no knowing where you can get to.' That weren't this master. 'Twere the other."

"Oh . . . the other?"

"This 'un's Pa. A big fine fellow, like Master. 'E were Master's Pa. And now it's for Master to get himself a wife and a little 'un or two so's the plantation goes on."

"I see. Master is Mr. Harrington."

"Oh yes, he's Master. Owns about everything here, he does. He's the big man. He's the master. We want to see him with a wife and little 'uns."

"So he has no wife yet."

"No, Missie Lady, no wife. We thought when he came back he would bring one of them with him. They always likes wives to come across the sea. Nothing here fits the likes of the Master . . . not for a wife, that is. Though there be Mrs. Manuel. But, you see, she wasn't free when he went away. Different story now."

Here was Mrs. Manuel again! I gathered she was a good friend of Milton Harrington. I felt a little stab of something like concern. Jealousy? Uneasiness? I really was letting myself become involved with that man.

"And what of Mrs. Manuel now?" I asked.

"Oh, well . . . we'll be seeing now. It's good. Master coming back without a wife . . . perhaps."

"You mean Mrs. Manuel is now free to become the Master's wife?"

"Master don't like talk about himself."

"Who does?"

He put his finger to his nose which I construed as meaning that he was realizing he had been a little indiscreet and he would prefer me to keep what he had said to myself.

I nodded in response and I went on, changing the subject: "Obadiah, can you remember back . . . about two years?"

"Two years. Why . . . what's that for?"

"You'd remember people who stayed here, wouldn't you? People from over the seas?"

Obadiah tapped his head and grinned. "It's all up here," he said. "I remember back years and years."

"Do you remember a gentleman who stayed here for a while? A Mr. Philip Mallory?"

"A Mr. Philip Mallory. Now . . . that seems to bring back something."

"He was a young man who stayed here. It was about two years ago."

Obadiah rolled his eyes upwards and said: "Surely. I can remember him. A very pleasant gentleman."

"He was my brother."

"Your brother, Missie Lady, you don't say!"

"You must have seen him often."

"Oh yes. I see him."

"And what happened?"

"Well, he were here . . . and then he weren't here."

"Where did he go? Have you any idea?"

Obadiah scratched his head thoughtfully.

"Wasn't he one of them that do charts?"

"That's right," I said eagerly.

"Oh well, he went off charting, I reckon."

"How did he go? Where did he go?"

"He just went."

"Did anyone go with him?"

"Oh, I couldn't say as to that."

"Try to think. How long did he stay here?"

Obadiah shook his head. "Could have been one week. Could have been two . . . and then again it might have been three or four . . . "

"But you just said he went away. He didn't say where he was going. He didn't just walk out. He must have paid his bill."

"Oh, I don't know nothing about that. Bills has nothing to do with old Obadiah."

I could see I was not going to get any further with him. But he did remember Philip. That was something. There might be others at the hotel who remembered more.

I talked to several of them that morning. Most of them remembered Philip, but there did not seem to have been anything mysterious about his departure. He had just come and gone as all other visitors to the hotel did.

I wandered down to the waterfront. But I could scarcely walk up to people there and ask them if they remembered my brother. I felt frustrated, wondering if I would ever discover anything. I had pinned my hopes on Cariba and now I was here I seemed to have come to a full stop. Moreover there was Felicity to consider.

I walked disconsolately back to the hotel. As I mounted the steps I was met by Milton Harrington.

"I've brought a horse for you," he said. "I've arranged for it to be kept in the stables here. Come and have a look at her. How is Felicity?"

"She seems a little better. She sleeps most of the time but she seems quieter in her mind."

"Good. That's what we want."

I followed him to the stables which were at the back of the hotel, and he showed me a pleasant little chestnut mare. "Her name is Excelsior. Don't you think that is rather pleasant?"

"Very," I said.

"Don't take her out in the afternoons. It's too hot for her and for you. She is sure-footed and understands the country. She's mild and friendly."

"Of excellent character. I don't know how to thank you."

He looked at me steadily and said: "You'll find ways of expressing your gratitude."

I was silent and he went on: "In fact it is I who should be grateful to you. I am very happy because you are here. I hope you will stay a very long time."

"But I have been here for such a short one. Who knows, if I stay too long, you might want to get rid of me."

"Never. I want to marry and that would mean that you would stay with me for the rest of our lives."

"Marry me!"

"Don't look so startled. Surely you can't be. You knew my intentions."

"I knew some of them, but I was not sure that they included marriage."

"Have you been listening to tales of me?"

"Are there such tales?"

"Aren't there always? No one is immune from scandal."

"Especially someone of your importance. I have been hearing about your power, this morning."

"Oh?"

"Someone called Obadiah. He seems to hold you in great awe."

He said: "This is no place to talk of serious matters." He led me into the hall.

Rosa looked up from the counter smiling at us.

"We are going through," he said.

"There is no one there, Mr. Harrington," she replied.

"We want to talk privately. See that no one comes."

"Very good, Mr. Harrington."

She was smiling her secret smile, speculating no doubt.

He opened the door of a small room which looked over the harbour. There was a balcony with chairs on it. He shut the door and we went onto the balcony.

"We can be quiet here," he said.

"You seem to command absolute obedience here."

"Of course."

"Your natural heritage, I presume."

"Now let's be serious. I want you here . . . with me . . . forever. I want you to marry me."

"Did you go to England to look for a wife?"

"I suppose every man is subconsciously looking for a wife as soon as he understands what life is all about."

"Your search was unsuccessful then?"

"On the contrary. I found my wife on the ship coming from England, so the mission—if mission there was—was highly successful."

"Not unless she agreed. You seem to have qualms about that."

He came closer to me and put his arm about my shoulders. "I never accept defeat."

"That's a bold statement. The most determined have now and then been disappointed in their hopes."

"I know you, my dearest Annalice. You really want me . . . but you won't let yourself believe it. Your experiences in Australia have affected you as well as Felicity. But life is not like that. That was not a real marriage."

"Naturally I don't think all marriages are like that—otherwise we should have a world of maniacs."

"Listen to me," he said. "You'll find the islands interesting for a while. My plan is to sell up the plantation and go home to England. We shall have to see about the children's education and we shall need to be home for that. We wouldn't want them to leave us and go away to school on the other side of the world."

I said: "I must remind you that I am engaged . . . in a way . . . to someone else."

"Someone who lets you go so far away!"

"There was a reason."

"What reason?"

"It is really between myself and my fiancé."

"*I* should never have let you go."

"I make up my own mind, you know."

"So you made up your mind to leave him. He must be what they call a laggard in love. You would find me very different."

"I have seen you here and on the ship and in Sydney," I replied. "Here you are like some little God. People are in awe of you, bowing down, almost worshipping you . . . and yet you behave like a callow youth in some ways."

"In love, you mean?"

"Yes. Imagining you only have to speak to me of marriage and I will thrust everything aside and say, 'Thank you very much.' "

"That's love," he answered. "Don't keep me in the dark. Why did you come here? And why did this fiancé allow it?"

"He helped me to come."

"Why did he want you out of his way for months?"

"He helped me to come because he knew how important it was for me to do so. I will explain."

I told him about the discovery of the map and Philip's obsession with the island.

"He came out here and disappeared. I want to find out why and whether he is alive. He is my brother and we were more close to each other than most brothers and sisters. I cannot rest until I know what happened to him."

"Didn't he write?"

"His last letter was from Australia. He mentioned in it that he was going to some island and I know now that he came here to Cariba. What I have to find out is where he went after that and what happened to him."

"You have a map, you say?"

"Yes, a copy of the one which was found in our house. I made it. It is an accurate copy. I have some knowledge of these things."

"Have you the map with you?"

"Yes. Shall I get it?"

He nodded.

I went to my room, found the map and brought it to him.

"The Paradise Island," he murmured. "This map is not correct. There is no such island."

"But it is there on the map."

"Who made the original map?"

I then told him how the room had been walled up and when it was taken down we found the map with the journal.

"You're bemused," he said, "because this girl had a name more or less the same as yours. My dear Annalice, you are a romantic after all. I am so pleased to discover this streak in you. There was a time when I thought you were all hard common sense."

"Wouldn't you have been intrigued by such a discovery?"

"Most certainly. So your brother came out on the quest and most mysteriously disappeared. He stayed here a short while . . . presumably he booked in like every other visitor. Where did he go from here? That is what is going to be difficult to find out. But this island . . . if it exists, should not be hard to discover. You have the map. Look at it. Here we are." He pointed with his finger. "Here is Cariba, and the other islands. Here is the one which is a little apart from us and then . . . how far would you say this Paradise Island is? Thirty miles . . . according to this map. I have sailed these seas . . . frequently. I would say there is no land— north, south, east or west for at least one hundred miles."

"What does it mean?"

"That whoever made this map put in an island which did not exist."

"I believe it is somewhere. There could be an error as to where. You see, the map was made from memory. Long ago the man who made the original visited this island when he was shipwrecked . . . and he made the map from memory afterwards."

"Coming from a family of map makers you would know that to trust to memory is no way to make maps."

"I know, I know. But there must be a reason behind all this."

"Unless your man dreamed up the island."

"That is a possibility. He was shipwrecked after visiting the island. He was picked up in an exhausted state."

"Dreams perhaps. Hallucinations."

"I had thought of that. But where is Philip?"

"Several things could have happened to him. He could have been wrecked at sea. You have been in the outback. You see that life is cheaper in some places than in others. He could have fallen among thieves. There are countless possibilities."

"What can I do?"

"Call in help," he said.

"Where from?"

"Here."

"Are you offering your services?"

"Didn't you know I was yours to command?"

I felt so happy that I could not hide the fact. I looked at him and I knew that gratitude shone from my eyes. I was going to shed a tear in a moment, if I were not careful.

He saw it and said: "How I love you. In all moods I love you. Determined and strong and sometimes faintly acid. And now tremulous and sweet—and let's admit it, rather helpless."

He put his arms round me and held me against him.

"Admit this, too," he said. "You'd be rather pleased if I came into the project."

"I just have a notion that you will succeed in everything you undertake."

"It could be well for you to remember that."

"I should be so glad of your help."

"Well," he said, "the first thing we must do is see if we can find that island. We need a fairly large boat . . . not like the one you came in from Sydney, of course . . . but not just a little rowing boat. We'll take the map with us and we'll go off. The first thing to do is to satisfy yourself that there is no island, at least not in the spot indicated on the map."

"Thank you. Oh thank you."

"There is one thing to be considered," he went on. "When you have solved this mystery, will you return to England?"

"That is my plan."

"And marry the young man who is quite happy to lose you for months . . . in fact has helped to arrange it?"

"He is very understanding. He knows that I will never settle down until I find out what has happened to Philip."

"So he lets you go off . . . "

"He understood . . . perfectly."

"I should never have let you go alone. I should have come with you."

"When shall we go on this boat trip?"

"It will depend on the weather. Leave it to me. In the meantime I shall try to find out all I can about your brother's stay on this island. Also I want to show you something of the island. I shall pick you up at five o'clock this afternoon. It will be cooler then. I want to show you the plantation, and you will dine with me. I advise you to stay in your room during the heat of the day."

He stood up. I rose with him. He took both my hands in his.

"If it is possible to find out where your brother is, we shall do it," he said. "Come with me."

We went out to the desk where Rosa was sitting smiling to herself.

He said he wished to speak to Mr. Selincourt and Rosa immediately left the desk to find that gentleman. In due course we were ushered into a room where Milton was greeted effusively by a short coffee-coloured man, to whom I was introduced and who turned out to be Mr. Selincourt, the manager of the hotel.

Milton asked to see the records of the last three years and I could see roughly at what time Philip must have come here. There was his name in the book. He had stayed here three weeks.

Mr. Selincourt remembered him. He had been a very agreeable guest. Yes, he had paid his bills; no, there had been no mysterious disappearance. He had paid his bill like anyone else and left.

"Did he leave on the boat to Sydney?" I asked.

Mr. Selincourt said that was the likeliest possibility. But according to the date of his departure he had not left on the day the boat called. He had left on a Sunday. That was strange.

No, Mr. Selincourt had not seen him leave. He would make enquiries of his staff to see if any of them remembered.

This seemed good progress—and it was all due to Milton Harrington. In spite of my anxiety about Felicity, I felt rather elated.

My hopes ran high during the days which followed even though Mr. Selincourt's enquiries among his staff produced nothing. No one saw Philip leave. He had just been there and then he had gone. But as he had left on a Sunday he could not have gone on the Sydney ship.

That was disconcerting, but Milton was sure we should find some clues which would lead to his discovery sooner or later. And at least I was doing something about finding him.

I was no longer so acutely worried about Felicity. She was very quiet and aloof, but she was better. She liked to stay in her room and had ceased to have those fearful nightmares. The doctor had warned me that they could return at any time and probably would, so I must be prepared. She needed to be soothed and assured all the time.

She slept a great deal which was what the doctor wished for her. She was mentally as well as physically exhausted, and she needed sleep and complete peace to recover.

I was seeing Milton Harrington every day; he would come to ask after Felicity and take me off somewhere. I rode round the island with him on my newly acquired mare and I began to enjoy the days.

He had taken me round his plantation which was an entirely novel experience. I had no idea how sugar was produced and because of the enthusiasm he brought to everything, he made it sound completely fascinating.

We walked on foot through the little paths between the canes— some of them dwarfing us by their height, for they were at least twelve feet high and about an inch and a half thick. He explained how the climate was just right for sugar—warm, moist, with sea breezes and some very hot spells. I had a peep at the roller mills which looked formidable, and at the boiler house. The people—mostly natives of the island—stopped their work to grin at me. One of them showed me a mongoose who was there to keep down the rats and the white ants which were the plague of the plantation.

I said: "You would hate to leave all this. It is your life."

"No, no," he said. "It's a means to an end. My father started the plantation. He made a success of it. He made the island what it is today. I have gone on with it. But his plan was to go home when the moment was ripe. That moment never came to him, but it will to me."

"All these people depend on you."

"I should not go until I found the right person to take over my place . . ."

"Then you will."

"You know, there is one thing—even more important—that I am determined on."

"What is that?"

"You."

"That is not so easy."

"No. But not insuperable."

"I know you believe you could never fail."

"It's a good way to live."

"Tell me more about the plantation."

Blithely he went on to explain the system of pan boiling.

After our tour of the plantation, I dined with him again.

He said: "When you are tired of the hotel you can always be my guests—you and Felicity."

"The hotel is comfortable," I replied. "They take good care of Felicity and really seem concerned about her. She only has to ring a bell and they are on the spot. And the view of the harbour is fascinating. It constantly changes."

There came the day when we took our sea trip. I could safely leave Felicity in the care of the hotel staff, so I set off without any fears about her and greatly looked forward to what we might discover.

It was not a large boat, but there were three men to manage it. I had the map with me. We made our way through the islands and for the first time I had a better view of that one which was a little apart.

"That's Lion Island," explained Milton. "You'll see why in a moment. There is a little bay and the cliff rises high above. From some way out it looks just like a reclining lion."

"There is a boat there. Is that a house?"

"Yes. The island is owned by a rich mining family from Australia. A sort of holiday island. They are not there very often, I gather. They keep themselves to themselves. There! You can see the reclining lion now."

We watched the reclining lion from afar and did not go any nearer to the island.

Soon we had left the group behind us.

"You need a fairly sturdy boat to come out here," said Milton. "A squall can blow up in no time. A flimsy boat could soon be overturned. Perhaps that was what happened to your brother."

I was silent. It was difficult to believe that now. The sea was so calm; there was scarcely a movement. I saw flying fishes skim the water and then rest lightly upon it. In the distance I caught a glimpse of dolphins at play. It was a beautifully peaceful scene.

Milton was holding the map in his hand.

"Now, according to my reckoning, this is where the island should be. You can see for miles. There's no sign of any land."

"Nothing," I said. "Nothing but the deep blue sea."

"We'll tour round a little if you like . . . but there is nothing . . . nothing at all. There has been an error somewhere."

I shook my head. "I think I shall have to come to the conclusion that there is no island. I can't understand it. That's an absolute copy of the map we found."

"I suppose your brother had the one you found?"

"Yes. He took it with him."

"Well, there it is. There is nothing here . . . We'll have to give up the search, I'm afraid. So . . . back to Cariba."

I looked at that vast expanse of water and I thought of the young man shipwrecked, dazed, drifting on a quiet sea. How long he had drifted, he did not know. Had he become delirious? Had he dreamed of an island where everything was perfect? Perhaps he had died for a few brief moments and gone to paradise and then had come back to life to dream of an island that was lost to him.

The sea was so beautiful, so calm on this day. How different it must have been at the time of his shipwreck. The deep blue sea changed in certain places where it appeared to be lightish green. Looking back I saw patches of that colour on the surface of the water.

I was about to call Milton's attention to this when he said: "We were lucky the weather was so good to us. Look. You can see Lion Island in the distance."

So I looked and forgot about the colours of the sea.

I felt vaguely depressed because I had to be convinced now that there was no island. It was a dream which had been conjured up in the mind of a shipwrecked man.

The days were passing—lazy days full of bright colours and the sound of continual chatter and spurts of laughter coming from the harbour where people ran about among the bullock carts. What excuse was there to stay? I could discover nothing of any significance about Philip. It had been proved that the island did not exist—at least not where it was supposed to be according to the map.

There was Felicity, of course.

I said to myself: "We cannot leave here until she is well."

And I wanted to stay—of course, I wanted to stay. I wanted to see Milton Harrington every day. I wanted to bask in his admiration, in his passionate absorption with me. It was vanity of course, but I could not help it.

I liked to watch him from my balcony window when he came riding up to the hotel. I was proud of the respect he inspired. People stood aside for him. In this island he was all powerful—the King among them all, the man from whom their comforts flowed, for the prosperity of the island came from the plantation, and he was the plantation; he was the island.

Then he would catch sight of me on the balcony and pause and smile and I would see the glint of his blue eyes in his bronzed face. I should scarcely have been human if I had not been gratified by the attentions of such a man.

To what was it leading? I was not sure. And the very uncertainty added to the fascination. But I should have to go home. I should leave this exotic life behind me. It would be something to remember all my life, but a life which did not include him would seem very dreary to me.

So . . . I did not want to think about the future. I just wanted to revel in the present.

Felicity was a little better. On the previous day she had sat with me in the courtyard in the late afternoon when the sun had lost some of its fierceness. She shrank a little if any stranger spoke to her; but at least she had left her room for a while.

She was still getting the occasional nightmare. I slept lightly. I think I was listening for the tap on the wall even when I slept. It came now and then and I would leap out of bed and go to her. The horror in her eyes when she came out of those dreams haunted me, and I knew that it was going to take a long time for her to recover.

But it was comforting to know that she was a little better.

She would talk to the chambermaid who looked after our rooms and brought up our hot water and food for Felicity. I often had my lunch with her. She slept late in the mornings so I breakfasted downstairs and if I was going out, which I often did in the company of Milton, I would ask Maria to keep an eye on her, and if she should ask for me tell her I should not be away long.

Maria was talkative and eager to help. She was perhaps not the best of workers but she had a pleasing personality. She was young and slender with long black hair and laughing dark eyes and a light brown skin; her bead necklaces and bracelets jangled as she walked.

She would roll her eyes round as she talked and life seemed a great joke to her. Even when she was recounting some disaster she would laugh. She liked to keep us up to date with what was happening in the island. We learned that a certain Sam had hurt himself badly when he fell on the stubs of cut cane. "Cut about he was," she told us with a high-pitched giggle. "Hands and face bleeding. He'll be marked for the rest of his days." Then there was old Mrs. Joppa who was knocked down by a bullock cart which provided the same kind of mirth.

This laugh followed every item of news—joyous or tragic. I presumed it was a habit and of no significance.

Maria had a lover. One day she was going to join him in Brisbane where he was working on a property. Sabrino was going to have a property of his own one day . . . just a little one for a start. Then Maria would join him. They were both saving their money to make that dream a possibility.

I listened attentively. Sabrino, it seemed, was the most handsome man in the world. He had been born in Cariba, but Cariba was no place for Sabrino; Maria lived for the day when she would join him.

The only time she was serious was when she talked of Sabrino.

She used to linger in my room. She was very interested in my clothes. Once I found her rummaging in my cupboard. I expressed surprise but could not really be angry with her, for her curiosity was so natural and she was so eager to please.

One morning I was sitting on the balcony when a very striking-looking woman came into the hotel. She was tall and her dark hair was piled high on her head; she walked with the exquisite grace such as I had noticed among the women of the island. But she was very different from the others. I felt she was of some importance and I had formed that opinion merely by seeing her walk through the crowd. She wore a white clinging gown and there was a gold chain about her neck.

I decided to ask Maria who she was when I next saw her. Maria would be sure to know.

To my amazement Maria came to my room. That was another habit of hers. She would come in without knocking, and although I had asked her to remember to do so, she often forgot.

"Miss Mallory," she said in a high-pitched excited voice and she appeared to be so consumed with laughter that she could scarcely speak, "there's a lady downstairs asking for you. She's come to call on you."

"Oh, who is she?"

Maria was so overcome that for a few seconds she was speechless.

"It's Mrs. Manuel," she burst out at length.

"Is that the lady I saw a little while ago? Tall, dark, in white?"

Maria nodded.

"I'll come down," I said.

Mrs. Manuel was seated in the reception area and I was aware of Rosa behind the desk, and several of them standing there, tense as though waiting for something extraordinary to happen.

She rose when I appeared.

"Miss Mallory," she said, "I have come to see you. I am Magda Manuel."

"Oh, how nice to meet you. I've heard of you."

"Everybody hears everything on these islands."

"I have heard about you from Milton Harrington."

There was silence about us. They were all listening intently as though there was something of great significance about this meeting.

"Perhaps we could go somewhere and talk," I said.

Rosa betrayed the fact that she had been listening by saying guilelessly: "Oh yes, Miss Mallory. Come this way."

She led us to the room with the balcony overlooking the harbour where I had once talked to Milton.

"You would like some refreshment?" I asked.

"Yes please."

Rosa said she would bring Lalu, which was the name of the local drink which was made of fruit and was only slightly alcoholic—the perfect drink for a hot day which was obviously why it was so popular.

We sat together side by side on the balcony.

"I have been meaning to call on you for some time." she said. "But we are so busy on the plantation."

"The plantation?"

"Oh, didn't you know. I come from Second Island. We have our plantation there. Not as big as the one here . . . but there is a great deal to do in it. I can't keep my work people in order as Milton does his. I lack the touch . . . so did my husband. Milton has taught us a few things."

"So you have a sugar plantation, too."

"Oh yes . . . It's a little too much. I lost my husband quite recently. I don't know how I could carry on without Milton's help."

The refreshment was brought by one of the men who seemed reluctant to leave us. I had a notion that beyond this room they were all talking about the meeting between myself and Magda Manuel.

"Milton was talking about you and I thought I'd call," she said. "You must visit me. Come to dinner. I believe you have a friend with you."

"Yes. But she has been very ill and still is."

"I heard about that terrible business in Australia." She looked at me apologetically. "You see, news travels fast here. It hasn't far to go."

"She is not well enough to see anyone just yet, but she is improving."

"You haven't been to Second Island yet, have you? I know you haven't or I should have heard."

"No, but I have often looked at it. It seems green and inviting."

"The green is the cane . . . "

"Are you managing the plantation yourself?"

"Not exactly. I have a good man. George Callerby. He was my husband's right-hand man. So many things go wrong in a plantation. Storms can beat down the canes; rats and white ants can eat them; the boilers give up at the wrong moment and the mills grind to a halt. Milton has all his under control and the best equipment . . . and most of all a way of handling people. He rules with the iron hand in the velvet glove. I have never known how people achieve that. Nor did my husband. He used to say Milton had a genius for these things. These people must know who is master. They've got to respect you, otherwise they'll slack and you'll find them half asleep with their cutters in their hands. But I am boring you with all this talk of business. What I want to know is, will you dine with us?"

"I should enjoy that."

"I'll fix a date. Milton will row you over. It is not really far. I've wanted to meet you so much but I have been busy. You see, my husband died only a few months ago. It was while Milton was in England."

"I'm sorry to hear that."

"He was ailing for a long time, so it wasn't unexpected. I'll let you know the date. It will probably be next week. That will be all right, won't it? You're not thinking of leaving us yet?"

"I shall have to go soon, I suppose. But I want to make sure that Mrs. Granville is fit to travel."

"Of course."

She rose. She was very gracious and graceful; the gold glinted in her ears and the sun caught it about her neck. She was a very beautiful woman.

I walked with her through the reception room to the door of the hotel.

I was very much aware of the eyes which followed us. I was sure that as soon as we were out of sight, the whispering would begin.

I went up to my room.

Maria was there, making a great play with a duster, but apparently doing very little.

I spoke to Milton about Magda when I saw him that evening. I wondered whether he had spent the day with her.

He had come to have dinner with me which he usually did. He often asked me to go out to his house, but I was wary of doing this and I did not care to leave Felicity alone in the hotel for too long. I wanted to be somewhere within call if possible.

We sat in the courtyard before dinner and I said to him: "I had a visitor this morning. A friend of yours."

"Magda," he said.

"She told you?"

"Yes."

"I suppose she called on you after she left me."

"She came up, yes."

"She tells me they have a plantation on that island."

"That's right. Smaller than this one."

"She told me that, too. She manages it on her own."

"She has a very good man in George Callerby. José Manuel wasn't meant for it. He should never have taken it up."

"She said you had been helpful to them."

"I gave a bit of advice . . . when José was alive."

"I gather that he died while you were in England."

"I can see she has brought you up to date with the news."

"Everyone here seems to be very amused that she should come to see me."

"They are easily amused."

"They seemed to find this especially hilarious."

He looked at me sardonically. "Magda has been almost a widow for some time. She had a hard life. José was injured in his mill. Something went wrong and he wasn't experienced enough to handle it properly. He was badly hurt and had been an invalid for four years."

"And you were a great friend of his and helped him a good deal."

"I found George Callerby for them. He is an excellent man."

I could imagine it so clearly. The husband who was no husband; the vibrant woman, young and beautiful, and Milton's going over to their island to help them, being the good friend . . . especially to Magda.

And of course the islanders would know. There was little they did not know. Perhaps they had thought that now José was dead, Milton would marry his widow. Then . . . I had appeared. Oh yes, it was very clear to me.

I had a rival. I could not stop thinking of her sinuous beauty, which made me feel almost clumsy in comparison. She had dignity and good looks. She fitted into this island life far better than I would. I wondered what he felt about Magda. I fancied his voice had softened a little when he spoke of her and I was aware of twinges of jealousy. It was absurd. I kept telling myself that as soon as Felicity was well enough I would go home and marry Raymond.

He was saying: "We are going to do a little bit of diving tomorrow. Would you like to see it?"

"Diving?"

"Yes . . . it's at sunrise tomorrow. We have some oyster beds on the south of the island. Occasionally we find a few really fine pearls. Not enough really to make an industry of it. So . . . we just amuse ourselves and hope that one day we shall come up with a pearl of great price."

"I should like to see it. Who does the diving?"

"We have divers. They have to be rather skilled. I have been down on occasions but I don't make a practice of it. It is quite exciting . . . sorting out the haul. We get all kinds . . . Quite a number of baroque—lovely colour but irregular; then we get blisters which are hollow and knobbly ones which we call *coq de perle*. Imagine the joy when we find a perfect pearl. The right colour, the right texture and the right shape."

"Have you ever found one?"

"Once. It was in my father's time. That was a real gem. I've never rivalled that. But there have been some that were rather fine."

"I had always thought of this as a sugar island. I'd never thought of pearls."

"Ah, there is a great deal you have to learn about us. So would you like to see us at work?"

"I should love that."

"Can you rise early enough? The boats will be a little way out where the beds are. They will start at sunrise."

"I shall be there."

"At sunrise," he repeated.

The next morning I rose early and went round to the south side of the island. I saw the men on the shore. I knew several of them because I had seen them on the plantation.

I said: "Is Mr. Harrington here?"

One of the men—Jacob—nodded out to the boat which was rocking gently to and fro in the water.

"Mr. Harrington's going down today," he said.

"What? . . . Diving himself?"

"Oh yes, he'll dive."

I stood there watching. I could see several figures in the boat. One was taller than the others so I presumed that to be Milton.

"How long do they stay down there?" I asked.

"Not long, Missie Lady. Couldn't stay long. Can't breathe for long. One minute about all time."

One of the men said: "Gemel he stayed six minutes once."

"Gemel very great diver. He stayed too long once though. Tried to break the record."

"What happened to him?"

"Can't live long down there, Missie Lady, not without air."

"You mean he died?"

"Diving dangerous work. That why they get money for it . . . lots of money."

"But Mr. Harrington has gone down."

"Master . . . he can do anything . . . better than anyone else."

"What is that noise I hear?"

"That's the shark charmers."

"Sharks! There are sharks in these waters?"

"Sometimes they come close. But they won't come while the shark charmer's there."

I felt a twinge of anxiety. I had no faith that those mournful ditties would deter the sharks.

I said: "Has any man ever been taken by a shark?"

"Oh yes . . . there have been."

"Then where was the shark charmer? What was he doing at the time?"

"There always be accidents, Missie Lady."

"How do they go down?"

"You see the man at the side of the boat? He's working with one of the divers. They work in pairs . . . one goes down and the other watches the cord that's tied to the diver."

"It seems very hazardous to me."

I was suddenly afraid as I stood there watching. He had gone down because I was here. He had wanted to prove again his ability to do everything better than anyone else. I thought angrily: I suppose he thinks he is going to return with his pearl of great price!

Pictures forced themselves into my mind. I imagined a monster shark appearing. I pictured the rope which was attached to him breaking. I saw him in my mind's eye down there gasping for breath.

"Let him be safe," I prayed. "Let him come back . . . "

I knew then how much he mattered to me. I just wanted him to be safe. Nothing else seemed to matter in that moment. I was arguing with myself. I have to go away. I have to go back to England and I shall marry Raymond, good, kind Raymond. But please God, let him be safe.

I might have known he would be all right.

I stood there rather angrily as the boat came in. He sprang out and ran to me. He was glowing with health.

"You came then?" he said.

"I expected to find you on the shore not at the bottom of the sea."

"It was exhilarating," he said.

"Did you find the fine pearl?"

"Probably. They have to be sorted out. You look a little distraught."

"I've been talking to the men about diving. It's dangerous."

"There is an element of danger in most enterprises."

"And particularly so in this."

"Perhaps it is rather specially hazardous. So you are rather pleased to see me back on dry land?"

"Of course I am."

He took my hand and pressed it. "Don't worry. I'll always turn up. I'll always be there."

There was triumph in his grin. I had betrayed myself.

ECHOES FROM
THE PAST

It was two days later. I had breakfasted and had taken my favourite seat on the terrace overlooking the waterfront. I seemed to have made a habit of sitting there at this time of day. Later I would go to Felicity's room and see how she was.

The scene never failed to interest me. It was constantly changing, never the same.

As I sat there a man came along. I had seen him on the previous day and guessed he was a visitor to the hotel. He was obviously English and as he passed my chair he said: "Good morning."

"Good morning," I replied.

He hesitated. "May I sit here?"

"Please do."

He took the chair close to mine.

"I have seen you around," he said. "Are you enjoying your stay here?"

"Oh yes, very much."

"The noise those people make down there! They don't seem to be able to do anything without shouting and laughing."

"Yes. It's amusing to watch."

"You come from England, do you?"

"Yes."

"I'm from Australia."

"Not so very far away."

"No. It's very convenient really."

There was silence for a few moments.

Then he said: "I have heard that you have been asking about a Mr. Philip Mallory."

I was alert. "Why yes," I said eagerly. "Did you know him?"

"I can't say I knew him. I called in here . . . it must have been about two years ago. I spoke to him then . . . just as I am speaking to you now."

"He was my brother," I said.

"Really!"

"Yes. I am Annalice Mallory. Did you ever hear anything about my brother?"

"Hear anything about him? No. I just spoke to him on one or two occasions. Then I went home. I did come back some months later and oddly enough I mentioned him and was told that he had gone away."

"Nobody seems to know where."

"I had one or two conversations with him. He told me something about an island he was going to visit."

"Yes . . . yes . . . that was so."

"He seemed to set great store on finding it. Apparently he had made some attempt to and had been disappointed."

I was feeling more and more excited. This man was telling me more than anyone so far.

I said: "We never heard what happened to my brother. We waited and waited for news of him but we heard nothing."

"That must have been terrible for you."

"If only I could find out what happened to him. If only I could find this island . . . "

"These seas have been well charted. It shouldn't be difficult."

"It seems this island is not where we thought it was."

"Have you come here to look for the island?"

"I really came to see if I could find out anything about my brother. I want to know what happened to him."

"How long is it since you last heard?"

"Two years."

"That's a long time."

"People here knew him. I have talked to them, but they can't tell me any more than you have. They met him. They talked to him. But he seems to have talked to you more than he did to most for he did tell you about the island."

"Well, that's all I can say. I suppose naturally he would talk to me. He was just out from England and I'm English, too, although I live in

Australia. We just got talking and it slipped out about the island."

"And you can't remember anything else?"

"There was nothing else. We just sat and talked for half an hour or so one or two mornings. That's all."

I was disappointed. It was the same as I had heard again and again.

"My name is John Everton," he said. "I hope you did not mind my speaking to you."

"Not at all. I am very interested to hear any little detail about my brother."

"I wish I could be of help."

We talked about the island and after a while I left him.

The next morning he approached me again.

He said: "I've been thinking a lot about what we said. This island ... It is intriguing, I find."

"It's non-existent apparently."

"How can you be sure of that?"

"Because I've actually been out to look for it and there is nothing where it should be."

"Did you have a map then?"

"Yes, I had a map."

"Depicting this island?"

"Yes."

"Well, then it must be there."

"It's a very old map ... or rather a copy of one."

"Where did you get this map? It seems so extraordinary that the place should be marked on a map and not be there."

"It is the copy of a map which was found in my home."

"Found in your home! What ...? Forgive me. I am being too inquisitive."

"No ... certainly not. We found this map in our house. It had been there for a hundred years or thereabouts. The island was marked on it."

"Do you have this map?"

"I have my copy of it."

"Could I ... would it ... Would it be asking too much to let me see it?"

"Of course not. I'll go and get it."

When I brought the map down to him he studied it with close attention.

"And that's the island," he said, pointing to it. "The Paradise Island."

"That is just the name which was given to it by the man who made the original map."

He looked at me with puzzlement in his eyes.

"It's a long story," I said. "The map was found in our house when some alterations were made. That was what gave rise to all this. My brother wanted to find the island."

"And so he came out here . . . " He put his finger on the island. "It is clearly there. I have sailed these seas and I am sure that there is no such island. The map must be at fault. Are you sure this is the actual map which was found in your house?"

"It is an exact replica. I made it."

"*You* made it?"

"Yes, from the one which was found."

"It's an excellent job."

"My family have been map makers for a very long time. I learned a little about it. I can assure you it is an exact copy."

"How very interesting!"

He gave the map back to me.

He said: "I really do find this most intriguing. I wish I could be of help to you."

"It has been very pleasant talking."

Conversation drifted on to other matters and I bade him farewell and left him.

He seemed to make a ritual of these morning talks for the next day he came up again.

"I feel so excited," he said. "Something has occurred to me. I woke up at five this morning with this idea. That is the time for my ideas. I've had my best then. I wonder what you will think of it."

"Do tell me."

"It's about the map and the island. The map is in error. I wonder who made it in the first place."

I hesitated, then I said: "It was made by a man who was ship-wrecked and thrown up on an island. He stayed there for a while and when he was fishing off the island he was caught in a storm and almost drowned. He drifted for a while and was picked up by a ship. Then he made the map."

"Good heavens! That explains a lot."

"You mean there was no island. He was just suffering from a form of hallucination. We have thought of that."

"That might have been so, of course, but I wasn't thinking of that. He made his map from memory. That could explain it. He could be miles out."

"Yes, that is a possibility. But after this group there are no islands for hundreds of miles."

"But what if his island was one of these?"

"How could it be? These are marked clearly on the map."

"There is an island . . . a little apart from these by several miles. Four of them are close together, but this one is some distance apart."

"You mean Lion Island? The one which belongs to the mining people?"

"I mean that one, yes."

"But that is marked on the map. There are the four islands and the fifth one apart."

"Exactly, but the shipwrecked man could have been thrown up on that island and thought he was a long way from this group."

I hesitated and he went on: "Don't you think it would be worth investigating?"

"That island belongs to someone."

"Why not pay a visit? The people there might know something about the history of the island."

"Do you think I might do that?"

"I don't see why not. Look here, I'm enormously interested. I've been thinking about it since five this morning. It's a calm day. Why don't I take you over. I could get a boat and we could leave right away."

I considered this. Why not? I had nothing to do this morning. Milton would call in the evening. I was sure that Felicity would be all right. I did not believe for one moment that Lion Island was the Paradise Island, and even if it were it must have changed completely now and how could I prove it? But I had promised myself that I would follow every clue, however remote it seemed.

I said I would go.

I went to Felicity who was still in bed. She said she felt like a lazy morning and would get up later.

I said: "I'm going out to one of the islands. I'll be away all the morning. So don't worry if I'm a little late back."

"To one of the islands?"

"Yes, just to have a look at it. I have been asked and I might as well go."

It was a feature of Felicity's illness that she was listless and indifferent to what was going on around her. She merely nodded and closed her eyes.

Soon we were skimming over the water. There was the gentlest of breezes and it was very pleasant. Looking ahead I could see the reclining lion getting nearer and nearer.

I was rather sorry when the boat touched land.

"Aren't we trespassing?" I asked.

"I don't think that will matter."

I stood on the sandy beach and looked back. There was no sign of Cariba and the other islands.

"I should have thought they were near enough to be seen," I commented.

"We're on the other side of the island."

I shaded my eyes and looked about me. There was a cove in which lay two ships. One quite big.

"What now?" I asked.

"Explore."

"How could we tell even if we are on Paradise Island?"

"I don't know. We just have to wait and see what happens."

Something was happening now. A man was coming towards us. He was of medium height with blond hair and light blue eyes. Did I have the feeling that I had seen him before—or did I fancy that afterwards?

He put out his hand and said: "Welcome to my island."

I put my hand into his.

He said: "Let me introduce myself. I am Magnus Perrensen."

I was in a state of bewilderment and incredulity and it is difficult for me even now to remember that day very clearly. From the moment he had taken my hand and spoken I felt as though I were living in a dream. I just stared at him. In that moment I was not myself. I was Ann Alice who had become me—just as he, the lover of long ago, now stood before me on Lion Island.

"I'm Annalice Mallory," I told him.

"At last you have come," was his answer.

"I . . . I don't understand. What does this mean?"

"You know who I am," he replied. "So there is a great deal we have to say to each other."

We both seemed to have forgotten John Everton who was standing by looking puzzled and uncertain—as well he might.

"Come into the house," said Magnus Perrensen.

We walked up a slope. I was trying hard to grapple with common sense. I am dreaming, I thought. I must be. How could he be Magnus Perrensen. He must have died years ago.

The house was magnificent. It was dazzlingly white in the shimmering heat and brilliantly coloured flowers bloomed in the gardens which surrounded it and my mood of bewilderment touched it all with an air of unreality.

He led us through a door into a cool paved hall.

John Everton who had not spoken so far said in awed tones: "It is splendid."

"You should have brought Miss Mallory before," said Magnus Perrensen.

"The idea that we should see the island only came to Mr. Everton this morning," I said, and as I spoke I felt more normal. The memory of meeting John Everton outside the hotel and discussing the trip brought me back to reality.

We went into a room with tall windows looking over the sea.

Magnus Perrensen turned to John Everton. "By a strange coincidence," he said, "Miss Mallory's family and mine were in contact years ago. We have a great deal to discuss. It was a stroke of good fortune that you brought her here today. Thank you."

"I'm glad of that," said John Everton rather awkwardly.

"We don't have many visitors here. We don't encourage it. It's by way of a retreat for my family. When we are here we like solitude."

"Perhaps," I began, "we should not have disturbed you . . . "

He looked at me reproachfully. "You are welcome . . . welcome indeed."

A servant appeared and he asked for cool drinks to be brought. His order was immediately obeyed.

I could not stop looking at him. I was taken right back to that night when I had sat up in bed reading Ann Alice's diary. Something had happened to me then . . . when I sat in that room . . . when I had tended her grave . . . and now here I was on a remote island . . . sitting face to face with Magnus Perrensen.

I was aware of course that this was not the young man who had worked in our shop and had planned to marry Ann Alice and take her in search of the island, any more than I was the girl who lay in that grave at Little Stanton. But some part of those people lived on in us, and I believed that I was on the verge of a great discovery.

At length Magnus Perrensen said: "Mr. Everton, you would like to see the island. Miss Mallory and I have a great deal to talk about because of our family connections. You will need a horse. I will arrange for someone to take you round. Luncheon will be served at one o'clock."

"I shall have to go back," I explained. "I have a friend at the hotel. She is ill and will be wondering what has become of me."

"If you go back immediately after luncheon it will mean being on the sea in the heat of the day."

"Then I must get back before," I insisted.

He smiled at me. "Very well. Just an hour . . . leave in an hour's time. I will tell them to bring you back, Mr. Everton, in one hour. That will give us a little time to talk and next time it shall be longer."

So I was alone with him.

"I see that you are bewildered," he said.

"I am indeed."

"You know something of what happened years ago?"

I explained about the night of the storm and our finding the journal.

"That Magnus Perrensen was my great-grandfather."

"So you know the whole story of what happened?"

"It is a story which has been passed down through my family. My great-grandfather told it to my grandfather, and he in his turn to my father and so to me. We were all named Magnus. It makes a kind of continuity. And you are Annalice . . . which is a little different from Ann Alice . . . and yet similar though."

I said: "This is not the island . . . "

He shook his head.

"Please tell me what you know," I begged.

"As I said the story has been passed down through my family. When my great-grandfather returned to Little Stanton it was to find his bride-to-be dead. She had died, he was told, of the plague which was raging nearby. At least that was the story. He didn't believe it. The matter was wrapped in such secrecy and there was the room. People talked a great deal about that. It was walled up by the local carpenter and builder who prospered from that time. My great-grandfather believed that it was because this carpenter had seen something in the room which must never be known and the price of his silence was money to enable him to prosper in his business."

"What did he see in the room?"

"My great-grandfather believed that Ann Alice was murdered. Her stepmother and her lover murdered her. She was probably shot. There would be bloodstains all over the room. Shooting is not a neat way of disposing of people. They daren't let what was significant in that room be seen. They were able to conceal the evidence of their crime because of the plague. There was a case of some tailor's rooms having been walled up because of the goods in them. They got away with that. They never would but for the plague and the bribable carpenter."

"It sounds very plausible."

"I believe when you saw me you thought for a moment that I was that Magnus Perrensen. Did you perhaps think you had become Ann Alice?"

"I had read her journal and it is still very vivid in my mind. Something seemed to happen to me after I had read it. I just felt part of her, and for a moment when I saw you on the beach and you told me your name . . . I felt strange and quite bewildered. Yes, for a moment I did feel that I had stepped back in time."

"Nothing so strange, I assure you. There is a logical explanation to everything that happens on Earth I feel sure. I suppose we all have something of our ancestors in us. Isn't that proved? Traits of character handed down from generation to generation . . . There must be something of that Magnus in me and something of Ann Alice in you. It seemed like a miracle to me when you came along this morning. For a moment I thought it was a fusion of the past and present."

"You said: 'At last you have come.' "

"I did, did I not? It was involuntary, as though someone was speaking through me. You felt it too."

"Yes, it was a very strange moment."

"Now calm reason is here."

"Tell me everything that happened. There was no island, was there?"

He shook his head.

"Let me tell you what I know and you shall tell me. This is the story we heard in our family. My great-grandfather, Magnus Perrensen, came back to Great Stanton. He had been to London to make arrangements for the journey back to his family. He was going to take Ann Alice with him."

I nodded. This was exactly what I had read in the journal.

"He came back to learn that she was dead. Died of the plague, they said. She was already buried, as people were quickly in such circumstances. They had walled up her room because of the fear that things might be infected. He would not believe it. He was highly suspicious of the stepmother and the man whom he suspected of being her lover. He was heartbroken. He wanted to know the truth and he wanted vengeance. There were no more cases of the plague. There had been only two men apparently and Ann Alice who were alleged victims. The men were tailors who had been buying materials somewhere in the Middle East. He could not rest. He wanted to know. He became suspicious. He questioned the carpenter and he was not satisfied. But there was nothing else he could do. He was young and a foreigner and the people at the Manor were rich and powerful. In time he gave up and came back to his family. He could not rest though. He wanted to go back and find that island."

"Did he find it?"

He shook his head. "No. There was no island. He wouldn't believe it at first. It was a long time before he had to accept it. He would not leave the area, so he went to Australia and there he became interested in looking for gold; he always believed he would find the island although he searched continually and there was nothing where he believed it must be."

"Do you think it was a hallucination? He was shipwrecked, wasn't he? And he was only on the island for a short time. It was strange that he was shipwrecked a second time. Do you believe that he imagined the whole thing? If he did he must have drifted for days and days at sea."

"I think that is a conclusion we have to come to—though he never did at heart. You see, the island was perfect . . . too perfect. Those lovable natives . . . the gold everywhere. It was a dream . . . an ideal. Perhaps he came to this conclusion in time, though I don't know. However, he discovered gold. He had great success. He went in for mining on a large scale. He was obsessed by gold because it was there on his island. Well, that was the start. He became rich; he married a girl in Melbourne; he had a son, my grandfather . . . That's the story. It was my father who bought this island. We use it as a sort of refuge. We come here for long spells sometimes . . . "

"You and the rest of your family?"

"Mostly myself. I have no brothers or sisters. My father does not come here much now. He leaves it for me."

"And your family . . . your wife and children?"

"I have not married . . . yet."

"Oh, are you planning to?"

He looked at me very steadily. "I suppose most people think of marrying sometimes. There have been occasions . . . but something has held me back. And you? But perhaps I am asking too personal a question?"

"As I did of you?"

He laughed. He said: "We are not really strangers, are we? How could we be in these very special circumstances?"

"That's true. You asked me if I was planning to get married. There is someone at home. I thought I might marry him. He has asked me, but as yet . . . "

"I understand perfectly. And you came out here . . . ?"

"I came with a friend who was going to be married. I wanted to find my brother."

"Your brother. So you have family."

"I had a brother. We were very close because of the family situation, I suppose. My mother died when I was born and my father married again and lives out of England. My grandmother took charge of my brother and me. When we were young there was a question of our being separated and that of course brought us very close together. He came out here in search of this mythical island . . . and we haven't heard from him since."

"How long ago was that?"

"Two years."

"Oh . . . that's bad."

"I came out to find him."

"How did you hope to do that?"

"I wasn't sure. I thought I might get clues and be led to the solution of the mystery."

"And have you found any?"

"None really. People knew him . . . remembered him . . . He was in Cariba. Then he left and no one has any idea where he went."

"And you have not found anyone who could give you an idea?"

I shook my head. "I am so frustrated. It seems so hopeless."

"It does seem a hopeless task."

"I really don't know what to do. I went out to look for the island.

There is a man in Cariba. You probably know him . . . Milton Harrington."

"Who does not know of him? A forceful character. He practically owns the place, I believe."

"He owns the sugar plantation there."

"And he took you out to where you thought this island should be?"

"Yes, there was a map. The one we found in the walled-up room after the storm. My brother took it. I made a copy. So we were able to see where it ought to have been. There was nothing there."

"Nothing at all?"

"Absolutely nothing. Mr. Harrington said there were no islands for a hundred miles at least."

"And you have this map with you, this copy? Are you sure it is accurate?"

"It's an exact copy of the one which was found in Ann Alice's room. I made it myself."

"*You* did!"

"You know of the family business. Your great-grandfather was in the same when he came over to England. I suppose that was abandoned when he went into mining."

"Oh yes, of course. Everyone knows of Mallory's maps."

"I worked in the shop now and then. I knew a little about map making . . . enough to make an accurate copy."

"I see. I wish I could be of help regarding your brother. I should have been so pleased to meet him. This has been a most exciting morning for me."

"For me too. I am still staggering from the surprise of hearing your name."

"And you now know that I have not stepped out of the past. You know I'm no ghost."

"It's all perfectly normal. You've explained so much. Isn't it extraordinary that we have met!"

"It seems miraculous. But when you think of it, the island—this non-existent island—is the focal point. You've come looking for it as all those years ago my great-grandfather did. It drew him here and he started our dynasty in Australia it's true, but we still thought of the island . . . and then we came here to this one. You found the journal and the map . . . and you're here too. There's a sort of pattern to it."

"Yes, that is what makes it so exciting."

"Do you realize that our hour is drawing to an end. Need you return just yet?"

"I must. My friend, Mrs. Granville, will be worrying. She is in rather a nervous state. She suffered a terrible experience in Australia. Her husband died violently."

"Oh . . . that Granville. There was a case. The bushrangers, wasn't it? He was after them and fell from a balcony when his gun went off."

"Yes, that is the case."

"The papers were full of it. Poor lady, I can understand that she is in a nervous state."

"I was in the house when it happened. I have brought her with me to Cariba. We shall go home together eventually."

"Not yet, I hope."

"I think we shall stay a little longer yet, though I can see that to try to find out what happened to my brother is rather a hopeless task."

"I fear so."

"And you understand I don't want to cause her anxiety."

"Of course. They'll bring your companion back very soon. You will come again?"

"I should like to. I am sure I shall remember all sorts of things I wanted to say after I've gone."

"And if I may, I will come to Cariba."

"That would be very pleasant."

"Now that we have found each other so miraculously that is a beginning. I hear them coming now."

"Then I must say goodbye."

"Au revoir," he corrected me.

John Everton came in looking flushed and rather pleased. "The island is beautiful. It is a pity you cannot stay and see it."

"Miss Mallory has promised to come again," said Magnus Perrensen.

He walked down to the beach with us. He took my hand solemnly and kissed it. I still felt a little light-headed.

"What a strange morning," said John Everton as we skimmed across the pellucid water. "Who would have thought we should have been so hospitably received! And what an odd coincidence that he should have known your family. Did you have a good discussion about all that?"

"Yes. It was indeed very strange that our families should have known each other a hundred years ago."

"That's quite amazing. I feel very gratified for having been the means of bringing you together."

"Thank you. It was a wonderful experience."

And as I sat back watching the reclining lion grow fainter and fainter, I still felt I was dreaming.

I was seated in the courtyard in Milton Harrington's house and telling him about my morning's adventure. I had asked Maria to look in now and then on Felicity and if there was any need to send for me. Maria had nodded, giggling. There must have been speculation about my visits to Milton's house.

He listened to my account of what had happened and clearly did not like it very much. I imagined he was a little piqued because there was a man in the neighbourhood as influential in his sphere as Milton was in his.

"You mean you went out in a boat with this man!"

"Well, I went out on another occasion with a man in a boat. Because his name was Milton Harrington does that make it all right?"

"Of course it does."

"You see, it seemed feasible and I did not want to leave any stone unturned."

"So you went out and met this mysterious gold miner."

"It was very odd—the most extraordinary thing that has ever happened to me. When I stood on the beach and he said he was Magnus Perrensen, which, as I told you, was the name of the man my ancestress was going to marry, I just felt as though I were dreaming . . . or I had been transported back in time. It was miraculous and then I discovered that he had descended from that man and he knew all that had happened . . . all that was in the journal because the story had been handed down from generation to generation in his family."

"And what happened then?"

"We just talked and talked . . . He wanted us to stay to lunch but I was thinking of Felicity. I didn't want to upset her. So we came back. Don't you think it is the most extraordinary thing that we met like that?"

"It's a little too extraordinary," he said. "I don't like it much."

"You don't like it because you weren't there and it doesn't concern you."

"It does concern me if it concerns you. I want to know more about this visitant from the past."

"He's not from the past. He has just descended. Oh, it is the strangest thing. I never thought of anything like this happening."

"You seem to be in a daze and you have been all the evening."

"I can't stop thinking of it."

"He has become very affable all of a sudden. I have always heard that he did not like people trespassing on his island."

"It was rather exceptional circumstances."

"I shall find out what I can about him."

"What do you mean?"

"I don't like these mysterious people. He comes here every now and then . . . He is supposed to be fabulously wealthy; he owns the only gold mines that are really producing these days. He must be something of a phenomenon."

"And if there are any of those about, you want to be the only one."

"Naturally. I hope you won't make a habit of going off with strangers. Promise to consult me before you do anything rash again."

"The suggestion for rashness might easily come from you."

"That is different."

"I see." I smiled at him. I was glad to see him sitting there. I still thought of the anxiety I had suffered when I had known he was on the sea bed and there were sharks in the vicinity.

"By the way," he went on, "Magda Manuel wants you to dine with her and suggests I take you over."

"I shall look forward to that."

"The evening after tomorrow. Felicity is invited if she is well enough."

I shook my head. "She still doesn't want to meet people. Do you think she is getting better?"

"I think it takes a long time to recover from such an experience."

"I'll ask her. In any case I shall be delighted to come."

He drove me back to the hotel in his carriage.

When he said good night, he added: "By the way I should like to take another look at that map."

"The map? But we've been there. There's nothing there."

"Still, I'd like to have a look at it again."

"Just as you like. I'll give it to you next time I see you."

I went to my room. I thought at once of the map. I would get it out so that I remembered it tomorrow. I kept it at the back of the drawer, I suppose because Ann Alice had done the same.

I went to the drawer. The map was not there.

I could not believe it. I had not taken it out and I never put it anywhere else.

It was very strange.

I turned out the drawer but I could not find the map. How very odd! I must have put it somewhere else. But where? I would make a thorough search in the morning.

I found sleep difficult. I kept going over that moment on the beach when he had said: "I am Magnus Perrensen."

I knew it was all logically explained, but somehow I could not accept the logical explanation. It was almost as though I had been brought here for a purpose and that purpose was to meet Magnus Perrensen.

I could easily believe that I was Ann Alice, that she had led me here because she wanted me to meet her lover, to live the life which she would have lived if she had not died so tragically, so violently on that last night she had written in her journal.

We had been brought together for a purpose. What purpose? What purpose could there be? It was more or less certain now that I was in love —physically in love—with Milton Harrington. I was excited by him; I loved to spar conversationally with him; I felt I could have died of fright when I had pictured him at the bottom of the sea. Was that love? I could have been sure it was but for Raymond. I loved Raymond too. I trusted Raymond. Did I not trust Milton? Perhaps not entirely and yet there was even an excitement in mistrust. Raymond would be a faithful husband. Would Milton? There was the shadow of Magda Manuel already to give me cause for speculation. I was sure there had been a deep relationship of some sort between them. Life with him would be a stormy one. With Raymond it would be gentle; I should be at peace. What did I want? I was unsure.

And now here was Magnus Perrensen. I had seen him only once but how many times had I thought of that other Magnus. I felt that I knew him. I had lived through those pages in the journal as though they were real. To some extent I *was* Ann Alice.

Life was becoming more and more complicated.

It was inevitable that night that I should dream. I was in the walled-up room and I was sitting at the dressing table writing in my journal what had happened to me that day. I was Ann Alice and I was listening all the time for a footstep on the stairs.

I saw the words clearly: "I thought I heard a noise. Footsteps . . . I can hear voices . . . Something is going on down there. They are coming . . ."

Then I heard the step on the stairs. I looked at the key in the door and it suddenly fell out of the keyhole. I heard breathing behind the door which was being forced open.

I screamed and awoke damp with sweat to find myself lying under my mosquito net. I was someone who had died a hundred years ago and had been reborn. I was Ann Alice as well as Annalice. Fantasy was still with me. She had willed me to come here . . . and here I was. This was what she wanted.

I stared at my door. It was being gently opened.

For a moment I thought I was still in the dream. I expected to see the wicked stepmother there with her lover, and the lover would have a gun in his hands.

"Felicity!" I cried.

She looked like a ghost in her white nightgown, with her hair loose about her shoulders.

"I heard you cry out," she said.

She came to my bed and I murmured: "It . . . was a nightmare."

"So you have them, too."

"We all do at times, I suppose."

She laughed suddenly. "This is in reverse," she said. "Me . . . coming to comfort you."

I felt a tremendous relief sweeping over me. Felicity was more like her old self than I had seen her for a long time.

I took her back to her room and sat by her bed. We talked awhile and finally she slept.

I went back to my bed.

I was fully awake now. Fantasy receded. There was a logical explanation to everything.

NIGHT ON
A LONELY ISLAND

Milton had rowed me to the small island where Magda had her plantation. Felicity had at first said she would come, which showed how much better she was; but at the last moment she had felt unable to face strangers. I did not attempt to persuade her because I felt she must be left until she was ready. She seemed to be progressing to some extent and I did not want to reverse that.

So here I was alone with Milton watching him as he pulled the oars with such ease that he made it seem effortless.

There was no wind. It had dropped that evening—but there was a faint mist in the air and the silence was broken only by the swish of the oars in the water.

I was intrigued at the prospect of seeing Magda Manuel in her own home. I have to confess that I felt a few twinges of jealousy. She had seemed to me so poised, so beautiful when she had called at the hotel.

I asked Milton as we rowed across: "She is a great friend of yours, isn't she?"

And he replied enigmatically: "A very great friend."

The distance between the islands was not great and in a short time we were there. Milton shipped the oars, leaped out and helped me to alight.

I was wearing a loose pale lavender-coloured dress which I had bought in Sydney for Felicity's wedding. It was cool and suited to the climate. About my neck was a necklace which Granny M had given me on my seventeenth birthday; it consisted of amethysts set in gold which matched my dress perfectly. I had taken great pains with my appearance.

The house was set back from the beach and, like Milton's, was surrounded by sugar canes. It was a white building, smaller than Milton's but otherwise not unlike it.

There were three steps to the porch and she was at the top of these waiting to greet us. She looked elegant in the extreme and was wearing white again. I wondered if it was a sort of mourning for her husband who was recently dead. I knew there were some people who wore white rather than the black we wore at home.

This white dress was low-cut; it accentuated her small waist and perfect figure. A thick gold necklace was tight about her neck—choker fashion—and she wore thick gold bangles. Creole earrings completed the picture.

Beside her stood a man, tall and if not conventionally good-looking, very pleasant.

Her welcome was warm.

"How glad I am to see you at last," she said. "I meant to ask you before, but I have been to Sydney on business. We have to make these trips now and then. By the way this is George . . . Mr. Callerby."

He said: "How do you do?" and bowed.

"I was afraid there was going to be a mist which would prevent your coming," said Magda.

"There is a faint one in the air," replied Milton, "but it would have to be very thick to deter us."

She laughed and took us into a room—very elegantly furnished as I felt everything about her would be. It had french windows opening onto a grassy lawn which went straight down to the sea, which at this time of the evening was touched with the red of sunset. The sun was now like a great red ball lying on the horizon. Soon it would drop from sight and darkness would be upon us.

She served us with the usual drink with which I was now familiar, and she asked about my impressions of the islands.

I told her how they fascinated me.

"What do you find most interesting?" asked George Callerby.

"The people," I replied. "Undoubtedly the people. They seem happy . . . and contented."

"They are not always so," she said. "Isn't that true, Milton?"

"We have our troubles . . . now and then."

"It's the sun. There it is up there shining down fiercely most of the time. Who wants to work when the sun is shining?"

"But they always seem to be laughing," I pointed out.

"Laughter does not always mean amusement," Magda explained.

"That's true," agreed Milton. "You'd never get to know these people even if you spent a lifetime here."

"You manage them very well, Milton," said George Callerby.

"I've found the recipe. They have to be a little unsure of you, a little afraid of you . . . and at the same time you have to be on friendly terms. It's the right mixture of the two. It takes some acquiring. I learned it from my father."

"And Miss Mallory is such a newcomer to the islands," said Magda.

"How long do you intend to stay, Miss Mallory?" asked George Callerby.

I hesitated. I was aware of Milton who was watching me rather ironically. I said: "My travelling companion has been ill. I want to wait until she is better before she undergoes the ordeal of a long journey."

"Yes, I heard how ill she was. Our servants discover everything for us. They go over to Cariba for the markets and there they glean all that is happening and bring the news back to us. So we heard about her and of course her involvement in that terrible case."

I could imagine that everything about us was known and that Magda was watching me intently—and Milton, too. I wondered what she was thinking behind those long languishing eyes.

"Shall we go in to dinner," she asked. "There has been great excitement in the kitchen. They have been discussing the meal all day long. I leave it to them, of course. Interference would be fatal. They would giggle if I suggested anything and if I insisted it would be spoilt . . . just to teach me a lesson. So I leave well alone."

We went into another room. It was dark now and big oil lamps had been lighted. A net was drawn across the windows and one of the servants drew the curtains. This shut out the beautiful view but I had been here long enough to know that it was better to forget the scenery rather than endure the intrusion of certain insects.

Turtle soup was served. It was delicious. Fish followed. I was getting used to the many types of fish on the islands which were quite different from anything we had at home. This was followed by alligator steaks which were palatable and no doubt owed much to the spices with which they were garnished.

But I was far more interested in the company than the food.

Seated at the head of the table was Magda, looking mysterious in the lamplight. Every time I looked up I caught her eyes on me speculatively. I imagined she was wondering about my relationship with Milton as I was about hers. There was no doubt in my mind that she entertained rather special feelings for him and she was very curious about me.

They asked a great many questions about England. George Callerby had come out about eight years before and had been working on a station near Sydney. He had apparently met Milton there and it was Milton who had suggested that he come and manage the plantation.

"George came at the right time for us," said Magda. "We were so grateful to Milton for bringing us George."

She smiled her seductive smile first at Milton and then at George. "It was wonderful for us," she added.

"For me, too," said George.

"My husband you see had had this accident."

Milton put in: "You were talking a short while ago about the contented workers. Well, these were not so contented. Do you mind if I tell Annalice, Magda?"

"No, please tell Miss Mallory . . . if she is interested."

"I am enormously interested."

"And may I suggest," said Milton, "that before we go any further we dispense with formality. Let it be Annalice and Magda . . . and George. We are all friends together. Miss This and Mr. That . . . it is quite unnecessary in the circumstances."

Magda looked at me. "Do you agree?"

"Why yes, of course."

"All right, then. Tell Annalice, Milton."

He turned to me. "One of the workers put a stone in the grinding mill. José did not understand what was wrong. He tried to put it right. The thing exploded and he was badly crippled."

"How terrible."

"I don't know how I should have lived through that time but for Milton," said Magda.

"I did what any neighbour would. I came over, sorted out the trouble with the men and put the fear of God into them."

"And made them feel," continued Magda, "that in acting against us they were acting against themselves."

"They believed that with any more trouble I would close down the plantations," said Milton. "They didn't want that. They have the sense to see that their prosperity comes with sugar and they need to keep the plantations going if they are to enjoy their present standard of living."

"Yes, Milton saved the plantation for us. Something for which I shall always be grateful."

She was looking at him with such tenderness that I felt: She loves him. He is her sort. There is something wild about her. They fit together. She would have the same outlook, the same ideas, the same morals which would be less rigid than those with which I had been brought up. I believed that like him she would stop at nothing to get what she wanted.

"And then," she was saying, "he found us George."

Now her smile was turned on him.

"It was the luckiest day of my life when I was found," said George.

"George is a natural for this sort of work," said Milton. "I knew it as soon as I set eyes on him."

He was looking at them benignly and I felt there was some deep emotion in this room. I thought: She has asked me here to have a good look at me. She is angry because she will have heard of his attentions to me. She is very beautiful, the kind of woman to whom he would be drawn.

But he was drawn to me and I was not in the least like her. I saw myself as quite different. She was softly spoken, experienced with men; she knew how to attract them with that subtle flattery which was irresistible to them and which I would disdain even if I could master it. I was prickly, terribly uncertain, quite inexperienced.

They were talking about hobbies.

"George, you know, is an astronomer."

George laughed deprecatingly. "A very amateur one."

"He came out to Australia because he was tired of the night sky on the other side of the world," said Milton.

"That," replied George, smiling at me, "is not exactly true."

"I've always liked to hear about the stars," I said. "It is so fantastic to think of them all those light-years away. I've always found that particularly fascinating. To think that when you look at a star you may be looking at something which is no longer there because it is so far away that its light is only just reaching you."

"It's all very scientific," said Magda. "And it is not only the stars, is it, George? It's the Earth and its age and everything. What was it you were saying about climates and the ice melting and all that?"

"Are you *really* interested?" asked George.

"I am . . . very," I told him.

"I was just saying what a difference climatic conditions make to the Earth. While everything is neatly balanced life remains predictable. But you only need a sudden change . . . a slight change . . . and there could be chaos. An ice age would freeze us all up . . . or suppose it became warmer. The ice at the poles would gradually melt. Imagine the influx of water all over the Earth. Continents could be submerged."

"Let us hope that doesn't happen," said Magda. "We complain of the heat but an ice age would be terrible. And the idea of being submerged by flood I suppose even worse."

"I believe within the last hundred years there has been change," said George. "I was reading that there was a period of excessive warmth which melted some of the polar ice and the seas did rise a little because of it. It wasn't all that noticeable as far from the poles as we are . . . but it did happen according to geologists."

"I hope there is a warning if it happens again," said Milton.

"It would probably happen gradually."

We had finished the creamed pudding and Magda suggested that we go back to the drawing room.

I complimented her on the excellent meal and she asked if I would like to see the house and I said I would.

"Then we'll leave the men to chat," she said. "They know the house very well and don't want to see it again."

She took a candle and led the way up a carved staircase. There was something rather Spanish about it which I supposed was to be expected. I guessed from his name that José must have been Spanish, and very possibly Magda was too.

"My husband built this house when he came here," she said. "I think he tried to make it like a corner of home. But you can never really do that in a foreign country."

She showed me her bedroom. There was a large bed with dainty white curtains about it. I thought of Milton visiting her here, and I wanted to get out of that room. She took me through to others. I was not paying much attention. All the time I was wondering about her and Milton.

I said: "You have made a charming home here."

"I wonder," she answered. "We are rather remote. I was brought up in a big city. It is very different here. There is very little on this island. We have to go to Cariba for everything. It is nice to have friends there. I could not have survived after José's accident without Milton."

"I can imagine that."

"He did everything for me. He is a wonderful friend. And José was fond of him, too. We relied on him."

"And now you have Mr. Callerby. I should imagine he is very efficient."

"George . . . oh yes. And I never forget that Milton found him for me. You see, he is my benefactor. He is a very good man although people don't always realize this because . . . Well, he rules Cariba with a rod of iron. They are all in awe of him. It is wonderful to be able to inspire such feelings."

I agreed that it was.

"They know that if there was trouble here Milton would step in. That is a great comfort to us. On him really rests the prosperity of Cariba. Well . . . I think we had better join the men. They will wonder what we are doing all this time."

We went down.

"I thought you had decided to desert us," said Milton.

"We were talking," explained Magda.

"Not about me, I hope."

"There," said Magda, "you see how important he thinks he is! Even when he is not present he thinks we are talking about him."

He looked at Magda intently and I guessed he was wondering what she had said to me.

"As a matter of fact," I told him, "you were mentioned."

"Don't look alarmed," put in Magda with a laugh. "I only told the nice things about you."

"What else could there be to tell?" He added: "It is time we went back."

"Must you? It is not eleven yet."

"My dear Magda, I have to take this young lady back to her hotel after rowing her across."

"Well, I suppose we must let you go."

"You will come and dine with me soon. You too, George. We will have a foursome."

My cloak was brought. It was a flimsy cashmere affair which I had brought with me because the night could be a little chilly.

As we came out of the house, Magda exclaimed: "It's still misty."

"Thickened up a bit," added George.

"Milton, do you think it is clear enough? I could put you up here."

"It's nothing," said Milton. "After all we only have a short distance to go and if anyone knows the way, I ought to. Heaven knows I've done it times enough."

A look flashed between them then. Was that significant or was I imagining it? I pictured his going over to the island at night, going quietly into the house. The invalid husband would be sleeping. Magda would come out to meet him. They would cling together passionately . . . and he would go into the house with her.

"Come on, Annalice. You're dreaming."

Yes, I thought, picturing you and Magda together and not liking it at all and despising myself for harbouring such feelings. What was his past life to do with me? But that past was impinging on the present.

He took my cloak and fastened it more tightly about me.

"It's chilly," he said. "It can turn really cold with the mist."

He helped me into the boat, pushed it out and leaped in. Magda and George stood on the beach waving.

"Are you sure you should go?" called Magda.

"Quite sure," replied Milton.

And then we were skimming over the water.

"Well?" he said.

"It was a most interesting evening."

"Yes, I could see you were interested."

"She is a fascinating woman."

"I agree."

"And she runs that plantation with the help of George Callerby. That's very unusual for a woman."

He looked at me almost maliciously. "She has good friends."

"You, for instance."

"I am gratified to be one of them."

"A very special friend, I gathered."

"Yes, you could say that."

I was silent.

"Cold?" he asked.

"Yes, a little."

"This mist is a curse."

"Is it unusual?"

"Well, it is not all that common. But if we once get it, it seems to be a feature of the season."

"It seems to be thickening."

"I believe you are a little uneasy. Haven't you learned yet that you can trust yourself with me?"

"I am not entirely convinced."

"Don't worry. Even if we drift out to sea you'll be safe with me."

He rowed in silence for a while. Then he shipped oars and looked about him.

"Where is Cariba? We should be there by now."

"So you are lost."

He did not answer but began to row again. After a few minutes land loomed out of the mist.

"It looks familiar," I said. "But it is not the harbour."

"It's not Cariba," he said. "I'm going to pull up here. It's no use going on in this mist."

"Not Cariba! What is it then?"

"It's the little one. We're some way from Cariba. It would be foolish to attempt to get there in this mist. It won't last long. It rarely does. I'm afraid you're going to be shipwrecked on an island with me."

"Oh no!"

"Oh yes. We have been around in a circle. I know exactly where we are now. We shall have to stay here until the mist lifts."

"That could be . . . all night."

He was looking at me with some amusement. "Perhaps," he said.

I thought to myself: I believe he has arranged this. I believe he knew where we were all the time. Excitement and anger were fighting with each other. It was typical of him. He was not to be trusted.

The boat scraped on the sand; he jumped into the shallow water and picking me up waded ashore.

"I'll have to pull up the boat," he said. "We don't want it washed away. Then we'll go and find shelter."

"Are there people on this island?"

He grinned at me and shook his head.

"It's about half a mile long and less than that wide. Just a rock really sticking up out of the sea. It used to be much bigger, but the sea encroached."

"Where could we find shelter here?"

"There's an old boathouse if I remember rightly. At least it used to be here. I came here in my extreme youth. We'll see if it is still there and if it is it will provide shelter. Come on. Give me your hand."

I did and he pulled me along with him.

Suddenly he put his arm round me.

"You're faltering," he said. "You're reluctant. You are just a little uneasy."

"It has hardly been a comfortable journey."

"I promise you comfort soon. Come with me."

We went a short way up the incline.

"A little hilly," he said. "Thank Heaven for that. If it hadn't been the sea might have claimed the lot. And yes . . . there is the old boathouse."

"Why should anyone want a boathouse on an island where no one lives?"

"It's a relic of the past . . . of the days when people did live here. That's what I was always told."

The sand was getting into my shoes and it was difficult to walk. He lifted me under his arm as though I were a parcel and carried me along.

"Put me down," I said. "I'm too heavy."

"Light as a feather," he retorted, ignoring my request. "Ah, there it is. A little more dilapidated than when I last saw it, but what can you expect."

He set me on my feet and pushed open the door. It was almost falling off its hinges.

A dark long object was there. I looked closer. It was a canoe.

"It's still here," he cried. "Leave the door open or we won't see a thing. I used to lie in this when I was a boy and pretend that I was sailing on the high seas. It's quite comfortable. They knew how to make these things. I reckon it is more than fifty years old. They don't look solid, but they are."

He put an arm round me and said: "We shall be comfortable here."

I drew away from him.

"Don't go out there. You'll be cold. It will be warm and cosy in here. We'll make a comfortable resting place in the canoe while we wait for the mist to rise."

"They'll be wondering where I am."

"They won't until morning."

"I should have said good night to Felicity. She'll be very worried."

"She knows you are with me."

"That might make her very uneasy."

He laughed aloud. Then he said: "They'll think we stayed at Magda's. They'll see the mist. They'll say no one would attempt the journey back in this."

"You did."

"Well, I attempt many things. Come on. We'll make it cosy. We'll make a bed for ourselves in the canoe."

"Oh no."

"Isn't it time?" he asked. "How long are you going to keep me at bay?"

"I believe you arranged this."

"You give me more credit than I deserve. Brilliant as I am, I cannot control the weather."

"I think you could have got us back to Cariba."

"Do you?"

"Yes, and I think you brought us here deliberately."

"And you would be pleased at that?"

"Pleased! I wanted to go back to the hotel."

"You will find our canoe a little more interesting than your virgin couch."

"You . . . planned this."

"I could not arrange the mist, as I told you."

"You seized the opportunity."

"I always seize my opportunities."

He put an arm round me and kissed me. Somewhat to my alarm I was responding before I withdrew myself with a show of indignation. I could not get Magda Manuel out of my mind and I was realizing that I did not trust myself any more than I trusted him. It would be so easy to forget everything but that I was here alone with him. In truth it was where I wanted to be . . . alone with him . . . but I was afraid. I was haunted, partly by my obligations to Raymond, but more I think by my experiences on Lion Island. It was almost as though Ann Alice was there urging me to be strong, not to give way to impulse. She had not haunted me, brought me across the world for this. I had met him once . . . and I should see him again. During that brief hour we had spent together something had happened to me. I knew as sure as I stood on this island that I had not seen the last of Magnus Perrensen.

I was not alone on this desert island with Milton Harrington; Ann Alice was there with me.

He went on kissing me. He was saying: "Don't be afraid. This was inevitable... from the moment we met. I knew you were the one for me... and you knew it, too, didn't you? It happens like that sometimes."

For a moment I lay against him. Go away, Ann Alice, I thought. I am not you, I am myself. Your life ended in that walled-up room; but I am here, alive and I want to be with this man, because it is true that I love him—if loving is wanting to be with him, close to him, sharing his life.

He was quick to sense my mood. He picked me up in his arms and set me down in the canoe.

He took the pins out of my hair and put them in his pocket which I thought fleetingly was rather a practical thing to do. I should need to put my hair up before I returned to Cariba. The thought crossed my mind that he had probably done this before.

He said: "You look beautiful."

I replied: "How many women have you brought to this island... to this canoe?"

"You have the honour of being the first and I swear here that there shall never be another. Perhaps you and I will make a pilgrimage here before we leave for England. We will remember this night... the true beginning."

"The beginning of what?"

"Of shared love."

"So you think that the seduction will be completed tonight?"

"It's an ideal spot. Very romantic really if you don't mind being a little cramped, and it may be that the canoe lacks that pristine brightness which it must once have had. Outside the gentle swishing of the waves on the sand and about us the gentle Heaven-sent mist."

"No," I said.

"No?"

"I don't want that."

"My dearest Annalice, do you think I don't know you? You do. You love me... you want me absolutely... as I want you. And you have for a long time."

"I have explained to you that I am almost engaged to someone else."

"After tonight you will realize that is quite out of the question."

I ignored that remark and said: "This smells of the sea."

"What did you expect it to smell of? The perfumes of Araby?"

He was beside me and his arms were about me.

"I want you to listen to me," I said.

"I am listening."

"I realize I am here at your mercy. You are physically stronger than I. If I resist you can overcome me. Is that what you intend to do?"

"You will come to me willingly."

"Yes," I said, "or not at all."

"But since you admit to my superior strength, how could I fail?"

"You could have a temporary success if you forced me. That would be rape."

"That is the technical term."

"I should never forget it and never forgive it. You might get temporary satisfaction but that would tell me what I have been trying to discover for a long time."

"You don't mean that."

"I swear that I do. I would leave at once. I would take Felicity with me. I would tell her what had happened. I believe that if she feels she has to look after me she would regain her strength. She would understand. Similar things happened to her. She had no redress. She happened to be married to her brute. I am free and I will come to you willingly . . . not on a makeshift bed because the opportunity was there, but because I want to, because it is of my own free will."

He kissed me gently. "Yes," he said. "Go on."

"This is a night for the truth, is it not?"

"It is."

"I will explain. I think I am in love with you. I want to be with you. I think I am happier with you than anywhere else. But I did care for Raymond Billington. He is quite unlike you . . . self-effacing almost, selfless. You are not like that."

"More human," he said.

"Indeed yes. You stride in and take what you want. You can take me now but that means you will lose me forever."

He said: "It wouldn't be like that. I would show you what joy we could give each other. I would make you see how well we suit each other. I would show you that we could have a lifetime of happiness together."

"How well do you know me?"

"Very well indeed. That is why I love you, because I know you so well and that tells me you are the one for me."

"Then if you know me well you will know my pride. I would not submit to you. I would come willingly or not at all. You see, I was with Felicity in that dreadful house where she suffered nightly. She was not the only one who was affected by what happened there. I was, too. And I know that when I married or loved a man I would never submit. I would be his equal. I would not be forced . . . as Felicity was. Do you understand?"

"Yes," he said. "Go on."

"I *think* I want to be with you more than anyone. But there is Raymond. I know Raymond well. He is gentle and kind. I think I could be happy with him. There would not be the excitement I should know with you. I am fully aware of that. It would be even . . . no heights . . . no depths . . . "

"Which you would find excessively dull."

"Not dull. Just pleasant . . . sailing along on an even keel."

"Squalls come along on the smoothest seas. Mists . . . "

"Yes, I know, but Raymond could be relied on."

"And I should not be."

"I should never be sure. You have known many women, I don't doubt."

"And Raymond has been completely chaste, of course. The perfect knight. Was it Galahad? I expect he is sitting at home polishing his holy grail and not worrying about what is happening to you."

I couldn't help laughing. "That is ridiculous," I said.

"It is your fault for introducing such a paragon on such a night as this."

"And don't forget," I reminded him, "I came out here for a purpose. I want to find my brother. I have an extraordinary feeling that I am going to solve the mystery."

"You are still thinking of the stranger on Lion Island."

"Yes," I answered. "I am."

"And where does he come in?"

"It is so strange. Sometimes I feel I am really Ann Alice . . . that she is part of me. That she lives again through me."

"You were bemused by this man. Do you know, I think he is more dangerous than the saintly Raymond."

I was silent. Was he? Here was I lying in a canoe with this man whose very presence excited me and it was as though Ann Alice was there with me, putting words into my mouth . . . telling me that I must keep myself chaste as she was . . . so that when the time came for her to marry Magnus Perrensen she could go to him as a bride should. But she had died. It was as though she had chosen me to play out the life which had been denied her.

"You have some very strange ideas," he said, kissing my forehead.

"I have been truthful to you. You were Magda Manuel's lover, were you not?"

He hesitated. Then he said: "She was lonely and there she was up there . . . her husband an invalid. I used to go often. We became very friendly."

"And the husband?"

"I think he knew."

"I see . . . a convenient arrangement."

"It was not meant to be a match, you know. I was still waiting for you to come along. It is a pity you delayed so long."

"I think she resents me."

"Oh no. Magda is a woman of the world. She understood. There was never a question of marriage between us."

"But you were in love with each other?"

"It depends on what you mean by being in love. We liked each other. We were good for each other. We suited each other. We're the best of friends. I'd do a great deal for Magda."

"You see . . . how I feel."

"You are hemmed in with conventions. It is not quite the same out here as it is at home. Maybe it is the climate. I am sure you will understand."

"And you and Magda now?"

"It's over."

"I don't think it is for her."

"I know her well . . . "

"She seems mysterious, secretive."

"That is because you are looking at her in a certain way. You don't like me to have been fond of any other woman . . . even before I met you. I like that. It comforts me."

I was silent and he held me against him, kissing my face gently. I thought: He really loves me. And I wished I could turn to him and tell him that I wanted to be everything to him . . . to stay with him forever. I almost did. I had only to say the word. It rested with me. I was happy that that was so. And I wanted to say that word . . . and yet, I was held back by forces I did not fully understand.

We lay there . . . close, for a long time. His arms were about me comfortingly.

I shall never forget it—the gentle sound of the water outside the hut . . . the silence . . . the comfort . . . the knowledge that he loved me enough to hold back that passion which I sensed in him because he believed that I was a woman whose wish was to be respected.

Love between us had to be perfect. No furtive affair in an old canoe because the mist had thrown us together. I loved him more for understanding.

I had no idea of the time but it must have been the early hours of the morning when the mist lifted. I was cramped. He helped me out of the canoe.

"It's quite clear now," he said. "You can see Cariba."

"We're very close," I replied.

I lifted my face to his and he kissed me.

"Thank you," I said. "I shall never forget this night. It will be one of my most precious memories."

"We'll come back every year we're here. We'll even come back and see the old place after we've settled in England."

"I wonder," I said.

"No need to wonder. It's a promise."

"Who can say?"

"I say," he said.

"And you are always right?"

He had returned to his old self, but I thought I had seen a new side to his nature on this night. And I loved him all the more for it.

I sat in the boat. He was smiling at me. He produced the hairpins from his pocket.

"I like it flowing," he said, "but I think you look more decorous with it up."

I took the pins from him while he took the oars and rowed us back to Cariba.

FIRE IN CARIBA

Everyone thought we had stayed the night at Magda's plantation. The mist provided a good reason for our doing so. Felicity had been anxious at first but had been reassured and I was relieved that next morning there appeared to be no undue excitement about the matter. Perhaps there was a little more surreptitious giggling, but I refused to notice it.

Felicity seemed a little better. We breakfasted together. I told her about Magda's plantation and she showed a little interest which was rare with her. I fancied she was coming out of her listlessness which was a move in the right direction.

I liked to watch the ship come in from Sydney and I would sit on the terrace waiting for it. There was always a great deal of bustle and excitement even though it was a regular occurrence. The waterfront was noisier than ever and there was general congestion among all the bullock carts and the people who had come from their houses with produce to sell.

It was becoming a familiar scene to me. I felt that I was indeed part of the island. Memories of the previous night were still with me and I was there, in my imagination, lying in that canoe with Milton. I treasured the memory because I believed he had shown that he truly loved me. It would not have been impossible for him to have overcome my scruples but he had not done so.

Then I began to think of Raymond and more perhaps of Magnus Perrensen. He aroused such strange emotions in me. He seemed remote; even his speech was a little archaic. If he had told me he was really that Magnus Perrensen, born again, I think I should have been ready to believe him.

The ship had arrived. People were coming ashore. Idly I watched, my thoughts elsewhere.

Then suddenly I was startled. It could not be. I must be dreaming. I had surely imagined it. But it was! Raymond was stepping out of one of the little launches which rowed people ashore from the ship. I stared. It must be someone who looked like him. People had doubles and one could be mistaken . . . especially from a little distance.

I left the hotel and ran down to the waterfront expecting the figure to turn into someone else as I approached.

But the nearer I came the more certain I was that I had not been mistaken.

"Raymond!" I cried.

He put down the bag he was carrying and looked straight at me.

I ran to him and he caught me in his arms. "Annalice!"

"Raymond! Oh . . . Raymond! It is really you."

"I've come to see you . . . and Felicity," he said.

"Oh Raymond, what a surprise! Why didn't you let us know? We didn't expect . . . It's such a surprise."

"I had made up my mind to come when you left," he said. "It was just a matter of arranging a few things. It was a business trip you see. I had to see people in Sydney."

"Why didn't you tell us?"

"Letters take so long. I have written as a matter of fact."

"Where to?"

"Australia."

"We left there some time ago. So you don't know what's happened. Did you get my letters?"

"I received one which arrived just as I was setting out. Something was wrong. Felicity was unhappy. The marriage wasn't a success. You told me that. I heard in Sydney that you and Felicity had taken the ship to Cariba."

"Oh Raymond, there is so much to tell. You will stay at this hotel."

"Where is Felicity?"

"She is here. She has been ill . . . very ill."

"Ill?" he said with alarm.

"She's getting better, I think. Raymond, I must tell you all about it before you see her. She is not herself. She came near to a breakdown. It was all that she suffered in Australia. You haven't heard about her husband's death? I suppose you wouldn't in England. It was in the Sydney papers."

"My dear Annalice, what is all this about? It is so good to see you. I have missed you so much."

"And you were planning to come out all the time."

"I wasn't sure. It was a matter of business. I didn't want to say I should be following you and then find it didn't happen."

"Where is your luggage?"

"They're bringing it ashore."

"I'll go and book you a room in the hotel while you see to it. And I do want to talk to you before you see Felicity."

"Is it as bad as that?"

"It's very bad. But she is improving. I'll go at once and see about the room. Get them to bring your luggage to the hotel. I've got to talk to you."

"It sounds so mysterious."

"Raymond . . . this is such a surprise. I'm so glad you're here."

He took my hand and kissed it. Then I left him and ran into the hotel. Rosa booked a room with an excited giggle. A friend of mine and Mrs. Granville had come. A gentleman. She found that of great interest and I could see was eager to impart the news to her colleagues.

When Raymond had his room and his baggage had been taken up I took him onto the terrace and called for a drink.

Then I told him everything, the marriage, the character of William Granville which had rapidly emerged, the terrible ordeal to which Felicity had been submitted, culminating in the shooting on the balcony.

"Poor child," he said. "How she must have suffered!"

"It is not surprising that she became a little . . . unbalanced."

"She is such a gentle creature . . . so carefully brought up and to go to such a brute."

"It was very unfortunate. She should never have agreed to marry him in the first place."

"I expect she wanted the excitement of travel."

"I don't think that was all," I said.

"When can I see her?"

"I think you had better come to her room."

He rose with alacrity and followed me upstairs.

I had asked Raymond to wait outside for a moment and I went into her room. She was sitting at her window idly looking out on the scene below.

"Felicity," I said. "Someone is here to see you."

She started up. I don't know what she expected. The ghost of William Granville? Mrs. Maken? Someone from the past. I said quickly: "It is Raymond Billington."

"Raymond! It can't be!"

He was in the room. She looked at him wonderingly and the joy in her face moved me deeply.

"Raymond," she cried and ran to him.

He took her into his arms.

She cried: "It isn't really you. I'm dreaming."

"I'm here all right," he said. "I've come here to look after you . . . you and Annalice."

"Oh Raymond!" She was crying now and I had not seen her cry for a very long time. She put up her hands and touched his face as though to assure herself that he was really there.

He held her tightly, rocking her to and fro. "It's all right now," he said. "I'm here. I'm here to take you home."

She put her hand against his chest and I saw the tears rolling down her cheeks.

I shut the door and left them together.

I went to my own room and thought: She loves him and he loves her too. Oh, what a mess we have made of everything. And what will happen now?

I was not surprised to see Milton. He had heard of Raymond's arrival and had lost no time in coming to the hotel.

I was sitting on the terrace with Raymond and Felicity when I saw him. He bounded up the steps and I rose to meet him.

I said: "Raymond Billington has come."

He looked rather grim.

"Come and meet him," I said. "Raymond . . . this is Milton Harrington. I've told you about him. He has helped us so much."

Raymond held out his hand. I watched Milton sizing him up. I could not tell from his expression what he thought of him.

"We were sitting here watching the harbour," I said.

"You look very much better, Felicity," said Milton.

"Oh, I am," she replied.

Milton sat down with us.

"This is rather a surprise, isn't it?" Milton turned to me. "Or did you know?"

"A great surprise," I told him.

"Letters take so long," said Raymond. "It makes communication difficult. I went to Sydney and made enquiries. Then I caught the first boat."

"Shall you stay long?"

"No. I can't do that. I shall be returning soon, I imagine. I believe the ship goes only once a week."

"You mean you are thinking of going next week?"

Raymond smiled at me. "I shall have to see about that. I've only just arrived. We haven't had time to discuss anything. It was a great shock to find that Felicity had been so ill."

Felicity lowered her eyes and flushed slightly.

"You must come up to the plantation and dine with me," said Milton.

"I hope you'll dine with us at the hotel tonight," I said to Milton.

"Thank you. I have to go back now. I'll come in at seven."

I walked with him to the stables where he had left his horse, leaving Raymond with Felicity.

Milton said: "You're not going back with him."

"I don't know. It's all so unexpected. I was astounded when I saw him getting off the boat."

"And you'd no idea that he was coming?"

"None at all."

"He should take Felicity back. She's much better since he's come. She seems like a different person."

"Yes," I agreed.

"Due to him, is it?"

"I think it must be."

"Let them go. You stay here."

"I don't know, Milton. I can't think what I should do."

"I'll think for you."

"No. I must think for myself."

He looked at me ruefully. "I might ask myself what hope I have," he said, "with a saint and a ghost for rivals."

"I don't think you would be overawed by either."

He turned to me suddenly and held me against him. I wished I could wave a wand and remove all the obstacles which stood in my way.

"I'll see you at dinner tonight," I said.

"I shall be there and perhaps I shall get to know this paragon of a man, this saint, and I am going to discover something about the ghostly one too. He's a queer character. Then I shall come to claim you for my own. You're going to stay here, you know. You're going to marry me."

I smiled at him and thought: That is what I want.

Then he mounted his horse and rode away.

There was tension in the air. Raymond's arrival had created that. Felicity had passed through the first stages of euphoria; she was very much aware of Raymond's feelings for me and there were moments when I felt she hated me for it. She was deeply in love with him. I could see that clearly. It was something she would never get over because he had been the hero of her childhood, whom she had dreamed of marrying. In fact she had implied that his family and hers had thought that a match between them was certain. Then I had come along. No wonder she felt less than kindly towards me.

I wanted to tell Raymond that I could not marry him. I wanted him to take Felicity home and leave me here. But I had not had a chance to speak to him at any length for Felicity was with us most of the time.

I wanted to explain to him that I could not go home. Perhaps I was not going to find my brother. Perhaps I had subconsciously accepted the fact that he was lost forever and the theory that he had drowned was correct. I had discovered nothing about him really. But what I had learned was that I was unsure of myself. That I loved Milton Harrington in a different way from that in which I had loved Raymond was certain and if I went back with Raymond I should never have a moment of real happiness because my heart would be in Cariba. Yet, if I stayed here I could drift into a state of blissful oblivion of everything but the moment.

All this I wanted to explain, but I must wait for the right occasion.

The previous night Milton had dined with us at the hotel as we had arranged. It had been an uncomfortable meal. Milton was inclined to be aggressive, talking about the plantation and the island and keeping the conversation to himself. Raymond, of course, deferred, which was exactly what one would expect of Raymond.

I was glad when the meal was over and Milton left.

"A very interesting man," was Raymond's comment.

I think Milton would have been less complimentary of Raymond. But that was an indication of their different natures.

I had been unable to sleep. I had another search for the map. I went through everything I had and could not find it.

The idea occurred to me that someone had stolen it. Why? Who would want it? What use was it to anyone? It was very strange.

Looking for the map I came across Felicity's pills. She hadn't needed one for some time now and I had almost forgotten them. I had regarded that as an indication that she was getting better. But I had made sure that I had some in case she should need them. There were ten still left in the bottle. I hoped she would not need them again.

During the afternoon when Felicity was resting I did have a talk with Raymond. We sat in the courtyard under a big sunshade. The heat was intense. The cicadas were making a great noise and now and then I heard the call of the fig-bird.

He said: "So you have discovered almost nothing about your brother's disappearance."

I shook my head. "Some people remembered him. He came and stayed here. Then he went away. That is really all I have found out."

"It was a long way to come for such a small reward and it has brought you no nearer to what you sought."

I shook my head.

"You've changed. And so has Felicity for that matter. Do you think she will ever be the same again?"

"I think she could in certain circumstances."

"You mean if she went back home."

"I mean if she had someone to care for her . . . someone loving and tender . . . someone who would show her that marriage was not what she endured with that man."

"I am so glad you were with her. She said she did not know what she would have done without you."

"It was a terrible experience for us both."

"Yes. It has changed you, too. Are you longing to come home?"

I hesitated.

"No," he said. "You're not. The life here fascinates you in a way. I believe I can understand that."

"Raymond," I told him, "you are the most understanding man in the world."

"And have you been thinking about . . . us?"

"A great deal."

"And are you still unsure?"

I was silent again.

He said: "I think I understand. That man is in love with you, isn't he?"

"Well, yes . . . He implies he is."

"And you?"

I said: "I don't know. You were so good to me. It was wonderful to know you when we were so desolate about Philip. And then . . . you arranged everything for me . . . so that I could do what I wanted to do. No one could have been kinder."

"I see."

"Do you, Raymond?"

He nodded. "Let's leave it, eh? Let's wait awhile. My arrival was so unexpected. I wish I could have let you know I was on the way."

"Life has been so strange. I have been worried about Felicity. Your coming has made all the difference to her."

"I've known her since she was a child."

"She told me. She is almost herself now. It's miraculous . . . the difference in her."

"She will get better. I'll take charge of that."

"When do you want to go back?"

"Very soon."

I nodded. Then I told him about my meeting with Magnus Perrensen. "You remember . . . the man who was mentioned in the journal. This is his great-grandson."

"What an extraordinary coincidence."

"When you consider all the facts it is not so very extraordinary. The family knew the story of Ann Alice and the island. The original Magnus came looking for the island, then settled in Australia and did some gold mining very successfully apparently. They then acquired this island. It was the nearest to that one for which they were looking. You see it is all quite logical when you look at it that way."

"It is strange that you should have met him."

"Yes, that was by chance, of course. But you can imagine how bewildered I was . . . and still am by all this."

"And you have not seen him since?"

"It is only really a short time ago. He said he would ask me to visit him or he would come here. I believe he will."

"I see. Annalice, let us wait a day or so. Perhaps you will know how you feel by the time the next ship leaves."

"A week?"

"Perhaps I could wait another week. But that would be the limit, I think. I have some business to do in Sydney. That was supposed to be the purpose of my coming out."

"Supposed to be?"

"Well, naturally I wanted to see what was happening to you. When I had that letter I was deeply concerned about Felicity. I thought from the first that she was a little unsure about that marriage."

"Yes. She rushed into it."

"I can't understand what possessed her."

I looked at him steadily. "She was really in love with someone else," I said.

He frowned and did not answer. Could it be that he who was so understanding about the affairs of others could be so obtuse about his own?

There was a silence of some duration. Then he said: "Well, all we can do is wait. In a few days . . . perhaps . . . "

I said nothing to that, and then after a while: "What a noise those cicadas make!"

Now I was wondering what he was feeling. Having basked in the torrid atmosphere of Milton's emotions I found Raymond cool and practical. His kiss had been gentle and swift. He knew Milton was in love with me and he would realize that Milton would not be the man to indulge in overmuch restraint. What did he see of my feelings for Milton? How obvious was that? And how much would it mean to him if I decided to marry Milton and stay in Cariba? His calm, his serenity, which I had found so comforting, might mean that his feelings did not go as deep as some people's—Milton's, for instance. I was not sure.

How strange that, in my state of bewilderment, I was not even sure of Raymond.

There were times when I began to wonder whether I had dreamed up that visit to Lion Island. I heard nothing more from Magnus Perrensen. I had thought he would come to Cariba. It was only a few days, I supposed, but it seemed longer.

After John Everton had brought me back to Cariba I had not seen him. I wondered whether he had left. I thought that after our acquaintance he would surely have said goodbye.

Then next morning I did see him. He was sitting on the terrace talking to Maria, the chambermaid. Maria talked to anyone when she had a chance. She was even more garrulous than the rest of the staff.

So John Everton had not left.

I considered the idea of asking him to row me over to Lion Island. But I could scarcely go without an invitation. It would come. I was impatient.

Milton had not suggested coming to the hotel for dinner that evening; nor had he invited us to the plantation. I felt this was due to Raymond's presence.

I missed him. I was restless. I should have to make a decision soon. I had been drifting along in a pleasant state of euphoria. I had refused to look at the facts. I had just wanted to go on enjoying my relationship with Milton and putting decisions aside.

Now I had to make up my mind. Was I going to sail away with Raymond and Felicity, or was I going to stay with Milton?

I knew what I wanted to do. My feelings for Raymond had changed and that was due to Felicity. If I had not come into their lives none of this would have happened. Perhaps if I were not there Raymond would marry Felicity and she would be happy. And him? I had convinced myself that his feelings did not go as deeply as some people's do; that was why he was able to face the world so serenely.

Soon it would be sunset and that lurid red light would colour the scene. The sea would turn pale pink and the sky blood-red. I should never grow accustomed to the sunset and I always waited for the moment when that great red ball seemed to drop below the horizon. It was spectacular and never quite the same twice.

I was restless and I decided to take a walk along the waterfront.

As I walked down marvelling at the colourful sky and sea I saw smoke some way inland.

I stopped to look at it and as I did so it spiralled upwards. I saw a great flame and then more smoke. Something was on fire. My heart began to beat uncertainly for the direction from which the smoke was coming was the plantation.

The plantation was on fire!

A terrible fear came over me. Milton was there. I could not think of anything but that I had to find him. I had to assure myself that he was safe.

I went to the stables. I mounted my horse and in my flimsy dress rode bareback to the plantation.

I was right. The place was on fire. I could hear men shouting. I had never seen such a sight. It was like an enormous tower of fire and the flames were racing through the canes. I saw men standing round the edges with buckets of water, rats and a mongoose scuttled out of the burning mass.

I tried to make my way to the house.

"Keep away," shouted one of the men.

"Mr. Harrington," I cried. "Where is he? I have to find him. Where . . . ?"

Then I saw him. He was coming towards me. I ran to him and he caught me in his arms and held me fast.

I cried out in relief: "You're safe. Thank God. I thought . . . I was terrified. I couldn't have borne it if . . . "

"Does it matter so much?" he said.

"You know."

He held me tightly. "You're committed now, you know. You've betrayed yourself."

He was laughing with triumph.

I looked at him in amazement. "Your plantation is on fire . . . and you stand here . . . "

He said: "This is the happiest moment of my life. Look at you. Distraught. Tearful. In a state of panic . . . and all because you feared you had lost me. Let this be a lesson to you."

"How can you . . . now . . . at such a time . . . "

"It is really very amusing. This is a great joke. It is the best joke I ever heard."

"You are mad."

"With joy. My love loves me. Look. She deserts all . . . even the saint himself . . . to ride to me . . . because she thinks I am in danger. Come into the house. I want to tell you something."

"Your plantation is burning down."

"I want to tell you how much I love you."

"I don't understand you. Don't you care. You are losing everything."

"What would that matter if I gained my love . . . which I have. You can't go back on this. You stand betrayed. You have revealed yourself. Admit it."

"Milton . . . "

"Well, let me tell you. The plantation is not burning down. Tomorrow all the canes will be cut the easier for the fire. This is what we call a field burning."

"You mean you deliberately set the place on fire?"

He nodded. "It's a periodic exercise. When the time is ripe we put a torch to the green sugar. It burns the cane to clear it so that it will be easier to cut in the morning."

"So it was all planned."

"It needs very careful planning. Waiting for the wind to be in the right direction . . . watching all the time . . . cutting firebreaks round the fields. We have to be on the watch all the time. If it got out of hand it could be disastrous. It could even destroy the whole of the island."

I was so relieved I could only laugh.

"And you rode out to save me . . . just like that. Oh Annalice, my darling Annalice, this is surely the happiest moment of my life."

"You said that before."

"Well, it is worth repeating. I shall always remember it. The day she came to me . . . If you could have seen the fear on your face . . . and all for me."

I could only cling to him laughing, I think, rather hysterically.

"I was so frightened," I said.

He kissed me. "And now you have no doubts."

I shook my head.

"You are going to stay with me. You let him know."

"I think he knows already."

"I am going to give you a drink and take you back to the hotel."

"They will be wondering what has become of me. I'll go back alone. You have to be here to make sure the fire is kept under control."

"There are men here to do that. They know what has to be done." He looked out. "It's almost over now. The blackened stalks will cut well tomorrow. The operation was a success . . . the greatest success I have ever known. Come along. I'm going to take you back in the carriage. I'll send your horse back tomorrow. You can't ride as you are. No saddle. How very indecorous. And all for me. I am so happy tonight. Tell me how very scared you were."

"You know."

"I saw it in your face. There was that other time. Do you remember when I went pearl diving?"

"I remember it well."

"You did not like my going down to the sea bed, did you?"

"I thought of sharks."

"I promise I won't dive for pearls when we are married."

I touched his face lightly. "You are a very forceful man," I said.

"Well, you are no meek Griselda yourself. After all it's you I have fallen in love with and you with me. Just as we are . . . warts and all, as they say. I wouldn't have one little bit of you changed and that's the truth."

"Nor I," I said.

"Come, take this. It will do you good. You were very shaken, you know."

"Yes, I do know that."

"Riding through the night . . ."

I sipped the drink and he sat beside me and put his arm about me. I felt suddenly happy. It was as though this evening everything had been resolved.

He drove me back in the carriage.

They had been wondering what had happened to me.

I explained and Milton went into some detail about the way in which they burned the canes every now and then when it was necessary to make cutting easier.

"Annalice was so worried on my account. She thought I was in my burning plantation and dashed over . . . just as she was . . . on horseback. I think she was going to plunge in and haul me back to safety."

"I don't know what I was going to do," I said. "I thought the whole place was on fire."

"Won't you stay and dine with us?" asked Raymond.

"Thanks, no. I must get back to make sure everything is all right. It's under control but one never knows. It's a tricky business."

"I can understand that."

"I should retire early if I were you," said Milton to me. "Take a little coconut milk before you go to sleep. It's very soothing. I'll tell Maria to take it up to your room."

He was already assuming a proprietorial air. I wondered if the others noticed it. I did not care if they did. I was experiencing a kind of exultation. Tomorrow I must speak to Raymond. I would explain and I was sure he would understand.

Milton left. "I'll see you tomorrow evening. I'll give you the day to set everything in order," were his parting words.

He meant of course my speaking to Raymond.

I wanted to talk to him. I even thought of doing so that evening. But I could hardly do so with Felicity there; and now that he had arrived she did not go to her room early as she had done before. She wanted to be where he was all the time.

I was glad. I felt everything could work out neatly after all. Raymond would go home and take Felicity with him. And in time . . . perhaps before very long . . . they would marry. I saw how suited they were to each other. Raymond needed someone to lean on him, that he might take care of her; and Felicity needed Raymond because he was the only one in the world who could wipe out memories of her terrible experiences.

I was happier than I had ever been, I think, on that night.

I was absent-minded during dinner and I retired early. The first thing I saw when I opened the door was the glass of milk on my table.

I smiled. He had spoken to Maria then. I did not want the milk, but it was his wish that I should take it and just because of that I would, I supposed.

I looked at myself in the mirror. I saw there was a smudge on the bodice of my dress. No one had mentioned it. My hair was a little loose too. My eyes were bright though. I looked slightly dishevelled but very happy.

I undressed, thinking of the next day. I must speak to Raymond as soon as I was alone with him. I would make him see that what had happened was inevitable. He would understand; and there would be Felicity waiting to comfort him. I think he loved Felicity more deeply than he realized. He had been so concerned for her, so eager to look after her.

Yes, it was all working out very satisfactorily indeed.

I undressed and brushed my hair.

I saw the milk by the side of my bed and remembered Milton's face, the brightness of his eyes which shone so blue in his sunburned face, his triumphant pleasure because I had betrayed my true feelings.

I picked up the glass and took a sip.

There was something rather sickly about coconut milk at times. I set it down again. I had no inclination to drink it.

I sat up in bed for a while thinking of the fire and that moment when I had seen him coming towards me.

I took more of the milk. I thought it tasted a little strange. I put it down and in doing so spilt some on the table. I got out of bed to find a cloth and when I came back to the table I saw that there was some sediment in the milk on the table.

I had never noticed that before.

I wiped the table. I was beginning to feel amazingly sleepy. I got into bed. The room was slipping away from me. I lay down and must almost immediately have fallen into a deep sleep.

THE DISCOVERY

Usually I awoke early, but the next morning it was the sound of Maria in my room which brought me out of a heavy sleep. I felt a twinge of alarm. Something had happened to me. My limbs felt leaden and I found I could arouse myself only with the utmost effort.

Maria was standing by my bed. She was looking at me in some consternation.

"Are you all right?" she asked.

"Yes, I think so. I slept very heavily."

I sat up in bed and put a hand to my head. Memories of yesterday came back to me. The fire . . . Milton . . . my arriving back at the hotel.

"I feel strange," I said.

I remembered Milton's saying that he would tell Maria to take up some milk for me. I turned my head. There was nothing on the table, and it looked as though the wood had been freshly polished.

"You did not drink your milk," said Maria.

"I drank some of it."

"You spilt some. I cleaned up."

"Thank you."

"Would you like hot water now?"

"Yes, please."

When she had gone I got out of bed. I felt vaguely light-headed. Something had happened to me last night. I had been emotionally shaken. I shall never forget that moment when I had seen the fire and how I had ridden through that acrid atmosphere and heard the crackling of the flames. I could still see the terrified rats scuttling frantically away from the burning canes.

It had upset me more than I had realized at the time. Mostly it was the horror of thinking something terrible had happened to Milton . . . and the joyous discovery that it was nothing at all.

Then the milk.

Oh yes, the milk. What an extraordinary thing to happen! Of course Maria would take it away and wash the glass. It was her job to keep the room in order.

I sat on the bed thinking . . . and I was still thinking when she came back with the hot water.

I washed and dressed.

There was a knock on my door.

It was Felicity. She looked at me in some surprise.

"Oh . . . you're just up."

"I overslept."

"That is unlike you. I have had breakfast downstairs with Raymond on the terrace. I want to show him the island. Will you come with us?"

"Not this morning. I have a slight headache. You two go on your own."

She could not hide her pleasure at the prospect.

"It must have been all the excitement of last night. That fire and everything . . . and you riding off like that."

"Yes," I said. "I expect so."

She went out.

How different she was! She had changed completely. If ever anyone was in love that was Felicity. Raymond must see it. It was so obvious. And he cared for her . . . deeply.

I sat down trying to cast off this feeling of vagueness. What was the matter with me? I had never felt like this before.

I must have been in a very drowsy state because I did not think immediately of the milk and it was only after I had been downstairs and had a late breakfast on the terrace that I remembered it.

The milk! I had taken only a little . . . and there had been a sediment.

I could not remain on the terrace and went back to my room.

I kept thinking: The milk. The sediment. Could it really be that someone had put something in the milk?

Why? To send me into a deep sleep? For what purpose? But I had only taken very little of the milk. If such a small amount could have such an effect on me, what would have happened if I had drunk the entire glassful?

I used to dissolve Felicity's pills in milk. That was the best way to take them, the doctor had said.

An alarming thought came to me. I went to the drawer. The bottle was there. With trembling fingers I unscrewed the top. There were only six pills in the bottle.

But only a few days ago I had looked at them and there had been ten!

I felt dizzy. Where were those four pills? I asked myself. I saw my reflection in the mirror. Pale face, eyes wide with speculation . . . alarming, horrible.

Someone had put those pills in my milk. Had I drunk all the milk where should I be now? Someone had tried to kill me.

I was remembering what the doctor said. One had been enough to give Felicity a good night's sleep. Never more than one a day, he had said. Two might not be exactly dangerous but it was not advisable to take them. More than that would be fatal.

And someone had put four pills in my milk!

I tried to think back. Milton had told Maria to bring my milk. I had found it waiting there when I came up. Maria? But why should Maria want to harm me? She had been very friendly. I had generously rewarded her for her services which had delighted her. She had seemed eager to look after me. She had been inquisitive, it was true. I had seen her examining my clothes, but that was natural curiosity.

Not Maria!

Felicity? Oh no. Gentle Felicity, Felicity who was frightened of so many things. She would never attempt murder. Murder? Surely no one was trying to murder me. But if I had taken four of those pills it would have been the end of me. Suppose I had. It could so easily have happened. If I had not become drowsy so quickly I might well have drunk the rest of the milk. I had thought it tasted peculiar . . . but things here often did. I might at this moment . . . be dead.

But Felicity? Impossible. But if I were not here Raymond would surely turn to her. She loved him wholeheartedly. He was everything to her. To see the miraculous change in her since he had come proved that. And I stood between them . . . so she thought. Would she go to such lengths? How easy it would have been! She knew of the existence of the pills. She did not know where I kept them, but she would know they must be somewhere in my room and she had had plenty of opportunities to find them. I had been away from the hotel so much, leaving her in her room. How easy it would have been for her to discover their hiding place!

No, I could not believe that.

Another thought struck me.

Magda Manuel. I could imagine her planning murder more easily than Felicity. Magda? She had a reason to want me out of the way and again it was a man. How far had her relationship with Milton gone? Did she hope to marry him? Had there been some understanding between them before I came? But how could she come into the hotel . . . into my room. She had not been there last night when the pills were put into the milk. She could have paid one of the servants . . . The more I thought of it the more possible it seemed . . . She knew the island. She knew the ways of the islanders.

I felt light-headed, unsure how to act.

Well, here I was, alive and well, and rapidly throwing off the effects of a night of heavy drugged sleep. True, I had a slight headache . . . nothing to take much notice of . . .

On the other hand I might say to myself: You had an eventful evening. You suffered a great shock. You thought the plantation was on fire. You rode over to it in a state of terrible fear. The reaction was tremendous when you saw him there. You accepted the truth. You committed yourself to action which you had been putting off for weeks. It was quite an experience and you exhausted yourself . . . emotionally. You slept deeply. And the milk? Imagination. Little pieces of coconut might be in the milk. That was your sediment.

It was all imagination.

But the missing pills? That was another matter.

You miscounted.

Ten? And then six? Had it been one less, even two, I might have accepted that. But four.

Yes, there were the pills to account for.

I sent for Maria.

I said: "You brought the milk up to my room last night."

"Why yes," she answered. "I put it by your bed. Mr. Harrington he say you should have it to make you sleep well."

"Did you bring it straight to my room from the kitchen?"

"But yes," she said, with an air of surprise at such a question.

I looked at her steadily and her eyes full of the habitual laughter met mine steadily.

I was sure Maria was innocent of any crime.

"You took the remains of the milk away," I said.

"But yes . . . this morning. You did not want last night's milk beside you."

"Some of it was spilt."

"It was nothing . . . just a little. I wipe up."

"I see."

What could I say? How could I ask her if she had put pills into my milk? She would go down and tell them about it. They would think I had gone mad.

I said: "That's all right, Maria."

I wanted to dismiss the matter from my mind but I could not forget the pills in the bottle. I took it out and looked at it again. Only six left.

I replaced it and as I did so, I thought: The map was there in the drawer . . . and that is missing. Where is the map of the island? Someone must have taken it. And whoever took it would have seen the bottle of pills there, for they were together.

I had another search for the map.

Maria came up to make my bed and do the room. I was sitting there waiting for her.

"Maria," I said, "have you seen a map of mine?"

"A map?"

"Yes . . . a map. Not very big. Like this." I showed her with my hands. "I've lost it."

"On the terrace. I saw you show a map to someone once. That was a long time ago."

I thought: They watch us all the time.

"No, I didn't lose it then. I thought it was here in my room and I can't find it now."

"I look," she said.

"I've looked everywhere."

"I find. Mrs. Granville she lose her scarf. Cannot find. Not in her room. I found . . . under the bed." She laughed as though that was a great joke. "I find map," she added.

No, I could not suspect Maria.

I left her and went downstairs. I sat there for a while wondering whether I should go to Milton and tell him what I feared.

He would immediately think I had spoken to Raymond and made it clear that I was going to marry him, Milton. If I told him what had happened he would want me to leave the hotel and go to his house. I smiled. Well, I should feel safe there.

John Everton strolled by.

"Good morning," he said. "How are you?"

"Well, thank you. And you?"

"Very well."

He did not stop.

I sat there brooding. What if the pills had dropped out of the bottle? I had taken them out to count them. I could have dropped four of them then. It was hardly likely but such things did happen. Those four pills might be lying in the drawer. How foolish I should look if I said that someone had put pills into my milk—and then they were discovered. And the map? Had I put that somewhere myself?

To say the least I had been in an excited state ever since my experiences at the Granville house. I might have been careless ... absent-minded; and now, after having been concerned in an act of violence, was I allowing my imagination to run amok?

Magda was coming up from the waterfront. She saw me and waved.

My first thought was: She has come to see if I am dead.

However she expressed no surprise to see me sitting there. Then of course she wouldn't. If she was clever enough to arrange my death she would certainly be able to control her feelings.

"Good morning. How nice to see you," she said.

"You're very early."

"I came with my cook to shop. He's gone on to the market. I thought I'd call and see you."

"How nice of you!"

"Are you well?" She was looking at me intently and I felt my suspicions rise.

"Yes, thank you, very well."

"I'm giving a dinner party tomorrow night and I want you to come. I'm asking Milton, of course, and I wonder if your friend would feel well enough. I hear you have another friend staying at the hotel. Perhaps he would like to come too."

"He is out now and so is Mrs. Granville. I will tell them of your invitation when they come in."

"It is something of a celebration."

"Really?"

"Yes. My engagement to George."

"Oh." I felt deflated. If she were going to marry George why should she want me out of the way?

"Well, it's the sensible thing to do. I wonder we didn't before."

"He is a very charming man," I said.

"I think so, too."

"I am sure you will be very happy."

"Then you will come?"

"I shall be delighted to."

"And ask your friends. I'm going up to the plantation to ask Milton when we've been to the market. I'd better be off now. I have a good deal to do. I'm glad I saw you. Au revoir."

I went back to my room. Maria had finished and was gone.

So Magda was going to marry George. I saw how foolish I was to have suspected her. Moreover, how could she have put the pills into my milk. There were only two people who could have done that. Maria or Felicity.

I wondered about Felicity. I had always thought she was rather ineffectual. Yet was she? What had really happened on the balcony that night? He had left me and gone down to drink. Then he went in to her. She said she had come to the end of her endurance. She had picked up the gun and threatened to shoot herself. Had she, or had she threatened to kill him?

She had never been able to shoot straight. But perhaps . . . My imagination was running on, playing tricks. I could see it all so clearly. Her fear, her loathing . . . and there he was lumbering towards her . . . drunk. I could imagine her rushing to the balcony. Did she shoot? Did she do it deliberately? I could not blame her if she did. But did she?

Whatever the reason, murder was murder and I reckoned that no one who had committed it—however provoked—could ever be quite the same again.

Was that how it had happened?

That shot had saved her possibly from a life of degradation and misery. Just one shot . . . Now . . . four pills could save her from a lifetime of frustrated longing; they could give her a lifetime with Raymond.

He loved her, I knew, in his quiet way.

Oh, it was fitting very well.

I wanted to go to Milton, but something held me back. I did not want to talk even to him of my suspicions of Felicity. My common sense made me reject them as ridiculous fantasy. But Felicity did have a reason to wish me out of her way . . . just as she had to be rid of William Granville.

There was a difference. He had been bestial towards her. I was her friend. How often had she said she did not know what she would have done without me? But I stood between her and what she wanted most in life.

It was impossible to think of Felicity as a murderess—that quiet, gentle girl. But what do we know of the hidden parts of people's minds. How well do we know each other?

I went back to my room. I turned out the drawer. Could those pills have been caught up in my gloves or scarves? I went through everything thoroughly. I searched for the map. What had happened to it? It was evident that someone had gone through my possessions.

Why should the map have disappeared? I could not accuse Felicity of taking that.

It was all very mysterious. I thought: I will go over to Milton, but not yet. Magda would be there.

What would that matter? She was going to tell him of her celebration dinner. What did a man feel about a woman with whom he had had a very special relationship when she had decided to marry someone else?

I felt simple . . . ignorant of the world. There was so much I had to learn, and what I had learned since I left England was how little I knew.

I thought: I will go to him this afternoon, after the intense heat of the day is over.

I went out to the terrace. The sounds of the harbour seemed some way off. I sat down, my thoughts in a maze of speculation.

I saw Magda among the stalls. Her cook was with her—a very tall man in blue trousers and a white shirt against which his skin shone like ebony. They were bargaining, after the custom of shoppers.

I watched them idly for a moment. Then I saw Milton.

Magda had turned to him. She held out her hand. He took it and I saw them laughing together.

Then he left her and was making his way to the hotel.

I ran down to meet him, relief flooding over me.

"I'm so glad you've come," I said.

"What a pleasant welcome! Have you settled things with Raymond?"

I shook my head.

"I have had no opportunity. Felicity is there all the time. They have gone off together. She is in love with him and in a way he is with her. I don't think it is going to be so very difficult."

"Are you all right, Annalice?"

"Why do you ask?"

"You look pale, strained . . . "

I said: "I want to talk to you. Something strange happened. Shall we sit on the terrace?"

When we were seated I told him about the milk. He was stunned. I had never seen him at a loss for words before. When he spoke he said: "You are sure . . . about those pills?"

"I've looked everywhere. I am sure I can't have been wrong. If it had been one missing . . . or even two, I might have thought I had miscounted, but four . . . "

"Four! That could have been fatal!" He had turned very pale and he looked at me with such deep feeling that I felt the ordeal was worth while to see him thus.

"It looks as though someone wanted to put me into a deep sleep."

"Why?"

"Something I had in my room. Someone who knew nothing about the power of the pills . . . "

He shook his head. "What could anyone possibly have wanted. They could easily have broken in without going to such lengths."

"The map was taken."

"The map of the island? It was taken last night?"

"No . . . no. Before that. I had already missed it. It was at the back of a drawer where the pills were."

"The map," he repeated. "That's odd." Then he went on: "You're not staying another night in that hotel."

"But where . . . ?"

"In my house, of course."

"But what about Felicity and Raymond?"

"They can stay here . . . or come if they like. There's room for them. But *you* are coming."

"Oh, Milton, I'm so glad you know. I was hesitating about coming to you. I felt it sounded so silly. I want to be very careful of what I say."

"Why should you have to be careful?"

"Because I think it may have been Felicity. You see, there is a reason. She thinks I will marry Raymond and she loves him . . . intensely. She came through that terrible shock. I don't quite know what happened on the balcony that night, but it unbalanced her. There was a time when I thought she might have lost her reason. I would never have thought she could do a thing like this except for that."

"Felicity," he said slowly. "And the map. You don't think she stole that?"

"Oh no. That would not concern her."

He was silent and I went on: "I feel so unsure. I may have imagined all that about the milk. You see, I thought there was some sort of sediment . . . and I thought afterwards it might have been the pieces of coconut. You know what the milk is like. I had had a very strange evening . . . the fire and all that. I was worn out . . . emotionally as well as physically. I think I may have fallen naturally into a deep sleep."

"And the pills? How do you account for those?"

"They may have dropped out of the bottle when I last opened it. It was opaque and I had taken them out to count. I could have dropped them onto the floor. They could have been swept up."

"Wouldn't you have noticed?"

"I should have thought so, but I am trying to look at this from all possibilities."

"And the lost map?"

"There are all sorts of ways I might have lost that. It was some time ago when I couldn't find it. It doesn't seem to have anything to do with all this."

He said: "I shan't rest until you are up at the plantation. Pack your things and come now."

"I must wait and see Felicity. I'll have to explain. I want to be very careful about this. If it is Felicity she needs very gentle treatment. I know her well. It could be something that snapped inside her brain. I do want to go very quietly on this."

He nodded.

"But you are not going to spend another night in the hotel."

"You are certainly taking charge of me," I said with a faint smile.

"I'm taking care of you. Isn't that what I'm going to do from now on? I see what you mean about Felicity. We'll play it quietly . . . but with the utmost care. When they come back you'll tell them you are coming up to the plantation tonight. If they want to stay here let them. You are coming. That is certain."

I said: "I want to. I should be afraid to sleep in that room again."

"Come back with me now."

I shook my head. "I must give them some explanation. I don't want this to seem too strange . . . too important. I'll think of something plausible. And I'll get Felicity at least to come with me. I feel I have to watch over her."

"Have you seen her this morning? Did she act strangely?"

"Only to be surprised that I was not up. I am really worried about her. How I wish everything was settled. I am sure Raymond would take her back to England . . . and they could be married. They'd be very happy together."

"You can't run people's lives for them, you know. They have to find their own way. I'm going now. I have one or two things I have to do. I'm expecting you before sundown. If you don't come, I shall come over to fetch you."

"Oh Milton, I'm so glad you know."

He held my hands firmly and kissed me.

"I'll take care of you always," he said, "for the rest of our lives."

I watched him until he had disappeared. I caught sight of Magda who was still wending her way through the stalls with the tall cook.

"Miss Mallory!"

It was John Everton.

"Oh . . . hello," I said.

"I'm glad I found you. I've got a message for you. It's from that man on the island."

"Oh?" I was alert immediately.

"The man who brought it couldn't find you."

"I was down here."

He shrugged his shoulders. "Well, he saw me and remembered me and gave me the message to give to you when I saw you. It was that you should go to Lion Island as soon as you could. Mr. Perrensen has something of the utmost importance to tell you. The messenger had to go back but I said if I could find you I would take you over as soon as you were ready to go. I said I would. I'll take you now if you like. I could get a boat easily."

"That would be troubling you."

"Oh, I have nothing to do. Holidays don't really suit me. I like to be doing something all the time. It will be a nice trip for me."

"If you are sure . . . "

"I am indeed. Could we leave now?"

"Yes. I'll go and get my sun hat."

"You'll need it. I'll be waiting here. Don't be longer than you can help. We want to get back before the heat of the day."

I went up to my room and got my hat. I had been waiting for something like this since I had met Magnus Perrensen. I forgot my lethargy. He had something important to tell me. Perhaps I was on the verge of finding what I had come for. Perhaps he had news of Philip. In the excitement of everything that had happened, I had forgotten the quest which had brought me here.

John Everton went ahead of me to the boat. Magda was still at the market. She turned suddenly and saw me. She waved.

Then John Everton helped me into the boat and we were off.

"Not such a bright day as the last time," he said. "The wind isn't in the right direction either, so it will take a little longer to get there."

"Let us hope there's no mist," I said.

"The wind would soon clear that."

I could see the reclining lion getting nearer and nearer. Now it was looming over us and the sandy beach was in sight. He took the boat in and, leaping out, helped me to disembark.

"Here we are. It didn't take so long after all."

We went over the sand to the house. At the top of the steps Magnus Perrensen was waiting.

He took my hands and smiled warmly. "Thank you for coming so promptly."

"I was eager as soon as I heard. You have news for me?"

"Yes, that's so. Come along in. We'll be comfortable."

The strange uncanny feeling was creeping over me. Being with him took me back to the journal. Phrases of Ann Alice's seemed to go on and on in my brain.

"We'll have a drink," he said. "They'll bring it to us."

He took me into the room with the french windows overlooking the sea.

"I have wanted to come to Cariba so often since we last met," he said. "And I wanted to ask you to come here. But there was something I had to make sure of first. I wanted to wait until I could tell you of my discovery."

"I am all eagerness to hear."

"First the drink . . . This is a very special concoction made by my servant. He is very clever with such things. You will like this. It is refreshing."

I tried it. "Thank you," I said. "I do want to hear . . . "

"Yes, I know. There *is* an island."

"You have found it! Where is it? How far out was the map?"

"The map was correct," he said.

"But . . . "

"Yes, I know you went there with the gentleman of Cariba, and there was nothing there. But you didn't look closely enough. It's understandable. You shall know everything. Nothing shall be kept from you. I do admire you so much. You are so vital. Far more so than most women. You are adventurous. You have set out on a journey round the world to look for your lost brother. You are a romantic too. The journal touched you deeply, didn't it? I believe there were times when you thought you were Ann Alice. And when you first met me . . . admit it . . . for a moment you thought you were back in the past. You thought I was the young lover who had promised to take you away from that sinister house. You did, didn't you? Confess it."

"Of course I never mistook my own identity."

"Oh, but I believe there were times when you thought you were Ann Alice reborn. That moment when I took your hand and said . . . What did I say? 'At last you have come.' That sent shivers down your spine. I know. I saw it."

"Oh well, perhaps. I am longing to hear about the island. You say the map is correct."

"Do drink up. It is so refreshing."

I took another sip. I was beginning to feel a little uneasy. He was acting so strangely. It seemed as though he was mocking me in a way. He was different from the man he had appeared to be at our last meeting.

"Tell me where the island is," I said.

"At the bottom of the sea."

I gave a startled exclamation. In a flash of revelation I remembered being in the boat with Milton, looking back at the lightish green water, that patch of a different colour in an expanse of blue. Had it meant that at that spot the land was closer to the surface of the sea? Could that be the meaning of the difference in colour?

"There is a simple answer," he was saying. "Eighty or so years ago there was a change in the weather pattern . . . just for one year. Most countries experienced excessive and unusual heat. A certain amount of ice at the poles melted and flowed into the oceans. Several lands suffered floods. It was even felt here, nearer the equator, though in a lesser way and some islands became just rocks jutting out of the sea, others were completely submerged. That is what happened to our island."

"Oh. I see it all now. I have heard about the possibility of that happening. Someone was talking about it . . . "

"In connection with the island?" he asked quickly.

"Oh no . . . just generally."

I saw John Everton walk past the window and it struck me as strange that he had not come into the house with me.

"Is he a friend of yours?" I asked.

"He works for me."

"But . . . I did not think he knew you. I thought we came here by chance . . . "

"He brought you . . . on my orders."

"You mean the first time?"

"Yes."

"Then why did he pretend that he did not know you?"

"You're going to hear everything in time. You are not drinking."

"I am not really thirsty."

"It is not unpleasant, is it?"

"No, very nice."

"You will find it so refreshing."

"I thought at first that you might have news of my brother."

"Oh, of course, your brother."

"Do you know anything of him?"

"He came here. He was a very inquisitive young man, and observant, too. He was very like his sister. And quite knowledgeable. He knew a great deal about charts and the sea. He guessed the island was submerged."

"So you met him?"

"He noticed the colour of the sea. It is not always like that. It happens only in certain climatic conditions. Sometimes there is no indication at all."

"So Philip discovered it . . . "

"It was discovered long ago."

"But when I last saw you . . . " I stared at him. He raised his glass and indicated that I should do the same.

I hesitated. Why was he so eager for me to drink? I had learned a lesson on the previous night. I believed I should not drink thoughtlessly for a long time.

There was something very odd about this. The manner in which he looked at me, the way he spoke, not giving clear answers to my questions. I was beginning to feel very uneasy indeed. It occurred to me that he might not be quite sane.

He looked so cold. His eyes were blue—so were Milton's. But how different! I felt an intense longing for Milton's protective presence and something like terror because an expanse of water divided us.

"I believe you have something to tell me about my brother."

"I know where he is."

I rose. "Take me to him."

"All in good time."

"What is this all about? Why are you so mysterious? Why don't you tell me outright?"

"I wish you would relax and drink. Then we could chat happily."

"No," I said, "I won't drink. I don't want to drink. I am not thirsty. All I want is news."

"Well, I'll tell you where your brother is. He is on the island."

"But the island . . . "

"Yes, it is at the bottom of the sea."

"You mean Philip is . . . "

"He's there . . . or what the fishes have left of him."

I said: "I want to go. I don't know what you are planning to do, but I don't want to stay here a moment longer."

"That is not very polite. What would Ann Alice say to that?"

"You have brought me here for a purpose. I want to know what."

"So you shall . . . I wish you had taken the drink. It would have been so much easier for you. I like you. You are very attractive. I don't think Ann Alice was as attractive as you are. She would have lacked your fire. You are a young woman of great spirit. You like everything to go your way. I think it was most commendable of you to come on this quest. That is why I have decided that you shall discover what you came for . . . before you join your brother."

"What?"

He nodded. "Not yet, though. You know the love of those two was never consummated. Did you know that? Ann Alice was a simple girl. My great-grandfather was a worthy young man, idealistic at that time. He changed. I daresay Ann Alice would have changed. People do. Circumstances change them. Don't you agree?"

"I want your man Everton to take me back immediately."

"This is my island. I have not gone to such pains to bring you here that you shall go when the whim takes you. I like that idea of going back in the past. I like to think of myself as the young map maker coming to England and falling in love with the beautiful young girl. You have to go, but before that I want a little make-believe. We will play the lovers . . . We will enjoy what they had not the opportunity to . . . or perhaps the courage. Conventions were very rigid in those days . . . so are they now, but here on this island I make the laws."

"I think you are mad," I said.

"No, quite sane. I have told you that I admired you from the moment I saw you. You walked straight into the lion's den, didn't you? You are rather careless. You are just like your brother. He was very gullible. He wanted to send divers down. He wanted to go himself. I had the equipment here. I took him . . . and I came back without him. He knew too much . . . discovered too much . . . just as I was afraid he would."

I stared at him in horror. Then I looked about me. He followed my gaze.

"Sea all round," he said. "There is no way out. If you had taken the drink you would have been pleasantly drowsy . . . that was how it should have been. I should have made love to you quietly . . . tenderly, just as my great-grandfather would have done with Ann Alice. But you are stubborn. You refuse to drink."

I said: "Did you try to kill me last night?"

"It is not for you to ask questions. And you may drink now. It would be better so. I want a sweet acquiescent mistress. I want her to be as Ann Alice would have been. You will fight. I can see that. Ann Alice would never have fought her lover."

I said: "You *are* mad."

"No, not at all. Everything I do is founded on logic. You are a danger to me as your brother was. You came to find him. Well, that is what you have done. So now you are going to join him."

"Do you imagine that you can kill me as you did my brother. He was unknown here. I am not. There are people who will want to know what has become of me."

"The big man of Cariba? That is taken care of. The boat will be found . . . broken. Everton will disappear and so will you. That will be indisputable evidence. Someone must have seen you leave with Everton."

"And they will know that he was taking me here."

"Why should they? No one knows of his connection with me."

"I have already told several people of that other occasion when he brought me over."

"That would not mean that he brought you here a second time."

"They will know that would be the only reason why I should go in a boat with him."

"You quibble. No one will know that you came here."

I was trapped. I thought, He means every word he says. He is cold and calculating. Why did I ever find the journal? If I had not Philip would be at home now . . . and I should never have met Milton.

"Milton. Milton." I said his name over and over again to myself. Where are you now? If only I could reach you . . . in thought . . .

I was trying to think clearly. I would not be missed for hours. Felicity and Raymond would come back and wonder where I was. Would they be anxious? They might think I had gone to the plantation for luncheon. Would anyone have seen me go off with John Everton. Magda had waved to me as I was about to get into the boat, but would she think of mentioning it . . . not until it would be too late.

It would not be until evening that they would realize that I had disappeared. If I could run down to the shore . . . get into the boat . . . row myself back to Cariba. How could I escape him?

I thought: He is mad. He is as obsessed by the past as I was. I had felt myself caught up in it—and so had he. Ann Alice had brought her tragedy to me just as his great-grandfather had caught him into his life.

When I looked into his cold blue eyes I thought I was looking at death.

And how I longed to live! I wanted to be with Milton forever. I wanted to enjoy that life he had talked of . . . going home to England, having children. I had wanted that for a long time ever since in my heart I had known that I loved him—but never had that seemed clearer to me than now.

Perhaps if I called to him. I felt my whole being trying to reach him. It must find some response. He must sense that I was in danger. Milton, Milton, where are you now? He would be there on the plantation supervising the cutting of the scorched canes. Milton . . . Soundlessly I called to him.

I wanted to cling to life. Every moment was important.

There was something coldly dedicated about this man. He was enjoying the scene too much to want to bring it to a speedy conclusion. There was no heat of passion in him, no over-riding sexual desire; it was to be a sort of ritual, a culmination of the story of Ann Alice and her lover.

If I could keep him talking . . .

"You promised to explain," I said. "You said I deserved to know."

"Well?"

"What is the secret of the island? Why do you want no one to know that it is there under the sea?"

"I will tell you," he said. "My great-grandfather, lover of Ann Alice, came out here searching for it. He never found it; but he was caught up in the fever of the search for gold. Gold, you see. There was gold on the island . . . so much gold that it was everywhere. He became obsessed by gold . . . and he found it in Australia. He became moderately wealthy. He married there and had a son . . . my grandfather who followed in his father's footsteps. But a gold mine is not a bottomless pit. The gold runs out. The affluence fades. My grandfather was no longer young when he went in search of the island. To find the island was an obsession in my family . . . as it became with your brother and yourself."

"Yes?" I prompted. I was looking for some way of escape. Could I get out of this room? Where could I hide. I suppose in moments of acute danger one's senses become more alert. My ears were straining. Did I imagine I heard the sound of movement . . . something out there . . .

He was intent on his story. "My grandfather bought this island to be near where he believed that other island might be. He made it his object in life to find the island . . . and he did. He sent divers down there. It was true about the gold. It seemed . . . inexhaustible. For fifty years we have been bringing up that gold."

"That is why you are one of the few successful gold miners in Australia. The gold comes from the island."

He nodded.

"It doesn't belong to you."

He shrugged his shoulders. "We do not want people prying into our affairs."

"You mean someone might try to get a share of the gold? Does it belong to you? I don't believe that it does ... by law ... "

"It belongs to my family," he said firmly. "And it is going to remain in my family. That is why we cannot have clever little spies probing around."

"I am beginning to understand."

"It is very clear ... and logical, you must admit."

I blinked. I saw a ship close to the island. I did not betray my exultation. He would not be able to see out of the window from where he sat. I must go on talking as though I had seen nothing. I must keep his attention focussed on me. The relief was almost unbearable. Someone was coming.

Surely some of his men had seen the ship. How many men were there on the island besides Magnus Perrensen and John Everton? The divers, I supposed; they would be necessary to bring up the gold, and the servants. There must be quite a few of them.

I said: "Suppose I offered to go away and say nothing about the island?"

"How could I trust you?"

"If I gave my word."

"What of your brother?"

"He is dead. I can't bring him back."

"I don't like violence," he said.

"Really? You surprise me."

"There was nothing violent about your brother's death. He wanted to go down with the divers. I sent him down and simply cut the ropes. We left him down there. It was very simple."

"Is that what you propose to do with me?"

"I wanted you to take the drink. That would have made it easy."

"I should have been asleep and you would have simply thrown me over. Yes, that would have been quick and easy."

"Why not drink it now?"

"It is not easy to drink to one's death."

"It has to be, you know."

Was that the sound of a boat on the sand?

"Nothing is certain," I said.

"This must be. I have thought of it since you came here the first time. Perhaps it should have happened then. But there was much to be discovered. You had the map. You told me that. I did not want the map to be found."

"So you stole it from my rooms. How?"

"Never mind. There is no map now . . . and soon there will be no one who has an interest in the island."

I heard a shout from outside.

I rose and ran to the window. I wrenched it open and was out before he caught me.

Wild joy possessed me.

Milton was striding up the beach and he was not alone. Men were scrambling out of the boat.

"Milton!" I cried. "Milton!"

I ran to him. He caught me in his arms. He was laughing, but I could see it was the laughter of immense relief.

I was safe—as I always would be with him.

He took me back to the plantation. Raymond was there with Felicity, Magda and George.

I knew the whole story now and how he had arrived just in time.

As soon as he had left me that morning he had found Maria. He had conjectured that she would be the one who could most likely have stolen the map and put the pills in my milk.

He had bullied her, threatened her, reduced her to such terror that he had forced the truth out of her.

Yes, she had taken the map; she had thought it was a silly bit of old paper. Not like a jewel . . . or money. She had put the pills in the milk. It was only to make Miss Mallory sleep well.

Why had she done this? Because Mr. Everton had promised her money if she did and she was longing to join her Sabrino in Australia. The sooner she had the money the sooner she could go, and for doing this she was going to have enough to join Sabrino. Mr. Everton had promised.

But it had gone wrong and Miss Mallory had not drunk the milk. She had spilt it and left it there on the table. So she had not been paid the money . . . only for the map.

Magda had seen Milton coming from the hotel where he had been questioning Maria and she had told him she had seen me go off in a boat with John Everton.

That was enough. Milton knew then that I was in acute danger. They had tried to kill me last night. He had set out at once for the island bringing with him a company of men whose duty it was to keep law and order on the islands.

While enquiries were made no one was allowed to leave Lion Island and later that day Milton sent his divers down to that spot where Paradise Island should have been and they explored the sea bed. They found the island below the surface of the sea.

I did not know what the regulations were with regard to the purloining of the gold; but there was the murder of my brother to be accounted for.

In the meantime, said Milton, I needed special care and he was going to be sure that I had it.

The best way he could do that—and the only way he could do it effectively—was by marrying me immediately.

I had already talked with Raymond.

He understood. When had Raymond not understood?

He said: "I saw how it was with you two as soon as I arrived."

"Raymond," I said, "I'm sorry. You have been so good to me."

"I want you to be happy. That is the most important thing."

"No. It is just as important for you to be happy. No one deserves to be more so than you."

"I'll be all right. He is your sort. I see that. I was a little slow, wasn't I? Not adventurous . . . as he is. Not forceful, not demanding."

"I love him," I said frankly. "I could never be happy without him."

"I know. So the only thing is to be happy with him."

"And you?"

"I shall take Felicity back to England."

"Take care of her. She needs a lot of care."

"I will," he promised.

And I knew he would.

There is little more to tell. I had travelled far since I had set out from England—and I don't mean in miles. I had broken with the past. I had come to some understanding of life, I supposed. I often thought that if I had not set out on that journey I would have lived peacefully in England, married, had children . . . comfortably, possibly happy. But I had broken away. I had faced death on more than one occasion. I had plumbed the depths and soared to the heights. I could easily have died violently as Ann Alice had. But whatever I had endured I should always remember that it had brought me Milton. Life is like that. It is not smooth and easy—and never will be. Often one must take risks to win the great prizes.

I am married to Milton Harrington. Raymond and Felicity have left for England. I fully believe that before long they will marry. She is quite recovered and I believe very happy. I am ashamed to think that I once suspected her of trying to murder me. Magda is now married to George Callerby and we are the best of friends.

One day we shall return to England. It will be wonderful to see Granny M and Jan and be home again.

Milton knows this. He reminded me the other day of how cool and formal I was to him in the beginning.

"I remember I said to you that one day you would say to me, 'I love you, Mr. Harrington.' You have never said just that."

"Well, it is true," I said.

"Soon we shall leave all this. We'll go home. Now that you have secured me I believe that is your next objective."

"I should love to see England again . . . to be there, but, Mr. Harrington, home for me is where you are."

He seemed very satisfied with that observation.